THE INFORMANT

THE INFORMANT

BY THE GORDONS

DOUBLEDAY & COMPANY, INC.

GARDEN CITY, NEW YORK

1973

All of the characters in this book
are fictitious, and any resemblance
to actual persons, living or dead,
is purely coincidental.

cop. 2

ISBN: 0-385-01433-3
Library of Congress Catalog Card Number 72–89414
Copyright © 1973 by Mildred Gordon and Gordon Gordon
All Rights Reserved
Printed in the United States of America
First Edition

For Velma and Bill Krauch,
with our love

THE INFORMANT

1

SAC, LOS ANGELES . . . INFORMANT ADVISES
ZERO SECTION, COMMITTEE OF PUBLIC SAFETY,
PLANNING ASSASSINATION TONIGHT OR TO-
MORROW IN LOS ANGELES OF UNKNOWN PARTY
AT UNKNOWN PLACE. FOLLOWING ALL LEADS
IN EFFORT TO IDENTIFY PROJECTED VICTIM . . .

SAC, NEW YORK

FOR A TIME it was touch and go whether Flight 901 would land at
Los Angeles International Airport, socked in by a heavy June fog, or
at Ontario, a good hour distant by airline bus. If it were the latter,
Stewardess Chris Roberts, twenty-five, dark-haired and slender, with
no visible hips, would have 159 unhappy passengers baying at her.
A few would hold her personally responsible for this dereliction in
the weather and consider a life sentence proper punishment. The
time was 11:16 P.M. with arrival at 11:28.

In the galley, Sarah Cashin, who was working Coach with Chris,
rattled along. "Politicians! They put an airport right on the ocean
when they could've put it out on the desert."

Chris had no time to discuss the matter. The little old lady in 14-A
needed an aspirin; 17-B had lost her glasses; and 23-A wanted his
coat that was on a hanger in the slot up front. As always Chris handled this madness completely unperturbed. Her car-hop experience,
after her graduation from the University of California at Santa Bar-

1

bara, stood her in good stead. Her parents had reacted predictably—with patient understanding—when she had taken the drive-in job, but she had known what they were thinking: "Four hard years in college for this?"

At the time, however, she had fallen into such mental and emotional confusion that she simply had to sit and ponder—or rather, run her legs off, which did more good than sitting. She had had what her mother called an ill-fated romance. She had loved the fellow. But in his own thinking, he was the center of the universe, everyone a slave to his bidding. Gradually it dawned on her that she would make a very unhappy slave.

She was on her way with the aspirin when 19-C yelled, "Hey, sister, how about a Scotch-on-the-rocks for your old man?"

"Sorry," she answered. "The bar's closed. We're landing in a few minutes."

He grew belligerent. "What d'ya mean, the bar's closed? You too damned lazy to get me a drink?" He raised his voice still higher. "I know the vice-president of this outfit. Old buddy of mine."

"We're only a few minutes from landing, sir."

She hurried on. She was uneasy. She had an inordinate fear of fogs.

When she gave 14-A her aspirin, she was conscious that the man in the row behind her had bent over, ostensibly to pick up something but actually to look up her legs. Quickly, she swung about, with the result that one kneecap struck one nose. "Oh, I'm so sorry," she said sweetly.

Up ahead 6-C held up a hand. He was in his late sixties. When he had come aboard she had noted the slight limp in his right leg. He had happy blue eyes, a gentle face, and a warm, kindly voice that she described later as "a sort of purr."

"Miss," he said, "could I have a glass of water, please? I must take my medicine."

She was in the galley getting the water when Sarah came alongside. "It's International after all, thank goodness."

The plane touched down lightly and smoothly. Mac, the captain, had a reputation for never jostling his passengers' kidneys. The A stewardess began her recital of the farewell ritual. ". . . please remain seated until the plane has come to a full stop. We thank you for flying United Airlines and hope to see you aboard again."

Chris stood at the door with the other girls. Outside the fog rolled

2

in thick waves, blotting out the lights one moment, parting the next. Wearily, the passengers trudged out. Even the seven-year-old monster with the rib-poking tommy gun seemed subdued by the late hour.

When everyone was gone, she got her two small cases and the moth-eaten rabbit-fur coat she had bought for $5.98 in New York. Sarah's eyes landed on it. "What the world?"

Chris beamed. "Remember that old bathtub with the legs that I sprayed with gold paint. Well, now I've got me a fur-lined bathtub!"

Sarah shook her head. "We get 'em all on this run."

Chris got her pink slip from the captain, a husky, big-boned individual in his late forties, married, the father of four, one a daughter Chris's age. The pink slip was her time card. She was paid from "block to block," from the time the block was pulled away from the tires for take-off to the minute another was shoved under on landing.

She hurried. She had told Jim Kendall she would call him before midnight, and if he weren't too busy drawing up a brief or doing whatever it is that young attorneys do at late hours, they would take a long walk. She loved strolling with Jim in the dark, block after block, both talking their hearts out, what they were going to do when they were married, which would be as soon as he earned a sufficient salary.

She was far from being perturbed by the long engagement. The delay postponed the final, irrevocable decision. She would wed Jim, of course, she told herself, but at night she would occasionally awaken in a sweat. Forever was forever was forever. She worried about herself and her attitudes, not about Jim. He was considerate, thoughtful, forever calling her up and buying surprise gifts that cost little but expressed the man. A wind-up turtle from a dime store, a big Mexican ceramic pig, a quaint Japanese door knocker.

Still, no bells rang, no organ music swelled, no magic carpet came by that she could climb on, and the longing that came and went could have been stirred by any likable male. Shouldn't something be happening to a girl?

She hastened to the Crew Desk where she handed in her pink slip and signed in for the next flight. There was the usual banter. She was a man's man, they all agreed—except when they looked at her. Next she reported, also on the run, to the check-in room for the stewardesses. There was nothing in her mailbox.

Usually she would have taken an airline tram at the back of the airport to the employees' parking lot and then driven her car to her Manhattan Beach apartment. But tonight Roz's parents—Roz Canaletto

3

was her roommate, a secretary at Columbia Records—were in town from New Jersey and Chris had loaned them her room and car. Roz had said: "The Mafia will always remember you for this."

Outside Chris edged her way through the metallic-tasting, eye-smarting fog, past slowly moving gunnysack forms. The fog had been clean when it moved in from the ocean but had swiftly absorbed the floating excrement of industrial plants.

In front of United Airlines she signaled a taxi. She would go to a nearby motel. A loud, peremptory voice came out of the fog from nowhere: "The white zone is for immediate loading and unloading of passengers only. No parking." The voice was cold, impersonal, merely stating a fact in relentless repetition but with the decided inference that if one did not want his head chopped off he had better pay heed.

As a yellow cab pulled up, she heard a man addressing her. Turning, she saw 6-C, the kindly old codger with the limp. He was exceedingly agitated. His face was working, and his lips trembled.

"Miss, may I ask if you are going to a hotel?"

"The Airporter."

"Oh, good, good. The Airporter. That's very good. Would you mind so much, please, to take these two pieces." He offered two attaché cases. "My taxi doesn't have room for them. I always bring too much gear but I'm so afraid I might leave something I would need."

Before she thought she agreed. He shoved them in the seat and carefully put hers on top of his and spread the fur over them. He continued talking as he took her elbow and gently propelled her into the back seat beside the cases. "I'll meet you at check-in but if I get held up, I mean, if my cab gets slowed down in traffic, please wait. Don't give them to anyone, please. Don't turn them over to the bellman, promise?"

Her mouth opened to protest but the entreaty in his eyes stopped her. Quickly he closed the door and motioned to the driver who took off. Now why had she done that? She knew better than to take custody of a stranger's cases. They might contain a million dollars in heroin. She was guilty of a universal urge; too inclined to say yes, to want to help one's fellow man.

A station wagon boxed in the taxi briefly and she glanced back. The old man limped away, his shoulders heavy with the years. Once he stopped as if to peer into the distance. With effort he gathered himself together to resume locomotion. The fog, heavy as a Lon-

4

doner, enveloped him, then parted to reveal a Japanese-like print of him climbing slowly into a taxi. A young man—she had the distinct impression he was young although she saw as through a milky glass—stood on the sidewalk watching. He struck her as acting furtive. That impression, though, could have been the product of her extremely active imagination. A fog invariably sent it out on an overkill.

2

SAC, LOS ANGELES. INFORMANT ADVISES ASSASSINATION UNKNOWN VICTIM ORDERED BY MAXIMILIAN HARTMAN, AKA MAX HARTMAN, SUBJECT OF YOUR CASE. NEGATIVE ON OTHER LEADS . . .

SAC, NEW YORK

SHE SAT AT the Airporter with her knees crossed and a leg swinging impatiently. Where was the old fellow? He should have arrived twenty minutes ago.

Airline personnel streamed in and out. She overheard one stewardess saying, "Don't ever, ever take the Baltimore run. Go to Nome instead. They put you up in this hotel, see, and well, I went out for a newspaper, it was barely dark, and some creep comes up and says, 'How much?', and I says, 'Ten cents.' Can you believe it? I thought he was talking about the paper! The hotel they put you up at, it's right around the corner from the prosties and you can't even go out in twos at night."

Chris signaled a bellman. Much to his annoyance, she insisted on carrying the passenger's two cases. It was ridiculous, she told herself. Why should she be toting a perfect stranger's cases simply because he had asked her not to let anyone handle them. A hangover from childhood, no doubt, doing automatically as one was told.

Once inside her room, and with the bellman gone, she kicked off

5

her loose, low-heeled pumps, aiming them for a chair. She hit the goal each time. Not bad. She was a basketball fanatic. She flopped and rubbed her aching feet.

She decided she could make it to the phone and dialed Jim who answered on the first ring. "I was getting worried about you," he said.

"I'm at the Airporter. Took a little time to check in."

"You all right?"

"Now don't go imagining things."

"You had trouble with someone on the flight."

She had never known anyone with such sensitive perception. He could spot her slightest change in voice or expression, and at times it nettled her. She was no prospective juror submitting to critical analysis.

Jim was combing law books this night for precedents that one of his firm's senior members might quote in court the next day. They agreed to meet for lunch in front of the Wilshire Boulevard building where he worked as low man on the totem pole.

In the bathroom she undressed, pulled on a gown Jim had given her at Christmas, spread out a magazine on the washbasin, studied a hair-do, and tried it out in the mirror. She grimaced and gave up. Some beautician had probably spent three hours achieving the effect with wires and epoxy.

She had carefully removed her false eyelashes and was creaming her face when the knock startled her. It was a determined knock, as if the party thought she might be asleep. Hastily she removed the cream, and on her way to the door, called out: "Yes?"

There was no answer and she stopped very still. "Who is it?"

The voice answering was a man's, pleasant and deeply timbred. "Max Hartman. You don't know me but I must see you. The hotel will vouch for me if you wish to call the desk."

Pulling her negligee about her, she opened the door, and looked into one of God's better designed faces. He was tall, well over six feet, with a muscular but loose hanging frame. His eyes—it was too dark to determine the color—she always looked for the color since she believed color revealed character—stripped her to the mole on her hip. For some reason, with this man she didn't mind. His smile was like his eyes, impertinent and disrespectful.

"Thank you, Miss Roberts," he said, making no attempt to enter. "Sorry to trouble you but my uncle gave you two of his cases . . ."

She nodded. "I've been waiting for him."

6

"He was hurt—in a car accident. He asked me to pick them up."
She started for the closet where she had placed them. "Badly hurt?"

"They don't know. At that age, anything's a shock."

She was propelled by the strong physical appeal of the man, then her reasoning surfaced and she turned about. He had followed her, and she noted he had closed the door. He was standing in the light from a tall grotesque table lamp, and his eyes were a deep, dark blue. That color indicated a strong, fine character. Washed out blues and rusty browns reflected weak people whom one should never trust.

She was reassured. She said: "I promised him I wouldn't turn over his cases to anyone. But I suppose . . ." He stepped nearer, and she was conscious of a drag-racing pulse. "He kept stressing that. Not even to a bellboy."

He smiled. "I'm not a bellboy, and under the circumstances . . ."

Stalling, she ran a hand over the rabbit-fur coat draped across a chair. She picked it up. "Did you ever see a fur-lined bathtub?"

"A what?"

"Five ninety-eight. And only nine moth holes. I counted them. I sprayed gold paint on the outside of the bathtub. It's got gorgeous lion's-paw legs."

He looked at her in utter bewilderment. She turned back to him. "I have a responsibility. It's almost as if he'd given them to the airline. I'll take them to him in the morning if you'll tell me where he is."

"Inglewood Hospital. But he needs them tonight. He's got to do something—and he has to have . . ."

He was pressing, and the bond between them snapped. He became only one more male to handle, as she would if he were a passenger. "At midnight he's got to do something—in the hospital—after he's been banged up?"

His smile disappeared. "If you think I'm a thief . . ."

She pulled her negligee tighter. "I'll see that he gets them in the morning. But darn it, I'd planned to sleep in."

"I'll drive you over now."

"If you'll kindly get out, I'm going to bed. I've had a day."

His eyes held hers. "You're a very beautiful woman. You look intelligent and sensible and yet—"

"You think I'm stubborn? Well, join the club—my parents, my boy friend, my supervisor."

He shrugged lightly and turned toward the door. "Tomorrow morning. Eight o'clock. I'll drive you to the hospital."

"Nine o'clock."

He closed the door quietly. She counted ten, then opened it. He was nowhere in sight.

At the phone, she dialed the airline's security office. Hank Garmuth answered.

"I don't know whether you remember me, Mr. Garmuth. This is Chris Roberts. I—"

"Christina Roberts! Flight 692. Over Kansas. Eight-forty A.M. April 17th." A psycho had pulled a gun on her and she had talked him into handing it over. "Do I remember! Talk about guts."

"It wasn't guts, Mr. Garmuth. I didn't know what else to do. But what I'm calling you about, I think I've got myself into a jam. I shouldn't've done it but I let a nice old character palm off a couple of his cases on me. He sat in 6-C, Flight 901. Last name was Jorgensen. J-o-r-g-e-n-s-e-n. I don't know the first name . . ."

3

FBI AGENT John Ripley, better known as Rip, sat his swivel as he would a saddle, his body pitched slightly forward, his ankles digging into the legs. He was lean, hard-packed, and sun-browned from years back when he had ridden the Arizona range. He squinted under the harsh light, staring at the teletype Peg had put before him. INFORMANT ADVISES ZERO SECTION, COMMITTEE OF PUBLIC SAFETY, PLANNING ASSASSINATION TONIGHT . . .

Peg said, "It came too late, didn't it?" She was a wisp of a girl with pixie eyes that the apparent tragedy of the moment had sobered. Efficient and conscientious, she manned the communications center. During the heyday of the miniskirted era, she had almost lost her job. She had maintained that a girl's legs, if properly tooled, should be seen, an opinion definitely not shared by the Bureau. "This Bureau," one agent had remarked, "believes that a girl's legs are the handiwork of the devil and all who look thereupon should be cast into hell and brimstone."

He was so cast, shortly after making that statement, by the Bureau.

Rip said: "God, I hope not." He rose six feet tall with muscles under taut control. "If I had any idea where he was. Any idea. It may not be him at all, of course. It may be somebody else. Still"—he glanced at the scarred surface of his old wristwatch—"the plane landed an hour and a half ago."

Sam Jorgensen should have called Rip immediately on arrival. That had been the arrangement. Either something had happened to him or he was an irresponsible individual. Of course, he could have changed his mind or panicked. Rip had never seen him, and as far as Rip knew, the man had never been in Los Angeles before.

Sam Jorgensen was an informant. A few weeks ago he had telephoned the New York FBI office to advise that he could produce information about the Committee of Public Safety, an underground organization dedicated to the violent overthrow of the government of the United States. He had insisted on delivering his information in Los Angeles. He said he feared he might be followed in New York.

When he had failed to call within the hour, Rip had dispatched two agents to search for him. Neither had reported back. In an airport the size of International, they could easily spend an hour looking for an individual, even one with a limp. The chances that anyone would remember him were slight. No one looked at anyone in an airport beyond searching out a relative or friend. In man's march through life, nowhere was he more of a lost soul, an anonymous face in an ever-shifting, confused, blurred mob of faces. Even for a trained hunter, the kaleidoscope sped by at a dizzy speed that left a man with deep frustrations and rhino-sized headaches.

"I've got to be going," Peg said. "Is there anything else, Mr. R.?"

"I don't like to ask it. It's so late."

"Your cat?"

"Could you?" She would be leaving shortly for home, which was only a block from his apartment. "He must be starving. I don't know why he doesn't pack up his fur and move, the hours I feed him." He removed a key from a ring. "It's to the back—"

"—'the back door.'" Peg took the key. " 'Leave it in the pocket of the old jacket hanging outside.' Anything for the FBI, Mr. R."

"And Peg, don't let anybody—"

"I'll only fall down over the garbage can and turn on all the lights."

Laughing impishly, she walked away. With difficulty, he pulled his eyes from the nicely compacted figure. She was some girl. He might marry her—if for no other reason than to stop his mother from

9

hounding him. She liked Peg. His mother, furthermore, said he was married to his job and he wasn't getting any younger. At twenty-nine, though, he figured he wasn't exactly over the hill.

He placed a yellow legal-size pad before him. He could plot investigative leads better if he wrote them out. Besides, the procedure had a certain therapeutic effect. It helped block frustrations. It could be a long night. He recalled an instructor at the FBI Academy in Quantico, Virginia, saying: "You'll risk your own life under gunfire but not too often. Only rarely, in fact. When you do, you will get no medals, no congressional awards. What you should get a medal for are the long hours on end when you work a case, the dark, lonely nights, the frustrating days—the hours that will drive you mad . . ."

He had tallied up years of such hours. On occasion, too, he had come under gunfire. He had no medals but he had memories, some of them searing.

Memories. An eighteen-year-old he had taken prisoner after a gun battle, an eighteen-year-old who had slain three men and a twelve-year-old boy when he panicked during a service station hold-up. A good youngster, everyone said, with good grades, but he couldn't wait to make money. He had to have it now. So many had to have it now.

A killer who had ambushed him as he walked down a dark driveway. Rip had turned quickly and killed him with the first pull of the trigger—and the man with his last breath had damned him to hell.

The mangled body of a police officer murdered by a bomb attached to his front door—and the twenty-year-old girl slayer who screamed in the courtroom she would kill the pigs until there wasn't one left.

An old Sicilian mother who collapsed and died in the courtroom while he was testifying against her Mafia son.

The extortionist he had killed at the Coliseum, at the end of a football game, an extortionist who had terrorized a woman bank teller and her teen-age sister, and would have murdered them if he had been permitted to play out his plot.

These were the memories, and sometimes the nightmares, to live over and over without any medals hanging on the wall to remind him.

A few minutes after 1 o'clock the call came from Hank Garmuth. "Rip," he said, "you know that passenger you called me about this evening, to see if he was on Flight 901? Well, I've got a screwball playback on that. One of our stews—name's Christina Roberts—we

10

call her Chris around here—swell dish—well, this Jorgensen character gave her two of his cases to take to the motel since he had more luggage than his taxi could hold, and then . . ."

He narrated in detail the events that followed. "This joker comes to get the cases, says his name is Max Hartman."

Rip felt his pulse leap. "Can you meet me at the Airporter? Say in thirty minutes?"

Hank Garmuth could. Rip hung up, and headed for the Chief Clerk's office where he asked the woman on night duty to run the indices on one Christina Roberts, also known as Chris Roberts, airline stewardess, twenty-five, current address in Manhattan Beach.

While he waited, he picked up a nearby phone. "Inglewood Hospital, please, Susan," he told the switchboard girl. Connected, he asked for Reception. "Do you have a party named Sam Jorgensen? J-o-r-g-e-n-s-e-n. Checked in about an hour ago."

"Who's calling, please?" She had a sexy voice that she obviously had taken pains to develop.

"The *Times*. Rewrite desk. We had a report he was—"

"No, sir. No Mr. Jugginson."

"Try Jorgensen." Again, he spelled it.

"You're cute," she said. "No, no J's. Try me again, will you? We get a lot of J's."

He dropped the receiver hard. Maybe he *was* over the hill. He was tired of playing games with sexy voices. The woman in the Chief Clerk's office reported there was no file on a Christina Roberts.

In the supply room he checked out picks to use on the locks of the cases and a photo copier. He held the car to forty miles as he took the Westwood on-ramp to the San Diego Freeway, and then accelerated to 65, the legal limit. The Bureau would frown if he broke traffic laws, and recently he had had a few frowns. Even inside the Bureau he found it difficult to obey every rule. There remained the kick and snorting of the maverick. Assignments to New York and Chicago and now Los Angeles only intensified the loneliness of being far away from starry skies and the first red glow of morning.

He remembered he must write his mother. She was the lonely one. She raised chickens and scratched vegetables out of a plot of hard caliche soil she and his father had cleared south of Tucson. She still lived in the house they had built together. She had nailed boards, heated roof tar, helped make adobe blocks, potted desert growth in the hard struggle to relieve the starkness of the place, and sewed up

11

flour sacks for drapes. That was long before he was born, back in the days when flour actually came in hundred-pound cloth sacks. She was the wiry kind, indestructible, and he liked to think he had inherited her stern, unyielding refusal to bow to weather, man, misfortunes, or time.

She had taught him the old virtues. The year his father died, when he was fourteen, he had found a dollar bill in front of the general store at Twin Buttes, and she had ordered him to walk the mile back to leave it with old Mr. Marshall whose face was as deeply crevassed as the mountains from which he came. When no one claimed it within a week, old Mr. Marshall returned it to Rip. But it was an anxious week.

Some of his boyhood was still back there. The old car that he was assembling when he left for college, from parts picked up here and there, still sat out back of the house. His old cat, Pancho, though, who had slept his life in it, was long gone.

Shortly after he left the freeway, the radio came alive. The agents looking for Jorgensen reported in the negative. Another agent, whom Rip had asked to run the police department's criminal indices, advised there was no record on Christina Roberts.

He found himself chafing at stop signs, gunning the motor on GO. He tried to temper his fear and anxiety. He had counted on Sam Jorgensen to provide a breakthrough in the toughest, most frustrating case he had ever worked. For nine months he had headed a special detail, known around the office as the Subversive Desk. He had twenty-two agents working with him full time, and could call on as many others as he needed. They had run surveillances around the clock month after month and followed hundreds of leads. And all the time the pressure from Washington mounted.

At the Airporter's newsstand he found Hank Garmuth riffling through a magazine. He was a heavy-set, squat ex-Marine with a bold nose, squinty eyes, and stained teeth, what there were of them. He was tough, aggressive, and smart.

Hank followed several steps behind Rip, running a careful surveillance with his gimlet eyes on room doors, to make certain none was open a crack. When Rip tapped at 120, he went past him checking doors to the end of the dark corridor.

Chris was still in her negligee and barefooted. Rip liked the squareness of her jaw, the uptilt of her head, the quick, discerning

12

eyes, and the subdued scent of her perfume. Neither said a word, nor did Hank until she closed the door which unexpectedly groaned.

"I've never tried to slip through a door yet," Hank said, "that it didn't yell, 'That man's here.' This is Rip, John Ripley. Miss Roberts."

In her nod Rip sensed hostility, faint but unmistakable.

"The cases are over there." She indicated the foot of the bed.

"May I take them into the bath?" She nodded slightly.

In the bathroom he sized up the locks, found the right pick, and quickly opened them. Most luggage locks served primarily to prevent the cases from opening if the catches sprung under rough treatment. Yet he was always surprised when any lock yielded. He had never become proficient with picks. His fingers were too big and awkward, the result of ranch work, one summer changing tires in a service station, stringing eight miles of fence another summer, and running a caterpillar one winter. He had no scruples about examining the baggage. He was searching for a clue that might lead to a missing informant, perhaps a slain one.

Opening the cases, he found Xeroxed sheets of correspondence and reports, and many newspaper clippings. His eyes swept a notation in English at the top of one news story in Spanish: "I think this seems the best way. What do you think, Nan?" His border Spanish, learned as a tattered kid playing with Mexican Americans, served him well. The story, from a Montevideo, Uruguay, newspaper, reported a recent, particularly brutal kidnaping by the Tupamaros, possibly the best-organized, most ruthless terrorist group operating anywhere.

He set up the photo copier, and working swiftly, finished in a half hour. When he emerged, Chris and Hank were talking animatedly about air travel. At sight of Rip she dropped a sentence halfway.

"You can turn the cases over to Mr. Hartman when he comes in the morning," Rip told her.

"Give them to him?" She was surprised and nervous, constantly twisting a princess ring from Thailand. He dropped wearily into the chair adorned by the rabbit fur, noticed, and started to get up.

"That's all right," she said, "if you don't mind a few old moths. I don't suppose you're going to tell us what's in the cases?"

He settled back. "I think you'd better let him take you to the hospital—rather than give in readily."

"He isn't at the hospital. Not at Inglewood. I called."

13

"I think I'll hire her," Hank said to Rip. "She's not a bad dick."

"Where is Mr. Jorgensen? Why didn't he show up?"

"We don't know."

"You're not telling me."

"I'd tell you."

"But if he isn't at the hospital and I go along with Mr. Hartman . . ."

"It won't bother Max Hartman," Rip said. "He'll figure you'll stay in the car while he runs in and gives them to a friend. If you follow—but please don't—if you did, you'd discover you were left talking with the receptionist and he'd be chatting with a nurse out of hearing, and giving her the cases, which she would turn over to a party as instructed. He'd come back and tell you that his uncle—but he's not his uncle, no relation at all—had been given a sedative and was out cold."

He rose, restless, and pulled aside the drape a crack to glance out. "Max Hartman is a fast-moving, glib-talking, intelligent operator, brilliant in anything he tries."

"Say," Hank said, "how long you been working this guy?"

Chris asked: "Mr. Jorgensen's dead, isn't he?"

"Was he scared on the plane?"

"Not at all. Who is he, anyway?"

"He's a confidence man with an arrest record that takes up two sheets."

Chris gazed at him in disbelief. "He couldn't be! Not that nice, thoughtful, polite old man!"

Rip nodded. "One of the best—as you'll have to admit." What he didn't tell her was that Sam Jorgensen was an ex-convict who had served three terms in prison for an aggregate of thirteen years, that he was a big-time operator of the flamboyant, imaginative old school of swindlers, who in his own world was known as Cadillac Sam since he drove that make of car, purchasing a new one each year.

Chris considered the news a moment. "Then if he isn't Mr. Hartman's uncle, then the cases . . ."

Rip sat opposite her. In the light her cheekbones were prominent. She had what his mother called good bone structure. His mother thought that indicated a strong character. In his years in the FBI, Rip had reached the conclusion that it did reflect a strong character, though not necessarily a good one.

He said: "I want you to play along with Max Hartman."

14

She frowned. "What do you mean, play along?"

"Just act the way you would with any man. Don't ask questions you wouldn't usually ask. Listen mostly, and tell me what he talked about, what he said. He'll ask you for a date. He does every girl he meets. And you'll go to lunch or dinner with him—"

"Now wait a *minute!* I don't—"

"Please," Rip cut in. "I—the Bureau would appreciate it deeply."

"I'm signed in for the twelve forty-five P.M. to Washington." It was a flat statement, intended to end the subject.

"I can arrange that," Hank said.

"Mr.—what was your name?"

"Ripley."

"Mr. Ripley, I don't like your walking in here and telling me what I'm going to do. I'm in the habit of making my own arrangements."

Rip felt anger begin to surface, so he smiled and battened down the hatches. "I apologize. I was overanxious. I'll tell the SAC you won't—you aren't available."

"What's the SAC?"

"S-A-C stands for Special Agent in Charge—of the local office, that is."

"Oh. I thought it was pronounced 'sack.'"

Rip groaned. "He'll be disappointed. Most disappointed."

She calmed. "I'd lose my pay—and I need it. I'm taking my two nephews to Ringling Brothers circus. You know what a circus costs today? It's outrageous. Only rich kids can afford it. When I was a youngster—"

"It *is* outrageous," Rip said, agreeing too readily. "Now, if you'll—"

"No. I've never been a rat fink and I'm not going to start now. What's he done?"

"I can't tell you. You might give yourself away if you knew."

Color rushed into her cheeks. "You expect me to risk my neck and tell you everything he says but when I ask a simple question . . . Is he dangerous?"

"No. Well, he is. Very dangerous. But he wouldn't be with you. Not with someone outside of his sphere of operations."

"He'll want to make love to me, won't he?"

Rip was jarred. She persisted: "He's that kind. I could tell."

"You've handled situations like that before."

She was silent a moment, then shook her head. "I was in this protest group at the university. We made placards and signed petitions. We didn't do anything illegal. But there was a girl in it who reported everything to the FBI. She was a stool pigeon."

Rip took a deep breath. "Believe me, Miss Roberts, this is nothing like that. This is a matter of possible death to a great many people. A great many. If I could tell you about this case, you wouldn't hesitate."

"You said he was dangerous."

"Not to you. He would have no reason to harm you. He's not a psycho, if that's what you're thinking. I'm not asking you to *do* anything. Only listen. You may hear something that will save Mr. Jorgensen's life—or someone else's."

"But if he found out I was reporting to you . . . ?"

"I don't know how he could find out . . . but if he did, well, I got to be honest with you, Miss Roberts, I must admit he'd try to kill you."

4

THAT NIGHT, what there was left of it, she tossed about until the covers the next morning were as askew as her nerves. Occasionally she awakened in a sweat. Once she dreamed that she met Max Hartman in a long, black, freezing cold tunnel far beneath the earth. Before anything could happen, she escaped from the dream, and listened then for the reassuring faint ticking of the travel clock by her head. There was no ticking, and alarmed, she switched on the light. In her half-consciousness she feared someone had stopped the ticking, someone was in the room. No one was, and she wound the clock and set it by her watch which was highly unpredictable. She kept it running ten minutes ahead of the correct time.

She took a roller out of her hair that was jabbing her, replaced it with bobby pins, and turning out the light sternly ordered herself to sleep. Tomorrow she had only to act herself. It was only one more date. She was not rationalizing. She was being quite logical.

Her thoughts, too, spun like a July 4th cartwheel around Mr. Ripley. What was there about that man? He irritated her irrationally, yet she wanted to impress him. He was so demanding, so sure she would do his bidding. She disliked him, and yet . . . The "yet" made her furious, too. She didn't understand it. He had not trusted her. He had provided her with no protective information. He had asked her to run a certain risk without briefing her. A woman assuming this kind of risk, even though minimal, needed all of the knowledge available.

She admitted that the risk was no greater than that of a few summers back, but that was different. Different? Yes—because she had taken it on her own volition.

From her car-hop pay checks she had saved sufficient money to buy a round-trip air ticket to Europe. She had hitchhiked all over the Continent, sometimes with a girl her age she would meet, more often by herself. She would stand by the side of the road, often at night, in tired, old jeans and a checkered blouse, a heavy pack on her back, and long straight hair blowing in the wind. Mostly truck drivers picked her up. They would inventory her, and there was always the latent fear. But none had ever threatened to molest her.

Eventually she needed money. In Zurich she mopped floors in a clinic, and in the little town of Kriens, near Lucerne, where the cable car came down from Mount Pilatus, she waited tables at the Restaurant Schlossli. By now she spoke a little German. For wages she got the 10 percent service charge collected on all orders, plus her board and room. She shared the latter with two Swiss farm girls who were accustomed to laboring in the fields from sunup to sundown, and were happy with the luxury of a ten-hour-a-day job and an attractive room.

At 9 o'clock, her heart beating hard, she waited at the curb. Max Hartman brought his freshly bathed Porsche up with the flourish of a horse lover showing off a beautiful yearling.

When he started to get out, she called: "Never mind." Hastily she tossed in 6-C's two cases and with a swirl of skirt and show of bare leg slipped in alongside him. He looked admiringly at her with that faint impudent smile that was his trademark. "Hey," he said, "you look devastating with clothes on."

She laughed unsteadily. He, too, looked better in the daylight. He was in a sport shirt unbuttoned halfway down with a medal around his neck that boldly proclaimed PAX. The medal lay against black heavy chest hair. His eyes were bright and warm with life and his shifting, restless body had virility and abandon. He looked far from

17

dangerous. Certainly he had no gun or knife concealed in the dark, skin-tight trousers.

He gunned the Porsche into the heavy street flow. She groped for something to say but could think of nothing that did not sound unnatural. She dared not analyze every word, every move, for he would be quick to realize she was acting. Finally she asked about his uncle.

"Can you believe it," he said. "I gave you the wrong hospital last night. I've never made a mistake like that. I don't make mistakes."

No, you don't, she thought, and you didn't this time. "He seems like such a nice old gentleman."

He shrugged. "He's okay I guess."

At the Daniel Freeman Hospital he parked in a tight space a considerable distance from the entrance. She noted there were closer ones. He said he would run in with the cases, and left her. She sat in a kind of stupor, trying to reconcile the components of the situation. If he were dangerous, if a good many people might die because of him, then why hadn't the FBI arrested him?

In about ten minutes he returned. "They doped him up last night and he's still sleeping. The nurse says he's coming along okay."

He asked if he could drop her off somewhere and she suggested her brother's home which was close by. En route, each talked about himself, divulging backgrounds, the way strangers revel in telling well-worn facts and stories that even the best of friends no longer will tolerate.

She painted a cameo of Clinton, a town of 8,500 in North Carolina, and of a father she adored who sold real estate, and how she still squandered money in record shops, a holdover from her teen years. In turn he talked about the "think tank" at Aerospace Engineers where he worked, and his love for the sea. "I've got a live-aboard boat down at Marina del Rey. A 36-footer. How about lunch and we'll take a run down there?" He was a teen-ager anxious to show off his new Honda.

"Not lunch. There's this friend I promised."

"What then? You're flying out this afternoon, aren't you?"

Her heart threatened to stop. How did he know? Act natural. "Hey, what are you, some kind of detective?" She put on what she hoped was a faint, pleased smile. "I've been put on another flight. Nine tomorrow morning."

"Great. Then how about dinner at the Lautrec? Have you been there?"

18

"I should say not. I can't afford Lautrec."

"I take all my girls there."

She looked at him curiously. He was not joking but stating a fact. "So you want me to join the club?"

He turned on the charm. "For tonight—for what you did for my uncle. Eight o'clock all right?" After a proper hesitation she agreed.

He said a little too casually: "Why didn't you ask me how I knew you were flying out this afternoon?"

She felt a lurch of fear as she groped for the right answer. She smiled and let her glance touch him briefly. "It's been done," she said lightly. "I mean, finding out."

"Hum-m." She felt his eyes studying her. "I told United I was your brother."

"You're awfully good at inventing relatives." She could have cut her tongue off. He shot her an inquisitorial glance. She pretended not to notice.

"What d'you mean by that?"

She managed an offhand look of surprise. "Mean? About what?"

His eyes said he knew that she knew or suspected that 6-C was not his uncle. But which is it, she asked herself: Do I know or do I merely suspect? If I know, then I have learned it from someone or some source.

As she came up the walk, her brother's nine-year-old twin boys rushed her, yelling. She bent to wrap her arms around them, and they chattered as if they hadn't seen her in years. She loved them passionately. "If things ever get rough at home," she had joked, "I'll adopt you." And a time or two they had camped on her doorstep. Her brother Dan, a big, no-nonsense kind who believed in discipline, took an ill view of this, and in very explicit terms had told her so.

Now they had news to tell her. Their big Saint Bernard dog, named Keg, a bone crusher and smotherer when he sat on one's lap, had got stuck in the mud while pulling the two in their wagon. Somehow they had extricated the jack from the car trunk and proceeded to jack him up.

"That was very clever," she said.

"No, it wasn't," answered one, tears coming into his eyes. "We hurt him. We had to take him to the vet."

She brushed aside his tears and assured him that Keg would be all right. She reconfirmed for the nineteenth time that she would take

19

them to the circus, an event which they had lived for since the end of the school term.

In the house, her brother's wife, Leona, met her with a kiss on the cheek and family gossip. When Chris could, she asked if she might use the phone extension in the bedroom. Leona looked at her curiously, obviously wondering about the secrecy. The slightest deviation from the norm invariably aroused suspicion.

When Rip came on the line, she steadied her voice and reported the conversation as factually as she could. She failed to tell him about her one slip, the flip remark that tipped Max off to the fact she either knew or suspected that 6-C was not his uncle. She hadn't meant to hold back this bit of information, and could not explain even to herself why she had. Somehow it had not fallen easily into the conversation.

5

SAC, LOS ANGELES. WHITE HOUSE LIAISON ADVISES PRESIDENT HAS REQUESTED SUMMARY OF INVESTIGATION TO DATE RE COMMITTEE OF PUBLIC SAFETY. THIS CASE TAKES PRIORITY OVER ALL OTHERS IN YOUR FIELD DIVISION. ALL LEADS MUST BE WORKED IMMEDIATELY UPON BEING SET FORTH. ALL FIELD DIVISIONS NOTIFIED LOS ANGELES OFFICE OF ORIGIN. TELEPHONIC CONFERENCE BETWEEN BUREAU, WASHINGTON FIELD, NEW YORK, CHICAGO, BOSTON, AND LOS ANGELES SET FOR 2 P.M. TOMORROW.

DIRECTOR

SUMMARY REPORT

The Committee of Public Safety was founded on or about Oct. 20, 1971, by 13 individuals, whose names and backgrounds are set forth below, in a meeting held on a boat owned by Max Hartman, anchored off Marina del Rey, California, with the avowed purpose of forming a conspiracy to overthrow the government of the United States by violent means, according to Informants C-119 and C-123.

C-119 and C-123 subsequently reported that the Los Angeles organization had established branches in Chicago, New York and Washington, D.C., but that all decisions and operations were controlled by the Los Angeles group, and no one could be accepted into membership without the approval of Max Hartman, the organizer and dominating figure in the Los Angeles organization.

C-119 and C-123 advised, furthermore, that the principal aim of the Committee was the destruction and seizure of Washington, D.C., the overthrow of the present government, and the establishment of a dictatorship with Dr. George Henry Beaumont as the temporary head of government, who subsequently would resign and make way for Hartman to succeed him.

C-119 disclosed that the Committee was modeled after the Tupamaros, the well-organized, efficient and disciplined band of terrorists who have operated in Uruguay for several years.

(Note: The Tupamaros have engaged extensively in kidnapings, bank robberies, assassinations, and terror tactics. Their record has included a six-million-dollar robbery of Uruguay's Bank of the Republic, the capture of an entire town, defiance of the United States by the murder of the American embassy aide, Daniel Mitrione, and the kidnaping of another American, four political assassinations in one day, and the freeing of 106 fellow Tupamaros from a maximum-security prison. They take their name from gaucho rebels who operated early in Uruguay's history, who in turn took their name from Tupa Amaru II, a Peruvian Indian chief who led a revolt against Spanish forces in 1790.)

C-119 advised, however, that the names chosen for the American group were those used during the French Revolution (1789–1799). The name of the organization, the Committee of Public Safety, derives from the Comité de

Salut Public which took final shape July 10, 1793, with the exclusion of Danton and the addition 17 days later of Robespierre. C-119 also reported that several code names for individuals in the Los Angeles-based organization have been drawn from the French Revolution, such as the assignment of the code name Robespierre to Dr. Beaumont.

While the Committee has modeled its organization, tactics and strategy after the Tupamaros, the leaders have stated, according to both informants, that the movement will have more appeal to Americans if it is cloaked in terms of the French Revolution, and the idea implanted that the United States has reached a period in its history, the same as France did, when the only way to achieve *liberté, égalité* and *fraternité* for all peoples is through revolution.

C-119 said that, like the Tupamaros, the Los Angeles organization consists of several groups calling themselves sections. C-119 stated that the members of one section have no knowledge of the identity of the members of another, and often no knowledge of the entire roster within their own section; that only Hartman, and possibly Dr. Beaumont, know the names of all members and the sections to which they are assigned.

BREAKDOWN OF THE SECTIONS

C-119 advised that the following sections are in operation at present:

THE PLANNING SECTION which consists of the key leaders, including Hartman and Dr. Beaumont, who direct the entire operation, including the activities of the branches.

THE FINANCE SECTION that raises money by means of bank robberies, kidnapings and similar crimes of violence.

THE INTELLIGENCE SECTION that primarily spies on the police, the FBI and other law enforcement agencies with the purpose of discovering their weak points and learning about their investigations of subversive groups.

22

This section also spies on Committee members who are suspect.

THE PROPAGANDA SECTION that develops rumors and factual reports with the intent to spread them in the course of the revolution as a means of creating fear and panic.

THE LIAISON SECTION that maintains loose contacts with militant organizations, and prepares appraisals of militant leaders who might be helpful in some capacity to the Committee at the time of the revolution.

THE ORDNANCE SECTION that raids police headquarters and ordnance supply depots for weapons and explosives.

THE ZERO SECTION that kills police officers, persons considered dangerous to the organization, and liquidates members who defect. C-119 stated that Hartman maintains a tight control over this section and orders to kill must have his approval. C-119 advised, furthermore, that all such orders in the past, to his knowledge, have originated with Hartman.

PRINCIPAL LEADERS

Informants C-119 and C-123, members of the Committee of Public Safety, advised that the principal leaders are:

MAXIMILIAN HARTMAN, aka MAX HARTMAN, 28, six feet three, 180, blue eyes, wavy brown hair, unmarried, small birth mark behind right ear, teeth uneven, stands very erect, a commanding figure. He informed C-123 that he practiced speaking in front of a mirror two hours each day. He has a highly persuasive voice, all informants have advised. C-123 reported that Hartman told him he would call himself prime minister when the Committee seized power, and he would model his appearance and actions after Nasser and Fidel Castro. He has read extensively about leaders who have come to power through the violent overthrow of governments. He is a Northwestern University graduate *cum laude,* 1968. He was student body

23

president, campus newspaper editor, quarterback for three years. Northwestern authorities advised he took part in three peaceful demonstrations during his sophomore year. He was inactive during his junior and senior years, and fellow students reported he had told them that he considered the protests a waste of time, "the whole scene was ridiculous," and he planned to set up a highly efficient organization of professional revolutionaries who would talk little and achieve results. His associates said he ridiculed the demonstrations at the University of California at Berkeley, the burning of the Bank of America at Isla Vista, California, the riots in Chicago at the time of the Democratic Convention in 1968, and other situations where "the violence leads nowhere, is only a one- or two-night stand, and achieves nothing more than to incur the wrath of the Establishment and show off the theatrical talents of the leaders." He dresses well, likes gourmet foods, night clubs, has expensive tastes . . .

DR. GEORGE HENRY BEAUMONT, 66, five feet ten, 148, blue eyes, white hair, a widower, has military bearing, wears eyeglasses, smokes a pipe, suffers from emphysema and pinched back nerve, holds anti-Semitic, anti-Negro, and anti-Chicano beliefs, and likes to quote classic scholars. He is a retired University of California at Los Angeles professor, a historian highly respected in education circles. Scholars consider him the foremost authority on the French Revolution. He has written numerous volumes, "The Reign of Terror," "The Great Fear," "Charlotte Corday," "The September Massacres" and others. He lives alone in the home he and his late wife (who died in May 1967) shared for about 25 years. According to his associates, he has a keen, analytical mind. For 20 years he taught a popular course at UCLA, History 178, known to the students as "The Guillotine Course." He was known as an extremely caustic professor who would expel students from his classes if he thought they were not displaying the proper interest. C-123 has advised that Dr. Beaumont stated on one occasion that whereas 40,000 went to the guillotines during the French Revolution, it might be neces-

24

sary to purge a half million in the key cities of the United States, and that he did not consider this an excessive number for a modern revolution in view of the fact that the Russians purged millions in the Ukraine and Mao, millions in China. C-123 disclosed that it was Dr. Beaumont who gave the Committee of Public Safety its name, and that he christened the Washington, D.C., group The Directory. (It was The Directory that ruled France toward the end of the fighting.) C-123 and C-119 reported that Dr. Beaumont and Hartman work closely and amicably, and that there appears to be mutual admiration. C-123 advised that Hartman depended on Dr. Beaumont's knowledge of history as a blueprint in planning the proposed revolution.

WILLIAM RANDOLPH BOONE, 24, five feet eight, 147, brown eyes, light brown unparted hair distinguished by a "crock" cut, thin faced, pock marked, single, a Vietnam war veteran with a dishonorable discharge for failure to follow orders, a munitions expert, highly unpredictable. C-119 advised Boone is a fanatic about explosives, that Hartman has to exercise tight control to keep him from prematurely blowing up or fire bombing a place or persons that would bring the authorities down on the Committee before the Committee was prepared to act. A check by the Washington Field division of U. S. Army records disclosed he had been given a dishonorable discharge shortly after he was ordered to mine a road and subsequently mined the entire countryside, endangering the lives of scores of civilians. He was born in Los Angeles, of a good, upper middle class family, the last of five children, attended Birmingham High School, dropped out in his senior year, had numerous jobs that he quit after working at them only a short time. He had a job repairing motorcycles when he was drafted. He is withdrawn, moody, has estranged himself from his family, refused to attend the funeral of his father and mother. He owns the Junkery, Ventura Boulevard, Sherman Oaks, where he builds plastic bombs and other explosive devices. C-119 stated that Hartman and Boone often quarrel, and that Dr. Beaumont has acted as peace-maker. C-119 said that Boone carries a hand grenade

25

in a coat pocket at all times and Hartman feared he would blow up the group at some meeting. C-119 said, furthermore, that when Hartman had demanded the grenade on one occasion, Boone had threatened to pull the pin.

C-119 died of gunshot wounds inflicted by an unknown party Dec. 24, 1971. C-123 died of lung cancer April 19, 1972. At present the Los Angeles Field division has no informants working inside the Los Angeles Committee of Public Safety.

6

AT 6 A.M. Rip awakened, stretched, and in so doing punched Pandemonium at the foot of the bed out of a dead sleep. Rip turned over, stared out of the window, and met eyeball to eyeball a hummingbird working the flowers. He rolled back and came to focus on a dusty, faded photo of his mother and the dog that had shared his first fourteen years. In her last letter she had written: "I hope you still love me as much as you did that dog." That was her little joke. In the first grade he had written a description of his mother: "My mother has brown eyes like my dog and gray hair like my dog and she is nice like my dog."

While the cat yawned and surveyed his world beyond the window with the jaundiced eye of an old rake, Rip dropped his rumpled pajamas on the floor and dressed. He had a well-disciplined body with a flat belly. He kept the fat content low by jogging, tennis, surfing, and karate. The bedroom had the same lean look. For three years he had been intending to hang pictures.

After feeding Pandemonium half a can of chopped kidney, Rip burned four slices of bacon, fried an egg, procured a can of orange juice from the refrigerator, and sat down at a sun-dappled breakfast nook. Outside the window a golden-yellow butterfly with delicate black markings landed on a plant. Slowly Rip's hand reached for the camera he kept on the padded bench. He brought it up, but as he focused, the butterfly flitted away. "Blast!" he muttered.

While he ate he listened to a tape playback. Christina Roberts had called at 1:07 A.M. to report on her evening with Max Hartman. Rip had informed her that he was taping the conversation. Now he heard a voice, one moment vibrant with youth and the next, subdued by fear.

ROBERTS: He picked me up at my apartment. I was waiting outside since I didn't want my roommate to see him and start asking questions. I'd already had troubles with Jim—my boy friend, Jim Kendall. When Jim learned my flight had been canceled he was determined to come over and I had to tell him I had a fierce headache. That's the first time I've ever lied to him—

RIP: Did he say anything about his uncle?

ROBERTS: Yes, we had barely started when he said his uncle had disappeared from the hospital. Said he had slipped out and with the condition he was in . . . Is that true? Was he at Daniel Freeman?

RIP: No more than he was at Inglewood Hospital. We haven't located him.

ROBERTS: He said his uncle had a thousand dollars in cash on him, if the police officers investigating the accident hadn't taken it. He was collecting old Buck Jones movies.

RIP: Collecting what?

ROBERTS: Buck Jones. He was an old Western star and it seems there are all kinds of collectors of old film prints, and his uncle specialized in Buck Jones. He paid one hundred and ten dollars a print if the print was in good condition. He had most of Buck Jones but was missing a few and thought he knew a place that might have them.

RIP: Did he say where?

ROBERTS: In San Fernando Valley. He didn't mention the name of the place and you said not to ask questions. Hold it a minute, will you? . . . I thought I heard Roz out in the hallway. I'm in my room with the phone. Her folks took off this morning. The phone's got one of these long cords. I should've told you something. I made a bad slip. I don't know how I could but when he said he had told United he was my brother I said he was awfully good at inventing relatives, joking of course. But I'm sure he believes that I either know or suspect that his uncle was not his uncle. I couldn't think of anything else all day. I almost called off dinner.

27

RIP: Don't let it throw you. He can't be sure.

ROBERTS: He said I didn't seem concerned about his uncle's disappearance. I said I was but what was there to say except did he know any place to look for his uncle because if he did we should right after dinner. He said no but did I know anything about it? How would I know? I asked him. He was suspicious. I got a feeling he was reading my thoughts.

RIP: It's an old ploy—get you to panic and drop something.

ROBERTS: He wouldn't if he didn't suspect me.

RIP: Not necessarily. Put yourself in *his* place. He's *got* to suspect you, to test you—until he's sure. Just act natural.

ROBERTS: Natural, he says . . . I told you, didn't I, that he lives on a boat at Marina del Rey? He suggested we drive down after dinner but I pleaded I had to get up early—but what I wanted to tell you was that he rents a power craft some weekends and he asked me to come along this Sunday but I said Roz and I were going to San Diego. I didn't want to tell him it's Jim and me. Oh, yes, I have an invitation to spend the night on his boat any time I want to. There's a full moon next week . . .

RIP: What'd you tell him?

ROBERTS: I'd have to see what my flight schedule was. I got to thinking on my way home, I'm not going to be able to break it off, am I? He's going to call me, and I can't stall forever. What'll I tell him? . . . Is he going to get threatening? You said something about people being killed. What people?

RIP: We'd better talk about it.

ROBERTS: I'm due back in Los Angeles Thursday afternoon . . . It's Roz's night to go bowling with a fellow. Jim and I said we'd go along but I could plead I had to get some sleep.

RIP: I'd better come over. Does your place have a back door?

ROBERTS: Yes, but be careful not to knock over the rubbish can. The sweet, little old lady in the next apartment—she must be seventy —she puts her liquor bottles in it.

RIP: Nine o'clock?

ROBERTS: You didn't answer my question.

RIP: I have no reason to believe you're in danger but we'll put agents on you, following you, until I see you.

ROBERTS: In Washington, too?

RIP: Yes—and on the plane each way.

ROBERTS: I'm scared. I don't think I can sleep.

28

RIP: Two agents are on watch now outside your apartment.

ROBERTS: You're scared, too!

RIP: No, but we're not taking chances. Try to sleep. I'm sorry I've frightened you. You've handled this very well.

ROBERTS: I'll be all right. I didn't mean to—but it isn't something you forget . . . it sure isn't. Good night.

7

HE COULDN'T FINISH breakfast. He gave Pandemonium the rest of the bacon, which he refused, and gulped down coffee that had an old cistern-water look. He said goodbye to the cat, opened the door, and decided he was safe. He wasn't. He had taken only a few steps when Mr. Lancaster, who lived across the way, shouted, "Hey, Rip!" He was short, waddling, and had a barrel stomach. "I won't hold you up. I know you've got a bank robber to catch before nine o'clock." He went into a loud guffaw, then sobered, and his voice fell to a low confidential rumble. "Did you look into that woman down the street I told you about?"

The woman in question had point-blank refused Mr. Lancaster's request that she display the American flag every day. Obviously, she was a subversive.

"We're working on it," Rip said, lying. He scarcely knew what the conversation was about. All he could think about was Christina Roberts.

"Can't say anything, huh? I wouldn't be surprised if she isn't a Chinese agent. I asked the postman to watch her mail. If she gets anything from Peking—"

"Good move."

At the Federal Building in Westwood, Rip rode up the elevator with Agent Ray Bunker, a slow-moving hulk of a man, big chested and big stomached, who lived in dread that the Bureau would terminate him. He was fourteen pounds overweight and the Bureau had sent him a terse memo to the effect he had sixty days in which to reduce.

This morning Bunker was all smiles. "Three pounds off in four days. Three pounds!"

In the office Rip signed in, then looked in the communications center and said hello to Peg. Even in the harsh, artificial light that bounced off the walls and converted everyone into a rogue's gallery suspect, she looked stunning. They had a date for the Hollywood Bowl on Saturday night. "I just put a teletype in your file folder," she said.

In a vast room that contained rows of highly polished, and for the most part, bare-topped desks, he stopped by a tier of files, pulled his open, and saw the teletype was from the New York Field division. It read:

SAC, LOS ANGELES. RE SAMUEL JORGENSEN. IN-
FORMANT BELIEVED TRUSTWORTHY. COM-
PLETED TERM ELMIRA PRISON 8-17-70 FOR
FRAUD. ENROLLED IN NEW YORK COMMITTEE
OF PUBLIC SAFETY 5-13-72 BY FRIEND ON BASIS
HE HAD BEEN OUTSPOKEN AGAINST GOVERN-
MENT DURING PRISON TERM. CAME TO THIS OF-
FICE 5-20-72. ADMITTED HE HAD CONDEMNED
GOVERNMENT BUT HAD QUOTE ONLY BEEN
LETTING OFF STEAM UNQUOTE. SAID HE WAS A
PATRIOT WHO OPPOSED MILITANT ACTIVI-
TIES . . .

That followed, Rip thought. He had never known a confidence man who was not fiercely patriotic. He would prey on his fellow men but not on his country. Maybe he appreciated the opportunity his country gave him, Rip had facetiously told Peg.

Although the time was 7:34, and sign-in was not until 8:30, many agents were working. Two were strapping on holsters. They had a lead, they said, in a flight to avoid prosecution for murder. Another had a map out. He was investigating the $150,000 hijacking of a truck loaded with furs. Another was preparing notes to use in dictating a report on an anti-racketeering case. At a far desk, an agent was interviewing a call girl in a washed-out yellow summer dress who looked more like a housewife. She didn't appear nervous. In her work a woman hardened quickly. He remembered the first time he had brought a prostitute in for questioning. He had had the impression then that most prostitutes had been forced into the work either through entrapment or poverty. It had come as a shock when the girl told him frankly she had had a good job as a secretary, but prostitution paid much better, and besides it was more fun. In the years since, he had discovered that that was the case more often than not.

At his desk he called the SAC's secretary to request an appointment. She said she would call him back. A girl from the stenographic pool placed a log before him, a report from the agents who had run the night surveillance on Christina Roberts. Nothing worthy of note had taken place.

He continued reading the New York teletype:

RE YOUR REQUEST HABITS OF INFORMANT, REPORT THIS OFFICE DATED 5-16-64 REFLECTS INFORMANT MAKES FEW CONTACTS OUTSIDE HIS CRIMINAL ACTIVITIES, SEES ALL NEW MOVIES, COLLECTS PRINTS OF OLD FILMS, PRINCIPALLY BUCK JONES WESTERNS, BUYS DIAMONDS FOR INVESTMENT, BUYS AGED MOTHER DIAMOND PINS, PLAYS GOLF DAILY WHEN POSSIBLE, LIKES GAUDY TIES . . .

He set forth several leads for the agents working the case with him to cover: (1) show informant's photo to all film print sales shops and old print distributors, (2) to all principal jewelry stores in Los Angeles, (3) and around all golf courses. He doubted if he would find a trace of Sam Jorgensen. Certainly he wouldn't unless Jorgensen had double-crossed the FBI or panicked. Rip believed Jorgensen had been murdered. The Bureau rule, though, was that all leads must be worked, no agent must ever assume anything. The Bureau dealt in facts, not in hunches.

He took from his bottom desk drawer the prints of the papers he had photographed in the two cases Jorgensen had turned over to Miss Roberts. The contents had consisted principally of (1) newspaper accounts of kidnapings by the Tupamaros in Montevideo, (2) lengthy analyses in Spanish by one Rodríguez Calle of Buenos Aires, (3) several books and pamphlets on explosives that Rip had not photographed since they were available in book stores, (4) the floor plans of several Washington, D.C., government buildings, and (5) a large street map of the city marked with code words. Rip would send the photo copy of the map to the Bureau Laboratory. He was finishing

31

compiling a list of the documents when the SAC's secretary advised the SAC would see him.

The SAC was a tall, robust man with broad shoulders, a narrow waist that had been well dieted over the years, and an awkwardness many big people have. He finished reading a report, then looked up but said nothing. He was not a man given to amenities.

He listened intently while Rip briefed him. "It was very foggy. She couldn't tell you whether the taxi was green or purple. She didn't notice the driver, maybe couldn't see him, although she has a hazy recollection of a young man looking on from nearby. We've got some leads to work. If he ran out on us, he may be searching for a print of a Buck Jones film."

"Buck Jones?"

Rip explained, and the SAC shook his head. "Who would want a print of a Buck Jones picture? A Clark Gable movie, yes. But Buck Jones!" He rose. "You should have put a surveillance on him on his arrival at the airport. You know better than to let a key informant come in without cover."

Rip tensed. "New York said the informant specifically asked that no tail be put on him. He thought it would be too dangerous. The subjects might spot it if we worked it tight and if we played it loose, well, we couldn't on a foggy night."

The SAC scowled. "Who's conducting this investigation, you or the informant?"

Rip's voice tightened. "It was my considered judgment that a tail job was a high risk—to the informant."

The SAC dropped back down in the swivel. "I'm the one who gets the heat. I've got to tell the Bureau that we made an error in judgment, that we may have lost another informant because we sat on our butts when we—"

"I'll take the heat," Rip said, "but I figured the subjects might have two or three of their men running their own tail. They would have spotted another surveillance."

The SAC could be right. If he—Rip—had run a surveillance, agents might have surprised a gunman in the very act of assassinating the informant. It was highly unlikely but still, an outside chance, a $2 bet on a long shot to win. This was a judgment call an agent had to make, and then pray the break would go his way. As a matter of fact—and the SAC knew this only too well—not much could be done to lay down a protective cover around an informant who by the very

32

nature of his assignment lived constantly within a danger zone. To prove effective, he had to be free to move around with the least possible outside contact. He had to become what he appeared to be to the group in which he operated. If the group learned his true identity, he usually had only his two legs to carry him beyond the inevitable gunfire.

Aside from Sam Jorgensen, the New York Field division had one other informant, classified as weak and reluctant. He was a runner for the Mafia who delivered their messages and looked after miscellaneous petty tasks. The New York District Attorney's office could prosecute him at any time it wished. He had been witness to a murder and failed to report it. The DA had agreed to go into court eventually, provided he turned informant, and ask for a suspended sentence and probation. But whenever agents questioned him, he appeared an unfriendly, hostile witness. Only by lengthy, extensive cross-examination could they extract information.

The Los Angeles Field division had fared little better. C-123, who had died of lung cancer, had been a heroin addict who was being treated with Methadone. He had been a member of the Intelligence Section that spied on the Committee's own members and law-enforcement agencies.

C-119, a weasel type and congenital liar whose every statement was suspect, had worked with dynamite crews on heavy construction, blasting through tunnels and on highway projects. He had belonged to the Ordnance Section and once had reported a proposed raid on the ordnance depot at Camp Pendleton near San Diego that Rip and other agents had successfully blocked without the Committee knowing. Late one night, when returning home, he had been riddled from ambush with a shotgun blast. He had been a heavy drinker and Rip believed he had talked too much, giving away his work with the Bureau, of which he was inordinately proud.

The Bureau, hence, had no informants in Los Angeles, Washington, D.C., or Chicago, which left only Sam Jorgensen, if he were still around, and the hostile witness in New York. The arrival on the scene, therefore, of one Christina Roberts was a godsend. Rip proceeded to brief the SAC about her background. She had never participated in any violent demonstrations or riots on the University of California at Santa Barbara campus, according to a resident agent, and had had an excellent scholastic record. Her instructors advised that she was of good character. Both the personnel people and her supervisor at United Airlines knew nothing derogatory about her personal life. Under Rip's direction, agents had checked out her roommate, Rosalind Canaletto, her fiancé, James Somerset Kendall, and her brother, Daniel Greene Roberts, and all sources interviewed had vouched for their character and loyalty to their country. None had a criminal record.

Rip continued: "She's worked out very well twice with Max Hartman. She's scared but cool. She can take pressure without panicking. Those are the pluses.

"Now for the negative side: She's an outgoing person, warm, human, loves people and life, very thoughtful and kind. It will take considerable work to change her into the hard, brittle individual that we'll need. It'll be a kind of Pygmalion in reverse. It won't be easy, but she can do it. She's intelligent and seems adaptable. Without a doubt, Max Hartman is interested in her. He has asked her down to his boat and she can probably swing an all-day trip next weekend. It'll take time but if she can work her way in, she'll be worth six other informants."

"When can you see her?"

"Tomorrow night. Nine o'clock."

"I hope she goes for it. But I wouldn't blame her . . . We've already lost one informant, and now maybe two. Be honest with her. Tell her she runs a great risk. Put it in so many words."

8

RIP SAT SLUMPED in the unmarked car, his eyes barely above door level, casing the dark street and the apartments across the way. The usual night noises came over: the low rumble of tires punctuated by a motorcycle roar, the exasperated calling of a mother for an errant child, an antiphonal dog medley, a television set turned too high with gunfire resounding in the canyon pass, and in the background the subdued roar of the ocean.

When the dashboard clock read 8:55, he roused himself, shook his hair into place, and stepped out. The night was warm, starlit, and redolent with all kinds of pleasing odors: roses, pork chops, sea weed, fishes, star jasmine.

Crossing the street swiftly, he lost himself in tall, overgrown hibiscus bushes that crowded the narrow, broken walk to Chris Roberts's back door. Before he could tap, it opened, and her low voice said: "Come in." He stepped quickly into darkness and was conscious of her perfume, light and pleasant like the girl herself. "This way," she said.

She opened a door into a living room lighted in the subdued manner of the better bars. A basket seat, painted chartreuse and crowded with pillows, hung from the ceiling. The sofa was a vinyl-covered foam pad swathed in gay pillows on a slab door supported by concrete blocks. The drawn drapes, which were patches of cloth sewn together, looked like Jacob's coat.

"I don't know why I'm whispering," she said. "No one can hear."

She noticed him staring at a moose head projecting from the wall with a beflowered straw hat perched thereupon. "That was Grandpapa's." She adjusted the hat to give it a rakish angle. "We were very close. Used to go walking in the woods hand in hand, and once I looked back and saw an ogre, and Grandpapa picked up a stick to do battle but when we turned back, the ogre was gone. That's the way with ogres, you know. They're all cowards. You pick up a stick and whoof . . . I'm scared. I never chatter like this. Please sit down, Mr. Ripley."

Rip lowered himself gingerly to the slab door. His knees stuck up higher than his chin and he tried in vain to arrange them comfortably.

"You wanted to ask me more about Mr. Hartman?" She sat on a faded Moroccan ottoman and leaned back against the wall in a provocative but innocent pose. Her glance lightly appraised him.

"Not exactly. I couldn't tell you much about the case the other night. I didn't want to be evasive—"

"But you didn't know me, and now you've investigated me . . ."

"I must ask you to hold this in confidence, everything we talk about."

"Of course." He had a nice, easygoing way about him, even when he was deadly serious, which he was now. She appreciated the fact that he had never played the big, important FBI agent with her. Now that banker in first class today who had demanded . . .

He said slowly, objectively: "To put it briefly, we're investigating a group of people—we don't know how many but it's sizable—who are plotting to kidnap high government officials, assassinate others,

35

blow up Washington, create anarchy, and seize the country. They call themselves the Committee of Public Safety after an organization that functioned during the French Revolution, and the brains behind it is Max Hartman."

She gazed in disbelief. "Max Hartman! I know there are some nuts running around who want to blow up things, but—"

"—but Max Hartman is no nut. You're right. He is an extremely intelligent revolutionary who operates with meticulous precision and fanatical dedication. His organization is not unique. There are similar ones in practically every major world power. You remember the massacre in the Lod Airport in Tel Aviv some time ago? Twenty-six innocent people were senselessly slaughtered and more than eighty wounded by three Japanese, hired by another terrorist outfit, the Palestine Guerrillas. They were members of a small group known as Rengo Sekigun in Japan of all places—one of the most stable, industrial nations in the world. Their self-stated goal is the destruction of Japanese society. They are dramatically akin to the Committee. They hold no rallies, no demonstrations, no protest groups. Their job in Israel stated their purpose. We can't just sit on our hands and let it happen here."

Deeply shaken, she spoke softly: "I didn't take you seriously at first . . . when you said many people might die."

He hurried on. "We want your help. We need it desperately. I'm not asking you to do anything but play along with Mr. Hartman, date him, talk sympathetically when and if he starts discussing militant ideas, and eventually simply drift into his confidence."

He was honest, she could say that. He put it on the line. In other circumstances, she could have liked him. Now she felt he was the hunter and she was a female fox at bay.

"No!" She rose swiftly, and stood erect and tense. "I would be too terrified . . . I couldn't. I wouldn't. Never!"

"Let me finish."

She broke in. "If you know all about them, why don't you arrest them?"

Patiently he explained: "We haven't identified a tenth of them. We don't even know a single leader in Washington and Chicago. We don't know their plans beyond vague generalities. We don't have the kind of evidence necessary for successful prosecution of the ones we do know here and in New York. And even if we did have the evidence, we would be tipping off the others. They would reorganize

36

and go deeper underground. We might not discover where they were or what they were doing until it was too late. That's why you would be so valuable. When we get it all put together—with your help—we will move in on them."

"How long . . ." She hesitated, finding it difficult to dredge up the words.

"Six months, if we get the breaks."

She flared up. "What do I tell my fiancé? 'Don't worry, I'm going to marry you but I'm going to be playing around with another guy for the next six months. Nothing to worry about, darling. Just routine.' "

"We'll work that out."

"Not with me you won't. You know something? I think you're crazy—and I'm crazy to be listening to you."

She punched the basket seat, making it spin. "You can get someone else. If I hadn't come along, if he hadn't given me those cases . . ."

He took a labored breath. "In World War II British Intelligence recruited spies on a quality basis. They sent trained men into enemy countries. The Nazis operated exactly the opposite. They recruited spies by the droves and flooded them into enemy nations on the theory that many would be caught but a few would not. But the Nazis discovered that most of the few who remained free failed to produce."

He shifted uneasily. "The FBI operates on a quality basis, Miss Roberts. Yes, we can find someone else but it would be a stroke of luck if the party was as well suited as you. Your temperament, your intelligence, your judgment, your background, your potential as an actress—"

"An actress!"

"I'll get to that. One asset you have that the next person wouldn't have, you're an airline stewardess. You can serve as a courier for them. The way it is, they're up against a communications barrier."

He explained that they never used the telephone for fear of a tap, or the mails since their letters might be intercepted. Hartman and the key leaders refused to fly to Chicago, New York, or Washington. If the FBI were running a surveillance on a Committee member in one of those cities, and Hartman was seen with the party, then the FBI would check out Hartman, and in running a surveillance on him, would identify others.

He continued: "They'll take you into their confidence quicker than someone else because they need you. Not that they won't in-

37

vestigate you thoroughly, and check you out, and test you. They will, and since they will, we've got to give you a new background, a new life, and a new personality, and that's where the acting comes in. You'll have to become a different person, even to yourself."

"I don't want to seem rude, Mr. Ripley, but I came out of the university without a very high regard for the FBI. There were these stool pigeons all over the place reporting back what we said. We had a right to peaceful dissent without the FBI building up dossiers on us."

"I don't know what that situation was." He spoke carefully. "There may have been a reason for an investigation you didn't know about, or it could have been an error in judgment. We're not infallible."

He spoke more intensely. "But this is no student dissent group. These are adults who will bomb and murder to overthrow this government. One of them, an eminent historian, estimates that a half million persons will die in this revolution. He has said that he doesn't regard that number as too high. There will be women and children shot and burned as well as men. There will be anarchy if these people have their way."

"That's impossible."

"It can't happen here? That's what the German people thought in pre-Hitler days. Just because the United States has never had a revolution—a dictator seizing power—doesn't mean we can't have one. Look around you . . . country after country . . ."

He leaned forward. "Let me tell you about these people. Take Max Hartman. He sees revolution as an opportunity to become a dictator, another Castro or Nasser. He doesn't care about righting injustices or helping people. For him, it's solely a matter of personal power. Old Dr. Beaumont, too, seeks power but a different kind. He's the intellectual, the Karl Marx. He wants to experiment with government. He's after the power that will give him a chance to run tests, to put some of the theories he has been studying and dreaming about for years into actuality.

"And then a few, like the explosive expert, are in it for the excitement of the kill, the bombings, all of the violence. They're after the thrill of being on the scene of a tragedy, an earthquake, a flood, an auto going out of control at a race.

"The younger ones may fit in better with your conception of a revolutionist. They've got what you might call a kind of lunatic idealism. They are nihilists. They would destroy to create. They believe that

38

they must level this country and start over. But no matter how falsely idealistic they may be, the fact remains that tens of thousands would perish and we would have anarchy, hunger, perhaps starvation and disease on a scale never known in our history."

She shook her head. "It's too fantastic. They could never get that far. The American people—"

He broke in. "All right, so what do we do? Let them try?"

She was quiet a moment, thinking. "All of my life I've hated people who spied on others and sent them to their deaths. Be a friend one day and stick a dagger in them the next."

"I felt that way once," he said, remembering, "and then one day I asked myself: What is the alternative?" He paused, and his thoughts scattered momentarily. She is wholesome and kind and tender and intelligent. I can't blame her. No one wants to be an informant but there are times when someone has to be.

He continued: "What is the alternative here? Do we let these people destroy our country, run rampant killing and bombing, so that our consciences will not be bothered? So that we won't have guilt feelings?"

After a moment he added: "In this particular case, I don't think you'll suffer the slightest guilt feeling. They're too ruthless, too determined to bring a blood bath on this country. You will be shocked and repulsed."

She shook her head. "You're putting me on."

"Let me tell you about a man named William Sebold back in 1940. He was a naturalized American, and went to Germany to visit relatives. He was a brilliant fellow, the kind the Abwehr was looking for, and they called him in, and asked him how he'd like to work as a Nazi spy in the United States. The inference was that he'd better if he cared anything about his relatives. So he agreed, only he went straight to a U.S. consulate over there and reported what had happened. Our government asked him to be a double agent. Well, FBI men were waiting when he returned to New York, and they helped him build a short-wave radio station on Long Island. He sent and received hundreds of messages for Hitler's agents in this country. The Abwehr couldn't have been happier. In the end, because of his work, the FBI rounded up thirty-three Nazi spies working under one of the great spy masters of this century, Frederick Duquesne. Sebold's work helped to break the back of the Nazi espionage in this country, and they never recovered. He was one of the great unsung heroes of the war. An informant, Miss Roberts—an informant who daily risked his life for his country, and saved the lives of countless others."

After a moment, she nodded. "You've made your point. But I still won't do it *because I can't*. It's that simple, Mr. Ripley. I couldn't bring it off."

"Work with me for a week, and then decide. I know you can. There's something else. The Bureau insists that I be completely frank with you. If you do this, and somehow they find out you're working with us, well, I don't know how to say it except in so many words. They'd try to kill you. We'd do everything under the sun to protect you, but still . . ."

She said defiantly: "You're daring me, aren't you?"

"No, certainly not! I'm just—"

"I'm supposed to be noble and brave and say I don't mind the risk. Well, the hell with it, I do mind. I'm not about to take a chance of getting murdered doing something I don't know how to do. Get yourself another pigeon, one who's had some experience and training."

He got up to go. "I didn't expect you to jump at the job." He smiled and that infuriated her.

"Roz will be here any minute now," she said crisply, "and I don't want her finding you with me. She heard me tell Jim I had a headache. She wouldn't understand. And I don't either. I mean, understand why I'm here talking about killings and bombings. I'm getting back to my world where people are decent and kind . . ."

"Because we give them a chance to be decent and kind, to have homes where they can live without terror."

He started for the back door. "Think it over, Miss Roberts."

9

ON ARRIVING HOME, Rip found Lee Jetzel patiently awaiting him in a car parked before the apartment. Jetzel was five months out of the FBI Academy, young and enthusiastic but levelheaded, and possessed of a quick, analytical mind and an uncanny insight into human nature. He had been assigned the task of tracking down every taxi driver who had transported anyone from United Airlines between 11:30 P.M. and 12 midnight the evening Samuel Jorgensen had arrived. It was a plodding, onerous assignment but not an infeasible one. He had shown every driver a four-year-old picture of Jorgensen that the New York Field division had forwarded.

"There's this one driver," Jetzel said, "a young fellow with acne, nothing much but bones, scared, shifty-eyed, who took a party to the International Hotel, according to the dispatcher's records, but no one at International reacted when I showed them the picture.

"When I handed this driver the photo, he said that wasn't the man he'd taken. Said he'd never seen this man. But he denied it a little strong and got real shook up. But I couldn't budge him. He turns his cab back in at two A.M. and I thought you'd know how to handle him."

At 1:50 the driver brought his taxi into the garage, parked it in the proper stall, and started for the dispatcher's office to sign out. When Rip and Jetzel intercepted him, he backed up as if he might flee, then stopped and stared with what defiance he could muster.

Rip said: "I'm also with the FBI." He showed him his identification. "Ripley. John Ripley."

The cabbie looked swiftly from the one to the other. "I told your buddy here I never saw the old joker. Never saw him."

"Yeah," Rip said, "but we got to thinking maybe you might have remembered something while you were out pushing the cab tonight. Sometimes something comes back." Rip had never forgotten a rule propounded by an Academy instructor: If you are trying to get the truth out of a man, always give him a way out, to tell you that truth. Never box him into a corner by accusing him of lying.

The driver looked relieved. "Naw, nothing."

"He had a mountain of luggage. Gave a stewardess in the taxi up ahead of you a couple of cases. Walked with a slight limp."

He shook his head and started off. "Gotta check out."

Rip blocked him. "Maybe you don't hear well. We're from the Federal Bureau of Investigation."

"I heard."

Rip continued: "Sometimes a guy hands you a ten or a fifty to keep quiet." The cabbie looked as if shot. "Maybe he doesn't want his wife to know. But it isn't worth it, if he's trying to keep something from the FBI. It isn't worth the ten or fifty."

The fellow shifted his gaze about nervously. "I don't know what you're talking about."

41

"Tell us what we want to know and there's nothing against you."

He wet his lips. "You mean—?"

"Nothing."

"Let me see that picture again." Jetzel handed him the photo. "Lots of bags, huh?"

"Yeah," Rip said.

The fellow wiped the sweat from his forehead, returned the picture. "It's coming back to me. You know, I carry so many people, they're all blurred, the faces I mean."

"We know. We see lots of faces, too."

He snapped a finger. "Air New Zealand." He laughed weakly. "Came back to me like that." He snapped a finger again.

"You mean," Rip said, "you drove him around the airport from United to Air New Zealand on the international side?"

He nodded. "He told me to take him to International Hotel but soon's I reported to the dispatcher, he changed his mind. Said Air New Zealand."

At Air New Zealand the passenger agent on duty that night remembered Samuel Jorgensen. His luggage was $156 overweight. He offered no protest and paid in cash for the overage and a one-way ticket to Tahiti.

Rip could see the picture: Sam Jorgensen had learned that the New York Committee had discovered he was an FBI informant and had marked him for assassination. Terrified on arrival, he had delivered what he could to the FBI by giving his cases to Miss Roberts, certain that when he failed to call for them, she would turn them over to the authorities.

In Tahiti, he would hide out for a month or two, then surface and stay at a luxury hotel. He would bide his time patiently until he developed a quick but warm friendship with a wealthy widow or a bored millionaire. Then he would take his victim for at least $100,000, and probably a good deal more. One hundred thousand was Samuel Jorgensen's minimum. He had never bothered with petty cash. In due time, by the law of averages, he would be caught but since he had been kind to his victims, and they could afford the larceny, a jury would recommend leniency—he was, after all, such a nice, old fellow, misled, of course, but meaning no real harm—and he would serve about three years. He would consider his time in prison as time put in on his job,

42

and by averaging his income over the years, he would draw, in effect, a salary as good as or better than the average corporation president. And it was all tax free.

He had quit as an informant without giving notice, which was no crime. The FBI now had no further interest in him. Max Hartman might still have, if he believed it worthwhile to pursue the matter so far afield.

10

RIP SAID: "I want to make it absolutely clear that we're not asking you to have an affair with him."

She broke in sharply: "I don't like your inference—that I might—"

"Believe me," he said, raising his voice, "I wasn't inferring anything. I had to get it on the record."

"Okay," she snapped, "you've got it. But I still think—I'm engaged —and you know it."

"It was routine."

"Not to me, it isn't."

"I don't mean . . . I meant . . ."

"I know what you meant."

"Please, Miss Roberts, forgive me. I wouldn't have said anything—"

She laughed unexpectedly. "Forget it. I shouldn't've made anything out of it. Sorry."

He smiled in return. "Chalk up an error for me. I'm not good in the outfield."

They sat across a massive old Spanish cocktail table in the pseudo-Moorish living room of her brother's home. She was in purple down to her shoes. She had had her hair set that morning, and Rip thought he had never seen a more stunning woman. Not beautiful in the usual sense since her jaw overshadowed her other features. But stunning. She had pulled the semi-sheer drapes to shut out curious eyes but the midafternoon sun, diamond hard, shone through to cast a soft yellow glow over the room. Her brother was at work, her sister-in-law at a club meeting, and the twins at school.

Early that morning she had called. Her voice was haggard from the restlessness and indecision of a night of wrestling with her conflicting and highly charged thoughts. She said: "I'm ready whenever you are."

There had been a long pause on his part, and then: "You're sure?" He wanted her decision firmly anchored, wanted no regrets, no recriminations.

"Positive."

"Two o'clock?"

"Where? Not at my apartment. A neighbor saw you leave and asked Roz questions. I'll tell you. What about my brother's place? No one's home today."

Far into the night she had debated with herself. At breakfast she was still undecided, though there was the deepening conviction that she was using her conscience as an excuse to escape a frightening duty. She glanced casually at the newspaper, and there on page one was the account of a school bombing in the San Francisco area. A teacher blinded for life, a little girl with an arm blown off, a man paralyzed below the waist.

She phoned Jim who was coming by at 8. Her next flight was not until tomorrow, and they had planned to drive through mountain country back of San Diego where the last of old California still lingered. She told him she was ill, and he duly sympathized. Next she canceled a dental appointment. Shortly afterward a call came from her supervisor asking if she would take an afternoon flight? For the first time she refused. On her way out, she stopped by the refrigerator to get the grocery list, held on the door by a little beetle-shaped magnet. The door was their bulletin board, dotted with slips of paper and cartoons.

Roz called to her from her bedroom. Roz slept in a hammock stretched from wall to wall, a voluminous Venezuelan hammock called a *matrimonio*. She had acquired it when she worked for an American company in Caracas, and said she kept it as a dowry for her future husband, whoever that might be. Chris had expressed doubts that she would ever get a husband if Roz insisted he sleep in that.

Roz said: "Do you want to tell me what's going on?"

Chris looked puzzled, and Roz continued: "You're too sick to go with Jim but you're dressed to go out. You cancel a dental appoint-

44

ment, turn the airline down, and that old nosy Mrs. Brown reported you had a man in the apartment last night with the drapes drawn—which could result in Mrs. Brown suffering a heart attack from frustration."

Chris laughed. "Next time I'll leave the drapes open. I'm not breaking with Jim, the fellow here last night was an old friend who wanted me to help get his sister a job with United, and I'm going out now because I'm a bundle of nerves, the job's getting me down, and I want to be alone. Now does that satisfy you and Mrs. Brown?"

Roz swung out of the *matrimonio*. She wore a faded Inca print cotton gown that looked as if it had belonged to an old Inca. "My heavens, Chris, I haven't heard anybody lie like that since my father used to stumble home at two in the morning. You've got talent, girl. I love you, you know that, and if you want to play the field, I'm with you."

Now Chris told Rip: "I'm no good at lying. I'm going to wreck everything. I warned you—"

Rip interrupted: "We're going to do a lot of talking and work it out."

"I've got to tell Jim. I don't want to deceive him."

"If you do . . . well, everyone talks, all of us, and no matter how much we try, we drop things. It's only human nature. I'm not thinking of the FBI because if—"

"—if something happens to me, you can get someone else."

He shuddered. "Don't say that. But what I mean is—"

Her eyes flashed. "I won't do it to him. I'm going to tell him I'm working with the FBI but I can't tell him until it's all over what I'm doing."

"But—"

"If you won't buy that, get yourself another pigeon. Forget it."

"All right, Miss Roberts. But nothing about the nature of the case. You promise?"

He started to tell her that in Bureau jargon he was her blanket, that the contact agent was known as the informant's blanket, but thought better of it.

"I read in the papers today," she said, "that a judge threw a case out of court because an informant was accused of something called entrapment."

45

He took his time, explaining patiently. "To put it simply, and not legally, if we asked you to suggest or encourage the Committee to rob a bank, kidnap someone, or engage in any crime, then you would be guilty of entrapment. You'd be what is known as an *agent provocateur*. But the Bureau does not want you under any circumstances to do anything of that sort. The Bureau doesn't even go along with the idea of an informant discussing the commission of a crime. We want you to report objectively what goes on. In other words, you're a newspaper reporter and I'm the city editor. If you're caught up in a discussion about a crime, play it vague. Be indecisive. Tell them you're a woman without experience in such matters. And do only what you're told. Never volunteer . . . Now you'll be out money for expenses. Would twenty-five dollars a week be all right for the time being?" Noting her quick anger, he added: "It's customary."

She said tartly: "A girl can run around all she wants to but she isn't a prostitute until she accepts money. You tell the FBI—"

"Okay, okay," Rip put in quickly. "No money. I understand."

"I may be a rat fink but I'm not going to be a paid rat fink."

"I understand," he repeated, wiping his forehead with a handkerchief. This was just not his day. Most informants were happy to get expenses, and it was only right they did. The Bureau seldom paid out more than small sums, except when someone had to give up a job. The Bureau then made up his salary.

The room was stifling. She had closed the windows when she had drawn the drapes. He asked permission to remove his coat, and afterwards, sat at the opposite end of the divan.

"The most dangerous part of this whole business," he began, "is communication. We've got to keep in touch once you're on the inside, and this requires careful planning."

She should not use her apartment phone, he instructed, except in an emergency. There was too much risk she might be overheard, and a possibility that after she had been recruited, Hartman would hide a microphone in her apartment that would pick up her conversation.

"If you're desperate, and you have to reach me," he continued, "call either the FBI confidential number I gave you or my home phone, and then say, 'Sorry, I've got the wrong number.' That will tip us off, and we'll get agents running a surveillance on you, and I will attempt to make contact, if I can without endangering you. Remember that now, 'Sorry, I've got the wrong number.' "

He discussed the use of a pay phone. "Don't, unless you would do so normally. If you're at a supermarket or drugstore, good. But if you left your apartment at night, say, and went to a pay phone booth on a street corner, that would look suspect.

"If you do have to get a message through, and are blocked every way, go to Barney's Malt Shop, order something, and leave a message with Barney."

"You mean Barney's right down the street? I've eaten there!"

"Barney's a retired police captain. He'll get a message to me."

The next time they met, he said, he would give her a tiny, highly sensitive electronic device shaped to fit into a brassiere. Although no bigger than a small cigarette lighter, it was capable of transmitting 50 miles or more if weather conditions were excellent and the party carrying it was not boxed in by tall buildings. It had been developed by electronics experts especially for Federal law-enforcement agencies and was not on the general market. This particular model, which would transmit over an FBI band, could not receive, and Rip had chosen it for that very reason. He had foreseen that she might betray herself by accidentally leaving the two-way model on in the receiving position while with someone from the Committee.

"Again, though," he warned, "don't talk into it in your apartment."

He said that henceforth they should meet in different places, and never at her apartment or again at her brother's home. "Once Hartman starts thinking about taking you in, he's going to check you out as thoroughly as the FBI would."

He told her it would be necessary to give her a subversive background. "So that when Hartman does scrutinize your past he will feel safe about you. I'm going to draw up an arrest record, dating back to your college years, showing that you took part in riots and bombings. I'll plant the records with university police and the sheriff of Santa Barbara County. Of course, when this is all over, we'll clear the record."

He had borrowed the idea of creating a fictitious background from the world of espionage. He didn't like giving it to her. It went against the grain. But it was imperative to come up with every bit of strategy possible to persuade Max Hartman she was good potential material for his revolution. The Bureau would disapprove, and would censure him, and perhaps take strong disciplinary action. He had to expect that.

47

"But what if something happens to you?"

"We'll have a notation on file to the effect that your record is to be cleared the moment you cease acting as an informant."

For a moment his eyes rested on her. He sensed the concealed fear, the hard beat of the heart. "I hate to put you through this but it's necessary to convince Hartman that you have acted militantly in the past and that you are a revolutionary."

"But does it follow, just because I was a militant at the university— I mean, how many radical airline stewardesses are there?"

"How many truly radical aerospace scientists are there?" he countered. "Or history professors? They all have to have jobs within the Establishment—Oswald who assassinated Kennedy, James Earl Ray . . . No, once we give you a background, and they run their checks and test you out . . ."

She asked quietly: "Do you have other informants in this group? Maybe I shouldn't ask but—"

"No, we don't."

She persisted: "Have you had?"

Rip took a deep breath. "I'd rather not say."

"You mean they're dead?"

"One died a natural death. The other, he was killed."

"Oh, God!"

"If you want to change your mind—"

"No, it's not that. Don't worry about me. I'm going through with it."

Suddenly she let out a slight gasp. Her eyes were raised directly above Rip's head, focused on a spot directly behind him. He swung his whole body about in one swift, fluid movement, and came to his feet. He had heard nothing, but there stood a big, robust man in his early thirties, a hacked-faced man with a shock of upright black hair. His dark, sharp eyes, mounted on half circles, riveted on Rip. He had enormous fists that squeezed rhythmically.

"Hello," Rip said casually, pulling up his tie.

Chris recovered quickly. "This is my brother, Dan. Dan, this is—"

"Martin—John Martin," Rip said. "From the office. We were kicking around ideas for an ad campaign. We like to talk with the people who are up front, right in the action."

"Yes," she said weakly.

"Yeah," Dan said, grunting, and started for the kitchen. "Sorry to butt in."

48

"Not at all. We're finished. I was about to go." Rip struggled into his coat.

Dan disappeared. Rip said: "Thank you, Miss Roberts. You've been very helpful."

After closing the door behind him, she went to the kitchen. She had clearly read Dan's interpretation of Rip's presence. She had always known what Dan was thinking. In her teen years she had adored him. He had looked out for her in school, had once threatened to punch a teacher in the nose when Chris returned home crying over a C grade. He had passed judgment on her boy friends, and any time she needed help, she had gone to him rather than to her parents. But he had changed with the years, and become a morose, unhappy individual, quick to fault her—and his wife. What happened between brothers and sisters? How could they be so close in the growing-up years and unpleasant strangers once they were adults?

He was getting a beer from the refrigerator. "Dan," she said tentatively.

"Don't Dan me!" he shouted. "After what you've been doing in my home! If our parents knew, they'd die."

Chris struggled for control. "You know better. We sat a couple of hours exactly where you found us, talking."

"With the drapes drawn?"

"The sun was hitting my eyes."

"You looked guilty as hell. You both did."

"Shut up, Dan, and listen—"

"I wish to God I hadn't come home early. My little sister. Where're you going?"

She stopped at the door to the living room. He lowered his voice to a normal tone. "Hold it now. Maybe I've been a little rough. I know it's a new age but dammit, I don't go along with it. We were brought up differently. Our father and mother—"

"Oh, for Heaven's sake, don't give me that routine. I'll see you Sunday."

She hurried away, crossed the living room, and stepped outside into blinding sunlight.

A man stood across the street, and it was evident he was watching the house. At sight of her, he turned and walked unsteadily down the street. He was an older man, a little on the shabby side, but a vague impression was all that she had. Her glance had failed to snap a sharp picture.

49

11

ROBERTS, CHRISTINA, AKA CHRIS ROBERTS

GIRL FRIEND AND CLOSE ASSOCIATE OF HOW-
ARD SPELVIN, AKA HOWIE SPELVIN, UNIVER-
SITY OF CALIFORNIA AT SANTA BARBARA
STUDENT CHARGED GRAND JURY INDICTMENT
RETURNED 6-3-70, SANTA BARBARA, AS LEADER
OF "BLOODY WEDNESDAY" DEMONSTRATION
AND RIOT AT ISLA VISTA, CALIFORNIA. INFORM-
ANTS REPORTED ROBERTS ACTED AS SPOTTER
FOR SPELVIN WHEN, ACCORDING TO INDICT-
MENT, HE PLANNED AND DIRECTED BURNING
OF BANK OF AMERICA BRANCH, ISLA VISTA,
2-25-70.

ROBERTS PHOTOGRAPHED ENGAGED IN RIOTS
UC AT SANTA BARBARA 6-7-70. REPORTED BY
INFORMANTS SEEN MINUTES BEFORE BLAST
THAT DESTROYED COMPUTER IN AEROSPACE
RESEARCH LABORATORY, SAN JOSE, 5-3-70.

MEMBER, STUDENTS FOR DEMOCRATIC ACTION,
1968, 1969, 1970, AND THE WEATHERMAN, 1969.
ATTENDED BLACK PANTHER-WHITE COALITION
MEETING 1-14-70 IN LOS ANGELES. SIGNED PETI-
TION TO FREE FOUR BLACK PANTHERS UNDER
ARREST FOR SHOOT OUT WITH LOS ANGELES
POLICE.

WROTE PAPER FOR HISTORY CLASS, "THE DE-
CLINE AND FALL OF THE UNITED STATES."

DESCRIPTION FOLLOWS . . .

12

RIP TILTED HIS chair back against the wall and closed his eyes. A slow-moving, warm breeze harbingered another 90° day. Outside a mob of birds sang merrily while they could, before the hotness silenced their song. He remembered the last time he had brought an informant to this study room back of the stacks in the downtown library. He had recorded the conversation only to discover later that the bird chatter overlapped much of it. "Where'd you record this?" the steno had asked. "In an aviary?"

It was she who had passed along the news this morning that Rocky Minden was leaving the Bureau. In his eighteen years with the FBI Rocky had become a legend. His investigations had resulted in the convictions of numerous Mafia and racketeer leaders. He was taking a $40,000-a-year plant protection job with a corporation, and Rip couldn't blame him. Now and then, Rip would think about quitting. He could earn twice his salary in half the hours. He might marry Peg and they would take long drives weekends, hike in the High Sierras, boat in the summer, fix up a house, and play with the children. But the pull of FBI work was the pull of gravity. He was hopelessly hooked. In Washington the inspectors and supervisors talked about dedication but rather it was a compulsion to do a job a man liked better than any other. It was exciting and plodding, frustrating and exhilarating, maddening and satisfying. A man fired on the shooting range and was kicked by the recoil of a rifle. He dusted for fingerprints and knew enough about many sciences to take specimens that would condemn or free a suspect. He was an attorney reading the latest Supreme Court decision and the newest criminal statute, and often he sat the witness stand. He talked with panhandlers, petty, sniveling crooks, and hardened call girls, and with corporation heads, bankers, schoolteachers, and PTA mothers. He ran tail jobs and stood all night in a blizzard waiting for someone to leave a house. He plunged into swamps to track a criminal and staked out an entire desert. He knew the secrets of listening devices and when he could legally use them. He walked the gamut of human activity, from the sordid to the great.

51

Not a day passed, no matter how many years he served, that he did not encounter a new experience.

Still, many agents resigned each year. Most gravitated into what they knew best, investigation. They became sheriffs and district attorneys and State Department or other government agency detectives. Some became politicians: senators, congressmen, governors. And there was a scattering of writers, a minister or two, a rabbi. All told, they held down 150 different jobs. Eventually most joined the Society of Former Agents of the Federal Bureau of Investigation, and met monthly in their home towns to swap stories of the "old days," help community projects, and their own sick and jobless. They kept in touch, too, through a monthly magazine, *The Grapevine,* where their pictures ran when they did something newsworthy.

When he thought about leaving the Bureau, though, he knew he was deceiving himself. He liked what he saw in the next pasture but he would never cross over. One of these days somewhere or other he would die, normally or from gunshot, and younger agents would say in awe: "Did you know he was forty years in the Bureau?"

The door swung open, hit by a body, and Chris entered, breathing hard. Quickly she closed it. "I think I was followed." She had noticed two men behind her from the time she left a parking lot until she entered the library, and they had trailed her until she lost herself in the stacks.

Rip left and wandered out into a wing of the main library where he located the two searching the card index file. He pretended to skim a book but kept them within the periphery of his vision. Then one said something to the other.

Smiling, Rip returned to the study. "They're golf nuts. I read their lips." He had started studying lip reading his second year in the Bureau.

She glanced up in surprise, and he added: "You'd be surprised what I 'hear.' "

"That's the same as eavesdropping."

"Only no one's going to catch you at it." She looked haggard, but eventually she would settle down to the situation, terrifying as it was. Man was an amazingly adaptable animal. Still, if she didn't . . .

He resumed then where he had left off two days ago, before her New York flight. "How long did you know Howie?"

"Five-six months."

52

"Did you date much?"

"Two, three times a week. His check came Monday mornings from his parents but he wouldn't cash it until Friday and then we'd have a big weekend. We'd go scuba diving and have dinner and take in a movie. He was a film buff. Saw them all."

"Were you ever in his dormitory room?"

"Sure."

"Did you spend nights with him?"

"I don't think you have any right to ask me that."

Rip nodded. "Good. That's a good answer. Don't forget it. Keep Max Hartman guessing. What was his roommate's name?"

"George Allison. But I didn't see much of him. He was gone usually. He was working his way through college doing yard jobs."

"What other friends of Howie's did you know?"

"None. He didn't want me to meet his friends, and that's why we broke up. I got suspicious. It looked like he was engaged or married. I told him I wasn't going to be a back street girl friend."

"What kind of a car did he have?"

"An old Plymouth. But he never kept it in the garage because he was making plastic bombs in there, and there wasn't room."

"No, Miss Roberts, don't mention anything about a garage. We don't know what it looked like inside and you might trip yourself up. Now, do you remember anything about his room, what you saw that stood out?"

"He had a picture of his brother on the nightstand."

"What's the brother's name?"

She closed her eyes, trying to come up with it. "Ted," Rip prompted. "It's Ted. Be sure to remember that because his relationship—well, you tell me."

"They were close. He had looked after Ted all of his life, helped him in his fights at school, taken him on hikes. He wrote him every week." She hesitated. "I don't remember his parents' names."

"Doesn't matter. He would have referred to them as Dad and Mother. He didn't care much for them. You should remember that."

"If I'd ever seen this Howie it would help."

"You're doing fine."

"What if he shows up?"

"He's running a motorboat on the Amazon out of a town called Iquitos in Peru. We'll pick him up if he ever returns to the United

53

States. Now, about the night he set fire to the Bank of America building, did he tell you what he was going to do?"

"No . . . there was lots of excitement, hundreds of students milling through Isla Vista and deputies everywhere."

She remembered the night vividly. After her last class, she had hurried back to the apartment she shared with another girl in Isla Vista, a square-mile enclave of 14,000, mostly students housed in old buildings. Once it was dark, the mob swelled rapidly. She could hear the roar, like waves bashing against a seawall. Hundreds swarmed down the streets breaking windows, throwing rocks at patrol cars, setting trash barrels on fire, dispersing swiftly before the firing of tear gas barrages, only to regroup as quickly once the gas had lifted. There was the sound of squealing police car brakes, rocks thrown from rooftops, the thunder of bullhorns, and doors being smashed in.

She continued: "Howie asked if I would drive his car, and keep it running while he went off for a few minutes. He said there was going to be a big blast. Well, I knew I shouldn't but I was in love with the guy, and it was all kind of romantic. So I drove and parked near the Bank of America, as Howie told me to do, and he took a fire bomb and some Molotov cocktails from the back seat, and left. By this time the students had already smashed in the door, so Howie tossed them inside."

"Did you see him do this?"

"No, he told me he did when he came back. I kept the motor running and we got away—"

"Did the police question you?"

"Yes, an officer came around the next day and accused me of being a lookout, so someone who knew me must have seen me. But I said I was home studying and he left."

Rip handed her a brief on Howie Spelvin's habits and eccentricities to memorize: "He liked steaks, hash brown potatoes, salads with Roquefort dressing, chocolate ice cream, anything with alcohol in it, though never drank to excess . . . never used drugs . . . spent extra money on his car, kept it washed and the motor block clean as an old maid's kitchen . . . at one time played tennis but gave it up . . . wore old clothes, never took care of them . . . wore no jewelry . . . never wore a tie . . . shoes usually needed half soling . . . wore hair full but not too long, moderate sideburns . . . very serious, never joked, never smiled . . ."

54

She folded the brief and put it in her purse. "How do we know he'll stay on the Amazon? That he won't pop up?"

"The Iquitos police will cable us if he disappears from his usual haunts."

She wrinkled her forehead. "My uncle sent us a cable once from Brasilia. He arrived before it did. Cost him thirteen dollars. Funny that I'd remember that."

His shirt wet with sweat, Howie Spelvin sat slouched comfortably at a little sidewalk café table in the blistering midafternoon sun. He ordered one Coke and two glasses, and when the heat-weary girl brought them, poured a few inches in one glass and offered it to his dearest friend, a little jungle night monkey that had adopted him months ago. They both gulped their drinks down with the thirst of men in hot climates, then Howie, with the monkey riding on his shoulder, walked toward the Amazon which even at this point, not too far from the Pacific, stretched more than a mile. He passed a woman doubled up in the gutter, crying either in pain or grief. Maybe she was dying. One never knew. He continued past the old Iquitos Hotel where travelers stayed for $10 a day, breakfast included.

He dropped down a steep, curving path to an outboard motor. Two couples were waiting beside the small launch, one American, the other German. He was polite but said little. Once aboard he started down the river to the lodge 20 miles distant where he worked. He passed a little clapboard schoolhouse on stilts where the youngsters came by homemade dugout canoes.

The couples asked about the trips they would take out of the lodge to the Yaqua Indian village tomorrow morning and the Jivaro one in the afternoon. The Yaquas were a pleasant people, their village as neat as a Dutch housewife's. They were proud of their bodies. At the lodge's request, the women wore a palm-fiber "hula skirt" around their necks to cover their breasts. It was invariably off course but at least it was a gesture toward the white man's sense of propriety.

The Jivaros, however, were a different people, fiercer looking, more aggressive. A few years before, some of their kinsmen deep in the jungle had murdered missionaries. Howie preferred the Jivaros who had taught him to use a blowgun; and now he could hit a bull's-eye 50 feet distant. Every day without fail he worked out with

55

the blowgun. In another month, he would dip the dart in poison and try his luck killing a wild pig.

He had these dreams of returning to the States one day and taking his blowgun with him. And the poison.

13

THAT NIGHT WHEN she returned home from marketing, Max Hartman was waiting in his car. Her heart sank. She had had visions all day of taking her exhausted, worry-battered body to bed. She had canceled a date with Jim, the fifth straight, pleading exhaustion.

She saw Max first, took a deep agonizing breath, commanded herself to be light and gay, and called out: "Max! What a surprise! Come on in."

"Thought I'd run by and see if you were doing anything tonight."

"Mildewing." She laughed. "That was one of my grandpapa's expressions."

"Dinner?"

"Great."

She couldn't control her fingers when she put the key to the lock. "Something's wrong with the blasted lock."

Once inside she managed, without Max seeing, to slip an old photo album from a bookshelf to the cocktail table. He wandered about the room, teasing her about the moose head and the basket chair. She excused herself to change clothes. She thought her mind would blow a fuse, but eventually she whipped it into line and managed sufficient concentration to select a long-skirted, wildly frivolous print she had bought on an irresistible impulse.

Returning to the living room, she found him thumbing through the old album. "That's for laughs," she said. "Aren't old pictures fun?"

He failed to react. He was staring at a photo of Howie Spelvin. "You know Howie?"

"Howie Spelvin?" By will power alone she held her voice steady. "Yeah, we dated some in my senior year, then we broke up. You know Howie, too?"

"He worked with us at Aerospace for a couple of summers."

"Small world department." She busied herself noisily shutting windows and turning on lights.

Rising, he smiled. "I get reports on you. One of my friends saw you in Inglewood the other day."

She knocked off the hat she was rearranging on the moose head. "Yes, I was over at my brother's . . . How come *he* recognized *me?* Or do I know him?"

"You're a standout. Didn't I ever tell you? Name's Roger Wilson. Says he was at Santa Barbara when you were."

She turned about, shook her head. "Doesn't ring a bell."

He held the door open. "I'm thinking about going out in the boat Sunday if it's sunny. I've got something to show you but I won't tell you what it is. A surprise. How about it?"

She accepted, feigning excitement, but inwardly deeply disappointed that she would have to cancel out on Jim once more. Dear old long-suffering Jim. He had accepted her explanation that she was working with the FBI, not without protest, but on her own terms and with understanding. She guessed he had reached the point where nothing she ever did would surprise him. His concern for her safety and his consideration made the situation all the more unpleasant. She almost wished he had been angry.

"Howie," Max was saying. "I'd almost forgotten him. To be honest, I never cared much for the guy. But maybe to a girl he looked different."

14

THE BOAT DUG her bow deep and smashed resolutely into a heavy wave, her old hull shuddering, tumbling and yawing. The crash divided the waters into two sheets that climbed high with a sibilant roar and fell as quickly as they had formed. Each time Chris's body tightened into a fistlike knot. She had experienced worse turbulence in the air but here miles from the California coast there was the strange feeling she was alone in a world of thunder and crashing, a fragment to be tossed about and perhaps engulfed by the angry waters.

Taut as a fighter, Max sat beside her, gripping the wheel, his eyes glinting in the sharp, hot reflection of the noonday sun. He was caught up with the joy of a man's triumph over forces more powerful than his own.

He had said little. If he were trying to subdue her, he had let the sea say it for him. Once he had tuned in on the Coast Guard Emergency channel, then a moment later switched it off. She experienced a compulsion to turn the radio back on, to maintain that thread-slender connection with security.

Long ago the shore line had slipped off the horizon and the last boat had disappeared from view. She wondered where they could be that on a Sunday there would be no craft about. A half hour ago she had noted the rifle in its long knapsack strapped to the starboard side of the hull.

Out here in this lonely water vastness, the fears of a restless night had burgeoned into stark reality. What was she doing with this stranger? How could she have let herself be talked into this situation? She damned both Mr. Ripley and her own lack of judgment.

"Land, ho!" he yelled above the sound of the engines and breaking waters. Dead ahead an island grew rapidly in size, a small, rocky hand with stubby fingers pointing upward. Soon she saw great polished, serrated boulders guarding it and scrub trees high up. There was no sign of people or habitation.

"We'll eat first, what d'ya say? And then I'll show you the surprise."

She yelled back, "Okay!" She must rout her fears, and accept this virile brute beside her for what he appeared to be, a good-looking, intelligent, thoughtful guy any girl would like to date.

He eased the craft without wasted motion into a small cove. Here the water was a glimmering, rippling surface, and the roar and anger were gone. She continued to shout before she realized how quiet it was.

She was unpacking the lunch she had fixed when he came from the boat toting a small fold-up table and two fold-up chairs. Next he brought a bag, and took from it silverware, china, and table linen. He grinned. "I always travel first class."

Her thoughts did an instant flashback to her days in Europe, and a common Sunday sight: family roadside picnics, always with table, chairs, and tablecloth. "Where are the candelabra?" she asked.

Each time he returned to the boat, she watched him guardedly, but he left the rifle where it was strapped. She put out the food—fried

58

chicken and potato salad, slabs of baked ham and Swiss cheese between great slices of rye bread, pickles, fat, crusty apple turnovers and chewy brownies filled with pecans to munch on afterwards. It was a man's picnic, or so she intended it, and he took it all in appreciatively.

Before he sat down, he took off the light, cotton, Samoa-print shirt and was bare to his black trunks. "Gets damn hot here." He stood over her, his chest black with hair, his body lean. She imagined that a fist hitting the flat stomach would bounce off.

His look was unmistakable. "Why don't you get comfortable?" he asked, indicating her floppy gingham shirt.

She laughed. In her early teens she had learned that laughter was the best brush-off, a rejection that rarely incurred male wrath.

"Huh-uh," she said.

He poured the coffee, steaming hot, out of the Thermos. "I hope you didn't think—"

"Didn't you?" She felt her stomach knot up, the hunger vanish, the dryness in her mouth.

He cut a sandwich, gave her half. "Any man would be a fool who didn't—with you."

"And any girl would be a fool who didn't accept? With your charm?"

"That's about it." He tore into his half of the sandwich.

Again, she laughed. "So I'm a fool."

"Do you always put it right on the line?"

"Isn't that the way you want it?"

He stared at her a moment with that playful, teasing smile. She couldn't help herself. Much as she feared him, he did something to her. That smile, the flashing blue, boyish eyes that seemed so innocent, even his hardness stirred her. She hated herself, hated him for doing that to her.

He said slowly, "I didn't think you airline girls cared. I saw this movie, *The Stewardesses*—"

She lost her cool. "We're not tramps!"

He never took his eyes from her. "I can wait."

How long can you wait, she wondered, how long? Every male of his kind had a termination point. She imagined a woman and a boat were the same to him. If you knew your navigation, if you plotted your course properly, if you handled the throttles right . . . He could see a woman only as a sex object, and for that alone, she detested him.

59

She quieted. "I don't want to get involved with a man unless, well, you know, unless there's something there. Otherwise I'm not about to get involved. Not on that score."

"Is there another score?"

"Well, hungry people, people out of jobs, all that. Now you've got something going for you, to get involved in." She hesitated. "I got busted at Santa Barbara for marching in a hunger parade. I wasn't doing anything. Nothing at all. And these pigs came up and shoved me into a car and booked me for creating a public disturbance."

"Don't tell me you've got a record?"

"Show me someone without a record and I'll show you somebody who doesn't care whether people around them live or die."

He offered her a cigarette which she refused. He dug into his jacket for an expensive lighter. "But you did have something going with Howie Spelvin?"

She was prepared. "I was young then."

"He got into some kind of trouble, didn't he? Wasn't the FBI hunting him?"

"I wouldn't know. We dated just that one winter." Play it cool, Mr. Ripley had instructed her. You're not the type to snitch on a former boy friend. Always act as if you are protecting Howie.

"The winter they burned the Bank of America?"

She nodded but added nothing. He continued, "Whatever became of his brother—what was his name?"

"Hum-m, let's see. Began with T. Tom or Ted . . . They were very close."

"Yeah, Ted Spelvin."

They picked up the dishes. She scraped them with a fork and wiped them with a napkin. She was squatting, returning them to the bag, when she felt the centipede crawl of his eyes up her legs. She shot him a swift glance, and surprised, he laughed softly, a boy caught with his hand in the cookie jar.

He sobered then, and said unexpectedly: "I haven't heard from my uncle. Can't find him anywhere."

"He got his bags, didn't he?"

"Yeah." He mulled that over. "Why would he give them to you?"

"Ask him—if you ever find him."

"You mean something's happened to him?"

"I don't mean anything," she retorted. "I wish to Heaven I'd never

60

met him, he'd never given me his blasted cases. Let's get going. Where's the surprise? You've kept me waiting long enough."

She was climbing into the boat, and he was following when he said: "You've got the cutest little bottom."

"Damn you!" she said. Then she remembered to laugh.

He tossed the line into the boat and stepped in. She noted the race horse muscles in his legs. He kept in good condition, jogging, working out every morning.

He was feeling good. He hummed an old Czech song he said his mother had taught him but when Chris asked about her, he shrugged. "I scarcely know her," he said. "She was forty when she had me, and father, forty-six."

"You were born in Czechoslovakia?"

"No, no. In Chicago, Rogers Park. They had a little Mom and Pop grocery. That is, until a supermarket moved in and ruined them. I smashed every window in that supermarket. Funny the things you do when you're a kid."

Heading for the leeward side, he took the boat slowly along the desolate island, too barren, she thought, to sustain any form of life. She saw only sea gulls and other birds that used it as an aircraft carrier. Skimming and diving, they foraged the ocean for food. To avoid rock formations jutting above the water's surface, he kept far out where the waves slapped and jabbed relentlessly. She set her teeth against a slowly growing nausea. Never before had she been seasick but the tension combined with the choppiness contributed to her upset. Once again, she glanced over the horizon, seeking comfort in some evidence of human life, and far to the stern, found it. A craft appeared, a very small bobble. She took a deep breath, and slumped.

He talked along easily, enjoying calling up old though bitter memories. "They lost everything. Everything. They'd been a couple of cows until then. Content. But the erosion soon set in. Overnight they got old. The supermarket could have bought out my parents—but the lion eats the old wildebeest."

Eventually his parents went on Social Security and now he sent them $100 a month to augment that income. He had no desire to see them, never intended to go back. "But they put out on me when I was a kid—and I figure I owe them some money."

"And love?"

He took his time lighting a cigarette. Up over the bow, the sun was beginning its slow descent. Now the island was a darkening monster silhouetted against white, fleecy clouds.

61

"Mother, apple pie, and the flag." He shook his head. "You don't know what it's like to come from the old country. I never had a father. He was a stranger. I'd come home from university and he'd treat me like the village burgomaster. Respectful, patronizing, stiff in his talk. And Mother, by the time I got to high school she stood in awe of me. Proud but in awe. They could scarcely speak English—terribly illiterate—and here I was editor of the school newspaper and pulling down good grades. They couldn't believe I was theirs. You expect me to love them because they're my parents? They're just two tired old people to me. Strangers. I think a lot of parents become strangers to their children when the years separate them psychologically. Maybe they ought to shoot old people the way they do in some cultures. Take them out and shoot them."

He interrupted himself. "There. Look up there. No, over here. That big rock. Jeez, there must be twenty of them."

15

SEA LIONS RAISED their glistening wet heads all over an enormous, partly flat-topped boulder to stare curiously down at them. They were the kind seen on television and in circuses. They barked playfully and seemed to be waving, happy urchins, then they lost interest, children that they were, and returned to their basking. A couple with the high spirits of puppies slid down a steep incline, worn smooth by the pounding waters and many bodies, into the ocean.

"There!" Max shouted excitedly. "Look up there." He pointed to the boulder's highest point, where an enormous elephant seal reared majestically to calculate what dangers, if any, the bobbing boat below carried. Once his species had been common in these waters but then man had hunted him near to extinction for his blubber oil. Sometimes man got 100 to 200 gallons per animal.

Never taking his eyes from the great seal, he unstrapped the rifle, and with fingers tense with excitement, fitted a telescopic sight into position.

Oh, no, she thought, he's not going to kill it. Not that beautiful animal. She was on the verge of screaming when she caught herself. Ripley had told her: I want you feminine on the outside, hard on the inside. Death means nothing to you. If a child dies before your eyes in a traffic accident, you shrug and walk on. You've got to school yourself until death has no meaning.

Far behind her, she was barely conscious of pounding engines. She was too stunned to look around. Only later, she would recall that out of all the sounds assaulting her at that moment, there was that faraway one.

Quickly he raised the rifle. The crack was sharp in her hearing but absorbed immediately by the vast emptiness. The elephant seal, silhouetted beautifully against the sky, a picture postcard, seemed stunned. For a second he swayed uncertainly, then slumped gracefully. His inert body slid a few feet over the slick, wet surface before plunging off the boulder into the heaving foam below. Water shot up under the impact. The foam rushed in to fill the vacuum at the point where the body had slipped in to find its ocean grave.

"I got him!" he yelled. "I got him!" He was beside himself with the thrill of the kill. "Did you ever see anything like it? God, what a hit!"

She forced herself to say: "You're a terrific shot."

"No, I'm not. Not really. But I come out here every chance I get. It's great target practice. If you can hit one from a boat going up and down—at two hundred yards . . ." He swung the rifle back to his shoulder. "Pick one out. Any one."

Everything in her cried out that she couldn't. "Go on," he shouted. "A small one. Any one."

"That one." She pointed to the most distant one she could see, partially protected by the rocks.

At that moment a bullhorn voice roared at them seemingly out of the waters. It sounded like God himself commanding the earth to stand still. "Put that rifle down, mister. I said, drop it. You're under arrest. Heave to and follow me in."

The pursuer, a 20-foot power craft, was bearing down on them, manned by two whose faces were too spray-blurred to be read. The boat had a strange flag flying from the mast. She was to learn later that it signified the Wildlife Protection Patrol, a private agency. The patrol boats, manned and financed by civilians who loved sea life, carried no firearms, and those aboard had no police powers other than to warn violators and later file charges against them. Conceivably they could make civilian arrests but that would be difficult on the open sea. The Patrol had been born out of indignation arising from the bullet-riddled bodies of porpoises, seals, and birds constantly being washed ashore.

A stern voice came over a bullhorn: "I put you on notice. If you fire, I'll report it."

Max shot one scornful look at the patrol boat. Again, he raised the rifle and fired at the seal she had designated. Once, twice. The second time he scored, and she shut her eyes and bit her lips. A baby seal, maybe; a mother, maybe. Slaughtered.

The roar of the patrol boat swelled. Max swung the rifle about, waited until the hull was lifted clearly out of the water and fired. She thought he hit it. She couldn't be sure.

Handing her the rifle, he shot their own craft dead ahead toward the other boat. He was yelling, mad with the exhilaration of these minutes. He had slain a great seal, brought down a sea lion at an impossible distance, and now was racing to challenge an enemy. She was conscious of the warm metal in her hands, of the acrid smell of gunsmoke, and dropped the rifle as if it were a bad memory.

Heading straight for the patrol boat, Max screamed: "Bastards!" He was going to ram the craft, to sink it, she thought. She braced herself for the impact, but at the last possible second he veered away, and they cut across the bow.

He raced the craft straight for shore. Behind the stern, the island and the patrol boat receded rapidly. She picked up the rifle to hold until he could return it to its jacket. She couldn't remember when she had been so stunned. She wanted to cry and vomit and scream. That beautiful elephant seal rising up in all of his beauty to study them . . . happy in his glory, happy in the sun-flooded day . . . weaving ever so slightly, then trembling . . . sliding into the ocean . . . vibrant with life one minute, in a grave the next.

Max was talking. She caught only every few words. Something about target practice . . . the only practice better than seals would be people on the move.

16

At the police substation, Sergeant Jess McCready stared across the desk at Max out of watery, lifeless eyes. The sergeant was a big, pouchy man in his fifties whose facial flesh hung like an elephant's behind.

He rose with a lumbering effort, and walking toward a door, said gruffly: "This way." He opened a door to an anteroom. "There're some magazines over there. Be a few minutes."

Puzzled, Max followed instructions. The sergeant closed the door softly, but it failed to click, and stood barely ajar. A young officer ushered in Chris who took the straight chair the sergeant silently indicated. Carefully, she crossed her sunburned legs, and sat erect, on guard. Her sweaty hands tightened about each other. Even in her present dilemma, she was acutely conscious that she looked like a waterlogged waif. Her hair was so much string, her lips swollen, her shirt plastered to her hot body.

The sergeant began: "Miss . . . Miss . . ." He fumbled through a sheaf of papers.

"Roberts," she said crisply. "Chris Roberts."

"Roberts . . . ?" He located a memo slip. "H'mm, it is Roberts. Stewardess. United Airlines. Good record. H'mm."

He slumped back, studying her. Police officers had met them when they pulled into the harbor to tie up, and politely asked them to come along "to clear up a matter." The Wildlife Patrol boat had telephoned ahead a "hold" on them. Max had anticipated the move and had told her the story they would tell.

"I've been talking with your young man," the sergeant said. "How long have you known him?"

"Quite some time."

"A year, two years?"

She hesitated. Had he asked the same question of Max, and what had Max told him? "Not that long."

"How long then?"

She shrugged. "I'm not good with time. I take each day as it comes."

"I see. What is . . . uh . . . your relationship?"

"Friends."

"You are . . . uh . . . engaged?"

"No, sir."

"I see. Good friends. Are you . . . uh . . . having a physical relationship?"

She said hotly: "I'm not required to answer that!"

"H'mm. Now about that seal hunt—"

65

She broke in angrily: "It was not a hunt. Those men couldn't possibly see what we were doing. They were far away and what with the ocean spray and all . . . There was this white spot on the rock a few feet above the water's surface. Like a target. It was well below where the seals were. I—I couldn't have stood for it if he'd been shooting at them. I'm nuts about ecology and it's almost a religion with me, saving our wild life."

"Maybe accidentally?"

"No, sir! Absolutely not!"

The sergeant held focus on her a moment, then rising, said: "Well, now, I suppose that about clears it up. Come with me and we'll go sign a paper."

She said firmly: "I won't sign anything until my attorney sees it."

He opened a door leading to a short, narrow corridor. "This way, Miss . . . Miss . . ."

"Roberts. Chris Roberts."

Toward the end of the corridor, he swung a door aside and closed it behind her without entering himself. Rip arose swiftly from behind a desk, his eyes grave with concern. All day his thoughts had been with her. She was self-sufficient, yet no one—man or woman—could control every possible situation. He had risen early, much to Pandemonium's annoyance, and gone to church. Following the service, he had telephoned the FBI office to talk with the agent monitoring the tiny sending device she carried inside her brassiere. As of 11:10 she had been safe. A minute later, though, the bug had faded out completely. The distance between the boat and the monitor had become too great. As soon as the bug resumed, the agent would advise Rip.

He had Sunday dinner with Peg, and a time or two his thoughts drifted off station. She understood. She was that rare girl who never demanded a constant flow of conversation. She recognized a man's need for pauses. Too, she had been a part of the FBI too long not to know that at times an agent was totally absorbed in working out a situation in which he found himself or had placed another.

At 2:53, the monitor picked up the bug again, and for the FBI's benefit, Chris managed to work into the conversation the vital fact that Max believed police officers would be waiting at the pier. At the time Rip was helping Peg with the dishes. He had taken off without explanation and only a scant goodbye.

Now he indicated the intercom. "I was listening. I thought you

66

told me you couldn't act?" He sat on the edge of the desk near her. "The sergeant set it up so Mr. Hartman overheard everything."

She shuddered. "He's a monster. He killed two of those beautiful things, Mr. Ripley. For no reason." She was about to cry from exhaustion, and took a deep breath. "He said it was good target practice. And he went on the make for me. Not that I can't handle him—for a while anyway—until this thing builds up in him and he's got to have me. The first one he shot was a great big fellow . . ."

"I know what it's like," Rip said quietly. "I remember the first time I saw something killed."

"Oh God, why does anything have to be killed?"

She dropped into a chair as though her legs would no longer support her, and allowed herself a moment to relax. Then she took a deep breath, and braced herself to face reality. "I've got a dinner date with him on Wednesday. Don't worry. I'll be all right by then. I fly out in the morning for Chicago and I'll be so busy . . ."

Briefly, she reviewed the day, then told him of her distress over canceling dates with Jim. "He's upset and I don't blame him. I told him I was working with you but not what I'm doing. I promised you I wouldn't and I'm keeping my promise. But it hurts Jim that I'd keep something from him. It would me, too, if the situation was reversed. I'm not sure he believes me. He's the suspicious type—lawyer, you know, and people are always lying to him . . . What happens back there now?"

He informed her that no charges would be filed. "It's the word of two nice-appearing young people against two men who can't be positive of what they did see at that distance. They heard rifle fire, they saw him holding a rifle, but they didn't actually see him hit anything. I don't think there've been more than a handful of prosecutions in years for destroying marine life. It's just too difficult to prove."

"They looked so happy in the sun, frisking about, and the next minute . . . why, why are there people like him?"

Max was waiting outside, smiling broadly, his eyes warming at sight of her. He took her arm as if she were his property and swung her along in pace with his strides. He whispered admiringly: "You're the smoothest, little liar . . ."

She tossed her hair defiantly. "I wouldn't give those pigs the time of day, damn 'em."

17

MAX CANCELED OUT on their Wednesday date. He had to work overtime, he told her. Relieved and her old happy self, she telephoned Jim who deliberately let his pique show. She should not expect him to come running after canceling out on a date. "Please, Jim," she begged, "don't let this situation come between us."

"I'll be seeing you," he answered cryptically and hung up. She was devastated, and before Roz could catch her with tears welling up, fled to her room.

Roz followed. "If you want to tell me anything . . ." Turning away, Chris shook her head. Roz continued: "I'm not asking what's the problem but I'm with you, girl, all the way. You know that."

The old camaraderie between the two, though, had come apart. Roz felt rebuffed. She had always said they were one "big, happy Italian family." Jim would drop in whenever he felt like it, and Roz's boy friend. They would cook up spaghetti or hamburgers on the spur of the moment, talk excitedly and at the same time, phone friends, watch television, talk back at the commercials, collapse laughing when they told about the crazy people and incidents of the day's work, and on weekends would go surfing. Now Chris was gone most of the time, and not out with Jim but a stranger—and yet she swore she was still engaged to Jim.

The big difference, of course, was the sudden change deep within Chris. They saw a completely different person before their very eyes, and they couldn't understand what they saw. She struggled to carry on the old lighthearted approach but it was forced, and Roz, who was as sensitive as a violin, knew it. More and more Chris went straight to her room, pleading exhaustion. She jumped at the ringing of the phone, at any sharp, little noise. Constantly, she was on the defensive.

By the end of the week she realized she must ask her parents, who planned to visit her and Dan shortly, to postpone their vacation.

She phoned Dan. "I've got such a heavy work schedule coming up that I just won't be in town much for the next two months."

He blew up. "The hell you have! Roz tells me you're running around with some jerk. Listen, Chris, get some sense into that head of yours. You're no teen-ager gone boy crazy. You're a mature woman."

She pushed back the anger. "Listen, Dan, please. I'm engaged to Jim. I'm going to marry him. And I'm not running around! But the airline is short on stewardesses and they've asked me to work extra—"

"I don't buy it. I think you've gone ape."

He hung up, leaving her angry and exasperated. Forcing back the tears, she dialed her parents in Clinton, North Carolina. Her mother was her same, old sweet self. Chris could do no wrong. Yes, it was a disappointment but her mother understood, and so would her father. They could come in the fall as well as in the summer. "I'm crushed, Mom," Chris said.

For moments after hanging up, she sat in shock. Her legs wouldn't move, her body was an inert mass, her brain too fogged to command. Roz found her that way. "What is it, hon?" she asked, wanting to sympathize. Chris shook her head.

"You're not pregnant?"

"Roz! For Heaven's sake . . ."

Roz stared down at her. "We've had some good times together." When Chris said nothing, Roz continued: "I feel like scrambled eggs tonight. You stay put. Here's the paper. Skip the bad news, and read Peanuts and the Wizard of Id, and you'll feel better."

Rip had warned her: If a person changed her daily routine, she would inevitably ostracize herself. She would incur the wrath of relatives, hurt and disappoint old friends, arouse the suspicions of neighbors, start evil rumors, be assailed with cutting remarks, and possibly her entire house of cards—that frail, delicate structure she called her life style—would collapse. Her case history would be no different from that of other informants.

That weekend she was in New York. The return flight Monday proved a nightmare. Another plane developed mechanical trouble on the runway and transferred twenty-four passengers to her craft. The pilot, delayed 45 minutes already, decided to take off without requisitioning additional food. At Kennedy Airport, it took an hour to get delivery. So she and another stewardess worked furiously, cutting down on the servings they had so they could fill an additional twenty-four trays. She even contributed a roll of French bread she was taking home.

Unexpectedly, Max was waiting when the plane put down in Los

Angeles at 5:43 P.M. He wanted to take her to dinner. He was his usual spirited self. She pleaded she must wash up. She prayed that Roz would have been delayed in returning home from work but she had not. What was worse, Max would not come in. He never did when Roz was home. He did not like Italians, he had said once. So he would sit in the car by the curb, listening to the radio, and tonight was no exception. She showered and slipped into what she called her snakeskin dress—a reptile print on a silky knit in colors that changed with the light and danced in step with her movements.

They sat on the floor with their feet under them at the Yamato in Century City. He ordered sukiyaki, pronouncing it like the Japanese, sk'*yak*-ee, and the kimono-clad waitress looked impressed. He had Scotch-on-the-rocks but she never drank. "I've got to keep a cool head around you," she said, only half in jest.

"I like my women to drink."

"Think of all the money I save you."

Midway through dinner, he mentioned Howie, and she tensed. "I hear," he said casually, "that you acted as a lookout for Howie the night he burned the Bank of America."

"So what?" she said flatly.

He continued: "You didn't think anyone knew, did you?"

She took a deep breath. "Look. I put my old boy friends away in a file marked top secret and confidential, and not to be opened until the year 2000."

He didn't even smile. "You amaze me. You're quite a girl—but you're also a very discreet woman."

On the way home, it came to her that she should have asked him how he knew so much about her. Would not that have been the normal reaction? Surprise first, then curiosity?

18

(From report dictated 7-22-72 by Special Agent John Ripley.)

MISS MARTHA CRANSETT, registrar's office, UC Santa Barbara, advised at 1 P.M. 7-20-72 that one OSCAR PEDERSON, who said he represented Aerospace Engineers in Burbank, called on her at 10 A.M. the same day to request information concerning Miss Christina Roberts. (Note: Subsequent investigation reflected that the subject had no affiliation, and never had had, with Aerospace Engineers.) He informed Miss Cransett his firm was considering employing Miss Roberts on a highly classified project. Miss Cransett refused to permit him to read Miss Roberts's file but summarized it as follows: Miss Roberts completed her B.A. degree with a 3.6 average. She was offered and declined an instructorship in English. In her senior year she was an associate editor of the campus newspaper, the Daily Nexus, and a member of the Associated Students Legislative Council. A notation in her file indicated that additional information might be obtained from the university security office.

FRANK INGERSOLL, security chief, UC Santa Barbara, advised at 2:33 P.M. 7-20-72 that one Oscar Pederson, who said he represented Aerospace Engineers, called on him at approximately 10:45 A.M. the same day to inquire about Miss Roberts. Ingersoll refused to disclose information in her security file until Pederson signed a statement to the effect that her prospective employment was a matter of national security. The statement has been forwarded to the Bureau for handwriting comparison.

Ingersoll said he then summarized the information contained in the file. Pederson pressed for more information re Miss Roberts's association with Howard Spelvin and her activities the night the Bank of America was burned. Ingersoll advised Pederson he saw no reason to supply him with further data since her participation in the Bank of America burning should be sufficient to bar her from a job in which national security was at stake. Pederson agreed, thanked him and left. Ingersoll further advised that Pederson seemed quite nervous after signing the statement whereas he had been poised and confident before.

LT. MELVIN STEPHENSON, intelligence unit, sheriff's office, Santa Barbara, reported at 3:05 P.M. 7-20-72 that one Oscar Pederson, claiming to represent Aerospace Engineers, called on him at 1:30 P.M. seeking information concerning Miss Christina Roberts whom that firm was considering for a highly classified position. Lt. Stephenson referred him to a private report prepared by a citizens' committee which stated Miss Roberts was under investigation by the FBI for having served as a lookout for Howard Spelvin, her known

71

boy friend at the time, when he set fire to the Isla Vista branch of the Bank of America 2-70, according to an indictment returned 8-13-70.

Lt. Stephenson further advised Pederson that he understood that upon her graduation Miss Roberts left for Europe. He said he understood "authorities" had traced her to London but at that point she disappeared and did not re-surface until she boarded a plane in London to return to her home in Clinton, North Carolina.

Lt. Stephenson further advised Pederson that Miss Roberts had a clean record in Clinton and came from a highly respected family. He pointed out that once Miss Roberts left his jurisdiction he had no further interest in her, and he did not know about her activities since being employed by United Airlines.

MISS JANE MACKINAW, supervisor, United Airlines, telephoned at 11:42 A.M. 7-21-72 to report that one Oscar Pederson, who represented himself as an employee of the Cutter and Cutter detective agency, called on her to ask questions concerning Miss Roberts. Miss Mackinaw reported the following: He said his company had been employed by a government agency to conduct a background check. He asked if Miss Mackinaw had any information unfavorable to Miss Roberts. Miss Mackinaw said she did not as far as Miss Roberts's efficiency and her character were concerned. He asked if Miss Mackinaw considered Miss Roberts one who could be trusted with classified material. Miss Mackinaw advised that the FBI had been around ten days before to discuss Miss Roberts. She refused to disclose the nature of the inquiry, and referred Mr. Pederson to the FBI.

Miss Mackinaw asked Mr. Pederson for his business card. Subsequent investigation established that the name of the firm, the phone number and address were fictitious. Furthermore, a check of the indices for the name of Oscar Pederson has proven negative. A lead to establish his identity is being set forth.

A composite description furnished by the above three follows: Age, late twenties; height, 6 feet; weight, 170; complexion, dark (one advised he was swarthy); color of eyes, brown; hair, dark brown, quite heavy, inclined to wave, no part (one described his hair as looking like a wig).

Other descriptive points: one of lower front teeth jagged, small mole below right temple, small, white, hairline scar on left side of neck, walks on heels, giving him appearance of falling over backwards, breathes as if suffering from an asthmatic condition. Other observations: poised, courteous, glib, knows the kind of questions a trained investigator would ask.

(From teletypes received and dispatched 7-22-72 by Los Angeles Field division.)

> SAC, LOS ANGELES. WHITE HOUSE AND NATIONAL SECURITY COUNCIL REQUEST DAILY SUMMARIES ON ACTIVITIES OF COMMITTEE OF PUBLIC SAFETY. ABSOLUTELY NECESSARY TO EXPEDITE INVESTIGATION. ADVISE HOW SOON YOUR FIELD DIVISION WILL MAKE INSIDE CONTACT AND REASONS FOR DELAY.
>
> DIRECTOR

> DIRECTOR. ALL LEADS BEING FOLLOWED PROMPTLY. SA RIPLEY WILL FURNISH TELEPHONIC REPORT TO BUREAU EACH NIGHT AND IF DEVELOPMENTS WARRANT AT OTHER TIMES. EXPECT TO PLACE INFORMANT INSIDE COMMITTEE WITHIN NEXT FEW DAYS. DR. BEAUMONT TO INTERVIEW C-77 TOMORROW.
>
> SAC, LOS ANGELES

> SAC, LOS ANGELES. UNABLE TO FOLLOW LEADS RE COMMITTEE OF PUBLIC SAFETY, YOUR OFFICE ORIGIN. INFORMANT C-98 PLACED ON INACTIVE LIST. ALL EFFORTS TO LOCATE THIS INFORMANT NEGATIVE . . .
>
> SAC, NEW YORK

C-98 looked like an emaciated alley cat slinking his bones along. He was a nothing person, eyes lifeless, hair a faded brown, clothes rumpled. Although he was not yet thirty, he moved and turned slowly, from long habit.

He was dog weary and showed it. He had been all over New York, from Greenwich Village to the Bronx. The cops knew him as a runner for hoods. He bitterly resented that. He was a postal system. Someone would call him up and say: "Hey, you going Uptown today? Got a letter I gotta get there."

Now he was on his way to Brooklyn and it was long past midnight. But a relative of Crazy Joey Gallo—may he rest in peace—wanted a box of candy delivered. At least she said it was candy. He never looked inside. He had integrity and consequently was trusted. Take Crazy Joey. He had run his legs off for Crazy Joey, who had been all right.

Joey always called him by name, sent his mother flowers the winter she had had pneumonia, and had said he would pay for the funeral, only she didn't die.

He sat like a sack, getting a good rest. There was the roar of trains passing, the spinning of wheels, and at times a spine-shuddering scraping of metal on metal. He liked the subways. He could ride them all day.

Before he boarded, he had called his mother who was knitting him a scarf in anticipation of a cold winter. She was forever doing something for him. She said the D.A.'s office had phoned. He was to report at 10 A.M. the next day. The same old routine. The same FBI agents, asking questions, getting tough. Well, kiss them off. He passed along as little information as possible about the Committee. That was the way to stay out of prison. As long as he knew something, they would cajole and threaten but do nothing. He was very pleased with himself. He had the names of the members but dragged out only one a month.

At the Court Street station he left the subway and emerged into a hot, humid, bright, starlit night. He took a firm grip on the box of candy in fear one of the hoods from the old Colombo mob might try snatching it. That is, if it were something besides candy.

He walked around the Borough Hall. For the late hour, there was considerable car traffic but not too many people on the sidewalks. He sidled along watching the cars approaching and the ones coming up on his rear. Only last week a good friend had been run down. He turned into Joralemon Street which was very quiet, no one at all about except a garbage collector picking up a can and dumping it into one of those big, shredder, van-type trucks. The street was so quiet that when he started by the truck, alongside the dark green shoeshine

74

kiosk, he could hear the muted roar of the empty shredder running.

He scarcely knew when the slug hit him. Somehow the garbage collector brushed him in returning the tall can to the sidewalk, there was this muffled explosion very near, and the pain in his gut shot straight up. Then he was conscious he was flying through the air, and his body struck metal with terrific impact, and the pain was so intense he screamed.

And loud in his ears, growing ever louder, was the roar of the shredder.

19

MAX SWERVED THE car up alongside the curb before her apartment and slammed on the brakes. They had been to The Grove to laugh, be moved and caught up in the magic that was Sammy Davis, Jr.

Max was out in a second and around to open the door. His arms went about her as she stepped out, and his big frame pushed her back against the car until their bodies melded. His lips were hard against hers. She eased away from him, maneuvering deftly, never struggling. She had fended off too many dates not to know the technique.

How she hated him. Briefly he could excite her. The body reacted even when the mind commanded otherwise, and afterwards she would experience shame and guilt.

They walked to the door, his arm tightly encasing her and his strong fingers kneading her flesh. "I know why you're holding off."

She tensed and waited, and he continued: "Why didn't you tell me you're engaged?"

"What are you, the CIA?" she asked. "That was months ago. It didn't take."

"I heard—"

"I see him now and then but it's all over, the hearts and flowers bit."

He didn't pursue the subject and said good night. As she closed the door, she saw his car pull away and another that had been parked a little distance behind move into the space.

She was arranging the hat on the moose when there was a tap on the door. Thoughtlessly she answered it. In the same instant she realized she first should have asked the party to identify himself. A young man stood there backlighted. She could barely make out his features. She had the impression he had a well-turned face, nothing unusual, no accentuated nose or ears. He wore a dark suit and tie, which seemed out of place on a warm night in this beach neighborhood.

He said in a low voice: "I'm Compton—from the FBI. Your usual contact couldn't come—and he asked me—"

She hesitated, her heart pounding. Mr. Ripley had told her if ever there were an emergency, and he were not available, another agent would come.

She stalled. "My usual contact?"

"Why, yes, you know . . ."

"Do I?" She moved to get a better view of him. He shifted with her. In the distance, the ocean bellowed. It was angry tonight.

"Well, he said you'd know . . ." He seemed to breathe with difficulty.

"What was it you wanted?" She feared she sounded nervous, rattled. She gripped the doorknob hard.

"Any developments? He thought we ought to check you out tonight. He got tied up."

"About what?" She wondered if Roz were home yet, if she were awake.

He said irritably: "I can't go into details standing out here."

She answered in the same tone: "I can't help you if I don't know what you want." She closed the door a little and braced a foot and leg against the inside. A swimmer in trunks with a jacket flapping passed by on the sidewalk. His sandals scraped on the concrete.

"Do you have something to show you're an FBI agent?"

"Why, of course. I forgot . . ." He produced a wallet-type identification. In the faint light she saw a photo and the letters FBI. To the best of her memory, it looked the same as the one Mr. Ripley had produced.

Mr. Compton continued: "He said—"

"Who is this he?"

"You know. You've talked a lot with him."

"I talk with a lot of passengers. I may have talked with someone from the FBI. But not recently."

"But, Miss Roberts, he said he talked with you—what was it?—a day or two ago, a few days—"

76

"Not with the FBI, I didn't!"

He assumed a hurt tone. "You're making this difficult for me. He said you were covering developments . . . with this subversive group."

"Subversive! I don't belong to any subversive group."

"You're getting us information on them."

"Now wait a minute, Mr. Compton. I'm not getting information about anybody for anyone." She added quickly: "Look, I'm tired. I don't want to play cops and robbers tonight." She closed the door.

Roz called from her bedroom: "What was that all about?"

"Some nut."

She collapsed in the basket chair, her legs sprawling, her arms falling by her sides.

20

SHE REMEMBERED AFTERWARDS that she took the trip to Westwood Village with Max during the dark of the moon. Remembered, because the porch light had been on as always when the moon was new and thin. When it was full, she and Roz turned off the light to save electricity.

As she was leaving the apartment, Roz said: "I almost forgot. Sears called and said they couldn't fill the order. Some character seemed awfully anxious I get in touch with you right away. Like who cares?"

Chris stood in brief shock, then said thanks. The message was from the FBI. Translated, it read that the bug in her brassiere had ceased to function. She was on her own.

Max had said he wanted her to meet an old and dear friend, Dr. George Henry Beaumont, a retired University of California at Los Angeles history professor. "His wife died a few years ago and he's quite lonely. They had no children. But he's still got a great mind, still the foremost authority on the French Revolution in the country. Historians always go by to see him when they're visiting in Los Angeles. You'll like him. He keeps up with the times, although you get this strange feeling that he's standing off to one side and looking at the world but he's not a part of it."

Max had called for her in an old Continental bearing Colorado license plates. She had been curious about the plates but had asked no questions. "The Porsche broke down, and a friend from Denver loaned me this."

Leaving Manhattan Beach, he took the San Diego Freeway to the Wilshire Boulevard off ramp, then to Thayer where he turned right. He pulled the car up before a two-story Spanish-style home set back from the street. A magenta bougainvillaea gone wild half covered a small balcony on the second story. A nearby street light revealed a long untended yard pockmarked with small bumps. "He gave up. The gophers took over."

Max picked up the evening newspaper and several throwaways. "He never sees them. Walks right by them."

A hound dog approached with the lackluster of old age. He knew Max and allowed himself to be petted. Slowly he turned his attention to her and growled from long habit. A stranger should be forewarned, not set upon, not threatened, but merely advised to behave himself. "His name's Rousseau. He's a good dog, aren't you, old fellow." Rousseau wagged his tail in full agreement.

They took a narrow, winding sidewalk to a massive oak door that bore an antique Spanish knocker. Max lifted it and let it drop. "Don't let the drawn shades bother you. He keeps them that way day and night. Doesn't like the idea of neighbors spying on him. He treats them like peasants, and they put up with it good-naturedly. They put it down to the fact he was a prof."

Max dropped the knocker twice more, and when the door swung back, she saw a thin, white-haired man with military bearing, and military eyes that appraised her in one fleeting glance. He had a baby's pink skin that denied his age. Somehow the wrinkles had not come.

"Max," he said, putting a measure of dignity into the one word. Before Max could introduce her, he said: "Miss Roberts. What a pleasure. Do come in."

He led them across a red tiled hallway, rubbed to a high polish, past a great arched entrance to a living room with white walls, a high-beamed ceiling, and a fireplace at the far end, and into a small, cozy den lined with bookcases. Everywhere books staggered drunkenly, on the chairs, the sofa, the floor. "Max," he said, indicating the books on the sofa. "Would you, please? Put them anywhere." He turned to her. "I can't do much lifting. My back, a pinched nerve the doctor

78

informs me, although I imagine it is more arthritis than anything. Sit down, please. How good of you to come."

He started to pour tea and serve small cakes but she insisted on taking over. He said: "I always put in a pinch of jasmine and a clove. Gives it that *je ne sais quoi*."

Before closing the door, he invited Rousseau in. She said: "I had a dog like him when I was growing up back in North Carolina."

"A hunting dog?"

She nodded. "But I never hunted with him. I didn't care for hunting."

"Over here, Rousseau." He indicated a mussed-up blanket on the floor by a long, dark, carved desk, and the dog dutifully stretched out there. "He's absolutely incorruptible. A burglar attempted to feed him prime sirloin and he refused. He barked and stood his ground until a neighbor came to see what was amiss."

He picked up a heavy tome he had been reading, *The Decline and Fall of the Roman Empire,* and said: "I can't begin to estimate how many times I have read this. There is considerable to be learned. The United States is rather like Rome in its final days. Very much like it."

He let himself down easily, his back ramrod straight, into an old red leather chair as decrepit as the dog. He breathed heavily from the exertion. "Emphysema," he explained.

He said to Max: "I mentioned to you about writing my publisher, you remember, and I had an answer today. They are rather interested in bringing out another edition of *Charlotte Corday.*"

He turned to her. "Charlotte Corday was—"

Chris interrupted. "She assassinated Marat while he was taking a bath. I've always thought it wasn't very sportsmanlike."

"How remarkable that you would know that."

She laughed. "Jacques David's painting in the Louvre has stayed with me. Actually, I was a poor history student."

He sipped his tea. "I doubt that. Anyway, what do you think of our society, Miss Roberts? I am always interested in the observations of our young people."

"I'm an airline stewardess, and honestly, I don't know anything about government."

"You must have opinions. Everyone does."

She uncrossed her legs, leaned a little forward. "Someone asked me the other day if I was happy, and I asked him, 'Is that what we're

79

put here for? Just to be happy? Not to do anything? Not to care about others?' Yes, I do have opinions, Dr. Beaumont. Strong ones. But I also believe firmly that a little knowledge is a dangerous thing, and I'm afraid to go out on a limb—especially with someone like you."

Dr. Beaumont made a deprecatory gesture, and she added: "Max has told me all about you and to tell you the truth, your vast knowledge is intimidating."

He studied her a moment, pleased, then turned to Max. "You better watch her, Max. She is a very sharp young woman. She has mastered the art of subtle flattery."

"Touché," Max said, giving her a nudge with his eyes.

"Well," Chris began, "my opinions are the cry of the multitudes—down through the ages, I guess. Maybe just an echo, too simplistic. But with millions barely having enough to eat, and sick and no medical attention, and hovels for homes, I think something's wrong. Terribly, terribly wrong."

Dr. Beaumont nodded, placed his fingertips together. "The question is, what to do? How to right the outrages?"

She said: "I had a dream once when I was in college—like all kids—that we'd wake up some morning and we'd have all new people everywhere, in the government, running business, everywhere. People who cared, who weren't just out for power and money. I think the nihilists have something. We're never going to get anywhere trying to reform the politicians. The only way to build a good and just society is to wipe out the old, do away with it and start all over, clean. But I guess that's impossible."

There, she had said it, and with sincerity and conviction. She had gone over and over all possible discussion that she might have with Dr. George Henry Beaumont, to the point where she feared it would sound memorized. But it had rolled off as if she did believe it—and for the moment she had. Ripley had cautioned her: Enter into conversation with him as any young woman would, respectful of his scholarship, hesitant to express herself on his ground, but eventually permitting her pent-up feelings to spill out. This, they both knew, would be the acid test. Max would have no reason for her to meet Dr. Beaumont except to gain the professor's approval. And by taking her, Max had put his own seal upon her.

"Yes! Yes, it *is* possible." Dr. Beaumont's eyes took on the unfocused, fanatical brilliance of a flagellant. "We have in our society today the very causes that brought about the French Revolution—

corruption in high places, excessive taxes, utter disregard of the people by the government. And then there's hunger alongside luxury and waste, unemployment on one hand and overpaid sinecures on the other . . . Yes, it *is* possible. The time is almost here."

"But after the French Revolution, the poor peasants just got another set of oppressors."

"Ah, my dear," he said quickly as though waiting for the opening, "that's where we come in, Max and you and I—the intelligent ones. History speaks to those who listen and see with their minds. We won't make the same mistakes."

The words of a supreme egotist, Chris thought, and wondered which was the more dangerous, the old intellectual or the young activist. Dr. Beaumont poured himself the last dregs of cold tea and continued: "The oppressed and the militants think they start revolutions. They don't. They are too stupid. They shout and march and burn and destroy, yes, but they're just the tools of the intellectuals. Oh, don't get me wrong. They are necessary—to incite the populace. Revolution is not possible unless the people get aroused. The Establishment must become sharply divided."

He paused. "I'm afraid I'm boring you. I—"

"Oh, no," she said quickly. "Please. Please go on. It's all so—so new and exciting, like exploring a new land. Only a new way of life, a new concept is so much more thrilling, challenging."

"Good! As I said, the time is almost here, and it's up to a carefully chosen few with both zeal and intelligence. Because the whole operation will fail unless we have organization, leadership by a capable nucleus. We need the rabble, in fact, we must find ways to subtly encourage injustice in some areas, invite police brutality and overreaction, in order to shock the apathetic, contented majority. But the intellectuals must hold the reins.

"That is where we learn from the French Revolution. There were plenty of enlightened leaders who wanted to redesign the world, and some of them tried. I have made a careful study of their failures, and we will avoid them. Some of them were carried away by their emotions and didn't know how to bring about their goals. Some of the Jacobins got satisfaction out of the hue and cry of the mobs, the revolution per se. None of them had a concrete plan and the intelligence and capacity to carry it out."

As Chris listened with mounting shock, she had the feeling that the pounding of her heart must be shaking her body. She managed

81

to nod agreement. "When I was in college, I felt so strongly. And we protested, did what we could to make ourselves heard. But nothing ever came of it. And now, well, I just feel frustrated so I sort of rock along. What *is* the answer, Dr. Beaumont? How can anyone bring it off?"

"The guillotine! The guillotine's the answer."

Was he mad? Was he testing her credulity, her sincerity? Chris wondered. She had to go along, play it by ear. "But surely in this day and age—"

He cut in: "It worked in the French Revolution. Forty thousand went to their deaths on the guillotine. Yes, Miss Roberts, it will work in this day and age, as you put it. This is the age of visual effects—in education, in advertising, everywhere you turn. That monster television has made us conscious of seeing. It's no longer enough to read about something or listen, we've got to see it in order to laugh or cry or believe or be shocked. Think of heads falling—literally—before your eyes. Heads of Nixon, McGovern, Humphrey, Reagan, Kennedy. That's the way to turn things around and start anew."

Chris could not suppress a shudder, and did not attempt to hide her revulsion. "But Dr. Beaumont!"

"You are shocked, my dear. That's the normal reaction. That's the desired effect. But actually, it's the *method* that strikes horror, now isn't it? Not the deaths."

She took a deep breath. "I suppose death is death. I don't like to think of anyone dying but I know some of us must if we are ever to do anything about all of the horrible evils that man inflicts on man. I'd willingly die myself if that would help."

His eyes were on hers. "I thought so. I would point out to you that the very horror this visual factor strikes in you, it also strikes in others. That, I must say, is the overwhelming point in favor of using the guillotine—to terrify the oppressors of justice and righteousness. The Nazis used gas, and put to death the enemies of the state secretly. They bungled it horribly. What a spectacle—and what fear it would have instilled in the populace—if they had done away with the Jews in the Sports Platz. Other countries have employed the technique of using firing squads, usually at sunrise when no one's about.

"But no, the guillotine, with the mobs lining the streets, the thousands watching the actual knife falling, the blood gushing, and the severed heads rolling, that is the most effective technique of all. Imagine if we used the guillotine in the Washington Stadium. One hundred thousand watching. Imagine lining up the enemies of the state and guillotining twenty at a morning performance, another twenty in the afternoon, and perhaps more at night. Imagine television cameras carrying it into every home in the country so that millions could witness what happens to any person who attempts to thwart the wish of man through the centuries."

He was mad, mad, she thought. But was he? He was talking along in a normal, quiet voice. He could have been discussing pleasantries with neighbors who had come by for the evening. She glanced at Max but his eyes told her nothing, not a muscle moved across his face.

Dr. Beaumont continued: "I have mulled over this matter for months and have reached the considered conclusion that we must use the guillotine. There is no effective substitute."

21

At 11:43 p.m. Rip took the call. For three hours he had been sitting anxiously at his desk awaiting it. The chance that something might happen was slight. There had been no indication that anything would. Yet no matter how safe the situation appeared, there was always the possibility of a word carelessly dropped, a reaction not quite true, thus tipping off an observant person, or a happenstance that would explode the whole plot. The truth, strangely, was difficult to simulate or conceal, as the case might be. Even when the masquerade was well-nigh perfect, there was a sixth sense—call it mental telepathy, extrasensory perception or what you will—that could scent something amiss. He believed so strongly in this that he had cautioned her repeatedly: "Don't let the thought creep in that you are playing a role. Don't even admit to yourself that you don't believe this way. You are this person, and your beliefs are this person's."

So on nights such as this he sweated it out. He had tried assembling data for a report he would dictate the next day but was unable to corral his errant thoughts. He had struggled to review the case to assure himself that he had covered every possible contingency that Christina Roberts might find herself in, but his mind balked at being programed.

Barney was on the phone. Barney from Barney's Malt Shop. Rip could picture him calling from the john. Barney's place was so small and compact that when Barney wanted a telephone, he had only one place to locate it. Ever after he bragged to his friends that he was in the same class as those people in Beverly Hills with their pink French phones in the bathrooms.

Without preliminaries, he said: "She ordered a burger with everything, and said she was hungry enough to eat ten of them. Side order of French fries."

Rip dropped the receiver and collapsed with relief in the swivel.

Translated, "a burger with everything" read that she was inside the Committee.

"Ten of them" meant that she would meet Rip at the rendezvous at ten the next morning.

"Side order of French fries" was superfluous. It indicated everything had gone smoothly and she was in no danger.

22

THE SKY WAS stern as an old schoolmaster, a flat, slate surface devoid of feeling. Nothing had depth, neither the growling, churning ocean nor the fish-and-worms shack, nor the short, tottering pier with the boats bobbing alongside, nor the lonely, cut-out figures trudging slowly over the sand.

Rip felt closed in, as if the sky might lower and compact itself. His was the lone car on the lot, and accordingly, conspicuous. He himself was not. He was in old clothes, his grass-stained yard trousers, a dark, pull-over sweater thin at the elbows, and an open shirt frayed at the collar.

A gaunt figure with eyes that had no common focus asked how long he wanted to rent the boat. "A couple of hours," Rip said. "I got to get away from it all."

The fellow nodded heartily. "Know what you mean. Got off a couple weeks ago myself and went to the mountains."

Rip's gaze crossed the man's shoulder and traveled up and down the dreary scene, searching for someone who might not belong. He, though, appeared the lone alien.

He kept the runabout near the beach, and it rode the waves well. He rounded a stubby, thumb-shaped peninsula and put into a sequestered cove, named aptly in Spanish, Pequeño (Little) Cove.

From the shore, Chris waved to him. She was in jeans held up by a wide leather belt, and a loose shirt that flopped about her narrow hips. With her scrubbed face and hair blowing, she could have been a teen-ager.

She helped him drag the boat up on the beach alongside hers, and said: "I haven't much time. I've got a twelve forty-five flight to Washington."

"You're all right?" he asked.

"Nothing that a couple months in a sanitarium wouldn't cure. Here's the bug. I dropped it. I'm sorry."

Rip handed her another in a small box. "You had me worried."

He trudged awkwardly in his street shoes through the sand. She wore thonged, Mexican sandals. Here on the beach he looked taller, she thought, than in man-made surroundings, and in the sweater, his shoulders appeared broader and hips narrower. She could have liked this man in another place, another time, but she felt in part toward him as she had when quite young toward schoolteachers. They were to be obeyed, listened to, and yes-sirred and yes-ma'amed. She could never feel at ease around him, and she was a person whose happiness was nurtured by closeness to others, little ecstasies shared with them and disappointments shored up by understanding.

They sat a few feet across from each other on rocks polished by the tides. She pulled her legs up to wrap her arms around her knees, and said: "I don't know how much longer I can go on. I warned you I wasn't good at this. And don't tell me I'll get used to it!"

"Nobody does."

"Not even you?"

"Especially me."

"Will you put flowers on my casket if I turn in a bad performance? 'In memory of Christina Roberts, from the FBI.'"

"Don't say things like that!" he snapped.

"Sorry—I shouldn't've. But it could be . . . Well, before I get on with my report, you asked me to mention anything odd. Max—Mr. Hartman—drove an old Continental last night with Colorado plates." She gave him the number.

Rip thought the plates had been stolen. "He figured if we suspected Dr. Beaumont and were running a surveillance on his home, we

85

might be taking down the license numbers of cars parked in front of his place."

He jerked his head upward, listening, then signaled her to follow him. They ran for the cover of two huge boulders that met tip to tip to form an arch, and stood beneath them while a helicopter droned overhead. They were close, not an arm's length apart. In the intimacy of the moment a strong desire surged through Rip, stirred by this girl he admired. She looked up at him, and from her glistening eyes he knew she had experienced the same longing. Then a curtain fell and once more, he was the FBI agent. There was a barrier of officialdom that no contact, however close, could push aside. In her thinking, too, he realized, was an unreasoning, but now quiescent, resentment toward him, toward this man who through the accident of having been on the scene at a particular time was the one who had sent her forth on this mission.

They sank into the sand a short distance beyond the arch, and she began her report. She was nervous as she recalled Dr. Beaumont's discussion about the guillotine. "He wants to set one up in a coliseum somewhere with the television cameras grinding away. And he isn't kidding. He'd do it if he got the chance. I couldn't believe it. I asked Max about it on the way home, and he said to forget it. He said it pleases the old fellow to talk like that. But Max goes along with him. Maybe not the guillotine but a lot of people, tens of thousands, must be killed to bring the revolution off. I don't believe Max has decided whether to shoot them or go with Dr. Beaumont. Max admires him, says he's a great brain . . ."

Her somber eyes reflected the strain. If this goes on many months, she will age, he thought with a sharp thrust. He had watched others grow old, like children who have too many adult pressures placed on them. The mind and body could absorb only so many shocks before the whole being moved in a stunned state, the thinking slowed, the eyes deadened, the smile became forced and sick.

"They played a game with me last night," she said slowly. "Dr. Beaumont gave me the shock treatment to see if my convictions were strong enough to stand up under harsh realities, and then Max on the way home played it all down to calm me. Max wanted to cool me because he's got an assignment for me."

"An assignment?"

"Well, to tell it in chronological order, so I make sense, after all the talk about guillotining forty thousand, or whatever it was, Dr.

Beaumont got down to business. He said a few of them had banded together to change things. He gave me the old malarkey about how you couldn't bring off a peaceful revolution because it couldn't be done within the Establishment. Just like when I was in the university and some of the acidheads were sounding off. He asked if I would like to help out and I acted excited.

"He said: 'I do want to inform you before you come in that we have a strict rule, and you must understand that we have this rule for the protection of all of us. It would be for you, too. Nobody ever resigns or leaves us. You can readily understand why. We are a family, a very closely knit family that must stay together to protect each other. We have never had a member of our family betray us but if we should, we most certainly would be forced to put him to death. You must understand, Miss Roberts, the reasons behind these rules, and you must agree wholeheartedly. If you have any qualms, you must express them at this point.'"

She was breathing hard. "What do you say to something like that, Mr. Ripley? What do you say?"

"What did you?"

"I nodded. I guess I did. I'm not sure. By then I'd come unglued. But I don't think it showed. I do remember saying something about I'd never had any use for rat finks." She smiled wanly. "That's what I told you the first time, remember?"

She rose and stretched, a long, slender body silhouetted against the unfriendly sky. He got up and asked: "The assignment?"

"I'm to be ready at one A.M. Saturday. I told them Roz would be suspicious if I left the apartment at that hour, so I'm to leave earlier, kill time, then go to The Prow. It's an all-night fish shack. Someone will call for me there. Not Max but a stranger. I don't have any idea what it's all about. Max wouldn't tell me but it's something big. On the way home he said it was their first major move. He patted me on the leg—we were in the car—and I told him I had a rule, too. I said if I came in, it was strictly business between him and me. I said: 'If later on we get . . . friendly . . . but right now . . .'

"He took his hand away and said, 'Okay, okay.' I told him also I wasn't going to seduce anyone to help the revolution, and he laughed, and said I was awfully straitlaced to be an airline stewardess. I didn't say anything for a minute, I was so mad, then I asked him what my part was, what I had to do, and he said he wished he could tell me but the others had voted against it. The man who picks me up at The Prow, he said, would clue me in.

"I said I thought I should know what it was all about if it was a dangerous assignment, and he asked if I wanted out. I said no and shut up.

"If they ask me to set up a sex trap for someone—Max was telling me about reading a story in the *Times* about a woman in Santa Monica who lured men into dark alleys and then her boy friend slugged and robbed them—if they want to use me as a sex decoy, I don't know whether I could go through with it . . . I don't know . . ."

She left first, with Rip set to depart fifteen minutes later. They had come out of different harbors. While Rip had rented his boat, hers belonged to friends, an older couple from her North Carolina days who had moved to California. She could borrow it whenever she wished.

On the way back she saw a sailboat bobbing aimlessly and wondered idly who would be out on such a miserable day. Sea lovers, though, were irrepressible.

A short distance south of Manhattan Beach she put into a tiny harbor. She was tossing the rope over a piling when the Korean war veteran with the shot-off toes, who tended a fishing shack, came limping over. She knew he batched in a rather primitive fashion, and she never came this way that she didn't bring him some home-cooked food.

"Thanks, Joe," she said out of breath. He always helped her with the skiff. There was an easygoing camaraderie among sea people that she liked. She wished Jim cared for the ocean. Around it, though, he was miserable and irritable. The sand, the humidity, and the ramshackle look along the beach bothered him. He liked neatness, order, and cleanliness. She could see clearly that when she married him she would have to give up hanging wet bathing suits on the mailbox and kicking off shoes on entering the apartment. She would be adamant, though, about the moose. That was Grandpapa's. It was an heirloom.

Joe said: "There was a character around asking about you soon as you was gone."

She looked up in quick fright. "A man?"

He nodded. "Wouldn't tell his name. Wouldn't say anything except ask questions."

"Like what?"

"Was it your boat? Did you go every morning? Where'd you go? Told him people around here don't go no place most times. Just go out, fool around. Like going for a ride in the country, I told 'im. You don't go anywhere, you just go. Anyhow, wasn't none of his business and I told him so to his face. I'd watch it if I was you. Don't go fooling around too much by yourself. Some of these acidheads—but he wasn't, don't think. Didn't strike me as one."

He described the man, and the picture fitted the party who had called himself Compton. She shuddered. They were watching her every move. They didn't trust her. Not yet.

23

THE NEXT DAY, Tuesday, Edward Markinson of Domestic Intelligence, one of six assistants to the Director, arrived at 7:10 A.M. at Los Angeles International Airport and went directly to the field division headquarters where the SAC and Rip awaited him.

Markinson greeted the SAC and Rip warmly. He was large of frame, in his early fifties, friendly, energetic, incessantly on the move. That was one side of him. Once he settled down to work, however, he was cold, impersonal, analytical. He had a stripped-down mind. He could be ruthless with an agent or a report, could turn sarcastic with an agent whose thoughts tended to ramble. He demanded a printed circuit with transistorized responses. He himself had started with the Bureau twenty-eight years ago in Omaha, and served in Louisville, Albuquerque, Boston, Seattle, Dallas, and Washington, D.C. He had never handled a bizarre case or distinguished himself by daring. Neither had he erred on a single investigation. Steadily, without one stumble, he had climbed the Bureau hierarchy which was a corporate structure as much as any business. He had one advantage over others. He had no outside interests, no wife, no girl friend, no hobby. He looked upon the Bureau's work as a crusade, and seldom put in less than twelve hours a day.

In the SAC's office they sat down to discuss this "major move" the Committee of Public Safety had set for one o'clock Saturday morning, as reported by Informant C-77.

First, though, Markinson asked for the physical surveillance logs.

He would study them later. Rip's desk had run, and was continuing to do so, "loose" tail jobs on every known member of the Los Angeles Committee. By "loose" was meant: Do not under any circumstances permit the party under surveillance to discover or suspect your presence. Lose him before you do that. The logs reflected little information. Max Hartman had set up the operation so there was no casual get together of members. Markinson also requested the electronic surveillance logs that contained conversations developed through legal wire and telephonic tapping (as approved by a federal court). These, too, revealed little pertinent information. When Hartman or the others needed to talk by phone, they used pay phones and restricted their conversation to a minute or two. Hartman had figured out very effectively how to circumvent the FBI on all types of surveillances.

Markinson was quietly elated that Rip had succeeded in planting C-77. She was the Bureau's only productive source. Even before his disappearance in New York, C-98 had provided the Bureau with only a few names and little information about plans and operations.

On a yellow legal pad, the SAC listed the possible eventualities in this "major move." The most likely ones were: (1) a kidnaping, (2) the planting of a bomb, (3) a raid on a bank, or (4) the hijacking of a plane.

"The subjects may well attempt a kidnaping," said Markinson. "We know that they must raise big sums. If they do kidnap someone, I should think they'd use the procedures worked out by the Tupamaros who have about perfected the crime."

The Tupamaros would force a car bearing their victim, or driven by him, to the curb, usually at rush hour in Montevideo, seize him at gun point in a daring surprise move, and spirit him away. Invariably, the operation was well plotted and executed, and timed for three minutes.

Markinson continued: "They could use the informant in any number of ways—as a decoy, a lookout, to phone the ransom demand, perhaps even pick up the ransom payment."

The SAC cleared his throat. "I should think heisting a bank might fit in better with what we know. It's been used by so many revolutionary groups in this country—and all over the world. Remember those college girls in New England? Absolutely unbelievable!"

Markinson nodded. "A bank raid *is* a clean, quick way of raising big money. Kidnaping calls for covering many contingencies and may stretch over a considerable time. And in the end someone has to expose himself on a high risk level to collect the ransom. He takes the chance he will walk into a trap whereas the surprise element is all with the criminal in a bank hold-up."

"No matter what course they take," Rip interposed, "if we can checkmate them—keep them from getting a big hunk of money—we'll gain time and set them back on their schedule. And time's what we need badly. If we could only block every move they make, without their knowing it . . ."

Markinson nodded and idly ran fingers along a bookshelf, testing for dust, which the Bureau would no more tolerate than would a Dutch housewife. "I wish you could've planted the informant inside the Committee sooner."

"We used all expedition possible consistent with safety," Rip said in defense. "You play along, wait and hope for a break—and we got it. A highly intelligent woman—"

"I know, I know," Markinson interjected. "I'm not criticizing. Now about the hijacking of a plane. They could raise a big sum quickly in a very simple operation. Requires only one man and a weapon. They could seize the informant—and she would give them no trouble since she is ostensibly one of them—and demand a ransom through her. However, of all the four possibilities, hijacking would be the easiest to defense. We could place a tight security about all the airports and—"

The SAC broke in. "I should imagine they have thought of a hijacking and discarded it for two reasons. First, they know the security precautions are tight, and secondly, the scheme has repeatedly failed. It's not a smart operation for a man of Hartman's shrewdness."

"But the Palestinian guerrillas brought it off," Rip pointed out. "Got five million dollars in ransom out of one hijacking."

Markinson nodded. "We'll set up tight security at all airports in California for Friday night. We can make it so tight no one can get through. Now for the fourth possibility, a bombing—"

"I've gone over that." Rip handed him a sheaf of maps and papers. "Here are the principal targets—police stations, government buildings, computer centers, universities, airports, and so on. But I don't think a bombing fits in with what we've learned about the Committee's thinking, especially Hartman's. The Chicago Field division reported that when he was at Northwestern he ridiculed what he called one-night fireworks, and Informant C-119, who was killed, quoted Hartman as stating at a meeting that he wanted no hit-and-run set-ups.

91

Hartman said they accomplished nothing, except to get the Establishment excited, wasted time and money, drew attention of the police to the organization, and that they should gear themselves for the final putsch."

"Is that right?" Markinson asked. "That's interesting. Most of these groups hit helter-skelter. They have a theory that a bombing here and there will scare people—that it's a beginning."

"Don't you think," asked Rip, "that it gets down to the old business that people with a cause must be doing something? They can't sit and wait."

"Lenin and Trotsky did," Markinson pointed out. "The smart ones do."

Although all three were inclined to rule out a bombing, they would propose in a conference with the police, sheriff, California Highway Patrol and other law-enforcement agencies a defense that would call for: (1) guarding all key buildings or installations, which would require bringing more manpower into the greater Los Angeles metropolitan area, including police officers and sheriff's deputies from other cities, (2) forming a large reserve pool of officers for unforeseen emergency situations, and (3) asking every peace officer to check his informants, to learn if they knew anything pertinent. Moreover, they would request every security person employed by the key targets to report suspicious acts, such as a loitering stranger who might be casing a plant or locality.

Rip suggested that the emergency pool should be divided, with units stationed in the principal areas of the city. "If there is a kidnaping, then we would have back-up officers close by."

The SAC stressed the need for secrecy. "We must impress this on all agencies. We must ask that they keep their people out of sight as much as possible that night. If it looks like an armed camp, we will tip off the subjects."

Markinson asked: "Will it break the cover of our informant if the news should leak out?"

Rip thought not. "She doesn't know anything about the operation—and I should think, if this is a major move as Hartman told her—several inside the Committee would know the details and be more suspect.

"Our principal problem," Rip continued, "is communicating with her. I've warned her against phoning me, now that she's inside, unless she's desperate. She did phone me a few times before and once she thought she was being observed. With these glass booths on the street, so open, someone with binoculars could take down the number as she dials and if he had a friend inside the phone company who would tell him who has that number, well, it would be all over for her."

"Shouldn't we run a surveillance on her that night?" asked the SAC. "We might get a tip a few minutes before they set the operation in effect. Too, we might help her if she gets into a bad spot."

Rip tensed. "If they discovered we were running a tail on her, they'd do away with her right then and there. There's *no way* we could get to her in time."

Markinson said: "We could keep it loose . . . it wouldn't have to be tight . . . if we lost her, we wouldn't be any worse off."

Rip raised his voice slightly without being conscious of it. "She'll be wearing the bug and we'll be picking up more from the conversation than we could from a surveillance. She'll ask questions, too, that'll feed us information."

"All right," Markinson said with finality. "No surveillance. It's your case." What he was saying, Rip knew, was: "I'm holding you responsible. If something goes wrong . . . if we could have forestalled something by a surveillance . . ."

Markinson continued, thinking aloud: "Why one A.M. Saturday? Does the timing mean anything?"

"It might," Rip said. "The banks close at six Friday evening and don't open until ten Monday morning. A clever bank job might not be discovered for two days. If I were betting, I'd wager they're going to hit a bank."

"You're not betting!" Markinson said sharply.

24

AT 5:35 P.M. Thursday United's Flight 906 from Washington's Dulles Airport put down at Los Angeles. Chris bade goodbye to 166 passengers, then hurried without the usual chitchat for the Stewardesses' office. The flight had been smooth and the passengers pleasant, but her neck cords were tightly drawn. The night before she had slept but little.

In the Stewardesses' office she took her monthly weight check. She never varied more than a pound from 118. The supervisor reminded her that she had failed to submit her bid for flights. About three weeks before the first of each month, the supervisor posted a schedule of forty-some runs. The stewardesses bid for those they wanted, listing first, second, and third choices. The girls with seniority got the first choices, the best flights.

The supervisor studied her sympathetically. "If there's anything you want to talk to me about—"

Chris indicated in the negative. She was disturbed that her turmoil was so patently evident.

At the rear of United's building, where the baggage was being hauled in, she took the little airline tram to the parking lot. Unlocking her car door, she saw the small envelope taped to the windshield. A typed note inside read: *I'll pick you up at 9 tonight. Your place. M.*

Her heart beat increased rapidly with the thought that the Friday night date had been advanced. Had there been a change in plans? But Max was calling for her, not a stranger, and at her apartment, not The Prow.

She resented the proprietary sound of the note. He had not asked if he might call for her. He was ordering her. Now that she was a member of the Committee, he could command her. As long as the FBI permitted the Committee to exist, she was a pawn, a prisoner, subject to Max's and Dr. Beaumont's bidding. She could not quit, run away, or pretend illness. Only this minute did the enormity of her plight sink in.

She noted a blowzy man in rough work clothes watching her from across the parking lot. He was leaning against a new car, smoking a cigarette. She turned the ignition key.

En route home through heavy traffic, she talked to the bug. "I found a note on the windshield. Max will be calling for me at nine o'clock. I don't know what it's all about." She figured if Max did have her under surveillance, the party would be following her and not in a position to see her lips move. For that matter, some people talked to themselves, didn't they? But older people mostly.

On the trip to Washington and back she had kept the bug in her bra. She had no idea whether Washington had listened in.

She arrived home before Roz, got into a gay but inexpensive Japanese robe Jim had given her, and tried phoning him. When there was

94

no response, she was crushed. Slowly he was slipping out of her life. It had been ten days since she had seen him. He said he understood but he had been short with her a time or two, which was unlike him.

About 6 the phone rang, and a pain shot out of her neck cords with bullet effect into her cranium. But it was only Roz calling to say that her boy friend was taking her to dinner at The Sizzler and they would go directly to the bowling alley. She didn't suppose Chris and Jim would be bowling tonight. No, Chris said, they wouldn't, and offered no explanation. She had lied too many times.

She wrapped a silver pin that she would send her mother for her birthday, wrote a note to a close friend informing her she would be unable to attend her wedding, watered a small potted geranium that stubbornly refused to bloom, and harvested three onions from a set of twelve she had planted in a bowl in the kitchen window.

The next time the phone sounded, her oldest nephew's voice came over. "Aunt Chris?"

"Hi, Tommy," she said, and sprawled with relief in a breakfast-nook chair. "How're you, Tommy?"

"Don't you love us any more?" The voice was plaintive, not accusing.

"I love you bushels and pecks."

"You don't come to see us."

"I will, Tommy, I will. Soon."

"When's soon?"

"A few days."

"Our dog's home." He rattled away giving her news about the family, mostly about the dog, the cat, and the parakeet.

Her brother, Dan, came on the line. "Listen here," he said in a low voice, "the boys cried half the night when you didn't come to take them to the circus. I don't know what's bothering you—must really be something! Whatever, don't you think you could get over here at least once a week? That's not asking too much, is it?"

Near tears, she said it was not.

She cooked two lamb chops, cut up some greens for a salad and made her mother's favorite oil-and-vinegar dressing.

As she was finishing the meal, she again answered the phone. "Miss Roberts? This is Joe McDonald at Sears. I got your message when I got back to the office. I'm sorry about the drapes. I'm checking now to see what's holding up the order and I'll give you a call tomorrow."

95

She thanked him and hung up. Merely hearing Mr. Ripley's voice buoyed her.

She was placing a note for Roz on the refrigerator door under the beetle magnet, when Max sounded the horn. She hurried out into a warm night redolent with dinner odors, roses, fresh cut grass, and smog.

"We're having a little meeting tonight," he said, shooting the Porsche down the street, "and I want you to meet a couple friends. I'll bring you back before the meeting gets underway. Okay?"

"Okay." She was relieved the Friday night deal, whatever it was, had not been advanced. If she could sleep late tomorrow she might have sufficient courage to face up to it.

He said: "We're divided up into groups according to what each of us does. It's the Tupamaro system—but then you probably never heard of the Tupamaros."

She answered that she had seen the name in the newspapers. He did not elaborate but continued: "We call them sections, and no one knows who's in the sections other than his own. That's so if someone defects, he can't blow too many members."

He was talking along casually, easily. He could have been discussing PTA committees. "But don't worry about that. We don't let anyone forget that execution is the penalty for a double cross. This meeting tonight is the Planning Group which is made up of the leaders of the sections. We set the policy and make the major decisions. But I'm boring you."

She assured him he was not, and he continued: "You'll be meeting Winnie Tipton. A beautiful black girl. Intelligent. Friendly. A good sport. She's our secretary. Never takes notes or keeps minutes. Has a fabulous memory."

"Winnie Tipton," she said, repeating for the benefit of the bug. She hoped to high heaven it was transmitting. She had no way of knowing.

"And then there's Tico Sharman who's a bitch, an out-and-out bitch. Pay no attention to her if she gets rough with you. She tears into everybody. Like a baby wildcat I came across one summer in the Yucatán jungles near Chichén Itzá. He was snarling and spitting, defying the world, fighting to survive. And that's Tico. But keep in mind she's had a hard life. Her father raped her when she was fourteen, she had a baby at fifteen, and was charged with smothering the child to death at sixteen."

96

"No!" Chris whispered.

"We need her. She's tough, amoral. She'll kill on command. Hates society, the whole human race, and she'll do anything to wreck it. But you know something? She'll feel the same after we take over. We mean nothing to her in the long run, but for the short pull she sees us as a means of destroying a world she hates."

Miles droned by and Chris lost track of their whereabouts . . . the endless streets, the satellite communities merging into each other, and the garishly lighted shopping centers with their excessive use of electricity when much of the world still groped through the dark by candlelight and kerosene. Eventually he slowed to a crawling pace and they rolled down a dark alley, a partly soundproofed chasm between decrepit two-story buildings that had the sottish look of old winos. There was the smell of urine and decay, papers wisping about in the breeze, ashes piled high, a boarded-up window, doors sagging with the years, crushed beer cans and jagged-edged bottles, and the graffiti of sick minds. Then the lights caught briefly a brilliant scarlet mural, a nude, perhaps the work of a young artist who had no other canvas.

Not a light burned, and the dark on either side was a monster gripping her. Man could never quite shake off this fear that had been born in him while he was still lumbering about on all fours. In the dark were treachery, torture and murder, and rape, and being taken slave. The dark denied primitive man of his freedom, little that it was. And thousands of years later, when man said he had emancipated himself from Neanderthal taboos and fears, he awoke with a start in the dead of night to listen, hackles up, to the scrape of a tree against his house.

She remembered the bug. "You sure picked a beauty spot for your meeting. Where on earth are we?"

If he heard, he did not answer. He told her instead how he had given $10 to a security officer to leave open the back door to an empty store. He had waited until 6 o'clock that evening to "make the set-up." He said: "That doesn't give the FBI a chance to plant a tap on us." The Committee, he said, never gathered in the same place twice. He waited until forty-five minutes prior to the meeting to notify the members of the address. His own security staff patrolled the area, on the watch for a surveillance by the police, sheriff, FBI, or other law-enforcement agencies.

While setting forth this information, deliberately, since he wanted her to know the Committee's method of operation, he drove the car into a recess between two buildings, then took her arm and guided her over a rough, gravelly surface to a back door which opened into a long, narrow storeroom. A street light directly beyond two large, dirty plate-glass windows cast a faint glow. Gaping shelves, reaching halfway to a high, old-fashioned ceiling, lined the walls on either side, and between them was nothing except a floor littered with small boxes, stuffing, and odds and ends left behind in the haste of moving.

In the dim light two indistinct forms sitting about a card table emerged. Max steered her toward them and without greeting, introduced them.

Winnie offered a hand. "Max has told us about you." She was small and slender, a piece of fine sculpture done in obsidian. She had her hair pulled tightly back, pushing into bas relief a gentle-featured face.

Tico said a hello that was neither hostile nor friendly. She was in pants and a tight, pullover sweater that advised she wore no bra. She was big framed and had emphatic facial features: prominent nose, cheekbones, and jaw.

As Max seated Chris, the fold-up chair scraped noisily on the bare, splintering floor. He said: "Winnie's a vet's assistant. She's good at setting bones. Next time you break your leg if there's no doctor around . . ."

Winnie laughed softly. "It'll cost you just as much, though. Man in today said next time he'd take his dog to his M.D. Be cheaper."

Later Chris would learn that Winnie came from a good, hardworking family. Her father was a draftsman in an architect's office and her mother held a good position in the telephone company's accounting department.

Max continued: "Tico runs a psychedelic shop in Studio City . . ."

It was a shadow play out of her childhood. Shadows sitting around, scarcely moving. A shadow table and shadow chairs, some empty, waiting for other shadows. Soon the lights would come on . . .

"Come to think of it, you knew Howie Spelvin, didn't you?" Max addressed himself to Tico. "Chris was his girl friend in university."

"One winter," Chris amended.

"A stupid jerk," Tico said. "Nothing but a stud." Then she asked unexpectedly in a whipcrack voice: "Did you know old man Jorgensen?"

Max intervened. "I told you—"

98

Tico snapped: "I'm asking her."

The time lapse, before Chris could control the hard beat coursing through her, seemed telltale, but when she did recover, she said coolly: "I'm certain Mr. Hartman has told you that I saw Mr. Jorgensen for the first time when he boarded the plane . . ."

In the FBI communications room, Rip tensed.

TICO: I wouldn't give my cases to a perfect stranger.

CHRIS: Most people trust us—airline girls.

TICO: Didn't Max tell you—

MAX: There wasn't any reason to—

TICO: —that that nice old guy, the father figure, he was working all the time for the FBI, a damn stoolie, a whistle guy.

CHRIS: What!

MAX: I didn't want to alarm you.

CHRIS: Before God, I'd never seen him before that night.

TICO: Don't hand me any of that before-God bunk! How do we know you and him weren't working together?

Winnie said softly: "She wouldn't trust Jesus Christ." She put a hand on Tico's arm. "But I love you. We all do. You know it."

Tico was not to be assuaged. "Who was it that exposed that other guy? Caught him dead in the act of squealing. He'd be sitting here tonight if I hadn't—"

Max interrupted. "Tico's right. He might've blown us all." He turned to Chris. "Revolutions don't succeed by trusting people. You never trust anyone. No one. You're always suspicious. You can't kiss a sweetheart without wondering . . . have lunch with your best friend . . ."

He nodded toward a bulky, hatted figure barely discernible standing by the front door. She had no idea how long he had been there, whether he had been watching all this time. "He's the head of the Zero Section. I give him a call on the phone. A name. It's over in thirty minutes. Unless he feels like prolonging it. He should've been with the Inquisition. He loves to see how long it takes someone to die. I caught him and another guy making a bet one day. I put a stop to it. I don't like that kind of thing. Get it over quick, forget it, and go on."

"You're so noble." Tico said.

99

25

THE CONFERENCE BEGAN in the SAC's office at 3:30 P.M. Friday. Present were Assistant Director Markinson, the SAC, Rip, and Anson W. Remington, vice-president and security head for the Golden State Bank. Remington was tall and angular, with shaggy eyebrows and hair cropping out of his eagle nose.

Only that morning, as FBI agents completed their check of the banks in the Los Angeles area, did the fact come to light that the Golden State headquarters bank (11 branches) was being moved that night, starting two hours after midnight, from a location on Ventura Boulevard in Sherman Oaks to a new twenty-seven-story building six blocks west on the same thoroughfare.

Markinson, Rip, and the SAC had just come from a strategy session with liaison officers from the police, sheriff, and California Highway Patrol in which final plans had been drafted for assigning and co-ordinating the work of 1,200 peace officers. They would be under the direction of a mobile police communications unit, manned by both police officers and FBI agents, which would operate out of a downtown location. Once the Committee had struck, the command post would be moved closer to the scene of action. The sheriff's deputies and highway patrolmen, who cover the vast Los Angeles freeway system, were volunteering their services since they probably would be working outside of their jurisdictions. They would take orders from the mobile unit, as would security guards employed by industrial and other private firms. Markinson and the SAC would supervise the FBI operations from the command post. Rip would work in the field, taking over-all instructions from them but directing the actual on-the-spot movements of 250 agents.

In their discussions with the liaison people, the consensus was that the subjects would raid a bank. A new point was raised, however, in regard to a possible bombing attempt. A police lieutenant, a specialist in underground guerrilla warfare, said: "These outfits don't usually have too much know-how when it comes to demolition operations, and they want to make a few trial runs. It's been the history of bombings in recent years. They're out practicing—getting ready for the big day."

In the end they all agreed it would be dangerous to assume that a bank would be the mark. The subjects might blow up a building.

Now Markinson began the discussion with Remington. "We are undecided whether or not a bank in the process of being moved might be more vulnerable. In the course of the usual bank robbery or burglary, the subjects can control most factors, such as the timing, forcing people in a small area to obey them, and so forth. They lose these advantages in hitting an armored car. It's in the open, people going every which way, the timing indefinite. Still they could get a fantastic sum quickly."

Remington estimated that the bank would move about $300,000 in cash and $25,000,000 in securities, of which approximately $5,000,000 would be negotiable, almost the same as cash. Remington pointed out that while this was a considerable sum, it was small compared to the $5,000,000,000 that the Bank of America in downtown Los Angeles had recently moved a distance of seven blocks. Three Brink's trucks had conducted a shuttle operation, carrying $100,-000,000 at a time, the maximum permitted for each run by the insuring companies.

"We've copied their operation," said Remington, "even to doing a dry run to iron out the bugs."

He outlined the bank's plan: an armored car and five moving vans would be used. The operation, starting at 2 A.M., would be completed by 5 A.M., including time scheduled for loading and unloading. The police department would shut off six blocks to both foot and vehicular traffic. Barricades manned by officers would be set up at every street intersection on Ventura. A police helicopter would cover the area during the three hours. Security officers would check every building at 1 A.M. An all-night restaurant would close from midnight to 5 A.M. A telephone company building, in which several scores worked all night, and the Sherman Oaks post office would be sealed off. Workmen would place heavy lead plates over all manholes to guard against a person secreting himself below the street. Remington himself had called various city departments to assure himself no resurfacing or excavation or like work would be underway.

He said: "About the securities, even the theft of the non-negotiable ones could hurt us badly. It would cost us five percent of their face

101

value to replace them and since we have about twenty million dollars' worth, that's a million right there."

Rip asked: "What if they should take a police officer or one of your security guards hostage? What do you do then?"

"No problem there," Remington said. "We'll let them have the armored car."

When the three stared in astonishment, he smiled. "You see, gentlemen, the money and securities won't be in it. At the last minute —nobody knows this but three of us in the bank—we're going to let the armored car go empty and put the money and securities in one of the moving vans along with some furniture. But don't worry about it. We'll shift the men we have scheduled to ride shotgun on the armored car into the van. But even they won't know about the switch until we're ready to load the money and securities."

Remington cleared his throat noisily, then continued: "I don't see how we can postpone the move. We are set to open in the new location Monday, and people will be expecting us there. The confusion could be terrible. And, of course, we are insured."

"That's up to you, of course," Markinson said, "since the Bureau cannot advise in such matters. I might point out, also, that if they do plan to strike, and you postpone the move, they'll simply wait until you schedule another time."

Remington made a deprecatory gesture. "It's necessary, of course, to prepare for all eventualities, but I'm confident nothing will happen."

Nevertheless, a worried frown persisted.

When Remington left, Markinson said: "I would feel better if we had a surveillance on the informant from the very beginning. For her own safety and to brief us. If we knew by only a few minutes where they were headed, that few minutes might make all the difference. If it is a bombing—"

Rip interrupted. "I must repeat what I said before—if they spot a tail job—and they're going to be watching for one—I wouldn't be surprised if they don't run one themselves to see if somebody else has one on her—if they should spot ours we'd never get a chance to rescue her. They lost Jorgensen, he got away from them to Tahiti, and they are probably burning about that."

"You may be right," Markinson conceded, and dismissing the matter, continued: "Notify all participating agents that the briefing will begin at ten P.M. We'll go over everything one last time. One more point, we shouldn't concentrate during the briefing on the move of this bank. It is a very logical strike area, and we should establish that. But we have at least two thousand other possible targets, including those for demolition. Keep that in mind."

For the next two hours, Rip stayed at his desk. Agents came by, and others telephoned. They wanted to establish with certainty their locations and duties. Before midnight Rip would talk personally with most of the 250 assigned temporarily to the case. Each would review the eventualities. What to do if this happened, or that. They had been taught at the FBI Academy to plot, preferably on paper, every possible twist and turn. One of the worst derelictions of duty was to leave something to chance. The FBI was not a gambler at a Las Vegas crap table. With the mathematical precision that forethought and planning bring, the odds for the criminal were often negligible. No matter how the agents figured tonight, however, the Committee held a slight advantage since the Committee was deciding where the contest was to take place.

Shortly after 6, Rip went home to rest for a couple of hours. He had been an athlete; he knew the value of relaxed muscles and nerves. Pandemonium came streaking. He was never far away. Rip bent to rub his ears and Pandemonium scratched at the door. Inside Rip fed him cat tuna that smelled good enough to eat himself. The moment he stretched out on the bed, Pandemonium was on his chest. Rip was tempted to put him out since he needed the rest without a 17-pound cat using his rib cage for a mattress. Before he knew it, though, he was asleep, and when the alarm awakened him, Pandemonium was curled up beside him.

On the way back to the office he stopped for a hamburger and malt. The heat of the August day was losing its strength. He felt refreshed. He wondered—with the same twinge of fear he had experienced all day, every time he thought of her—what Chris was doing.

Max phoned a few minutes after six. "I'm calling to see if everything's okay."

"Yes, Max," she answered from her bedroom phone.

"You've got nothing to worry about. Nothing. Do whatever he tells you to. I should've told you, he's high-strung, so don't argue with him, don't cross him. Do what he tells you to and you won't have any trouble."

"Max," she said to a clicking receiver at the other end.

Roz came in, greatly upset. "I shouldn't've listened in. I've never done it before, and I keep telling myself it's none of my business. But it *is* my business. I love you—and these creeps you're hanging around with . . ."

"It's all right," Chris told her. "I'm going for a walk. I won't be in for dinner."

She left with Roz staring in bewilderment and hurt.

At Barney's she ordered coffee, then reminded herself she must eat. It would be a long night. She asked for a pastrami sandwich, and when it came, took out half the meat. No one could get his mouth around one of Barney's pastrami sandwiches.

She had hoped, with a desperation that seemed to envelop every thought and act, that he would have a message. But he only nodded when he took her order.

26

AT THE PROW she finished her third cup of strong black coffee. Across a counter of unwashed dishes and crumpled paper napkins, five fellows her age sneaked carnal glances her way. She was alone, the hour was late, and she looked like an easy pick up. She was in dark pants, a light blue shirt, and scuffed oxfords. About her neck was the tiny gold cross that she was never without.

When a short, young fellow sauntered in, intuition told her he was the one. He had glittering, darting eyes, caved-in shoulders, a small pursed mouth, and the appeal of a weasel. He wore a blue jacket, a blue, pull-over sport shirt and light blue slacks. The blues disputed one another.

"The car's around the corner," he said in a voice trained for drama. One more bit actor out of work, she thought. Putting the exact change on the counter, she followed him out.

At the car, an Impala, he went directly to the driver's seat. Repelled by his looks, she hesitated at the door. He was her stereotype of a rapist.

"Get in," he ordered, and when she still did not move, asked irritably: "What's the matter with you?"

As she slid in beside him, with misgivings burgeoning, he took her purse, dug through the contents in the dark, then dropped it behind his seat. "You won't be needing it." His nimble hands went over her so swiftly, frisking her, that she didn't have time to react. When she did, stifling a scream, he had finished. Her heartbeat shook her head to foot.

"What've you got in your bra?" he asked, starting the car.

She tightened her fists to control herself. Never had she been so terrified and at the same time so furious.

"Felt hard. Small object."

"Where've you been?" she countered. "They put framework in bras these days." She forced her voice up. "And keep your filthy hands off me! I wouldn't be here if Max hadn't vouched for me."

He grunted. "I take no chances. Nobody's word. You can thank me I didn't make you strip."

"That does it! I'm getting out! I'm not going I don't know where with a stupid jerk."

He laughed. "Cool it, will you? I'm only doing a job."

The gauge climbed to 65 as he took the San Diego Freeway in the direction of Westwood Village. He continued: "You're better-looking than Max said. You've got something up there. I like women with something up there. You didn't get a silicone job, did you?"

"Where're we going?"

"Airport."

"Now wait a minute! Max didn't say anything about flying. I thought we were doing something in L.A."

"Look, sister, when it's time for you to know I'll tell you. Right?"

He slowed the car when he drew even with a highway patrol cruiser. "Max said if I got a ticket . . . Didja ever see Max when he was mad? Nothing on his face, nothing at all."

At the far end of the Van Nuys Airport, he pulled the Impala in front of an incredibly small, all-glass office. A modest wooden sign read: HARSWORTH HELICOPTER SERVICE. "Wait here," he said, and went inside. An Oldsmobile rolled up in the rear, almost touching the bumper. Glancing back, she caught four men with their eyes riveted on her. No one got out.

She slumped in the seat, trying to relax. In her mouth was the bitter

105

taste of coffee. If she only had some idea where she was being taken, what she was going to be commanded to do.

Dropping her head, she said into the bug: "We're at the Van Nuys Airport, place called Harsworth Helicopter Service. He's inside now, could be renting a copter. There's a car with four men waiting behind us. Light blue Oldsmobile sedan. Maybe two, three years old. I can't see the men good enough to describe them, and the car's so close, I can't see the license number. The fellow I'm with—"

She broke off. He was looking oddly at her from inside the office. Then she saw him sign a paper and produce a roll of bills. When he exited, he held up a fish-limp hand in greeting to the four men. Once he was behind the wheel, she said: "I've played this silly game long enough. Tell me what we're doing or I'm getting off here."

He shrugged. "Nobody gets off. Not now, not ever."

The four men followed in their car. "Who're those men?" she asked. She was damned if she was going to take all of this like a good, little girl.

"I had a kid sister like you. Knocked half her teeth out once. What were you talking to yourself about?"

"How'd you— Was I doing that? I've always talked to myself since I was a little girl. It's like chewing your fingernails. I've got to break myself. I—"

"Cripes! I ask a question and get a record. Come on."

He parked near one corner of the airport and they made their way toward a helicopter. He got in and pulled her up. The men stayed behind in the Oldsmobile.

Once seated in the dark, he tossed a black scarf on her lap. "When we get there, blindfold yourself. If you want to see a little, okay, but make it look like a blindfold."

She shook her head in astonishment. He pulled a gun from a shoulder holster and pushed it into her side, squashing out a torrent of breath. "What're you doing?" she shouted, hurting.

He paid no attention. "I'm going to pull this .45 on you when we get there, and maybe rip your shirt down the front to let them think you put up one hell of a fight. I don't know for sure. I'll ad-lib it as we go along. Now, have you got all that?"

She nodded.

Across the field three men from the car hurried toward them, leaving the driver behind. They were garbed in black with their faces masked and carried tommy guns. As they climbed into the helicopter, one man shouted: "Come on, come on, get it moving. We're five minutes late."

The whirlybird moved gracefully out onto the field, and then with the clatter of a thousand dragons rose straight up toward the white clouds and the full moon beyond them.

27

NERVOUSLY, BECAUSE THIS was beyond his experience, Remington made a last-minute check. Outside the bank, three vans were lined up, then came the armored car, and then two more vans. The drivers stood around the cabs smoking and talking, waiting for the 2 A.M. deadline. The night was unexpectedly cool, the air clear, and with the street barricaded to traffic, unusually quiet. A media contingent, including a dozen newspaper photographers, numerous reporters, and three television crews, was scattered over the sidewalk and the street. Remington glanced apprehensively at them. They had been checked and rechecked but he was inherently suspicious of the press.

Returning inside, he made his way around stacks of cartons and office equipment piled high. The cash and securities were still in the locked vault. Shortly after midnight his tellers had finished packing the securities in special cartons, a little larger than legal size and six inches deep. Usually the securities would have been moved in the large steel safety boxes the bank kept them in but technical difficulties had developed that made that impossible. A demolition expert reported, however, that his men had succeeded in cutting away the customers' safe deposit boxes from the floor and the walls. These boxes, which were in sections bound by steel bands, had been placed on wooden platforms set on rollers. Remington remembered then, and called to a young man. Two bank officials and two police officers were to observe the moving of the customers' safe deposit boxes. Were they on hand? The young man left to check.

Overhead a police helicopter, a Bell G-5 with a two-man crew, cruised at 70 miles an hour at a one-thousand-foot elevation. Sergeant Hawley, who commanded Air 10, the code name for the helicopter patrol, kept careful watch on the miniature street below, the buildings and people. He was enjoying the assignment. Usually Air 10 found lost children, spotted car clouters stealing from parked vehicles, sighted burglars breaking and entering, and the like.

Below, the move had begun. He and his partner saw the first van pull out, and the second roll up. The operation was being carried out with precision and speed. He swung the craft around in a wide arc, using the powerful spotlight to check the immediate side streets, and then broadened the circles until he had meticulously inspected every house, yard, driveway, sidewalk, and street within a radius of a half mile. "Everything quiet," he reported in.

Returning to make sweeps up and down Ventura, he grew conscious of another helicopter flying several hundred feet above and a little behind him, where it was out of his line of easy vision. He was annoyed, and when it kept hanging in the same spot, disturbed. The radio and television station whirlybirds, used for news coverage, would be on the ground at this hour, as would be the ones ferrying passengers from International Airport. He asked the Van Nuys tower to request identification. To his amazement, the tower reported a few minutes later that the aircraft had not answered its call.

When he tried climbing to get a better view with his spotlights, the other copter fled and was soon only a speck moving across the distant, moonlit San Gabriel Mountains. He did not pursue it. He had the uneasy thought that it might be a decoy trying to lure him away from his assignment. Before the other pilot disappeared, however, the sergeant had caught a blurred snapshot of a woman seated beside the pilot. It was probably a couple out for a lark and frightened when the police craft appeared.

Returning to Ventura Boulevard, he and his partner continued to scrutinize the layout beneath. Only a very few minutes had passed—not more than five at the most—when the other whirlybird again took up the same position. This time the sergeant knew he was the epicenter of an unfolding plot. He said into the radio calmly, precisely: "I've got a chopper on my tail, a few hundred feet above me, that refuses to identify itself, and fled when I moved in for a look. There's a woman with the pilot and there may be others . . ."

The voice boomed out of two loudspeakers that had been set up to cover an area of about a block around the bank. They had been placed on the front of buildings, just above the first story, and were quite visible. No one had noticed them, or if someone had, had

108

thought nothing of it. Electronic gear had become such a part of American life that it was commonplace.

The voice said: "Now hear this, hear this. I'm right up over you in a chopper. I've got one of your tellers, Virginia Maple—and a gun on her. I'm coming down and I'll kill her if you fire or try any tricks. You got that? I've got a .45 in her side and a nervous finger. I killed a lot of gooks in Vietnam and she's only another gook to me. First, you pull off the pig chopper. You got that, you white niggers down there in the squad car? Tell it to tail off . . ."

He flipped off the transmitter, and never taking his eyes from the police copter below them, said: "Okay, get the blindfold on. Not a bad idea, huh? It was Max's. No telling what this Maple broad might do if she was here. But a friendly hostage—a very friendly hostage . . ."

He let out a shout. "Wow! Look at that bird tail out. Must think I'm going to pump lead into him . . . You ready?" He slipped on a black, Halloween mask. "Put up a little struggle down there if you want to. Not too much. But we mustn't let people think this Maple broad's a patsy. Here we go."

Four miles away, Rip heard the police broadcast, and the agent in the driver's seat beside him gunned the motor. At 80 miles an hour, with the siren going, they raced along the Ventura Freeway. Over the police band came a steady, unexcited drone, the voice of a veteran woman officer who had handled murders, kidnapings, shootouts, and the whole gamut of criminal violence. "Subject helicopter parking on Ventura Boulevard one half block south of Golden State Bank. Pilot holding female teller hostage beside him. Hostage appears blindfolded . . ."

To Markinson, on the FBI band, Rip said: "Ask all units to hold fire. Repeat, hold fire—and do not move in on subjects."

To the FBI units under his command, he said: "All units, all units. Hold fire. Repeat, hold fire. Unit forty—get into position if possible to keep subject under rifle surveillance. If subject leaves hostage—or she makes a break and gets into the clear . . . but open fire only if there is no possible chance of hostage being harmed."

Four miles, three minutes. How much can a man review in that distance, in that time? She had become more than a name, more than an informant, and by the time he arrived she might be lying sprawled on the street, the victim of a killer who had panicked or slain for no reason once he had the money. She had the courage he admired in a woman. She had stood up to him; she had stood up to Max Hartman. She knew full well what she was risking, which many informants did not. She realized she was putting her life on the line. And what was she doing it for? For love of country, through a sense of deep patriotism? He doubted it, unless one could call love for one's fellow man patriotism, and maybe that was what patriotism was. She had seen a picture of a little girl with an arm blown off, a teacher blinded, an old man who would never walk again, and she had decided. Yes, maybe that was what patriotism was all about.

Whoever this weasel was beside her, he certainly could put down a helicopter. She scarcely knew when they touched pavement. She could see through the black scarf as through dark glasses. Nothing moved, men and vehicles alike were frozen. It was like a snapshot, like some of the stills in *Butch Cassidy and the Sundance Kid*. The lens caught blurred images: a driver with a cigarette in midair, an older man with one foot on the sidewalk and the other in the street, a police officer rigid behind the wheel of a squad car, newsmen staring her way, a mover stopped with a box on his shoulder. It was a silent scene. She heard nothing from out there, only the incessant, clattering, nerve-explosive roar of the overhead rotors.

He caught a movement, a camera raised in the distance, fingers touching the settings. "You bastard," he yelled. "One more picture and I'll blow you to hell."

He had put down immediately after the second van had pulled away, and she heard him ordering the third to move up. She doubted if it could pass the copter. There did not seem to be that much clearance but then her vision was fogged.

When it was within a few feet, he commanded the driver to stop. "Everybody out of the back end," he said. He was shouting over the microphone. He had forgotten he was using one. She could tell he was shaking all over. The weapon was vibrating all the way to her navel. Now he was screaming. He has gone mad, she thought.

"Everybody out! Come on, come on. Where's the other guy? There were three of you in the back." The third man lost no time in jumping out. The driver and his companion already had stepped down.

"Okay," he shouted to the men in black behind him. "That's everybody." They left the helicopter, and it seemed they walked in slow

110

motion, their tommy guns cradled in their arms. Two climbed in the cab of the van, and the third hopped up into the rear . . .

A half block away, alongside a barricade, Rip sized up the situation: She could not escape, the pilot had no intention of leaving his craft, and any attempt to slip up on his blind side would prove fatal heroics for the agent trying it and for Chris Roberts.

Over the loudspeakers came the orders: "We're moving this van out. I'm warning you again, if you try to stop it, fire just one shot, do anything, I'm killing this girl. Okay, pull out, pull out. Let 'em through that barricade over there."

The van climbed the sidewalk and rolled past with no more than a foot of clearance. The security officers manning the barricade removed it, working swiftly, and the van disappeared down a dark neighborhood street. The voice continued: "I'm in radio contact with the van. I'll know it if the cops stop it or follow it. Keep away from it if you want to see this girl back in the bank. You got that? Keep away."

He counted to sixty. It had to be more than sixty seconds, she thought. He said then: "I'm going up but it's still the same for the girl if the police chopper follows me. Stay clear of me and the van, and she's okay. But if you don't, I'm itching to kill somebody. I feel good when I'm killing. I feel like God himself."

She started shaking. This was no play-acting.

28

WITHIN MINUTES AFTER the helicopter disappeared, peace officers sealed off San Fernando Valley with its million plus people—an integral part of Los Angeles on the other side of the mountains, away from the ocean. They erected barricades across the principal exit routes, but because of the heavy flow of traffic even at this hour, 2:35 A.M., it was deemed impossible to slow down vehicles on the freeways. On these routes cruise cars took over with officers flagging down vans and large trucks.

As Rip headed for his office, he got a relay from the FBI communications room of the most pertinent parts of the bug's transmission from the helicopter:

CHRIS: Is that Palmdale down there, or Lancaster?

UNKNOWN SUBJECT: (*answer unintelligible*) . . .

CHRIS (*five minutes later*): Gosh, it's lonely out here. No house, nothing. Is that your car over there?

U.S.: Crazy fool! I told him to turn off the lights. I don't need no lights to put down.

CHRIS: You just going to leave it here on the desert?

U.S.: The police chopper will come buzzing over in the morning and find it. Give me back the scarf. It's my mother's . . .

CHRIS (*ten minutes later, apparently reading sign from a car*): Devonshire. I went there once. They had an old English fair. I think it was Devonshire. Where're we going?

U.S.: You chicks are all the same. Questions, questions.

CHRIS: I got to get some sleep. I've got a flight out tomorrow. I've done my job, so take me home.

U.S.: Max wants to see you. Say, when Max gets tired of you, give me a ring. I can show you more fun than Max. I got more to offer—if you know what I mean.

CHRIS: I don't even know your name.

U.S.: Vince Dearborn. I run the Finance Section. Didn't do bad tonight, did I? Five million bucks! Wow, man!

CHRIS: Vince Dearborn—if that's your real name.

U.S.: Meaning what?

CHRIS: Meaning if that's your real name.

U.S.: Damn, I wish you weren't Max's girl. We could have a party. Five million bucks! Calls for a blow-out. I've got to find me a woman. You got a friend somewhere around?

CHRIS: Not this time of night.

At 2:55 A.M. an elderly insomniac, a Mrs. O. T. O'Brien, called the West Valley police substation to complain in a whining voice that three men had dumped desks and chairs "and everything" on her parking space and sidewalk from a moving van. Questioned, she informed the desk man that they transferred "some boxes" from the van into "a little kind of truck thing" and took off, leaving the van's right wheels up on a geranium bed that she cultivated between the sidewalk and the street.

112

"People don't have respect for property like they did in my day," she said.

"No, ma'am," said the sergeant, "they sure don't."

"When you catch them, you make them come back and fix up my flower bed. You hear me?"

At the address Mrs. O'Brien gave, officers and FBI agents conducted an intensive crime scene search. Since Remington had packed the cash and securities in the middle of the van, with office equipment fore and aft, the subjects had had to get rid of considerable furniture. This they had done by dumping it on the geranium bed where the sound would be muted. Mrs. O'Brien's meager observations indicated the getaway car was a small camper. She had been too excited over the tragedy that had befallen her geraniums to take more than a fleeting glance. Over the police band went a bulletin to all radio cars to stop every camper in Los Angeles and environs, a monumental task. "Approach with extreme caution. Subjects armed and may shoot to kill."

Before Mrs. O'Brien phoned, the police had established that the woman in the helicopter was not the teller, Virginia Maple. A phone call to her home aroused her mother who in turn awakened her. Miss Maple said she had worked at the bank until 11, then had gone home and to bed.

Neither the peace officers nor the 250 FBI agents working the case that night knew the identity of the woman in the helicopter. Only three persons knew—Markinson, the SAC, and Rip—and they were in conference in the SAC's office. They foresaw considerable risk in identifying her. They knew full well the truth of the old dictum: The more who know a secret, the more likely the secret will out. Not by design would their fellow officers give it away but a chance remark in a restaurant, talk in a barber shop, even discussion in a conference room where a caretaker or window washer was nearby could blow Chris Roberts as an informant.

Markinson remarked that the informant had guts. "Thank God, she came through okay."

Rip thought to himself: Now if she can only make it the rest of the way.

"I don't know why," he said, "they didn't take the haul up in the copter with them rather than risk driving the van even that short distance."

113

Markinson thought he had the answer. "The time factor. It would have taken ten minutes, maybe fifteen, to unload the van and carry the boxes to the helicopter."

The SAC conjectured that possibly they had a hideout nearby for the money and securities.

Rip then took the phone call. "I've got Peg on the line," the switchboard operator said. Rip tensed, knowing Peg would not be calling at this hour unless the matter were urgent. "Put her on."

Peg said without preamble: "I took a call at 3:26 from C-77. I quote the informant verbatim . . ."

29

CHRIS READ ALOUD from a wooden sign at the bottom of a hillside lane: "Four, four, three one. Top o' the road."

"Do you have to read every sign we come to?" Vince asked irritably.

"Why not? I talk to myself, I have good company."

He stepped on the fuel pedal and the car shot up a steep incline, past two houses on the left and one on the right. Then the lane narrowed with palm trees bordering it, their fronds waving in silhouette against a moonlit sky. A big orange-colored cat, its eyes gleaming, looked down on them from its perch in the crotch of a native walnut. Close by, an owl hooted. Now great pine trees towered over the trail and there was a good, woodsy smell. They passed a Volkswagen camper and came to a two-story, old Spanish house, its white stucco glistening in the moonlight. There was a half-circle driveway that encompassed a rose garden from which emanated nostalgic odors from her childhood. Vince parked alongside two other cars, got out and said: "Stay put until I tell Max you're here."

Muted voices attracted her attention toward a long, low archway that tied together the main house and another section. Beyond the archway, and only faintly visible, were several figures moving about what looked like an enormous sarcophagus. She identified the people as Max, Tico, and a strange man, and the immense coffin as an old outdoor barbecue.

Max advanced toward her, with Tico and the stranger following and getting into a nearby car. Neither Tico nor the man glanced her way. Vince disappeared as Max opened the car door. "God, I'm glad to see you. I've been worried."

"So have I," she countered, getting out. She must look a wreck. The heat of the helicopter and her own nervousness had left her clothes and hair limp as wilted lettuce. Her head felt as if it were disembodied.

He took her in the back door, into a long, narrow, red-carpeted kitchen. "You handled it beautifully."

"I could've been killed," she answered laconically, dropping to a bench at one side of the breakfast table.

Max nodded. "That's what it's all about. You shoot craps, and don't make your point, or you do and you've won a nation, one whole country. Coffee?"

She nodded, and he picked up a carafe warming on the stove. He remembered she liked cream and sugar. He programed details as a computer would. Idly she glanced at recipes someone had left on the table. She loved recipes. By the hour she would clip, read and file them, although afterwards she could never find one when she wanted it.

He continued: "You've got guts. Not many women have. Tico has but not Winnie. Too soft. Not bad in bed but a man wants more than sex from a woman."

The coffee revived her. "I'm going to show some guts if anybody ever frisks me again. I'm warning you, Max."

He appeared genuinely surprised. "I don't know what gets into some of these characters. Not that they aren't good for us. But they go too far."

He paced about, unable to sit, keyed up with the excitement of the night. "We've got an organization here, Chris, hand-picked. Nobody who drinks, no big mouth, nobody who picks up playmates in bars. Hand-picked. Do you know we pulled this off tonight with only eleven in the know? You get too many involved and you're in trouble. You've got to keep it tight and small, the way the Tupamaros do. That was the trouble with the French Revolution. No tight control. But Lenin and Trotsky had it, and so did Nasser."

"Can I use the phone?" she asked. "I've had it. I've got to get someone to take my flight out."

He indicated a red phone hanging from a wall in a corner.

115

"Who's place is this anyway?" she asked.

"Couple of crazy writers. They're in South America. I had to rent it for two months—to use it one night. But who would look up here?" His eyes followed her as she walked to the phone.

Dialing, she prayed she remembered the number correctly. When Peg's voice came over, she was relieved. "Susie—this is Chris. I'm terribly sorry to get you up in the middle of the night but I'm sick and I've got a flight out in a few hours. Could I trade? . . . You're an angel! I can't tell you . . . It's awful to call you like this. No, no, nothing serious. I'll be all right. It's the twenty-four-hour virus, I think . . . It's Flight 852 . . . No, not 285 but 852 . . . What's yours? . . . 784, Monday morning. Yes, I'm sure I can make it . . . And Susie, I left my purse by that whatchamacallit in the patio the other night . . . Gosh, I'm glad you found it. I've been worried. I'll run by the first of the week. And thanks so much. Awfully sorry about getting you up."

Hanging up, she turned to Max whose eyes had the glassy, fixed stare of binoculars. "Susie? Who's this Susie?"

She felt her stomach grab. "Susie? Susie Danton. We've known each other for years. We were in stewardess school together in Chicago. Why? Something wrong?"

Unexpectedly he dropped Susie. "You haven't asked any questions. Where the money is, how we got it out. Why aren't you curious?"

When he was playing the inquisitor, his face was a mask. She looked away, out the window to the parking area, and said quietly: "I'm glad about the money, Max. But forgive me if I don't wax excited. After what I've been through—you wouldn't know. Tomorrow I'll feel again, be curious. Now, I just want to go home and collapse." She shook her hair out and rose to leave. "Are you going to run me home?"

He relaxed and smiled. "Why go? I've got some liquor in the car . . ."

She shook her head. "I'm a zombie."

He shrugged. "Vince will take you home."

He took her in his arms, pushed her against a wall, and locked her in a tight embrace. This time she had no female response, such as before with Max, but only the horrible feeling she was caught in a vise.

116

30

R<small>IP</small> <small>SAT</small> <small>WITH</small> Lee Jetzel studying the information Peg had telephoned, which the bug had also reported. Peg had called in case the transmission from the bug had been garbled.

Scribbling the facts and figures on a legal size pad, Rip said: "She gave us an address, 4431, but not the name of the street which she didn't know. A dark street probably. Maybe one with few street signs.

"Then she gave us several numbers. Seven digits, all told, in three sets. They could be a phone number which also has seven digits. She may have been reading from the phone she was using. She may have known someone was listening, and scrambled the numbers, figuring we would put them together.

"She said 852, then 285, then no, it was 852. She could have been telling us that the 2 before the 85 was to be included somewhere. And we have a straight 784. She never altered that."

Intrigued, Lee Jetzel listened. In the five months he had been out of the Academy, this was his first assignment on a major case. He had handled an impersonation (a drunk had said he was an Army general), a $1,200 extortion, Selective Service violations, and a constant flow of leads brought to the Complaint Desk by concerned citizens who had heard or witnessed a highly suspicious act.

Rip continued: "Call our contact at the phone company and give them these numbers and see if they can come up with a street name that 4431 will fit."

He jotted down numerous combinations: 852–7842/ 285–2784/ 784–8522/ 784–2852, etc.

With Lee gone, Rip leaned back in the swivel, his eyes closed. He could have dozed—it was now after 4—but he was too disturbed by the situation in which he had placed this sensitive and lovely and inexperienced girl. He had said Max Hartman was ruthless, cared nothing about her, and if he must, would sacrifice her without a qualm. But what about one John Ripley who would let her go on a mission so fraught with hazard? Not only *let* her but assume it was her duty. If she had died out there somewhere, would he not have been as guilty as Max Hartman? With a different motive, of course?

With a highly righteous one? Should the fact she was a woman he liked and admired and had a fondness for—in the sense that any man has a fondness for a woman with qualities he likes—make a difference? Should he by any logic feel differently toward her than other informants in the past, some of whom were convicts, a few on the fringe of the law, and many stool pigeons in the worst sense of those words?

Within ten minutes, Lee returned, his eyes speaking triumph. "Simple. It's 784–2852. The address is 4431 Pinto Avenue in Encino."

"That figures," Rip said. "I didn't think they'd go far." He studied a map Lee had signed out of the Chief Clerk's office. "Here's a back route—runs through a residential neighborhood, probably dark, roughly parallel to Ventura. I doubt if the whole trip took them more than ten minutes. They switched the money out of the van at this point. By then they were halfway to the hillside house."

Rip pointed to a thin, black, curving mark leading up a hill. "If the money is up there, they'll have a guard hidden out on the lane leading up off Pinto, or around the parking space, and if I go up that way I'll run into an ambush. But around the hill on this side is a street called Chanson. You see, the house overlooks it although there's no lane up from Chanson. I'm going to case Chanson and see if I can get up that way on foot."

Preparing to leave, Rip put away his papers and ran his hand over the top of the desk to remove lurking dust.

"I'll come with you," Lee said.

"Thanks but it's a one-man job."

Lee's face dropped. Rip continued: "Lee—just between the two of us—what I have in mind isn't kosher, and if I get exiled to Butte, Montana, I don't want to see you up there."

Lee smiled. "I've got a pair of long johns left over from Vermont."

"Well, in that case . . ."

31

RIP PARKED THE black Bureau car at the bottom of the hill on Chanson. The old Spanish house sat directly on the hilltop above. Between it and the homes at the foot, fronting Chanson, was what looked like a wide stretch of undergrowth. At least, there were no structures but certainly there would be fences. Rip decided to worm his way through the undergrowth, and left Lee Jetzel behind with the admonition that if he did not return within a half hour to leave the scene and report nothing to anyone. "If something happens up there, I don't want the Bureau to know." Jetzel had protested but promised.

Stealthily Rip slipped past a darkened, low-slung, ranch-type house facing Chanson, and began climbing, foraging his way through heavy brush and struggling over the dead trunks of fallen walnut trees. The night was too quiet and the moonlight too bright to conceal his movements. Every step, guarded though it was, recorded itself in sound, and the soft light permitted anyone scanning the area to spot him.

Eventually he found a foot-wide dog trail that led straight up, and the crawling was easier. The path brought him to an area directly in front of the two-story home. Not a light burned. Slowly, he eased himself up on his hands, and saw a long patio extending the length of the house. Above the archway was a big picture window, and downstairs, where the dining room should be, was another. Someone standing a foot or two back from either window could be watching. In the patio was the usual outdoor furniture, a basket seat, an umbrella, plantings, and hose reels. His eyes went to a white-bricked structure at one far end, about three feet high and 12 feet long. It had to be the *whatchamacallit*. Nothing else around the patio could be. He recognized it as a barbecue from out of the 1930s, probably with the cooking grill in dead center and with each side designed to hold charcoal and wood.

A movement higher up, on a small, flower-decked balcony, caught his eye, and he sank back down into the high, dry, crackling grass, but not before he had noted with shutter speed a man sitting on the balcony with a rifle. From the guard's position, he could look down diagonally on the barbecue 25 feet distant.

After waiting a few minutes, Rip crawled on his belly and approached the barbecue from the rear. The patio, and hence the barbecue, sat on a flat pad that dropped off sharply into undergrowth. He slithered up to the back of the structure. The slope was so steep he had to raise up on his haunches to touch it. The barbecue itself formed a screen between him and the rifleman. Exploring the bricks, he found they were loose with age. He pulled one out, then another,

119

and feeling beyond them, touched the canvas money bags and the boxes containing the securities.

With a sharp thrust of fear, he discovered he was only a few feet away from an outside, wooden stairway that led to a second-story door. No one, fortunately, was on the landing outside the door. He realized that while the barbecue protected him from anyone watching from the balcony or the house, he could be spotted easily from the landing above.

Satisfied with the reconnaissance, he began the return trip. He was passing the house at the hill bottom when a dog awakened and barked tentatively at first, too sleepy to know whether the intruder was friend or foe. Dogs were his worst enemy. Never yet had he led a raid that a dog didn't sound the alarm.

The last hundred feet, he ran for the car, parked in pitch blackness under a great, old tree. He was panting. Tomorrow he'd better start jogging.

"Get to a phone," he told Jetzel, "call the phone company, get the number of a neighbor, and ask the neighbor where the owners of 4431 are and what they're doing. Then call the house and tell Max Hartman you're from the Los Angeles *Times* and something's happened to the owners and you need a photograph of them. Keep him on the phone as long as you can. That'll get him away from the windows and should distract the guard and any others since they'll be uneasy about a phone call at a time like this. Am I going too fast for you? Are you getting all of this?"

Jetzel said he was, and Rip continued: "I'll be working on the barbecue while you're on the phone but that won't be time enough for me to haul all that stuff down here."

"You mean . . . ? Holy Toledo!" Jetzel said, and forgot to close his mouth.

"Now as I said, keep him on the line as long as you can but before you hang up, tell him you're coming out to get a picture, that there's got to be one around somewhere, on a desk or a bedroom chest, someplace. Tell him if he doesn't want to co-operate you'll bring along a policeman friend.

"Okay, so in about twenty minutes you drive up there. I figure he'll meet you at the parking area, and if he can find a picture of the owners, he'll turn it over to you. Talk with him as long as you can. Try to kill ten minutes for me."

"Great Scott," Jetzel said, "what's the Bureau going to say when they find out you stole back the loot?"

"That," said Rip, "is a question I refuse to think about at this particular time."

He had thought this step out carefully, and decided he had no alternative. If the FBI or the police seized the cache of money and securities in a raid, which would be the normal, legal procedure, the Committee would suspect one of their members on the scene: Tico, the strange man, the driver of the camper, Vince, or Chris. Tico could be eliminated. She hated the "pigs," and if she had been going to betray the Committee, she would have done so a long time ago. Vince, too, would have no reason to blow the brilliant coup he had brought off. Rip did not know about the stranger or the driver but Chris most certainly would be highly suspect. She had been with the Committee only a short time. She had been accused by Tico of being a plant, and this suspicion would surface anew. There was no doubt in his mind but that Chris would be summarily executed. Aside from the personal tragedy, the Bureau would have no informant inside the Committee.

Another aspect was that with the arrest of Max Hartman at the time of the seizure, and subsequent sentencing to prison, the Committee would go even deeper underground under the leadership of Dr. Beaumont.

If, however, he could bring off the recovery of the cash and securities, Chris would be in the clear. It was unlikely that she could have committed the theft herself. She might have had a confederate, of course, but that, too, was farfetched. She was not the criminal type. Suspicion would fall primarily on Vince or the other men. Vince, especially. He had the daring and the strength.

It was a wild, insane idea—but wild, insane ideas had won battles and wars. Life had a way at times of trapping a man in desperate situations that required difficult, agonizing decisions, and when that happened a man had to go to his imagination and convictions. However, the Bureau, he feared, would terminate him with prejudice.

He took a deep breath of resignation. He loved the Bureau. He would never be happy in a 9 to 5 job.

But so be it.

From the trunk he took a small rubber hammer and chisel. After crossing the street, he skirted a high, fairly thick hedge, ready to step swiftly to the other side if he noted activity in the ranch house. The dog barked furiously, and while the warning covered the little, stir-up noises he was making, he expected momentarily someone would awaken. No one did, though, and he concluded the dog had barked wolf too many times.

He gained the barbecue, and was stretched out hidden in deep grass when the phone sounded. Endlessly it rang. Using the chisel, he pried out the bricks until he had a sizable opening. The incessant plea of the phone, though, was threatening to get to him. But working rapidly, he kept himself under tight control. Now he had one box out that he pushed with a foot. It slid a considerable distance down the hillside before grass and vines braked it. Desperately he wished he could see the balcony where the rifleman sat, and the picture windows. The barbecue shut him from view, and at the same time set up a potential trap. Someone might approach quietly, lean over the barbecue and spot him. Frequently he glanced up at the landing directly above him.

Suddenly the phone went dead, and so did his hands. A muted, protesting voice sounded inside the house. He could make out no words but a psychic sense told him Hartman was talking on the phone. No one could resist answering a phone.

He freed a canvas money bag about half the length of his arm and fastened at the top by heavy cord held tightly by a lead seal. It did not slide and he realized he would have to drag or carry the bags. The night seemed noisier but it was only that his hearing had grown more sensitized. The eerie hoot of an owl in the nearby pine told on his nerves. He could swear the hoot had been set electronically, with precise ten-second pauses. Close by, too, a mockingbird voiced his joy with the world. In the background a few crickets chirped away.

Then the grass crackled a few feet behind him and he whirled to find a black cat that obviously had not expected to meet one of the human species on his personal path. He hissed by reflex action, turned with fantastic speed, and noisily retreated.

On a street far below a tire screeched, and unexpectedly, Rip jerked. Any little, sudden noise would set him off. He was not the cool, unflinching stereotype of FBI agent as seen on television, who could walk without the twitch of an eyebrow into gunfire. He considered himself basically a coward who usually handled a dangerous situation quite well for the simple reason he was thrust into it and had no choice if he were to survive.

Working feverishly, he removed about half the cache, eight bags and boxes, and had them alongside him when the voice quit talking. He heard a noise above him, coming from the second-story door at the head of the outside stairway. Apparently the door stuck but yielded with much groaning under a sharp tug. As a gunman emerged on the landing above, looking ten feet tall, his holster prominent, Rip stepped out of sight under the landing. Another man called, perhaps the rifleman from the balcony, asking if the other had heard anything, and the gunman above grunted and said he guessed it was the cat. He went back into the house.

Pushing and dragging the packages, Rip slithered down the hill along the dog path to the car. Only when he had them locked safely in the trunk did he remember to breathe. Leaning against the car, he wiped the sweat and grime from his face on a shirt sleeve. With alarm, he noted the first light streaking the sky. He rearranged his twisted, binding undershorts, stuck his shirt back in his trousers, brushed them the best he could—and why he did that he would never know—and taking a long breath, started to retrace his steps. He limped a little, having turned an ankle during the descent.

This time he advanced slowly, stopping frequently to listen. He was several yards from the barbecue when he heard the car drive up, the slam of doors, and Hartman's and Jetzel's voices. Scrambling upward, he reached the barbecue. One bag, two. Three boxes, four, five, six.

He heard someone shouting very near. Then he placed the call. It was overhead, on the outside stairway landing. Barely in time, he was conscious of a heavy object hurtling down. He moved aside, rose, and with a quick karate blow, struck an arm, and a gun dropped at his feet. His right fist sank into a soft underbelly and a form crumpled up. As it did, his rock-hard, outstretched palm cracked down on a neck, and the form rolled at his feet. He fell flat then, and shoving the money bags and cartons before him with a speed he never thought possible, went spiraling down the hill. Behind him were a few shouts and calls for Jake. But the alarm he had anticipated never developed. Seemingly, no one knew that Jake lay crumpled up in the weeds back of the barbecue. It had happened so fast, so noiselessly.

32

MARKINSON AND THE SAC awaited Rip in the SAC's office. He had told them over the phone only that he had an "important development" to report. The time was shortly after 9 A.M. on a Saturday bright with a warm sun.

Both Markinson and the SAC were freshly shaved but their haggard eyes and slowness of movement told of a night that had taken a physical toll. At dawn they still had been working on the reconstruction, minute by minute, of the hijacking. One salient point stood out: Someone on the scene—a bank official or employee, a security guard, even a peace officer—had tipped off the helicopter pilot that the securities and money had been loaded in the van. The raiders had gone straight to it; they had ignored the armored car. As the whirlybird put down, the ground accomplice could have used a simple hand signal, or merely could have stood by the van. Scores of agents had interviewed everyone on the scene in an attempt to determine exactly where each individual was at that specific time.

Apprehensively, Rip entered the office, across which a wide shaft of sunlight slanted. The first elation over recovering the money had diminished. He realized he was in for a rough session.

Markinson and the SAC nodded, and waited. Neither was given to exuberance. The work in itself stifled emotion.

Rip reacted in kind, and said with detachment: "We got the money back. I've just come from delivering it and the securities to Mr. Remington."

Markinson stared hard. "Who recovered it? The police? Why weren't we notified?"

"I did," Rip answered. "You might say I found it. I swore Mr. Remington to secrecy—not to tell anyone we got it back since the informant's life wouldn't be worth a hoot if it got out."

They both interrupted with questions but Rip said: "I'd like to clear this point. Mr. Remington will deliver the money to the Federal Reserve in downtown Los Angeles—to be posted to the bank's account— and the Federal Reserve will send out new money by armored car, the same as it does every Monday morning. In that way, no one in the bank will know about recovering the money. We were worried about that since the Committee has someone in or around the bank tipping them off."

When he had finished, the SAC asked quietly: "You say you found it. How did you find it?"

"I'd rather not say . . . under the circumstances."

With the two closing in on him—not deliberately but unconsciously, with the training of years to get to the heart of an issue—a surge of memories came back to Rip, of his first months in the Bureau, the times he had been called in by the SAC to explain why he had acted as he had in an investigation. The SACs had varied greatly, as superiors do in every field. One had been casual in his approach, thoughtful, helpful; another, a stone-faced judge of the old school who considered himself a fair and just man but who rendered decisions with frightening gravity.

Markinson raised his voice slightly. "Are you implying you do not trust us? An assistant director, a special agent in charge, your own Bureau?"

"It's not that—but I may have violated Bureau rules . . . I don't know . . ."

"You mean," the SAC asked, "you don't want to tell us because of the manner in which you recovered the money?"

"That's about it."

Markinson's tone took on that of a prosecutor. "Did the informant turn it over to you?"

Rip shook his head.

The SAC persisted. "Did she tell you where it was?"

Rip took a deep breath. "Let me clarify a point. The subjects will think one of their own crowd stole it when they discover it's gone. And they've got to think that—and they will since they put the informant to bed, so to speak, and she was in her apartment at the time the money disappeared. But if they read in the papers that the FBI got it back, or hear it from any source, they're going to put two and two together and come up with the informant."

The SAC asked in disbelief: "Are you telling us that you stole this money instead of taking the usual legal steps that would have led to recovery?"

"I stumbled upon it," Rip said, "and picked it up."

"If you had been caught," the SAC said, "you would have involved the Bureau in a highly embarrassing situation."

Rip nodded. "Embarrassing situation for me, too."

"You should have consulted with us," Markinson put in sharply. "I want you to prepare a report immediately setting forth all of the facts."

"I can't. I'm sorry."

"Do you know what you're saying?" Markinson asked tartly. "Do you realize—"

"I'm guilty of insubordination—although I don't want to be."

"If you pursue this course, the Bureau will have to take disciplinary action. I appreciate fully that you are protecting the informant but your zeal is excessive and inexcusable—to conceal the facts from your fellow agents, the Bureau in general, the Director . . ."

"I have no choice," Rip answered doggedly.

"You mean," Markinson continued, "in your judgment you have no choice—but your judgment is in flagrant error."

"If I may be excused," Rip said, starting to leave.

Markinson stopped him. "One minute, Ripley. If there are further major decisions, you will consult with the Bureau."

"I will—if I do not jeopardize anybody's life in doing so." He paused at the door. "I'm not challenging the authority of the Bureau or the Director. I wouldn't do that. But you must surely see that I'm caught up in a desperate situation."

Markinson's intent, glassy stare followed him out. When he had gone, the SAC spoke up. "He may have a point. Since we don't have all of the facts, we must grant that possibility."

Markinson hammered the desk. "We don't have the facts because he refuses to give them to us. If he has violated Bureau rules—and apparently he has—the Director can't tolerate that, no matter how much justification there is. We can't have agents running around calling the shots. I'll talk with the Director about this when I get back to Washington."

He was scheduled to leave at noon. He would return to Los Angeles if there was a possibility of a major development. In a case such as this, however, the investigation would normally cover months, and he could not remain away from Washington that long.

"In the meantime," he continued, "we'll remove Ripley from the case."

"We can't do that," the SAC said.

"Why not?"

"The informant is skitterish as it is. It took some doing for Ripley

126

to gain her confidence. She's not an unfriendly informant, not that at all, but she's very suspicious of what she terms political investigations. If Ripley disappears and another agent comes into the picture . . ."

Markinson nodded. "All right, don't say anything to him until I've consulted the Director. We will have to terminate him with prejudice or take some kind of disciplinary action. We can't condone an open flouting of the Bureau. If he would write a report . . ."

"He won't."

"No, I suppose not." He paced about restlessly. "What are we going to do about the other law-enforcement agencies? We can't have them out beating the bushes when we know the money has been recovered."

They decided they would advise them that the Bureau had developed a lead that would result, most probably, in the recovery of the money. In the meantime, would they defer to the Bureau's investigation? The question, of course, was so much diplomatic phraseology. The others would be happy to be relieved of responsibility. The case load they all shouldered constantly exceeded the man hours they had available for investigation.

Markinson said unexpectedly: "Confound him! I like the fellow. Why does he have to be so stubborn?"

33

SHE WALKED THE lonely beach and cast no shadow. When she stopped to look far away, there was the old, mysterious fascination of endless water. She imagined herself at Alexandria in the days of the Ptolemies, staring out over the Mediterranean, and at Marseilles when the name Napoleon exploded over Europe. Since a very small girl, trapped by her first history book, Chris had stood and dreamed of herself in a thousand settings in a thousand other ages. It was a part of childhood she had never surrendered.

Max appeared out of nowhere. Even from a distance she noted the mean scowl, and with an increased heart beat, wondered what it portended. She walked toward him, her feet bare, her hair blowing in the soft wind. Close up, she saw the stubble on his face. He was always close shaven, his fingernails well kept, his grooming in general meticulous.

Now he said shortly, without a hello: "What'd you and Vince talk about on the way home?"

She stopped abruptly. "Talk about? Nothing much. He was still terribly excited. Said he was going to celebrate—if he could find a woman. I thought you said you hand-picked everyone and they didn't pick up playmates?"

"What'd he say about the money?"

"Nothing, except . . . Say, what is this? The third degree?"

He shook his head a little and his glance was an apology. "Something happened this morning. Something terrible. Someone got the money. All of it. Got it right out from under our noses. I know it isn't Vince—but I thought—I had to know if he'd said anything. We've got a thief somewhere in our organization. I can't believe it . . . I've got the Zero Section working on it. I gave them the authority to execute him on the spot when they found him. I told them I didn't care how they did it. If they want to torture him first, okay."

She couldn't control the trembling. "You mean . . . all of the money we got last night?"

"We hid it in front of the house—in a great, big, old barbecue. But I didn't tell you where it was, did I?"

"Now wait a minute!" she began angrily. "If you suspect me—"

"Not so loud . . . No, no, it couldn't've been you. It was a man. Jake jumped him but he got away. You don't know anyone in the organization. You couldn't've tipped off anyone inside. You're not the criminal type and you wouldn't have a confederate waiting. Besides, you didn't know where you were going until you got there."

"Well, thanks a lot! I go through hell for you and you take your mad out on me!"

"Now don't get excited. I suspect everyone. I've got to. But it doesn't work with you. Now don't crack up on me."

He looked far away. "I've never gone in for torture . . . but maybe once . . . as a lesson . . . when we catch him. I told you about Japan's Rengo Sekigun, didn't I? They stab you and leave you to bleed to death, or beat you, strip you and put you out in subzero weather to freeze to death. We could take him to the High Sierras. I don't know . . ."

As abruptly as he came, he walked away. She stood a moment un-

128

able to move, then very slowly trudged toward her car. She would stop by Barney's for a Pepsi. Hopefully, there might be a message.

But there was none.

On the sidewalk before the apartment building she stooped to console a whining mongrel dog, and he followed her. He looked hungry and her heart went out to him. Her life could be measured by her pets. Three to six was her turtle period; six to nine, a shepherd; nine to fourteen, a one-eyed cat; and fourteen to eighteen, the one great love of her teen years, a horse. She wondered if Jim would like to keep the mongrel, now busy lapping up milk, until they were married.

The idea had such appeal that she called him, and got a quick, decisive no. "But, Jim," she pleaded, "you had a dog when you were a boy and said you liked dogs and they won't let me keep him here."

The dog still got a no vote but the conversation did end with a date set up for that night. She would meet him at the Inglewood Theatre to see a movie. After hanging up, she sat worried. She had told Max she had broken with Jim, and if he, or one of his henchmen, should see them together . . .

Roz breezed in, her usual happy self. "Say," she said, putting a sack of groceries down on the kitchen drainboard, "you can have that carrot cake recipe. Gosh, it tastes great but do you know how many carrots it takes, and what was I doing while you were sawing away this morning? Peeling carrots. Thousands of carrots. A whole ton of them."

Chris collapsed into a chair and laughed uncontrollably.

Roz looked at her consolingly. "Things are that bad, huh?"

34

WHEN SHE PUT into the cove, the sun had not been up long. The sea gulls were feeding, the waves lapping sleepily, the distant sky pink tinged. Riding in on a soft crest, she shouted good morning.

He pulled her boat up on the beach alongside his, and she kicked off her sandals. "I like to feel the sand in my toes," she said. When he smiled down on her, she noted the warmth in his eyes, eyes that

129

skimmed over her appreciatively, not missing a curve beneath the simple purple sun suit.

"I've needed someone to talk to . . ." she began.

"I know, Miss Roberts. I know how it is."

"I'm Chris to most people. I'd like it if you'd call me Chris."

"And I'm Rip. Just Rip." He motioned to the two rocks. "Do you want the straight chair or the sofa?"

She dropped instead to the sand and asked the question that had hounded her curiosity. "It was *you,* wasn't it—got the money? Someone in the outfit could've stolen it. But no, I think it was you." She added: "I'm getting to be a fair actress. I'd react okay with them even if I did know."

"I'm sure you would but why take a chance?"

She leaned back against a rock and stretched out her long, slender, Indian-brown legs. "It's more than reacting, isn't it? They're not above torture. Max said as much—if they caught whoever stole the money. If I'm caught and tortured, you're thinking I'll talk."

He sat on a rock a few feet from her, looking down on her. He shifted nervously. She had stated quite unemotionally a fact, one he had pushed down into the dark, musty cellar of his mind. Yes, they would torture her; they would smash the lovely face. He recalled one girl who had been worked over until her face was a pulp, the jaw and cheekbones broken and crushed, and an eye blinded. If any man did that to the radiant creature before him, he would kill him. Never had he thought he could set out deliberately to kill another but he would.

"God, don't say that," he whispered.

"I won't talk."

"For Heaven's sake," he said firmly, "let's not anticipate. You're handling everything beautifully. There's no reason to think—"

They settled down to a review of the raid on the bank and subsequent developments. Rip sought descriptions of everyone she had met. He wanted to know details, such as glasses worn, if any; jewelry, if any; oddities in speech; manner of walking, sitting and holding the head; scars or birthmarks; if the person smoked and what; slang and unusual words; and height, weight, complexion, et cetera.

"When you were putting down on the street," he asked, "did you notice anyone looking up, raising a hand, taking out a handkerchief to blow his nose or wipe his forehead, anything that could have been a signal?"

She couldn't recall such an act. "I guess I was too scared. You heard that Vince frisked me?"

He nodded. "I don't know, maybe you shouldn't have a bug on you."

She was touched by his concern. "No, it's okay. It's scarcely noticeable with the kind of bra I'm wearing. You'd have to press to find it."

"You're sure?" He smiled. "I'm not much of an authority on bras."

"I'm sure. What about this Howie Spelvin character? I got to thinking last night—"

"Don't worry, he's still on the Amazon. He won't show his face around here."

"Nights are the worst. I wake up and get all kinds of worries."

She had awakened last night to the crack of rifle fire. But it was no rifle fire, only a car backfiring. She had begun then to have dark thoughts, and resolutely got up and padded about, whistling softly to herself. Since she could remember she had whistled when alone to fill the silence, the same whistle, an old song popular when she was in her subteens. Pulling aside the drapes, she discovered it was sunrise, and outside her window a hummingbird was bathing in the spray from a lawn sprinkler. Her thoughts went skimming to Europe where she had been a bird watcher that summer she had hitchhiked, and then to Venice, and the warm afternoon when she had been sitting on the great square having a Coke. A gamin, about seven or eight, had darted by her table, dropped a rose in her hand, and raced on. She had never seen him again. Had it been a gesture of love born out of lonesomeness or was she a fantasy image to dream about, someone to love and care for him? That was it! She would go back to Venice when this was all over, and find the boy, and do something for him. It would be the perfect escape from the memory of these weeks, a memory that never could be erased but with a little boy's help in a faraway place might be stilled.

She continued: "I must tell you about a character they call Boone. You don't get conversations at a distance from the bug, do you?"

He indicated in the negative. Constantly he scanned the ocean and the sky but this morning they were as alone as if they were on a far-off, uncharted island.

"I don't know what they're cooking up," she continued, "but they've got to raise money fast and they've called this Boone fellow in who's head of Ordnance. But they're scared of him. I heard Max

131

say, I heard him talking in a low voice to Dr. Beaumont, that he would blow them all to kingdom come if they didn't watch him. They talked about how to control him. Dr. Beaumont said he thought the guy was a madman, and would blow up half of Los Angeles some night. Max then said Boone had become an expert ammo man in Vietnam."

She doubled her legs under her, and knitted her brow in concentration. "Somebody's given Max a rundown on him. Said his superior officers in Vietnam classified him as brilliant with explosives but one who could not take orders. They'd send him out to destroy a road and he'd mine the whole countryside. Said that once he blew up a village instead of the target spot. Shall I go on? Is this important?"

"Everything's important. You never know how it may fit in."

"Max told Dr. Beaumont that Boone is a child wanting attention. He craves it—and gets it when he's holding somebody's life in his hands. Max said Boone came to him a few weeks ago and begged to plant a few bombs in crowded places. Said he wanted practice. Dr. Beaumont said they had to do something about him before he went berserk. Max argued that they needed him and Dr. Beaumont agreed and said he would talk with him but Max didn't think that would do much good. Oh, yes, I almost forgot. Max said he carries a hand grenade around in his coat pocket and plays with it when he's nervous. Like counting beads. This hasn't gone over very well with the Committee."

"I bet it hasn't."

"He doesn't get along with people, Max said. He's a loner. Well, that's about all on Boone."

She rose, sat on the rock across from him, and ran sand through her toes. "This girl, Tico, I met the other night—you heard the conversation—she said Mr. Jorgensen was an FBI informant. I'm hurt, Mr. Ripley—Rip—that you didn't tell me. She said he was safe in Tahiti and here I've been worrying about him. I think there are some things you should tell me, especially if I know someone and like them. I don't go along with this how-I-react business when I have a right to know."

She offered the comment quietly. He could remember when she would have put a karate blow behind the words. By now, though, they liked and respected each other.

He took a deep breath. "I apologize—but it wasn't entirely that I was concerned about how you'd react. The Bureau protects the identity of its informants even when they are no longer informants, even when they walk out on us like Mr. Jorgensen did, even after death."

"Even after death," she repeated in a whisper, her face a sober study.

"I didn't mean—"

"I know you didn't."

He said softly: "I want to tell you something. I suffer when I sit and listen to the bug or read the log. I'm helpless, and there's nothing I can do, and there you are—I'm not putting this well . . ."

She nodded in understanding. "There're some things that can't be put into words, but we understand better than if they had been. Take me. I'm scared all the time, of course, and terrified, but the scare and the terror pass when it's all over. It's not that part of it that's so bad. The part that hurts is knowing what your friends and relatives are thinking about you when you cut them off."

She sat up straight; she was very intent. "Papa called last night. His twin brother, my Uncle Grant, died, and Papa wanted me to come back to the funeral. We've always been very close, Papa and I. He's not old, about fifty, and he's a lot of fun.

"I don't think in all my life he's ever asked me for anything but I knew he didn't understand. He mumbled about how much Uncle Grant had loved me, and it's true. When I was a kid, Uncle Grant was always doing something for me, buying me dolls and playing with me when he came visiting.

"No, it's not the scare part. It's the hurt that stays with me."

35

Shortly after 9 o'clock three nights later, Chris parked her car on a dark, deserted side street in an old industrial district. For a long moment she sat very straight behind the wheel reconnoitering. In the pitch blackness she could make out only the squat hulks of small plants, ramrod straight power poles that walked in a dwindling line far apart, a few nondescript cars, and a half block distant a weathered, swinging, rattling sign under a weak light that read: *THE JUNKERY* —B. Boone.

Neither man nor dog nor car moved. Yet strangely she felt certain she was being watched. She left the car and locked it. This, she said to herself, was no place for a lone woman. Max, however, had been unable to call for her and when he had offered to send Vince, she had turned him down, a decision that had pleased him. This would be her first Planning Section meeting. She had had her doubts that she would be invited to one.

Rip had been certain she would. "Hartman likes exciting women around him. He put Winnie in as secretary—and fixed Tico up with a job. But with all his women, it's more than the sex angle. That's a nice bonus—but he's hard, pragmatic. His women have to pay off by doing a job. And you—as a courier—could take care of a weakness in the organization. You're the biggest break they've had."

"I'm afraid," she said slowly, "you're underestimating the personal angle. I think I'm probably the first girl who's ever told him no, thanks. He's become obsessed with me. I'm a wild mare to break— to prove to himself he's simply irresistible to every woman."

She had known nothing about the meeting until she had arrived late that afternoon from Boston. As she made her way through a milling throng in the passenger building, a determined boy thrust a note into her hand, then scurried away before she really noticed him. In a few terse words, Max ordered her to keep the night free. He would phone at 8 o'clock.

That had been her first minor shock. The second came when she found a memo in her box from her supervisor. A passenger had filed a complaint alleging that Chris had been rude about heating her baby's bottle. Chris recalled that first the bottle had been too hot, then too cold, and again, too hot. At that point Chris had had to serve dinner. She had returned as soon as she could to the woman who accused her of endangering the life of her child. Chris would write an explanation which the airline would accept. Still, as with all airlines, every complaint was given consideration, and too many complaints looked bad on the record.

She picked her way carefully over a disintegrating sidewalk. Long-dead leaves crackled loudly in the stillness. Once she stifled an outcry when she kicked a beer can that went clattering with great noise. She stopped very still, scarcely breathing, then realized that heavy feet dead behind her had also halted. Turning slowly about, she found a man, immobile, a hundred feet distant, who made no attempt to hide or to advance on her. He merely stood and watched. He must be one of Max's men, from the Security Section.

134

Beneath *THE JUNKERY* sign, she passed a strange assortment of bric-a-brac and paraphernalia from another era: a cigar store Indian who had fought one too many battles, an old chest with a good mirror, two tall white Roman columns from a movie set, a bathtub, and a big black iron cauldron. They were lined up along the sidewalk like a ragtag army.

Pushing through an enormous iron gate, she was blocked by a figure in black. Then she remembered. "Nine Thermidor," she said. They were the code words that Dr. Beaumont had provided. Thermidor had been a month in the French Revolutionary calendar. Nine Thermidor was July 27, 1794, the date of the *coup d'état* which ended in the guillotining of Robespierre.

Still not speaking, the figure stood aside, and she walked slowly through a junkyard, past staircases from wrecked mansions, elaborate, costly ironwork from Los Angeles's Spanish period in the 1920s and '30s, expansive but stained marble slabs, impressive fountains topped with statuary, and the usual washbasins, tubs, toilets, washing machines, stoves, and other tired fixtures.

She was drawn by a single light burning over the door stoop of a small stucco house to the far back. The paint was peeling, the house itself listed to the right, and on the left was a broken window. She was about to knock when the door opened and a white-haired but young-looking woman asked in a deep mannish voice: "Miss Roberts?" Chris nodded and repeated: "Nine Thermidor."

From the vestibule, she entered a surprisingly large but cluttered area. A wall separating the living and dining rooms had been torn out. About ten persons sat sandwiched in between old phonographs, unpainted chests, pseudo Chippendale chairs in varying degrees of health, and ornate bed posts. From the cracked, spidery ceiling hung grotesque and delightfully nostalgic lamps, chandeliers and mobiles, dusty, streaked, and cobwebbed.

Obviously, the meeting had been underway for some time. The bodies were well settled, and there was the weary look induced by much talk. Max had given her a later meeting time and there could be but one reason: he hadn't wanted her sitting in on one certain discussion.

Tico was talking in that strident, brittle way of hers. Scooched far down in a chair, she had her sandaled feet on a low chest, her skirt above her knees, her legs wide apart. Max admitted he had found her exciting at first although recently he had repelled her advances.

135

He was repulsed by women who were sexually aggressive. Chris recalled Max telling her that Tico had had a rough past. After her father raped her when she was fourteen, she had run away from the tarpaper shack on the lonely railroad siding in the Arizona desert, the only home she had ever known. Subsequently she had worked as a waitress and part-time prostitute. Then she had had the baby she was later accused of smothering. About running away, she had told Max: "At that age you want to get into the future as fast as you can and out of the now." Max thought she was still trying to get into the future.

She was saying: "We've got to live revolution every day, right now. Tear down society. Kill a policeman here and there, blow up a government building. Terrorize the whole damn lot of them. Pile one horror on top of another, and then when we do strike, they'll welcome us as saviours. They'll shout hosannah, and take one look at Dr. Beaumont and believe anything he promises. But all of this take-it-easy, no-guts business . . . I could throw up."

Leaning wearily against a wall, Max listened intently, his features devoid of emotion. For him, Chris thought, this was one big poker game. Too bad he was such a handsome devil, and when he wanted to be, a charming one. She had been brought up on Westerns—her father loved them—in that era before Westerns became involved with social justice, and she liked her villains all evil and her heroes all good.

Nearby Dr. Beaumont was seated comfortably in a dirty brown easy chair from which the insides spewed. His seemingly casual gaze moved from person to person, scanning each carefully, a college professor taking precise notes. When her turn came, she was unaccountably disturbed. She had no reason to think he might suspect her, and yet she did. He was more observant than Max, and more objective, too, when it came to a woman. She was a girl to Max, but to Dr. Beaumont, a new student.

From behind her came a man's wispy, slightly high-pitched voice. Turning, she saw a short, thin-faced, pock-marked, balding individual hunched up on a bench. If Max had not told her his age, she would have guessed he was ten years beyond his twenty-four. He was Bill Boone, head of Ordnance, the ammo expert, never called Bill but always Boone.

"I'm ready," Boone said to Tico. "How many places you want blown up a night? One, two, three? How many cops you want killed? You tell me and we zero 'em. We blow up California."

"No, no!" Winnie Tipton cried out. "We aren't going to kill peo-

136

ple." She turned to Max. "That's what you told me—except when there just absolutely isn't any other way. We've got to educate people, teach them—"

Tico cut in: "And how long do you think that would take? A thousand years, ten thousand—"

Winnie ignored the interruption. "It's all a matter of teaching people that they have been thinking wrong about how they live. We must explain to them as if they were children that competition is wicked, and the weak ones who cannot compete, fall by the wayside and live in ghettos and starve and die. We must teach them that we should co-operate with each other, and love each other, and help one another, and not fight for every dollar in sight, and run over and trample the weak. We must eliminate money because money is the reason people are starving and dying. But we mustn't go around killing policemen. Why should we kill them? They don't know what they're doing. We've got to get through to them."

"I'll tell you how you teach people," Tico said. "You bury the ones who get in your way. That's how you get justice."

"Now, now, Tico," Dr. Beaumont chided, and said to Winnie: "You must remember, my dear, that many of our most learned men were high in their praise of revolution. Carlyle said—and I quote— 'Men seldom rebel against anything that does not deserve rebelling against,' and someone—I've forgotten his name—said that rebellion against tyrants was obedience to God."

Tico snorted and turned to Boone. "How much does it cost to blow up a place?"

"A plastic bomb? Three dollars and forty-six cents. Blow up one room. A good job that'll knock out a wall, about seventy-five dollars."

"How much a computer? If we could knock out all the computers in this country—make them a symbol of what's destroying mankind . . . ?"

"Twenty bucks." He dropped to a conspiratorial tone. "I know where we can hook some nuclear warheads—"

Max spoke up sharply. "We're killing no policemen, bombing nothing, and stealing no nuclear warheads. Not now, Boone. You understand? Not now." He turned to Tico. "You know how I feel about this—but if you want it on the agenda, we'll put it on for next time but tonight we've got this matter about using a mob. Dr. Beaumont has been studying the question. Will you give us your findings on this?"

137

With effort, Dr. Beaumont pushed himself up out of the sunken chair. Calmly, he looked from one to another until he had their attention. "In the entire course of history, I doubt if a mob has ever been used as effectively as it was during the French Revolution. The Jacobins used it, the Girondists did, and others, including Napoleon Bonaparte when he came to power. The employment of the mob at that time, and still today, is principally psychological. A mob terrifies the viewer who imagines himself caught up in it, his wife and children, his home and place of work going up in flames. And a mob calls attention to a cause in a dynamic manner and can swiftly crystallize public opinion."

He talked slowly, a professor lecturing students. "You will raise the issue, as Max has done, of the effectiveness of a mob in this era. I acknowledge that conditions have changed drastically since the French Revolution. We have tear gas that will quickly disperse a mob, and other means. But we have counterchecks for all of these. I have given much thought to the pros and cons and I recommend strongly that we employ a mob to loot and sack and fire Washington a few hours before we strike.

"I would suggest the following logistics: The mob—which should number no less than one hundred thousand—gathers at noon to hear a speech by a firebrand. The more radical the fellow, the better. While he is speaking, one of our men will assassinate him. We will have *provocateurs* planted in the crowd who will immediately spread the word that he was killed by the FBI, and start the mob moving down Pennsylvania Avenue toward the Department of Justice.

"The *provocateurs* will urge the crowd to set fire to everything in sight, principally buses and government cars. At the moment the crowd runs riot down Pennsylvania Avenue, Boone's men will set off explosives in certain key buildings, and these explosions will be blamed in due course on the mob. They must not appear to be the work of an organized group. In other words, when I assume power, I will be coming out of nowhere, and neither I nor any one of us here will have blood on our hands. This is very important and calls for astute timing.

"One more thought: We should ask our Washington allies to establish protection squads for the television crews that will cover the events. These squads should appear offhand. There should be no previous arrangement or we will give ourselves away. They should seem to be people who happen to be on the spot and want to help. We will need the best television and radio coverage we can get."

Tico cut in. "Where are we going to get a hundred thousand people?"

"We've discussed that. Mr. Pederson will give you the logistics on that."

Oscar Pederson, who had masqueraded as FBI Agent Compton in an attempt to trap Chris, rose from behind a filing cabinet where he had been hidden from her view. He smiled slyly at her and nodded.

"This won't be any problem," he said. "There's always some cause that would like to stage a big rally in Washington. If it's not for peace or a poverty program, it's for something else. And there's always a leader who's itching to make a name for himself, but doesn't know how to go about it or doesn't have the financing. We'll supply the money. These productions usually take about one hundred thousand dollars but we should budget at least a hundred and fifty thousand. It's one thing, of course, to get a hundred thousand people there and another to turn them on. The trigger in this plan is the assassination of their leader. Dr. Beaumont came up with that and it's a bit of pure genius."

"What do you think, Max?" Dr. Beaumont asked.

"I can't see that it would do any harm and as you point out, it may have tremendous psychological value. As for seizing power, though, we all have studied recent revolutions—those in South America, Egypt, Libya, Syria, Indonesia, the Bolshevik take-over of Russia—and they have been won by getting control of the key points in a capital—all law enforcement agencies, including the counterparts of the FBI, and radio, television and newspapers, the telephone, telegraph and other communications of every kind, and the military, or neutralizing of it.

"We cannot depend on the people. The Black Panthers did a few years ago in Los Angeles when they staged a shootout with the police. They fought for hours thinking the people would come to their aid. But not one solitary person did. The guy who won't help a girl being attacked on a street corner isn't going to fight for you behind barricades.

"The secret of a revolution is in seizing the key points in a lightning thrust. You don't win with mobs or by prolonged fighting, not in a modern nation—and I can't repeat that often enough. You win by surprise, by moving fast, usually at night. We'll activate our plan at one A.M. and we must be in control by five."

For the next hour, they discussed the "employment" of a mob. The

139

eventual vote stood at eight for, one against, the one being Winnie Tipton.

Tico glared at Winnie. "You make me sick to my stomach, you little nigger slut, always whining around—"

"Hold it right there," Chris said in a voice she could barely control. "I'm new here, and maybe I shouldn't be talking, but I don't like what I just heard."

"You want to make something of it?" Tico shouted.

"Like what?" Chris hurled back at her.

Not a person moved or seemed to breathe. Only Max smiled. He enjoyed watching women devour each other. "They're all savages," he had said.

"What the hell business is it of yours?" Tico asked, now livid.

"She's my friend! That's what the hell."

Under the stare of the others, Tico weakened. "She knows how I talk."

Max interrupted. "Let's get on with the business at hand."

Uneasily they resumed talking. Max was instructed to request the Chicago chapter to investigate the background of a young, upcoming black rebel who was commanding considerable attention. Max had heard he was a remarkably persuasive speaker. He might be the one to lead a mob, and if a black were slain, the repercussions might be even more intense than if a white were.

"On this subject of mob employment, there's one interesting historical fact," Dr. Beaumont commented. "You know, of course, that Washington was laid out by a Frenchman but not many people are cognizant of the fact he reputedly planned the circles with the French Revolution in mind . . ."

The Frenchman was Major Pierre C. L'Enfant, engineer and architect, and Lafayette's associate. The major supposedly believed, Dr. Beaumont said, that every nation must consider a revolution a constant threat. Accordingly, he designed circles where artillery could be mounted to fire on a mob racing down the avenues and streets intersecting them.

"This country's leaders and Army men have always secretly been very revolution conscious," Dr. Beaumont continued. "Why, shortly after they planned the White House they dug a tunnel from it to the Octagon House and from there to the Potomac so the President could escape if the White House came under siege.

"And more recently we had the consternation immediately follow-

140

ing the assassination of President Kennedy. The people in his party—
Lyndon Johnson, all of them, and the FBI and military in Washington
—feared the assassination was part of a plot to seize control of the
country, and steps were immediately taken in Washington to thwart
any such move."

Max interrupted. "That's why surprise is a key factor in our plans."
He turned to Chris. "We took a vote before you arrived, and named
you Co-ordinator. You will serve as our liaison with the other cities."

She forced a smile. Rip had prophesied correctly. At last they had
named her their courier.

Shortly afterwards the meeting broke up. She learned later that before she arrived Max had reported the investigation into the theft of
the money was "proceeding in a satisfactory manner." He had said
there would be no discussion and no progress reports since this was
an "inside job." When the guilty party was apprehended, he would
be summarily turned over to the Zero Section. Max advised that the
Planning Section had no authority in the matter, and the members
were forbidden to discuss it among themselves.

On the way out, Chris put an arm briefly about Winnie. "Do you
bowl?" she asked, and when Winnie nodded, Chris continued: "Let's
get up a foursome."

Tico appeared at her side. "I want to talk with you," she said
brusquely.

Chris pulled away. "There's nothing to talk about."

"It's not about her. It's Max's idea."

Tico led the way into a bedroom crowded with so much junk that
there remained only a catwalk around the bed, half of which was itself
piled high with boxes. From the looks of it, the bed had never been
made. Here Boone slept in the kind of rat's nest a man like him would
enjoy.

Tico said: "Take off your clothes. Everything."

36

CHRIS STOOD PARALYZED, staring. Tico wavered before her and the
room swayed. It was as if she were in an earthquake. The floor

141

dropped, jolting her, and the floor raised up, buckling, and she buckled. Within seconds, the quake ended, and her mind took over again, telling her where she was and warning her to think and act swiftly. There were aftershocks but she was more or less stabilized. Even though her body trembled, she could think. Still she stood perfectly rigid. The bug was a paperweight inside her bra.

"You heard me," Tico said, lighting a cigarette. "Get out of your clothes—and hurry it up. I haven't got all night. This is an inspection."

"Inspection?"

Tico blew the smoke out. "Didn't Max tell you? We pull these little surprises on everyone—because if there's a rat among us, we could end up hanging, some of us."

From deep down, Chris tapped a reservoir of strength she never knew she had. "Go to hell," she said, not believing it was she talking. It was another person, a fictitious Chris. If you get in a tight spot, Rip had counseled, attack. Get angry, tear into the party, engage in histrionics, remember some of those old Bette Davis and Joan Crawford films. "I'm not stripping for you or anyone else. Go ahead and kick me out if you think I'm a rat fink. I don't care. I've got other things to do besides play games with you."

"Or Max?" Tico taunted. "Maybe you'd rather strip for him? Not that you haven't, you bitch! Give me that purse."

Yanking it out of Chris's hands, she dumped the contents on the bed. Out spilled a wallet, lipstick, key chain, coins, receipts, slips of paper with notes on them, a perfume atomizer, nail file, silver Mexican earrings that hurt her ears and she had removed, a long letter from her mother she hadn't had time to read, a gas bill, eye make-up she had bought that morning in Boston, and a handful of S & H green trading stamps.

Carefully, Tico examined each item. "I voted against you. Max didn't tell you that, did he? And I wasn't the only one. Some of us got you figured for a damn stool pigeon. Why would a girl who's never been kicked around, never gone hungry, never been pawed over by a man because she had to have a place to sleep, why would she want a revolution? Maybe you're in this for the kicks—but you don't look the type."

Chris started to scoop the contents back in the purse, then thought better. She shouted at Tico: "Do I have to starve to death to want to help the hungry?"

142

In the FBI Communications room, a monitoring agent told the FBI switchboard to locate Rip quickly. "Tell him C-77's about to be blown. She's at this address . . ." He gave the address, then turned back to listen.

CHRIS: You can get kicked around too much. I bet you've never cared about anything in your life except your own stinking skin. Get out of my way. I'm coming through.

TICO: I know you're a stoolie. You got a tap on you. You wouldn't be raising so much hell if you didn't.

CHRIS: Sure, I've got a tap on me. Go ahead. Try to find it.

Now she yanked off the top of the blue polyester pants suit and threw it across Tico's face.

"There! Try to find it. I dare you. We're children, playing children's games, aren't we? I dare you. That's what you say. I dare you." Tico crunched the garment in her hands, and started to toss it on the bed. "Wait a minute! You missed a pocket. Don't be so sloppy. Max wouldn't like it."

Tico gave her a murderous look, then dropped the garment. Chris unzipped the back placket of the pants, and as she started to wriggle out of them, tripped and fell face downward on the bed, aiming herself for the exact spot where the purse contents lay. Her right hand went swiftly inside her bra and as she gasped and moaned with pretended hurt tore the bug out. She dropped it among the other items, rolled over on her back, and sitting up, finished removing the pants. She threw them at Tico. "This is where I always hide the bug!"

Chris slid a quick glance at her other belongings on the mussed covers. There lay the bug among her keys on the key chain. If Tico looked carefully, if she decided to examine the purse contents again . . .

"Damn, you've got a figure," Tico said, checking the pants. "I bet Howie Spelvin really went for you, knowing Howie."

Chris's hands, unfastening the bra, hesitated but a second, then Tico grabbed it almost before Chris was out of it, and examined it closely to assure herself nothing was hidden in the lining.

"There!" Chris said. "I hope you're happy."

Tico stubbed out the cigarette as if killing something alive. "I've got a feeling about you—a feeling . . ."

143

37

SAC, CHICAGO. C-77 ADVISED TODAY COM-
MITTEE OF PUBLIC SAFETY WILL ASK CHICAGO
AFFILIATE, EXACT NAME UNKNOWN, TO RE-
PORT ON UNIDENTIFIED YOUNG BLACK MALE
REBEL LEADER POSSIBILITY OF ENLISTING HIS
AID IN RECRUITING MOB OF ONE HUNDRED
THOUSAND TO STAGE DEMONSTRATION IN
WASHINGTON, D.C., PRECEDING SEIZURE OF
GOVERNMENT. C-77 WILL ARRIVE SHORTLY IN
CHICAGO TO DELIVER MESSAGE RE ABOVE
FROM SUBJECT MAXIMILIAN HARTMAN. WILL
ADVISE ARRIVAL TIME OF INFORMANT AS SOON
AS SET UP. PHOTO OF INFORMANT, DESCRIP-
TION, AND INFORMANT'S WHEREABOUTS DUR-
ING CHICAGO STAY FOLLOW.

SAC, LOS ANGELES

TAPED TELEPHONE conversation at 1:10 A.M. between SAC, Los
Angeles, and Assistant Director Markinson at Bureau:

SAC: . . . Hartman told the informant that they planned to create
nationwide panic by blowing up key buildings in a score of cities the
same night they move on Washington. He mentioned the Los Angeles
aqueduct which furnishes part of the water for the city and O'Hare
Airport in Chicago. We don't have any details. Hartman wanted to
know how soon she could be in Chicago and she told him she'd try
to trade runs with another stewardess.

MARKINSON: Was any date mentioned for activating the plot?

SAC: Not even the time of year. They seem inclined to move
slowly. In regard to the bank robbery, we've now interviewed every
bank employee, security guard, and police officer to determine where
he was positioned at the time the helicopter came down. We've cross-
checked the information and developed no leads. One bank employee

144

and three security men were standing by the van in question but all are of excellent reputation—and yet we're positive someone signaled the pilot as he put down. We fingerprinted the copter and took off several excellent latents that we're forwarding. Also, some very good plaster of Paris casts of footprints on the desert around the helicopter. What about Ripley? Have you reached a decision on him?

MARKINSON: I've recommended no action at this time. Has he changed his attitude?

SAC: He still insists he'll take whatever action he believes is appropriate—without advance consultation with the Bureau—if he thinks the informant's life is in jeopardy.

MARKINSON: I don't like that and neither will the Director.

SAC: Nor do I. But I've brought all the pressure I could on him, even to informing him that he is subjecting himself to possible dismissal with prejudice, and with that on his record he'd have trouble getting another job in the investigative field.

MARKINSON: The Bureau will hold you strictly responsible for his actions. I don't care how effective he is, the Bureau cannot tolerate—

SAC: I'll keep a tight rein on him.

Taped telephone conversation at 1:50 A.M. between Assistant Director Markinson and Ted Somerset, White House liaison with the FBI:

MARKINSON: . . . O'Hare in Chicago and the Los Angeles aqueduct—that's all we know to date . . .

SOMERSET: What about the Washington group? Do you have anything on them yet?

MARKINSON: Not yet.

SOMERSET: I don't mind telling you the President's terribly upset that you haven't infiltrated them. He can't understand the Bureau's failure to do this.

MARKINSON: We're close—very close.

SOMERSET: When?

MARKINSON: Nobody can give a time in these situations.

SOMERSET: Ed, I know the President well enough to know he's going to raise hell about this—if the Bureau doesn't get cracking.

Taped telephone conversation at 2:20 A.M. between Assistant Director Markinson and the SAC, Los Angeles:

MARKINSON: Look, when Ripley sees the informant tomorrow, ask

145

him to find out whether she can get anything at all on the Washington group. We're coming under stiff pressure from the White House—

SAC: I don't think she should ask questions—

MARKINSON: Not at all—but if there was some way she could lead one of the subjects into a discussion of the Directory . . . The President thinks he may be sitting on a powder keg, and we don't know, maybe he is. It's darn important that the informant be instructed to concentrate on this. Does Ripley have a good cover for meeting her?

SAC: He says he does.

MARKINSON: You don't know what it is? Where he meets her?

SAC: I didn't press him. It didn't seem to be absolutely essential that I know.

MARKINSON: I suppose not. But for his own good . . . He could be murdered and we might not find his body for weeks. Has he considered that?

SAC: Agent Ripley considers everything. He said if he were murdered he would not be particularly interested in when we located his body.

38

THAT NIGHT Oscar Pederson stayed up until past 3. Slight of build, lacking only a half inch of being 6 feet, he sipped cheap wine while he hunched over a battered portable typewriter on a straight chair. He sat on a whining pull-down bed in his rabbit-hutch apartment, located in the respectable but aging Larchmont district.

Occasionally he would rise and stretch and think about this new girl, Christina Roberts. In some vague way he knew she was a new breed among them, but his analysis went no further, nor did the thought bother him. With a body like that, who cared where it came from or where it would lead. He thought he would ask for a date. Max, of course, might have pre-empted her but she did not appear the kind who would enjoy Max's fast, earthy approach.

Pederson knew quite a lot about her. Last year she had earned $8,480. She had a savings account at Security Pacific bank of $700, owned 20 shares of A.T. & T., and 10 of Walt Disney. She had no dependents. She had contributed $250 to a church, $50 to United Welfare, and $65 to Go-Vap, an orphanage in Saigon.

146

He knew all of this since he was with a credit agency. He knew considerably, too, about other people, mostly about wealthy individuals. Tonight he had turned over to Max three photostated copies of their credit reports. One had $290,000 in savings and loan, and owned $360,000 in marketable stocks. The man's family, hence, could easily pay a quarter million in ransom. Pederson himself, however, had no intention of kidnaping anyone. He assured himself he was not the criminal type. He would furnish copies to Max and leave the rest to the Finance Section.

Tonight, though, he was pursuing work that eventually should net him a fortune. Since grade school he had longed to be a writer but his efforts had been consistently rebuffed by editors. In time he realized he needed a subject so sensational that it would sell itself. The revolution would provide him with that. He would write a day-by-day account which should bring him an advance of a half million. So nights he typed out every scrap of information he had collected during the day.

From the time he first met Boone, he had been fascinated with him. While Max had instructed Pederson to build up a dossier on Boone, the same as Pederson had prepared on every member of the Committee, he had gone further. Max was not interested in why people were what they were, only in what they were. But Pederson, even though he had never sold any of his writings, was sufficiently perceptive to realize that readers were intrigued by what went into the making of a person.

He reread what he had typed about Boone:

"He comes from a good, upper middle class family. He was the last of five children. The other four are all highly successful, the oldest sister a professor at USC, another sister, a real estate broker, one brother owns a furniture store and another, a clothing store. His father owned two drugstores, kept buying and selling real estate.

"Boone has always felt he was left out of the family. He was a kid when his brothers and sisters were the center of attention. They were getting good jobs, buying properties, marrying, having children, and he was—or at least so he felt—the forgotten one. He became more and more withdrawn. He hates his brothers and sisters, never sees them. When his father and mother died within months of each other, he refused to attend the funerals.

"When he came back from Vietnam, his brothers and sisters offered to buy him a business or pay for an education. He wouldn't talk with them. He hung up when they phoned, walked away from

147

them when they made efforts to see him. For a time, he was their project. They were determined to 'save' him but eventually gave up.

"His older brother, George, said, 'I guess we didn't pay much attention to him when he was growing up. He was just the kid brother. If he'd needed anything, we'd all been in there helping but he had everything he could want and was in good health and we were busy doing this and that. I remember in freshman year in high school he made the B football team but I don't think any of us ever went to see him play. I guess it was a big deal to him. Seems that one of us could have made it to a game. We would have if anyone had pounded it into our heads we should but we were caught up in this and that— and a frosh football game, who wants to sit through one of them? But we should have. We should've known.

" 'He dropped out the next year, and tried repairing motorcycles but gave up on the job. He might have succeeded with something if he had persisted but with only one tiny failure, would quit and move on. He seemed to want to go off to Vietnam. Never heard him say much about it. When his draft number came up he just disappeared one day. We all wrote him and the girls sent him boxes— cookies and candy, that sort of thing. He wrote them and thanked them for a while and then he quit and we never heard from him after that. We thought he'd been killed or was sick and asked the Red Cross to find out for us. He just never wrote.' "

Finished reading, Pederson took the pages to a closet where he slipped them into a big, cardboard grocery box. It was almost full of manuscript. From the pocket of a coat on a hanger, he took a copy of a credit report, studied it a moment, shook his head, and returned it to the inside pocket. He would like to give it to Max but the couple, who had income from more than two million dollars, had three children, aged two, four and six. He did not want that crazy Vince Dearborn kidnaping one of them. Not a child. An adult, that was all right. An adult could cope.

39

RIP THOUGHT HER eyes lacked luster. Prolonged fear could do that. Without doubt, the long, harrowing weeks were telling.

She moved uneasily under his study, sensing what went through his thoughts, and he shifted his gaze out to sea. The ocean, that had been in a tantrum yesterday, roaring its fury, was today in a languid mood. The water barely lapped at the hot sand. Even the sea gulls were in slow motion, describing lazy arcs in the sky.

"Do you have the bug on you?" he asked quietly. They sat in their accustomed places. He had arrived first, and a ripple of apprehension had run through him on finding a crushed cigarette package and burned matches. There were footprints, a solitary man had been that way.

"I don't want you wearing it again," he continued. "I never dreamed they'd strip you."

In taking the bug from her purse, her fingers trembled. "I haven't been getting enough sleep." But that was not the trouble and both knew it. She tried laughing. "If I hadn't had all that gear in here"—she indicated the purse—". . . and men are always poking fun at what's in a girl's purse. You won't know what's going on if I don't wear it. How will you know, Rip?"

He liked the warmth of his name on her lips. "We'll manage."

"I don't want to give it up. It's my security blanket, I guess you'd call it. They won't search me again."

"They might."

"I've felt you were listening or someone was who'd get to you if I needed you. And now . . ."

"I've another idea. Do you remember that day you thought the men had followed you into the library, and I went out and read their lips? Well, this is what I want you to do, if it's all right with you."

She smiled to herself. There was a time when he would not have added, *if it's all right with you.* The turbulence within was subsiding. He was good for her.

"I want you to sit somewhere in the open and pretend to read a newspaper or a book to yourself with your lips moving silently. Some people do that. They call it audibilizing. But instead of reading you will be telling me what's happening. I'll get word through Barney where you should go each time."

She nodded. "Can we come here sometimes? . . . I hope we can."

He said they would. He did not mention the crunched cigarette package.

She began her report. "On the way home last night, Max said he wished I could meet one of their men in New York. Said he raised

149

money for politicians and once had for a presidential candidate. Said he'd gotten a friend to give a hundred thousand to the Committee. Max called him Boogie or Woogie or something ending in oogie."

"No mention of what he did?"

She shook her head. "I said I'd like to meet him but Max didn't pursue it."

They discussed her Chicago assignment. She would be flying out at 8 A.M. day after tomorrow with Sarah Cashin, and the two would share a room that night at the Palmer House.

"Max said he'd get the message to me at the airport. I explained I had to be there an hour in advance of take-off and aboard the plane thirty minutes before."

Rip said a Los Angeles agent would be aboard. "He'll identify himself by asking you if the plane will be flying over Four Corners."

Four Corners was a wild, rugged terrain of fantastic gorges and mesas where Utah, Arizona, Colorado, and New Mexico met. One summer, with a Navaho friend his age, he had ridden up on its mesas and through canyons so still not even a bird called out and so narrow he had to lift his legs high out of the stirrups. He had learned to talk a little Navaho and how a people communed with this stark world and found faith and beauty and peace of mind. It was a memory to think about during long stakeouts when the pollution of men's minds and environment lay heavy.

He outlined what he wanted her to do after the agent had identified himself, and added: "I wish I could go along but sometime in the future I may need to be around you—and if my face is seen too often near you . . . Keep in mind that Max Hartman may have a party on the flight watching you."

He continued quietly: "Our Chicago office will run a surveillance on you from the time you arrive until you leave. But don't try to spot the agents following you. Just pretend they aren't there."

She said hesitantly: "I wanted to go shopping in Chicago for my nephews." She smiled. "They want a live mouse. Costs fifty cents. They're going to name it after me. A real honor. Crazy, isn't it, but a mouse from Chicago means more to them than one from here."

He laughed, and the tension broke. "Go ahead and get the mouse. Do anything you usually would. But give the agents following you a break. Don't go racing out for a taxi or get on an El train just as the doors are closing."

A strange, distinctive clattering sound, that could only indicate a helicopter, came over, and without a word, they hurried for the rock

150

overhang. The copter flew low over the cove, circled and then returned. They watched the pilot scanning the water and land beneath him—and the fact they could see him meant that he could them. Rip pushed her against a boulder and with his back to the helicopter, pressed against her, concealing her and pretending to kiss her. Then the odd bird was gone, and he released her, and took a half-step back but their eyes continued to cling in embrace, sharing the sudden longing.

He took out his handkerchief and ran it around his neck and face. "You said once you didn't think you could go through with this . . . and now I feel . . . I don't know. You came so close to being found out, and I got to thinking: What am I doing to you? If anything happened to you . . ."

She touched her hand to his cheek. "And here I thought all the time you were very much the FBI man."

He turned abruptly. "We'd better get going."

Before he pushed her boat off the beach, he said: "I liked what I heard a Jesus freak say the other day. God be with you."

"He will," she answered confidently. Taking a long, deep breath, he watched the skiff ride the first small crest. She lifted her hand in goodbye, and seconds later, was out of sight.

40

SAC, NEW YORK. INFORMANT C-77 HAS ADVISED KEY FIGURE IN NEW YORK COMMITTEE IS WEALTHY CAMPAIGN FUND RAISER FOR POLITICAL CANDIDATES, INCLUDING PRESIDENTIAL. HE RECENTLY PERSUADED UNKNOWN PARTY TO CONTRIBUTE $100,000 TO COMMITTEE. NAME UNKNOWN BUT FRIENDS CALL HIM BOOGIE OR WOOGIE OR SIMILAR NAME ENDING IN OOGIE.

SAC, LOS ANGELES

THAT NIGHT Chris had dinner with Winnie Tipton who lived in a commune-type home with nine others about her age. The half-century-old house was big and rambling, a mansion long gone to seed, the yard overgrown with weeds, the floors rolling and creaking, great slices of plaster missing from walls, and extension cords worming every which way.

Like Winnie, the four fellows and five other girls, all single, had good jobs. They divided the expenses and housework. They looked like the flower children they had been before discovering that working for a living was more pleasant than sleeping on pads, going hungry, and selling the *Free Press* on Hollywood street corners. While they banned the use of drugs and hard liquor, they considered morals a personal matter.

After a hamburger dinner with lettuce salad and Roquefort dressing, and an inexpensive California wine, Chris sat with Winnie on the splintering steps leading to a wide, old-fashioned porch. It took Winnie time to work into what she wanted to discuss. She began by relating a little about the background of her fellow housemates. "We're like many kids today. We want to help people. We see all of these horrible things going on, and we want to do something about them. But there aren't many places where a person can do something, and so we get sucked up into things like Max's idea of taking over the government."

Tensing, Chris stared in surprise. "I wouldn't say I got *sucked in.* I went in because—"

Winnie didn't hear. "I guess it was partly because I loved the guy. Man, how I loved him. But I woke up—and how I woke up! When they began talking about killing people and the guillotine, and all that. Max said it was going to be a peaceful revolution and I believed the guy and went along with him. I still love him. I can't help it. I spent every weekend on his boat—until you came along."

She hastened to add: "Not that it's you. That's why I wanted to talk with you. I know people are saying things—that Max dropped me for you—"

Chris broke in. "I'm not sleeping with him!"

"—but you've got to know you didn't do anything. I'm not mad at you. I don't hold it against you. I crossed him too many times. The last time was after the meeting at the Junkery. He and Vince went out to the car to talk. I got in the back seat and they forgot I was there. They talked about holding up banks—one every day. Max said they would use only expendables. That's what he called the kids they'd send out with a gun. Max figured they might lose three or four.

152

They're hitting a bank in a couple days, their first one, the Crenshaw National. They've got to raise a lot of money fast. Max said if they had money, they've got all kinds of opportunities, such as getting some of the white mercenaries who fought for Tshombe in Katanga."

"Katanga?"

"You know, when they tried to break away from the Congo some years back. Well, I got to thinking after hearing Max talk about expendables, got to thinking they were no better than the corrupt politicians and all the others. I thought to myself, why, Winnie, you fool, you're just trading one crowd for another—"

Chris interrupted. "You're all mixed up, Winnie. You're—"

"Am I? You're saying that because you're supposed to. They don't care about the poor or the blacks or the ghettos. I've been going out to Saugus and listening to the Jesus freaks. They're with it, and maybe I'll work with them. I got to thinking about Mom and Dad, and how they'd worked hard to put me through school, and maybe they had something when they said the way to do it was to get into community affairs and politics and scrap and fight to change things. I don't know, maybe I'll try that."

"I think you are confused," Chris said quietly. "You don't know what you're saying. It's dangerous what you're saying."

"I don't care. I don't care about anything since I lost Max. I had to talk with someone, I've been so wound up. I couldn't with Tico, that's for sure. Did you know she carries a gun in her purse, a Saturday Night Special? Did you know that? I've been doing a lot of thinking about you, trying to figure out why you're in this. You're quiet and considerate and kind. I thought maybe it was Max . . ."

For a moment Chris was thrown. "Considerate and kind? I hope so. But kindness is helping the most people, helping them even if some die in the doing. That's what kindness is, Winnie. To die, that many may live."

"You sound like Max," Winnie retorted. "Like you're repeating him. Not like you. I don't believe it's you. You're someone else acting a part. Now aren't you?"

Chris felt the coldness creep through her body. "I don't know how to tell you—"

"You needn't. I know. Why don't we both haul out of here? I've got friends in Seattle—"

"For Heaven's sake, don't talk like that! You know what'll happen."

"Who cares? Anyway, Max wouldn't do anything, not after what we've been to each other."

Long afterwards, long after she had got the message to Barney about the Crenshaw National Bank, she sat in her car, rigid behind the driver's seat, the doors locked, in the pitch dark of a moonless night, wondering about Winnie. She had appeared very much herself, very natural, and while outspoken, that was her way. Yet the thought could not be pushed completely out of mind that Winnie had been instructed by Max—or more likely Tico, since this was Tico's kind of trick—to test Chris's reaction to a proposal for defection.

41

SAC, WASHINGTON FIELD. INFORMANT C-77 HAS ADVISED SUBJECTS REPORTED IN CONTACT WITH WHITE MERCENARIES RECRUITED 1960–1963 BY MOISE TSHOMBE FOR KATANGA SECESSION FROM DEMOCRATIC REPUBLIC OF THE CONGO. FOLLOWING LEADS SET FORTH: REQUEST STATE DEPARTMENT TO ASK U.S. EMBASSY IN KINSHASA IF PRESENT WHEREABOUTS OF SUCH MERCENARIES KNOWN. REQUEST NAMES, HOME ADDRESSES AND NATIONALITIES OF MERCENARY LEADERS IF KNOWN. REQUEST CHECK OF OTHER U.S. EMBASSIES THAT MIGHT HAVE KNOWLEDGE OF CURRENT ACTIVITIES OF AFORESAID MERCENARIES.

SAC, LOS ANGELES

WHEN CHRIS CAME up the ramp at 7:30 A.M. carrying her small overnight case, the plane was a burst of golden light. The sun's slanting rays, casting a sheen over the immediate world, dispelled her vivid dramatization during the night of all that might happen to her.

The first girl aboard, Chris examined the stewardesses' kit. Everything was in place, the aspirin, the earplugs (for those passengers who

154

needed them for take-off), the acid counteractants for hangovers, the baby kit with the nursing bottle, and other sundries. Walking to the coach galley, she checked the magazine racks and the upright seats, and arriving in the kitchen, tallied the breakfast trays which numbered 125.

For the last half hour she had loitered about the passenger counter but no Max had materialized, and she had grown increasingly nervous. He had awakened her about 1 A.M. to inform her he would meet her at 7:15 at check-in to give her a small package for delivery in Chicago. She had been in a foul mood. "You call me in the middle of the night to tell me that!"

For the next three hours she tossed, then at 4 dragged herself out, showered, dressed, drank a pot of black coffee, and put a note on the refrigerator door telling Roz they were out of bacon.

A puffing Sarah Cashin, her midriff tire showing through her uniform, arrived, followed within minutes by the other girls. At 7:45 A.M. the "peeps" trooped in, yawning, sleepy-eyed, and heavy tongued. Each had had his baggage examined in a routine search for weapons and explosives, and had personally been steered past a metal detection device.

A few minutes before take-off, the passenger agent entered to report that the manifest showed 119 passengers on the flight. He handed Chris a quarter-inch-thick, four-by-six envelope addressed to her that had been mysteriously left on the check-in counter.

He was curious, and even more so when she did not open it. "I brought it in without putting it through for examination."

She smiled weakly. "It's a birthday gift."

"Mind opening it?"

She hesitated a moment. "It's . . . it's quite personal."

He thought that over, then shrugged. "If you say so," he said and left. She leaned against a seat, breathing hard, and had to ask a passenger talking to her to repeat himself.

Then the ramp door was closed, a quick thrust of power vibrated through the cabin as the pilot tested, and the A stewardess in first class was saying over the intercom: ". . . seat backs must remain upright and seat belts fastened . . . please observe the no smoking sign until we are airborne . . ."

As senior B stewardess in coach, Chris demonstrated the use of the life jacket and pointed out the exit doors. She went quickly then to the lavatory where she carefully examined the package. The clasp was fastened but not sealed. She opened the envelope, and using tissue, extracted a small carton that held a reel of magnetic recording tape. She had an instant reaction: Why would Max Hartman risk placing his voice on tape? Did he not know that his voice pattern could identify him almost as conclusively as his fingerprints?

Returning to the passengers, she picked up a raft of magazines from the rack, slipped the envelope inside *Esquire,* which she kept on the bottom, and started passing them out. Midway, a conservatively dressed man, nondescript except for a Charles de Gaulle nose, asked if the plane would pass over Four Corners. Handing him *Esquire,* she said she would inquire of the pilot. He was seated next to a big-eyed, restless, overweight teen-age girl whose curious gaze followed and unnerved Chris. All she needed was for a child to spy on her.

While Chris helped Sarah get breakfast organized, the agent went to the lavatory where he remained several minutes. On his return, he handed her the magazine and thanked her. Without moving, Chris removed the package and dropped it into the purse she had placed on a bottom galley shelf.

So far so good.

The flight was smooth, the passengers pleasant, and Sarah was laughing and bantering by the time they had finished serving breakfast. Chris, mentally and physically exhausted, had to force herself to respond. If she could get away for a few days . . . but she was a prisoner, a prisoner of the Committee, the FBI, and her own conscience.

With rapidity, Chicago shaped up below as a child's very bad plaster of Paris model. In the distance lay a deceptively quiet Lake Michigan with a packed expressway curving along its shore, the Chicago River a dark polluted ribbon unrolling through a downtown area, and two fantastic, circular skyscrapers called irreverently the Corn Cobs by the natives.

"We welcome you to Chicago," the A stewardess said. ". . . please check on your personal belongings and remain seated until the plane comes to a complete stop . . ."

The FBI agent left with the other passengers and disappeared. Exiting by Gate F-3, Chris turned right and passed under a white-on-solid-blue sign, To TERMINAL AND BAGGAGE CLAIM, then along a concourse lighted on both sides by colorful advertisements. Carrying her case, she took clipped, decisive steps, but did not unduly hurry. Any minute she expected a stranger to intercept her. With effort, she kept her eyes straight ahead. Her heart beat increasingly hard and her lips were dry. The weeks of tension, punctured with sudden fright, were telling on her. Even more telling at the moment was the fear she might err in following instructions. She alone, if she played her role right, could provide that first contact for the FBI that eventually would lead to exposure of the Chicago operations. She was in a pressure cooker, a field goal kicker in the last seconds of a tied football game.

The loudspeakers never ceased chattering. They reflected an era of noise: traffic at rush hour, jets thundering overhead, the deafening hard beat of rock, television sets turned high, everywhere a level of noise that man never before in history had had to tolerate. "Mr. Kittredge, please contact passenger service counter for a message." . . . "Miss Brown, please return to ticket desk." . . . "Miss Christina Roberts, please pick up white courtesy phone. Miss Roberts, please pick up . . ."

The voice over the phone was a girl's, pleasant but businesslike. "I'm Judy. We're happy you're here, Miss Roberts. Here's what you're to do. Keep walking and you'll come to an open space, a waiting area. You'll find a gift shop on your left. Go into it and leave your purse—you know, act like you put it down and forgot it. Put it by a big, lavender stuffed dog. Must be three feet high. Has a tag on him, twenty-eight dollars. So you forget your purse. Leave it open. You go across the way to the Blue Yonder and have a cup of coffee—but you don't look back, not once, that's very important—then you remember your purse and return for it. Have you got that, Miss Roberts?"

When Chris said she had the girl abruptly hung up, and Chris experienced disappointment. She had thought she would meet the party in person, perhaps be invited to a conference. She came with Max's blessing but apparently that was not sufficient. It was every man for himself, to test another's loyalty, integrity, and intelligence (since one might be fiercely loyal but yet betray his comrades through stupidity). She was reminded of a documentary film she had seen about the Resistance movement in France during World War II when a man chose his companions fearfully and cautiously since any one of them could be his ultimate executioner.

Pacing herself slowly, thinking, she passed a mother wheeling a baby in a stroller, an old man carrying a hang-up bag, pilots, a woman so loaded down she looked like a moving junkyard, and people speaking unidentifiable languages. Once her gaze fell and she saw nothing but attaché cases bobbing along at the end of tired arms. At last she came to a gift shop jammed with games, perfumes, model cars, belts, purses, and myriad other items that left little space for customers. The lavender dog stood out, a dog with a rascal look designed to ease the process of parting with $28. Putting her purse down between the dog's front paws, she turned to look at a belt, then sauntered out.

The Blue Yonder proved a stand-up snack bar. She got her coffee, took it to a tall, round table, and sipped it with her back to the gift shop. Only a few customers were about. A hefty man in his early thirties who wore a dark suit and tie, and avoided her glance, could have been an FBI agent.

When she returned to the gift shop, the purse was where she had left it. She patted the dog and wished he cost half of what he did. Her nephews would love him.

She headed for the main concourse, a spacious, high vaulted area where the passengers checked in. She thought O'Hare with its spotless marble-like floors, its many unique shops and pleasant restaurants, and its floor-to-ceiling glass-walled concourses, where one could look out in all directions, the most beautiful of metropolitan airports.

Casually she reached in her purse to dig out a lipstick. Her hand quit fumbling; her heart missed a beat. The package was still there, with the envelope still clasped. Stopping in the midst of traffic, with hurrying people making their way about her, darting curious and occasionally irritable glances, she nervously unclasped the envelope to find the reel of tape. Taking it out, she looked it over. As far as she could determine, it had not been disturbed.

She was mystified, bewildered, and suddenly frightened. Had she heard the instructions wrong? Had the FBI agents somehow exposed themselves?

42

ON THE BUS that took the Kennedy Expressway, she struggled to organize her jumbled thoughts. Outside the dusty window the suburbs of Chicago came into view, little two-story brick houses only a half-story wide with three and four drain pipes that created the illusion of added height, and high gable roofs to shed the winter snow, with a window in each gable, giving the homes a one-eyed effect. In the distance, rows on rows of brick chimneys stood like markers in a cemetery. Close by passed Dad's Root Beer bottling works, a homey touch on a dreary scene. No matter in what part of the world, she thought irrelevantly, big cities had the same look. They dehumanized and depressed man, and regardless of the smile mask he wore all day, his talk about opportunities and the excitement of the milling throngs, he was a fool on a dilapidated, old stage crowded with too many actors. Suddenly she wished she were with her parents in Clinton, North Carolina, back in her teen years. She knew she was not alone, that many who walked the pavements wished the same but sensed they would never return. The city grabbed and held one and few escaped. Even in death one was packed away in a sardine cemetery.

At the Palmer House, a lavish, elegant reminder of an era when opulence had not been prohibitive in cost, she learned that Sarah had already signed in. In their room on the fourth floor, Sarah had dropped clothes and spread her gear with thoughtless abandon. She was showering, a ritual good for a half hour. Each day she scrubbed as if she had come out of a coal mine.

No sooner had Chris opened the travel case than the phone rang. Thinking it would be Judy, she was unprepared for the tough, arrogant man's voice.

"Roberts?"

Instantly she resented him. "This is Christina Roberts," she answered quietly.

"Listen, the place was lousy with FBI men."

"Who's this?" she asked sharply.

"None of your damn business. We figure you tried to suck us into an FBI trap."

She was both angry and frightened but her mind ordered her to cool it. "You're crazy. I did what I was told to do. I didn't see anybody who looked like cops . . . but if you pick an airport with people everywhere . . . out in the open . . ."

Conscious Sarah was listening, she lowered her voice. "You're going through a switchboard, you know."

"I was told to kill you if I thought you were—"

"In that case, I'd better go to the police." There was no response. He had worked himself into a dead end. She continued: "Let's talk

159

sense. For one thing, I don't scare over silly stories about the FBI being around. You don't trust me, and you think if you scare me, and if I'm working with the police, I'll panic and run off."

She was paraphrasing Rip. In briefing her, he had warned that *they* might accuse her of collaborating with the authorities. It was an ancient ploy dating back to the days of the Romans and probably beyond that to Stone Age man. Accuse someone of a double cross, and in the terror of the moment, he would admit guilt by fleeing.

"Remember," Rip had said, "if they actually thought you were an informer, they wouldn't accuse you of it and give you a chance to escape. They would take immediate action."

She continued curtly: "You want the delivery and I want to make it. I've some shopping to do and I don't want to be bothered carrying it around. Tell me where you want it and I'll be there."

"Okay. I was told to give you another chance if I thought . . ." He trailed off, then said slowly, as if reading from notes: "Eleven o'clock tonight. Walk to the Washington subway station. Don't take a taxi. Go down and stand on the North Side train platform. On the wall, you'll find a wire hanger with insurance leaflets and a sign over it, *Take One.* Put the delivery back of the leaflets and take the first train north. Get off at Chicago and State and you're on your own from that point . . ."

43

IN THE Los Angeles Crenshaw area, Operation Holdup began at 5 that morning when two FBI agents in work clothes pulled up in a dilapidated pick-up truck before the Crenshaw National Bank, and unloaded three carpenter's horses. They proceeded to block the bank's front door, and post a sign that read: *DOOR BEING RE-PAIRED—PLEASE USE BACK ENTRANCE—SORRY FOR IN-CONVENIENCE.* Few customers would read the sign since most entered from the parking lot through the big, glass back doors.

At 6 A.M. twenty agents gathered in the field office for a briefing. Rip used a floor plan chalked on a blackboard to indicate where each agent would post himself and what his moves would be during the holdup. Rip himself had awakened the bank manager at 2 A.M. who informed him that the tellers had been instructed, if confronted by a demand for money, to turn over all cash quickly, and as they did so, to press a button beneath the counter which would flash a red light on the desks of two officials and activate overhead cameras at each end of the bank. In turn, one of the officers would push a button that would notify a branch bank that a holdup was in progress. At the co-operating bank, officers and secretaries would immediately call a long list of numbers, starting with the FBI and police.

At the briefing conference, two different plans were formulated: One in case the holdup was conducted by a lone person, the other if more than one were involved.

At 7 A.M. Rip and two other agents sauntered through the back entrance, one at a time, and settled down for the grueling wait. Rip seated himself behind the vice-president's desk, out in the open, behind a railing, where he could see every teller's window. (They still called them windows although in most modern banks, such as this one, tellers worked behind a counter.) He pretended to study an assortment of papers provided him by the manager.

The tellers and other employees drifted in a few minutes before 8:15, and were admitted by an assistant cashier who locked the door after each person entered. A bank official watched the door from his desk, ready to push the silent alarm button notifying the branch bank if a holdup man burst in along with an employee. For the most part the tellers were young and laughing. They remarked about what a hot day it was going to be, and what a morning it would be for the beach, and why couldn't weekends be like this? Since none knew about the possible holdup, they wondered about the agents. They looked too young to be bank examiners or from downtown headquarters.

From 9:30 on, Rip grew increasingly taut. He was fearful that despite all the planning, an innocent person might be hurt, and fearful, too, the gunman might somehow escape. These were touch-and-go situations. The unforeseen could happen swiftly, and split-second decisions could be wrong and perhaps tragic. He didn't fight down the fear. A little fear was good for a man. It kept him mentally alert. Errors came more from complacency and overconfidence.

Ten o'clock came, and a small swarm of customers who had been waiting restlessly, entered, and for the next ten minutes the tellers were busy. Then the traffic slackened.

161

At 10:28, he came, young, slight of build and slow-moving. Despite the heat, he wore a jacket with a turned-up collar, big, dark sunglasses, and a floppy hat that partly concealed his face. He was in faded, patched blue jeans and had hair to his shoulders. Rip could not have told how he knew this was the man. Perhaps it was because he appeared up-tight, not casual the way a customer usually is, and kept darting glances about. Perhaps it was the small cardboard box he carried. He made his way directly to the commercial window and waited for a matronly woman to complete her business.

Not moving, Rip looked about for an accomplice but found none. When the red light came on next to the intercom, he headed straight for the back door, and pushing one of the big glass panels aside, shouted: "I'll be right with you, Joe." He went then to a nearby writing table, almost directly behind the holdup man, and pretended to add up a column of figures. The teller, a buxom girl with a big, round face, turned to an older woman who was working the adjoining window, and Rip lip read what the girl said: "I need fifty thousand. Would you get it for me, please? I can't leave my window."

Rip was certain he had a gun on the girl, probably held close to him, partly concealed. Barely nodding, the older woman locked her cash drawer and disappeared in the direction of the vault.

Outside, once Rip had shouted the code words, agents cleared the parking lot of everyone in sight. One agent stopped cars from entering. Another ran to a car in which a mother holding a small child was waiting, identified himself, and ushered her and the youngster to one side of the building. Other agents were intercepting people leaving the bank and herding them to the same spot. The operation went smoothly. Sometimes it didn't. An individual might be hard of hearing, or rebellious by nature and refuse to follow orders, or think the agent was trying to rob him.

Inside, the older woman returned with several stacks of bills, each bound by a paper band that had the denomination printed on it. Offering no comment, she handed them to the girl who started to count out the bills. "One hundred, two, three . . ." She stopped abruptly, and Rip knew the man had reached for the money. He turned swiftly, at the same time stuffing the bills into the box, and passed Rip.

162

Rip followed him out of the bank. The plan was to take him outside in the cleared parking lot, where no uninvolved person would be hurt if a struggle or gun battle should develop.

As agents approached from each side, Rip called out: "We're Federal officers. Hold it where you are. Don't move."

Rip's command pulled the man about in one swift turn. He stared, petrified, then conscious of an agent moving in on his left, broke into a run. The agent tried to seize him but missed. The man swung about, raised a hand, and fired at the agent, then at Rip who crouched low and ran for the protection of a car. Far out on his periphery of vision, Rip caught a boy of about ten entering the parking lot, and heard an agent shouting at him to get back. But the boy only stood and watched.

Once more Rip called out for the youth to surrender, shouted that they were FBI agents, but swinging about, the man fired wildly. Rip saw the boy drop.

Slowly Rip took aim, and with one shot, brought the man to a slow, staggering fall, first to his knees, then he crumpled, and a spasm shook his body, and he released the box and some of the money fell out, and he lay still on the hot asphalt.

Rip's insides clutched. He had killed a man, and in the years ahead, in the dead of night, he would awaken, sweating, to remember this sun-scorched morning, and it would be as sharp of focus as it was this moment.

With effort, he walked toward the lifeless form lying face downward. He heard an agent calling that the boy was all right. At the first shot, the youngster had dropped of his own volition. For a moment, Rip stood over the fellow looking down on him. There was no breath. He stooped beside him, and gently, turned him over. The denim jacket fell apart, revealing a reddish stain on a tight, white pullover sweater. It seemed too small a stain for death. And then Rip saw the small, rounded breasts with the nipples showing through the thin sweater.

In time he would get her name, the address where she lived with her parents, their names, the campus where she studied, the cold facts that people would read in their newspapers. In time he would forget the facts, even her name, but never the sweet intelligent face, the boyish body not yet fully matured, the dark stain creeping across the white sweater.

163

And he wondered: Wasn't there anyone close to her who could have talked with her, stopped her? Told her that her cause was to be admired, and her wild longing to help the hungry and needy, but her method was wrong, that destruction in itself destroyed the very ends she sought? That love died under the trampling of hate? That in Northern Ireland the hate of centuries had polarized an entire people, and more centuries might pass before the love of one's fellow man, regardless of beliefs or faith, might return?

Someone. A history or philosophy or sociology professor? He guessed not. Some of them were preaching revolution. He wished to God they could have watched the ambulance attendants come and tie her up in a bag and cart her off.

And the exploiters! The Max Hartmans who sucked them up into the vortexes of their ruthless bids for power.

An expendable. A kid with a cause.

44

DESPERATELY, Chris longed for Rip. She needed his reassurance. She was certain she had analyzed the threat correctly: that *they*— those unseen, mysterious revolutionists she invariably termed *they*— hoped to strip her mental processes naked by a machiavelian scheme of pure terror. Yet she could be wrong. She had no background for intrigue. She knew nothing of the psychology of one individual turning the screws on another.

All of a sudden she realized she wanted more from Rip than his counsel. The bright memory of that moment yesterday when the copter turned and headed back toward them suffused her with a happy glow. His arms were about her, he was pressing her softly, his lips near hers, the warmth of his breath on her cheek, his big frame covering her from the sight of the pilot. She tried to remember: Had he backed off the second the copter disappeared, or had he held her a brief moment longer, as if he could not let her go? Her body grew warm with the memory which was as vivid as the event itself.

When she returned she would break with Jim. For a long time, she had known she no longer loved him, if she ever had. She liked and admired him, and enjoyed tremendously being with him, but a friendship, no matter how close, was far from the love of a girl for a man. She had longed to be in love, and Jim had happened on the scene. She had liked him better than any man she knew, and slowly had persuaded herself that she loved him.

Sarah emerged from the bathroom in bra and pants. Scrounging around in her case for a freshly laundered slip, she cast curious glances at Chris. Unlike Roz, Sarah would ask no questions and offer no advice. Chris struggled for a total recall of what Sarah had heard, then decided to offer no lies by way of explanation.

The question of how to escape from Sarah tonight was solved when Captain Mayberry called. Sarah answered and the captain, a pleasant quiet individual in his late forties, asked if she and Chris would like to dine and see the show at the Ambassador East. The three had often gone Dutch on their layovers, the two girls insisting on paying their share down to a penny. They needed an escort to a night club, and appreciated it when he offered to accompany them. Some stewardesses took advantage of the men aboard their craft. They would let them pay the bills, to the point where many captains ignored the girls. Chris begged off, reporting that she was dining with old friends but Sarah accepted.

When Sarah went shopping a short time later, Chris stretched out on the bed to study the situation. Surely the FBI must be monitoring the phone calls to the room, and hence, would know of the arrangement for the delivery. Surely, too, the Chicago Committee would have no reason to harm her if she made the delivery as instructed and if *they* had no reason to suspect an FBI trap. Surely the FBI agents running the surveillance on her would be discreet.

Surely, surely—but not all the surelys were that.

Since she had never ridden the Chicago subway, she had no idea what the physical lay-out would be. She would take it slow and easy, and subdue her usual compulsion to hurry. By nature, she had to move fast, do everything in a rush, whether it was washing dishes, serving meals in the cabin, or sewing.

It occurred to her that a thief might grab her purse with the package inside. If she struggled she might be slugged. After mulling this over, she decided she would carry the package in the open. A nondescript package would have no allure.

It was possible, of course, that she might be intercepted on State Street before reaching the subway. Why, otherwise, had she been ordered to go to a station several blocks from the Palmer House when only a short distance away was an entrance?

She fell asleep, and was still sleeping when Sarah returned at 5.

At 10:30 P.M. she walked out of the State Street entrance to the Palmer House. The heat from the pavement struck her as if she were stoking a smelter furnace. No air was stirring and with the high humidity, she felt as if she were in a Turkish bath. In her left hand she carried her purse and in the right, clutched tightly, the package.

State Street lacked the glamour of New York's Madison or Fifth avenues, and the history and romance of Paris's Champs Élysées but it was beautiful in a modern, Midwestern fashion, the street wide, clean, well lighted, and by day crowded with more shoppers than in most downtown areas. Here there had been no flight to the suburbs by the big, fashionable department stores and shops.

Not too many people were about. It was too early for the show crowds, too late for the night shoppers. Passing her were a young couple, hand in hand, four high school fellows talking animatedly, two middle-aged men speaking Spanish, an Italian woman with a scarf about her head, a college-age student with a guitar who was idly plucking the strings and singing softly to himself, and two older couples discussing an R-rated movie they had just seen. ("Anyone with a shape like hers ought to wear clothes," said one woman.)

Then her eyes were drawn to a girl standing before the Carson Pirie Scott department store. The girl, in jeans and deck shoes, with her shirt hanging out, and her hair below her shoulders, walked toward her. She seemed little more than a child, surely not more than fourteen, with the saddest face Chris thought she had ever seen.

"Ma'am," said the girl in a low voice, "I hate to beg but I'm hungry. I'm awfully hungry."

Unprepared for this, Chris hesitated. "Did you want anything else?"

The girl looked bewildered, then started away. "Hold on," Chris said, reaching into her purse.

"Where're you from, hon?" she asked, handing her a dollar bill.

The girl was near tears. "Thank you, ma'am. Thank you very much. Down in Indiana. Near Crawfordsville. I'll send you the dollar back if you'll give me your name and address."

Chris shook her head. The girl was looking past Chris, to the right of her. "I think a man's following you, ma'am. He's looking in a window but he's faking it."

166

"A young man?"

"About fifty, I'd guess."

"By himself?"

"I'd say so."

"Thank you for telling me. Have you a place to stay tonight?"

The question startled the girl. "God bless you," she said. "I gotta go now. God be with you, ma'am." She darted away, a fugitive, one more flower child, like other thousands roaming the streets of the cities.

Continuing to the subway, Chris fought down an urge to glance back. She was convinced the party following her was from the Chicago Committee. Behind him somewhere, or across the street, were FBI agents who by now would have detected him. She prayed he had not spotted them.

Suddenly she was alone in the tile-lined stair well leading down into the subway. Her shoes tapped out a warning. She should have paused at the entrance until others were going down. She must never let herself be caught anywhere alone. Nearing the bottom, she heard footsteps joining hers. In a fleeting, backward glance, she saw a middle-aged man lumbering down toward her.

Then she was in the subway proper, passing columns encased in black marble, with fluorescent lighting that was bright as day. She bought a ticket to Chicago and State, and following the signs, came to the North Side platform. A train was pulling in with mounting clatter of metal on metal and rush of air as the electropneumatic mechanism automatically brought the train to a stop. As if drawn by a magnet, her eyes went to the pamphlet rack, then scanned the waiting passengers: a man in shabby-looking clothes, a college-age fellow, a young Japanese couple, an Indian woman in a sari, three girls chattering away, several workmen finished with their shifts, and a big, heavy-set man with a violin case.

Her feet heavy, she walked to the rack where she turned her body to block out the view of the passengers. She suffered a moment of panic when she discovered the rack packed tightly with brochures. She removed a handful, enough to work the package in. Turning back, she surprised the college-age fellow ogling her, but realized he was interested only in her legs.

Alone in a subway office, deserted because of the hour, an agent watched her on a closed circuit television set. There were no agents

167

on the platform, only a television camera hidden high above. He said into a microphone: "The informant is boarding the fourth coach from the rear. No one has approached the rack. The train is pulling out. Time: 11:06."

His voice reflected his tension and that of other agents working the double surveillance. Washington had given strict instructions: Under no circumstances were they to be *made*—that is, discovered— by the subject or subjects, that the case was of the utmost importance to the security of the nation and penetration of the Chicago Committee an absolute must. If they could identify one link, then usually that link would lead by surveillance to others. If they blew it tonight . . . no one wanted to think of the consequences.

At the next stop, Grand and State, two agents boarded the train to continue the physical surveillance of the informant. They entered the third coach from the rear and one made his way to the fourth where he sat down at the far end, on the same side as Chris who was midway. The coach carried only a scattering of passengers.

The agent monitoring the television set said into the microphone: "A man is heading for the rack, stopping a few feet from it, looking around. Now he takes the package from the rack and slips it inside a folded newspaper. He is in his fifties, about six feet, slender build, receding hair, high forehead, prominent nose, dark bearded, wears glasses, regular shirt open at collar, pen fastened in shirt pocket and something that could be a glasses case, trousers pleated with cuffs, narrow belt. Subject is boarding third car from rear. The train is pulling out. Time: 11:36."

At the Grand and State station, one agent boarded the second coach from the rear, one the third, and another, the fourth. They began a drifting pattern. The agent in the second car moved to the third, the agent in the third to the fourth, and the agent in the fourth to the second. The subject sat near one end with a middle-aged couple on his right and a family of four, including two teen-age daughters, on his left. He sat hunched, his head on his chest, pretending to doze. He held the newspaper on his lap, both hands resting on it. The agents noted that he was younger than he had appeared on television, possibly in his mid-forties, and most likely wore a wig. He had a bad, knife-like scar on the lobe of his left ear. The agents scrutinized the passengers in each car they entered for an accom-

168

plice, and kept on guard for a surveillance being run on themselves.

At the Clark and Division stop, he continued to doze, seemingly, then a second before the doors closed, darted out. The agent in the same car made no effort to follow. The agents in the second and fourth cars, who in anticipation of such a move had positioned themselves at the doors at each stop, stepped out. One went ahead of the subject up the steps, the other was only a few feet behind. The one ahead stopped to buy a newspaper. The one behind, hurrying, passed the subject, and now the one with the newspaper became the trail man.

For the first time, the subject appeared nervous. Repeatedly he stopped to glance furtively about. He appeared unsure of the direction he should take. His delay was welcomed. Mobile units had followed the subway route on parallel streets but they had been delayed by traffic, and it would be a few minutes before they arrived and could begin their maneuvers.

The agents passed out of the subject's view. The one ahead turned into an all-night grocery, the one behind took off in the opposite direction, eventually to step into a recessed store entrance.

Apparently satisfied, the subject headed west on Division. He walked slowly, as if his feet hurt. Stopping once before a store window, he covertly reconnoitered his rear. Then a heavy gust sent papers blowing along the street, high as face level, forcing him to bow his head and quit his reconnaissance. The agent emerged from the grocery with a small sack. The other agent appeared on the opposite side of the street, far in the rear.

Shortly afterwards, the subject turned down a dark, almost deserted side street which was flanked with apartment buildings, a few old, most of them contemporary.

The agent with the sack followed at a discreet distance, and was greatly relieved when Unit 10, a dark, dusty sedan driven by a lone agent, passed him and then the subject. At the next corner, it turned to the right and disappeared from sight. At the same time Unit 17 turned into the street and headed toward the subject. It parked directly opposite the subject and the driver took his time getting out and locking the doors. The agent on foot came up to him and kidded him as one neighbor might another, remarking loudly that it was a great time of night for him to be getting in, how was Betty and had they heard from Bill. The subject continued to plod ahead, doggedly now, his feet apparently hurting him more with each step. The driver of Unit 17 started for the apartment house but dropped to a step where he sat quietly watching, partly hidden by shrubs. The agent resumed walking. The second foot agent entered the street on the other side.

Unexpectedly the subject turned right, and within a few steps was inside an old but well-kept brick building sandwiched ludicrously between two tall, modern ones. He entered a dimly lit vestibule, checked a bank of mailboxes, and disappeared down a corridor to the right.

45

SAC, LOS ANGELES. INFORMANT C-77 DE-LIVERED MESSAGE AT WASHINGTON AND STATE SUBWAY STATION AT 11 P.M. MESSAGE PICKED UP AT 11:32 BY UNIDENTIFIED SUBJECT. SUR-VEILLANCE CONTINUING ON SUBJECT . . .

SAC, CHICAGO

LEANING BACK in the swivel, Rip tried stretching the weariness out of his long legs. The tension of the wracking day eased, and a great, good feeling surged through the lean body that had been taut for so many hours.

Picking up the receiver, he asked the switchboard to put him through to the SAC's home. He wished instead he was calling Chris. He wanted to hear that deep, low voice, tell her of his concern, and how courageous she was. She would laugh quietly and abruptly change the subject. She didn't believe in heroics and rebuffed sympathy. She had a risky job to do, and was doing it, and that was that. She was uncomplicated, unlike girls he had known who suffered from identity and other complexes. A man would always know where he stood with her. She would never secretly nurture hurt or disappointment.

Teletype dated the next morning:

SAC, LOS ANGELES. SUBJECT WHO ACCEPTED DELIVERY FROM C-77 IDENTIFIED AS RONALD

ASTERISKAN, FREE LANCE NEWS PHOTOGRA-
PHER. ARRESTED CHICAGO POLICE 8-24-68
RESISTING POLICE OFFICER, ACQUITTED. AR-
RESTED CHICAGO POLICE 9-17-68 INDECENT
EXPOSURE IN CONNECTION WITH DEMONSTRA-
TION IN RANDOLPH PARK, ACQUITTED. AR-
RESTED WASHINGTON, D.C., POLICE 10-6-69
INCITING TO RIOT, ACQUITTED. APPEARED
12-7-69 BEFORE HOUSE COMMITTEE ON IN-
TERNAL SECURITY IN JEANS, BARE WAISTED,
WITH BREASTS AND NIPPLES PAINTED IN PSY-
CHEDELIC DESIGN. DESCRIPTION FOLLOWS . . .

SAC, CHICAGO

Teletype dated two days later:

SAC, LOS ANGELES. SUBJECT RONALD ASTERIS-
KAN CONTACTED JAMES RANDOLPH LINCOLN
AT 9:40 A.M. TODAY. LINCOLN IDENTIFIED AS
FOLLOWER MARTIN LUTHER KING AND LEADER
IN POVERTY MOVEMENT. CHECK ALL INDICES
CHICAGO PROVED NEGATIVE. FRIENDS AND
LAW-ENFORCEMENT OFFICERS DESCRIBE LIN-
COLN AS NON-VIOLENT MILITANT ENGAGED IN
CAUSE OF WELFARE REFORM AND MORE HELP
FOR NEEDY AND GHETTOS. REPORTED TO HAVE
CONSIDERABLE FOLLOWING AMONG BOTH
BLACKS AND WHITES. REPORTED GOOD POSSI-
BILITY COULD ENLIST ONE HUNDRED THOU-
SAND IN MARCH ON WASHINGTON. ALL SOURCES
ADVISE LINCOLN WOULD OPPOSE ANY REVO-
LUTIONARY MOVEMENT. RESULTS OF CONVER-
SATION BETWEEN SUBJECT AND LINCOLN
UNKNOWN. LINCOLN'S DESCRIPTION FOL-
LOWS . . .

SAC, CHICAGO

Taped telephone conversation the same day between the SAC,
Los Angeles, and Assistant Director Markinson, Washington:

171

MARKINSON: We have a report from the State Department, out of the embassy in Kinshasa, reflecting that an individual by the name of Henri Brouay who lives in Brussels acts as a mail drop and a clearing house for European mercenaries. Tshombe was in direct contact with him, both at the time of the civil war and again in 1964 when Tshombe became Congo premier and called back his hired soldiers. State reports, too, that Brouay recruited additional mercenaries when an unsuccessful rebellion was staged in the eastern provinces of the Congo in 1967. Some of the mercenaries are dead, of course, but many have worked here and there, a few in Angola, some in Mozambique, and some in the Sudan. State advises that some are from the French Foreign Legion and all are crack professionals. State says it has a contact in Brussels who has furnished accurate intelligence in the past and he may be able to identify the party who is recruiting for the Committee or acting as a go-between.

SAC: I don't suppose it would be any trick to get quite a few mercenaries into this country if they came in through different ports of entry one at a time . . .

MARKINSON: Not at all—unless we can get photos. They'll be coming in under aliases on forged passports with forged visas, and I imagine some will move across the Canadian and Mexican borders. If the informant does come up with pictures or has descriptions setting forth scars, birthmarks, or other highly identifiable characteristics—

SAC: It's possible. We believe she's definitely established as a courier and will be carrying messages regularly to the affiliates. Ripley thinks the Chicago delivery was a final test—to assure themselves of her loyalty and that she was not being followed. He believes the messages after this will be written or typed, and that they sent the reel through to Chicago because they didn't want her to know the contents before they were sure of her. By the way, the agent on the plane doesn't think a voice was on the tape. He thinks—from a quick examination—that it contained a message written on it with a non-visible chemical solution.

MARKINSON: Any chance the informant might fly to Washington soon and make contact with the Directory? The President's about to blow his stack.

SAC: She's due out in two weeks but she's trying to switch dates with another stewardess and get out sooner.

MARKINSON: Couldn't you ask United to help . . . No, I guess

172

you better not. If we start asking favors, the word might get around. We're furnishing the Secret Service with summaries since this may involve the security of the President.

SAC: Have you considered the risk involved? It wouldn't take much deduction by Hartman, if somehow he got hold of a summary, to figure out where the information was coming from. I'm not inferring that the Secret Service . . . but if there are too many summaries floating around . . . after all, we don't know but what someone high in the government may be involved.

MARKINSON: The Bureau has impressed upon the Secret Service the absolute necessity for secrecy, and the Secret Service has advised us that the summaries will be available only to the highest echelon.

46

WHEN SHE WAS settled in the car seat beside Max, she said: "Some guy threatened to kill me in Chicago."

Play-by-play she reported on her trip while he raced the car over the Harbor Freeway toward downtown Los Angeles. He heard her out, then sympathized. "I don't go for that, Chris, and I'll find out who the guy was who threatened you, and tell him off."

He took his time lighting a cigarette. "You do need all kinds in a revolution, of course. Intellectuals, naturally, to guide the movement and lay out the plans, and technicians to organize and plot the mechanics—and thugs and terrorists and anarchists. And the wild ones are important. Somebody has to blow up places, and kill, and get shot at. If you study revolutions, you discover, though, that when the intellectuals and technicians take over, they phase out the thugs and terrorists.

"Take Tico. She's got guts, drive, and determination. But she's got to settle down once we get in, and between us I don't think she can. She's a born anarchist, and I'm sure we'll have to get rid of her. Do I shock you, darling?"

She laughed nervously. She didn't understand, and never would, how any man could admire a woman and have sexual relations with her while knowing all the time it might be necessary one day to

173

murder her. She could understand how a man might compartmentalize his mind but how could he regiment his feelings? Did he have none? Did he only simulate laughter and anger and pleasure in sex on orders from a highly disciplined mind that programed the emotions?

She recalled what Rip once had said about Tico. "She has a blind, raging hostility toward authority. We all, of course, have ambivalent feelings toward authority. We recognize we must have it to protect ourselves from being hurt or killed by criminals, for an orderly, stable organization that makes possible the movement of goods and the conduct of business necessary to our daily living, and that guards our homes from being raided and burned and our bank accounts from being seized. Yet we also dislike authority when we disagree violently with something the President has said, a law Congress has passed which hurts us economically, when a traffic officer gives us a ticket, when taxes seem too high. With the anarchist, there is no ambivalence. It is all hate. Miss Sharman's utterly blind to any benefits of authority. Slowly through the years she has built up emotional responses that block out her intellectual processes."

Now she smiled. "Let me know when you're ready to zero that woman."

He shot her an amused glance. "You put on a good act. You wouldn't kill her if she were coming at you with a tommy gun."

"What about you? You'd fold if she stripped."

He smiled. "Thanks for reminding me. There's going to be a full moon on the ocean tonight—and from my boat—after the meeting?"

"Not tonight."

"What's the matter? Don't you have feelings for a man?"

"What about Winnie?"

He gripped the wheel tightly. "That's all over."

"Since when?"

He didn't answer, a stratagem he employed to show displeasure.

He drove down a dark, wide alley somewhere in the wholesale district, and pulled up near a large furniture-moving van. From inside came muffled voices. After parking well to one side of the alley, behind several other cars, he helped her out and up a short ladder that led to the van's interior.

Inside, seated on office chairs around a card table dotted with beer and soft drink cans, coffee cups, a plastic bowl of potato chips, and a stack of thin sandwiches, were the members of the Planning Section. They said casual hellos, the way neighbors would who had dropped

174

in for the evening. The air was stagnant with smoke. Tico was never without a cigarette and Dr. Beaumont enjoyed thick, pungent cigars. Boone did not smoke. He was an inveterate gum chewer. Oscar Pederson had brought along a bottle of California wine.

Winnie Tipton was not among them. No one was to mention her absence, then or ever afterward.

Chris sat by Dr. Beaumont who patted her hand affectionately, the prerogative of an older man for a girl he liked. There was no question about his fondness for her. But if she should make a slip, would he intercede? The answer was no. He would send her to the guillotine along with the others, and find scholarly pleasure in comparing her plight to that of a historical figure.

Bill Boone pulled in the ladder, closed the back door, then walked the length of the van to tap on the partition behind the driver. Slowly the van rolled forward. A van that had no windows offered maximum security, Max would point out later. No one could eavesdrop, no neighbors could see who came and went, and the Committee need not worry about an electronic surveillance since no one, not even the members, had known until forty-five minutes prior to the meeting that a van would be the site this night.

Max said sharply to Boone: "Put that damn thing away!" Shooting Max an insolent glance, Boone shoved the grenade he had been absent-mindedly tossing, as one would a pencil, in his left trouser pocket where it bulged ominously.

"You're going to blow us all to hell some night," Max continued, then called the meeting to order. He reported that the investigation into the theft of the money was continuing. Did he intend to advise the Planning Section before the guilty party was turned over to the Zero Section? No, he did not. There would be no discussion once the guilty party was apprehended.

He reported matter-of-factly that the Committee had suffered one casualty during a bank holdup. In this particular case, the FBI had had the bank staked out. The Intelligence Section, through an informant in the police department, would determine whether the FBI had received advance information or was engaged in random stakeouts.

Chris had difficulty holding her eyes on him. To avert them, though, might indicate guilt.

Dr. Beaumont cleared his throat which indicated he wished the floor. He proceeded to deliver a lecture on the fact that other revolu-

175

tions had welcomed outside rebellious elements. Finally he got to the point. "We have set up a separate group that we will call our Friendship Section. We will invite in the manpower and the guns of the Mafia, the Black militants, the Maoists, Communists, Trotskyites, Nazis, Klansmen, and other dissident groups."

He nodded to himself, giving the matter his approval. "The inherent danger in taking into our movement such varied and often violent leaders is that each one will secretly conspire to take over, usually by assassination, once we have effected a successful revolution. If you study history carefully, you will note that such counter-coups are invariably launched—and sometimes with remarkable success—in every overthrow of a government."

Again, he nodded in concurrence. "To forestall such a counter-revolution, we have set up a time schedule. On the second day after we have seized power, the Zero Section will hunt down and assassinate every leader of these collaborating groups. There will be no exceptions. No exceptions whatsoever."

The church was vast and high-vaulted, in the tradition of the turn of the century, and the Biblical scenes in multicolored glass were brought alive on the east side by a hot, brilliant midmorning sun. Chris was alone, facing the enormous cross back of the altar. She had her eyes closed.

She moved her lips, and it was difficult to move them and utter no sound, not even a whisper. She remembered to talk slowly and not to use contractions. "They are going to raid an ordnance depot. They did not say where and did not discuss details. Max asked only for approval which was voted. Bill Boone will be in charge. He said all the plans had been worked out. He talked like the raid would take place soon, maybe in a day or two."

She stopped. Someone had entered. Covertly she glanced back. An older woman had seated herself in the last row.

Chris continued: "Max said they had somebody in the police department who would find out if someone tipped you off so you could stake out the Crenshaw bank. Could the police know? Did you tell them? If Winnie remembers she told me . . ."

She moistened her dry lips and shifted her position to relieve her aching leg muscles. "Tico brought up the subject of kidnaping for ransom, and Max has always been opposed, but he said he would reconsider. He said the Tupamaros have raised millions. He asked Pederson to pick out the best bet and draft the mechanics."

A personable young couple, barely out of their teens, passed down the aisle, and seated themselves in the front row. The man glanced back at her, and for a fleeting moment she thought she recognized him from somewhere, then decided her hyperactive imagination had gone too far.

"One more thing. I must talk with you. I need your help. I told you about the black girl, Winnie. Well, she told me she was getting out. Max would call it defecting, and would expect me to tell him or he would think I was covering for her. I cannot tell him, Rip, because if I did I would be condemning her to death. I thought you would know some way out—for me and for her. If you think we should talk about this, will you leave a message at Barney's? I am terribly worried."

Taking a deep breath, she rose unsteadily. She waited for the blood to course smoothly again in her legs and for the muscles to work out the knots. Head bowed, she said a silent prayer, asking God to give her strength, repeating long-forgotten phrases from out of her childhood.

As she started for the door, she observed the young man watching her. Averting her eyes, she continued walking softly down the aisle.

What was it that Rip had said? "You are a striking woman, Miss Roberts, and people are going to stare at you, both men and women. You've probably taken it in stride in the past, not noticing especially. So don't think now that every time a man looks at you he's a threat. Don't worry because someone stares at you."

Nevertheless, she did.

47

WHEN SHE RETURNED to the apartment, the phone was ringing. Max demanded to know where she had been, and she answered truthfully. He appeared satisfied. He had only contempt for organized religion. He would take his boat out on the ocean until he was out of sight of men, and find solace in the quiet, the sun, the air, and the great waves.

"They are my gods," he said. When she remarked that this was nature worship, he agreed. "I'm a savage in many ways. I think primitive man was a great man. He was direct, took what he wanted, worked only enough to live, and worshiped gods he could see, not a mythical creator floating around somewhere up in the heavens."

Max asked if she would like to go for a ride, and she was dressed and waiting when she thought to check the refrigerator door. There she found a message from Roz: "Chris—I love you, gal, but things have changed and I'm leaving the first of the month. Got another apartment six blocks from here. Sorry. Roz."

She dropped into a breakfast table chair and closed her eyes. Slowly the world she loved was slipping away. Roz was her last close friend. She had stalled the others too many times. She had even lost her nephews. They never phoned, and when she did, they had little to say, hurt in the belief she no longer cared for them.

When Max honked—she detested men who demanded that a girl come at the sound of a horn—she stood up and stretched, took a deep breath, and slipping on a smile, went hurrying to the car. He drove straight to the Junkery. He was in one of his ugly moods and by now she knew better than to engage in random talk.

At the Junkery, two young people were looking over a Roman column from a film set. Without explanation, Boone informed them he was closing. The man insisted he wanted to buy the column. Boone repeated he was closing, and the couple, angry and puzzled, left. Swinging shut the rusty iron gate, Boone padlocked it, and nodding to Chris and Max to follow, led the way to the ramshackle, old house at the rear. In daylight it looked even worse. Not in decades had a paint brush been put to it.

"Reason I asked you along," Max said to Chris, "I want you to know our entire set-up."

Nervously Chris fondled the cross at her throat. She was fully aware she had worked herself into an even more dangerous position than she had originally anticipated. Each day, because she was Max's favorite of the moment, she learned more about the operation.

"Are you all set for the ammo raid?" Max asked Boone who nodded. He did not like to be checked on.

Inside they followed a path through the junk-crowded room where the Planning Section had met weeks before. At the far end, on the left, Boone pulled out an ornate, antique highboy that covered an opening only three boards wide. It was low and they bent to step into

178

a long narrow room that reminded her of a high school chemistry laboratory. It reeked with acrid odors. Gasping for breath, she glanced about for a window, but there was none. A lone, low-wattage light, with an old-fashioned office shade, hung high in mid-center.

"Been making TNT," Boone said proudly, addressing her. He took two beakers from a table. "You put 76 percent sulfuric acid, 23 percent nitric acid and a little water in this beaker, and in this one—"

Max interrupted. "Damn you, Boone, how many times have I got to tell you, don't make the stuff. We'll buy it. You're going to blow yourself up one of these days."

Boone glowered at him, then smiling at her, picked up a receptacle. "Tri-iodide. You have to keep it wet. You let it dry and breathe on it, and . . ."

Max shuddered, took a map of Washington, D.C., from his inside coat pocket, and spread it out. "Here are the bridges I told you about. These two are the most important—the 14th Street ones. They carry nearly all the traffic between the Pentagon, which is over here in Virginia, and the capital."

The Pentagon, the world's largest office building with its seventeen and a half miles of corridors and 30,000 employees, housed the Department of Defense. Max believed if he could control all lines of communication emanating from it, he could partly control the Army, Navy, and Air Force. Only partly since the Department of Defense had spilled over into fifty other buildings in Washington.

He continued: "You don't have to blow them up but just put them out of operation. If you start work after dark that night, how long do you think it would take if you had ten or twelve men who knew explosives?"

"Hour. Maybe two."

"All right. Now we are trying to isolate the Pentagon for a few hours. If the people can't get across the 14th Street bridges, they'll go north to the Arlington Memorial, Theodore Roosevelt and Francis Scott Key bridges. So you'll knock them out in that order. Now, here, miles to the south, is Woodrow Wilson but forget it. You won't have time. But I'd like you later, if you've got the men, to blow up the approaches to the bridges over the Anacostia, starting with the Douglas and the 11th Street ones, and moving north—"

Boone interrupted. "I gotta know what kind of bridges they got back there. Makes a difference in how I tamp 'em. Some fellows don't

179

know how to tamp." He walked over to the wall where he had taped crude sketches of T-beam, concrete cantilever, truss, and other types of bridges. Indicating one of the drawings, he continued: "With a stringer bridge, I put the charge here and here. And I tamp them here with wooden braces and this one with sandbags. You understand, Miss Roberts, why I have to know what kind of bridge?"

She nodded.

"She'll bring detailed photographs from Washington next week," Max told him, "and we'll have about forty soldiers of fortune coming in who fought in Katanga. Some are experts with explosives and others at seizing and holding bridges."

Boone was disinterested. "Bridges are harder to blow up than buildings," he explained to Chris. "They build 'em to stand up under stress. You set a charge not right, and the explosion goes out into the air."

"I wouldn't have thought of that," she said. "You sure have to know what you're doing."

Boone brightened. "Buildings are hard to blow up, too. Some of these fellows put a plastic bomb in a rest room and all it does is blow a coupla johns out the window. You don't do it that way. You put your charge at the weakest point of the foundation and tamp it so the explosion hits the foundation."

He turned to Max. "Just one thing . . ." He hesitated, frowning. "I didn't have any buildings in Vietnam anything like as big as we're talking about. Only way I can be absolutely sure is to try one or two here first."

Max shook his head. "That would alert the authorities and get everybody shook up. We'll get pictures and plans of the buildings we want you to blast—the Department of Justice, the police head-quarters, the others—and you can work it out on paper."

"Watch it!" Boone exclaimed when Max touched a gallon bottle with his foot. "Methyl nitrate." He pointed to eight jars on the floor. "Enough to blow everything off a city block. Made it all myself."

"I wouldn't insure this place for a wooden nickel," Max snorted.

Boone picked up a plastic bomb to show Chris. She backed away and Boone smiled. "I wouldn't hurt you, Miss Roberts. I wouldn't hurt you."

His eyes were full of adoration. He touched her hand with his fingertips. "No, I wouldn't."

48

THEY SAT ON the warm sand of the cove, Chris and Rip, under a fog cover so thick that they "saw" only with their hearing. Her dark eyes were heavy with worry. She was in jeans, a Hawaiian shirt and sandals, and her hair was loose and blowing with the wind.

"Time means so much now," he was saying. He looked thinner than when she first met him. He lost weight on a major case, and he had little weight to lose. He was a worrier like herself but unlike her, worry was his business, to anticipate troubles and when and if they came, how to meet them.

He continued: "We block them here and there, keep them temporarily from getting the money and weapons they need, and then they've got to put off D Day, and we've bought a little extra time and can get a few more names and a little more evidence."

Wisps of fog drifted over her where she half lay in the sand with her head against a rock. Her long slender body seemed to float. He remembered the moors of *Lorna Doone,* and the heroine of his boyhood.

He told her that the man who picked up the package from the Chicago subway rack was a free lance news photographer, and a surveillance run on him had resulted in the identification of several Committee members. In turn she filled him in on details of the meeting in the van and with Boone in his laboratory. She had no further information about the raid on the unspecified ordnance depot.

"Get word to me at once through Barney if you learn anything on it, anything at all," he said. "If they get a big supply of arms and ammunition . . .

"Now about the bank holdup in which the girl was killed," he continued, "some time ago we informed the Los Angeles police we were going to stake out certain banks at random, which is true. We're doing just that. We had no occasion or reason to tell the police we had a tip on this particular bank. I have to tell you"—he hesitated a long moment—"that I killed the girl."

"Oh, Rip!" Her eyes told him that she understood his anguish.

181

"She was twenty—and I'm only nine years older—but in feelings I could've been her father. I don't want to talk about it. When do you go to Washington?"

She would be flying out at 10:30 the next morning, and Max had asked her to carry a message.

"We'll have a different agent on the plane with you," he told her. "We don't want them to see the same face twice in case they're watching you. But we'll keep the identification code. Four Corners . . . About Miss Tipton—Winnie—you can't take a chance. This could be a plant. Max Hartman may have set it up. She tells you she's going to defect and asks your advice. If you're loyal, you'll counsel her against it and then tell Hartman."

She rose and sat very straight on the rock. She said slowly, intensely: "If I went to Max, I'd be sending Winnie to her death. Don't you see that, Rip? He can't afford to gamble on a girl who knows so much."

"Neither can you. If you don't go to Hartman, and it is a plant . . . Why would she tell you all this if it isn't?"

"Look, Rip, she's a young girl and terribly emotional. She had to talk to somebody and we hit it off from the beginning. But she wouldn't have said what she did to me if she'd thought she was in danger. She doesn't think Max will do anything because of what they meant to each other."

"It could still be a plant," he repeated stubbornly. "You've got to go to Hartman."

"I can't do it," she answered, her voice rising slightly and the wind carrying it partly away. "I won't do it. I—I think you're being—"

"Heartless?" He took a deep breath and glanced anxiously about. "I am heartless. I have no choice. I've got to be cold and objective—even though I don't want to be, even though it goes against everything inside me. We're playing a game, a life-and-death game . . ."

"And Winnie doesn't matter?" She couldn't restrain her quick anger. It rose fast, and she let it show even when she knew she should not. "She doesn't matter any more than all the thousands going to their deaths matter to Dr. Beaumont? We condemn him and Max but it's all right if we kill Winnie. It's all for the good of the cause, we say. Well, that's what they say. I think we're being hypocrites. Just plain hypocrites!"

For a moment he said nothing. The hurt showed in his eyes, and transferred itself to her. It grew in her, the hurt did, but she could not and would not compromise what she believed so deeply. She hadn't known Winnie Tipton long but Winnie Tipton was a human being, not a fox to ride to the hounds. For that matter, she would not kill a fox, or any living thing, and blast all the rationalizing of man when it came to destroying life of any kind.

Rip said softly: "I know how you feel because I feel the same. But look at the facts. Miss Tipton is an intelligent person. She went into this knowing the consequences if she defected. I'm sure Dr. Beaumont and Hartman pointed them out to her just as they did with you."

She interrupted. She could not hold herself in. "She went into it because she loved a man, and she believed in it because believing is a part of love, and it was easy for her to believe because she'd gone to college at a time when some of the thinking on the campus was to wreck the Establishment, and she hadn't really thought much about what revolution meant until Max told her to get lost, and slowly it dawned on her what she was a part of. She's not a deep thinker and—"

Rip broke in impatiently. "She has been an accomplice in the commission of several criminal acts. The law doesn't care much about a person's reasoning. You're guilty of murder even if you committed the murder for love."

"Don't be ridiculous! She didn't commit murder!"

"I didn't say she did! You're being very feminine about this."

She exploded. "I don't go for women's lib, and I don't go around calling men male chauvinists—but when you say something like that . . . I'm being human, that's all, and for your information it's as much a male trait as a female one . . . I'm sorry. I shouldn't have said that. I didn't mean it the way it sounded but I get so . . . anyway, she made a mistake and she's ready to risk her life to get out and be the decent person she is. And you would arrest her—even though she changes?"

"It's not my decision," he said coldly.

"Don't tell me that, Mr. Ripley. You can recommend."

"Believe me, we're an investigative agency, not a prosecuting one. It's up to the United States Attorney to decide whether prosecution is warranted, and he makes that determination based on the facts we give him. But usually with a jury, repentance would be a mitigating factor when they consider the case."

She hadn't heard a word. "I've got it! Why don't you arrest her for speeding or marijuana possession or something. If she's in jail, Max can't get to her . . ."

"Look, Chris, I can't fake a case—and even if I did she'd be out on bond in a few hours."

His voice softened. "But that's neither here nor there. You've got to decide if you're going to Hartman, and I beg of you, Chris, in the name of God, and I say that reverently—"

"The answer's no."

"Don't make a rash decision! Give it some thought."

"Oh, sure, think about it a couple of minutes: do I risk Winnie's neck or my own?" She stopped short. "Or is it that? Maybe it's that I might wreck your case!"

He looked at her intently as though to force her to understand. "Now that you've brought it up, yes, it's the case, too. But it's not because it's my job—although it is that—but I care for my country, and a lot of people getting killed and hurt, and another generation coming up that might never know anything about being free. I know it sounds corny but where I come from we *are* a little corny. Besides—" He broke off.

"Besides what?"

"Besides—I love you."

"Oh, for Heaven's sakes!" she exclaimed in exasperation. "You drive me up the wall . . . I don't know how it's possible, but I love you, too!" After a moment she added: "I broke with Jim yesterday."

Her voice rose. "But I'm still not going to Max about Winnie. I think love is when two people disagree and still love each other, and if that isn't what you think love means . . ."

She could not finish. His arms were about her and she had little breath.

49

MEMO MARKED URGENT dictated at 1 P.M. by SA John Ripley to agents running the surveillance on Winifred Tipton:

> We have received information to the effect that the above
> subject may have defected and may be marked for assassi-
> nation. This information may be a plant in an attempt by

184

the Committee to test the credibility of the informant. However, if during the course of surveillance you have reason to believe the subject may be in danger of her life, take whatever steps necessary to protect her if you can do so *without divulging your identity to her or anyone.* It should be stressed that you are not under any circumstances to take action that might create a suspicion you are with the Bureau or working a surveillance.

SA RIPLEY

The passengers had been courteous but demanding. There had been more than the normal complement of children, mostly in the aisles. But Chris did not mind. In fact, she was only vaguely conscious of people about her. She was up in the clouds, seemingly flying without benefit of the plane. Rip loved her! The buoyancy inside her made her light-headed, dizzy. It was a joy that possessed her, and she let it flow in, deliberately screening out reality.

Shortly after she had checked in at Los Angeles International, Max had come by to hand her a plain, white, legal-sized envelope. He had said nothing, only smiled, and gone on. She left the envelope on the counter, the sealed side up, and a few minutes later an FBI agent had sauntered by, glanced casually at it, and wandered on. He had approximately forty minutes in which to obtain a duplicate envelope to give the agent boarding the plane.

Soon after take-off, the latter identified himself with the code words, Four Corners, and in the john had photographed the contents—three pages—and placed them in the new envelope. When she had left the plane, she had dropped the envelope on the macadam, stepped on it, and turned, crunching it under one foot. If Max had sealed the original in a telltale way or the texture was different, a comparison would be difficult.

In the cab from Washington's National Airport, she sat beside the driver, an older black man resigned to the tedious pace of traffic. Delivery was set for 9:30 P.M. It was now half-past 8. She reviewed the instructions: From the Hotel Sonesta at 14th and Thomas Circle she was to take a taxi to a newsstand on 14th in the I and H Street area. At the newsstand she was to place the envelope inside the front cover of the fourth copy down of *Sports Illustrated.* Max had ex-

185

plained: "I don't like personal contacts for my people. The FBI may be following the man or woman the Washington people send—and then you're identified."

While these instructions were simple, she disliked going out alone at night in a city where the statistics for rapes and muggings were unbelievable. In Washington, the stewardesses tended to venture forth in packs, and preferably in the company of the male crew.

Her thoughts drifted to Winnie. Occasionally she met someone briefly and yet experienced the feeling she had known the person for years. Could it be that she had met Winnie in a previous life? Chris liked to think she believed in reincarnation. It was exciting and frightening wondering who you had been in past centuries. A murderess? A queen? A whore? A peasant with big buttocks wed to a bore? She could understand Winnie, understand how a young, unthinking person could be swept up into something evil by one she loved. Chris herself was not too many years out of the growing-up process, and remembered how difficult it was to say *no* to a friend. Of course, with Winnie it was more than that. It was a failure to study a situation. And then, too, the thought patterns of an era would influence a girl like Winnie. So often the thinking of a people in a certain year was a fad, a hanging mob setting forth to string up all of the old idols, whether good or bad.

The driver swung around Thomas Circle, and idly she wondered who the green general was on the handsome green horse. One day she would walk over from the hotel and read the plaque. Washington was filled with green generals on horseback. Across the way was the little basement grocery where she went to buy apples. Just seeing familiar scenes reassured her, and she took a deep breath, and steadied her thinking.

She was prepared to make the delivery.

The area proved largely a honky-tonk district that should have been located on the waterfront of a bygone era. Small night clubs and bars with garish lights and cheap signs hawking liquor and sex offered rock bands heavy on the drums and weary, bored, and bloated topless dancers who would have been more erotic covered. A couple of head shops paraded the accoutrements of the drug scene, and tiny movie parlors advertised nudity, sex acts, and perversion. "You'll never see more." "This one will blow your mind."

186

Not many people were about, and most were not the habitués common to such streets. Some were smartly dressed couples out for a lark, college fellows wanting to shock their girl friends, or vice versa, and older people seeking vicarious thrills.

Slowly, the taxi cruised by a hole-in-the-wall newsstand, jammed to the ceiling with papers and magazines. Three doors beyond, she asked the driver to wait. Walking at a quick pace, she brushed by people without seeing them. She wanted no awareness that eyes were following her, if any were.

Stepping into the newsstand she saw the attendant at the rear, hunched over a racing form behind a small, beaten-up counter. He was a sawed-off, heavily bearded, long-haired runt, wrinkled and rheumy-eyed beyond his years, with a drooping cigarette and a talent for picking his teeth while he smoked. He appeared totally absorbed. She glanced hastily over the magazines, of which there were hundreds in many languages. She suffered alarm when she failed to locate *Sports Illustrated*. She picked up a copy of *The New Yorker,* and pretending to thumb through it, continued her search. Except for the man, she was alone, and growing ever more conscious that she was. At the backfire of a car outside, she jumped a little and turned. In the distance a police siren sounded. The man never looked up.

Then she located a stack of *Sports Illustrated* on the floor, and stooping, picked up three copies and slipped the envelope under the front cover of the fourth. Rising, she was conscious someone was behind her, and turning, found the runt staring up at her. How he had materialized in that spot without sound, blocking her exit to the door, she never could explain.

"What're you doing?" he asked in a little, whining voice as repulsive as his appearance. Before she could answer, he continued: "You put something down there, didn't you? In that magazine? Four down, wasn't it? Well, you're not going to get away with it. Somebody tried that last week—and the cops were all over the joint, looking into every magazine. Wrecked the dump. Accused me of being a mail drop. Said they'd drag me in if it ever happened again."

He backed toward the door. "Stay where you are. I'm calling the cops. If you try anything . . ." He flicked open a switch blade.

Never before had she been threatened with a weapon, but her thinking and her nerves, surprisingly, were steady. She heard herself talking as if she were listening to another woman. "Go ahead and call the police. I'll tell them I came in here to buy a magazine, and you drew a knife on me, and I'll sue you for everything you've got."

He pondered that a moment, then blurted out: "No, you don't! No, you don't! A fast talking dame, huh? You ain't getting away with it."

Behind him a woman's high screechy voice cut in, sounding like a record gone bad: "He was raping her when I came in. Had her down on the floor with a knife at her throat and her clothes half off . . ."

He turned in amazement, his squinty, watery eyes swelling cat-like. The woman was a kindly looking, grandmotherly type in her seventies with a sharp, aquiline nose that sniffed now and then. Chris remembered her. She had been across the street when Chris entered, an anomaly in this kind of a district. She had been walking fast in a falling-forward fashion, like a bird going for a worm.

The woman continued: "That's what I'll tell the judge, mister, and with a sweet, old grandma like me tellin' him and the jury, they goin' to believe me. Got a powerful imagination. Good at details. If you've got a lick of sense, you'll mosey back into the woodwork, and"—she squatted with the agility of a ballet dancer and swept up the fourth copy down of *Sports Illustrated*—"I'll get my magazine . . . Well, they got a piece on Joe Namath. Too bad I ain't forty years younger . . . Just charge this to my account, mister . . ."

His eyes were riveted on her. He could not get his mind or body into locomotion.

The woman said to Chris: "Come on, let's buzz out of here."

Leaving with Chris, she continued: "I shouldn't've busted in. I'll catch hell from the Directory for showin' myself—but I can give it as good as I get. Your taxi's waitin' for you and I'll watch you to it."

By now they were on the sidewalk, and when Chris hesitated, in a daze over the swift turn of events, the woman said: "Go on now, you pretty thing. No need to bother yourself about me. I always carry a hat pin. Should've given that fellow a jab in the butt. But that's me. Always thinkin' of what I should've done when the train's down the track."

Getting into the taxi, Chris glanced back. The woman was heading in the opposite direction, walking fast, still going after the worm. On the other side of the street, a lone man hurried in the same direction, cutting in and out around people.

188

50

THE BUREAU REPORT setting forth the message delivered to the Directory, Washington, D.C., by C-77 carried the following synopsis:

. . . Subject Hartman requested names and addresses of Pentagon generals and admirals who could give commands that would neutralize the Army, Navy and Air Force.

Subject recommended the following procedure: that on night of coup a unit of three Directory members be assigned to each key military leader to instruct him to give such commands as the Committee desires, and if the leader refuses, to assassinate him. Subject advised that if this procedure were followed, then it would be necessary to have at least two lists of back-up militarists. According to subject, if first leader refused to give proper order, and was assassinated, then his second in command would be served with the same request, and if he refused and was shot, then the third in command would be approached, etc.

To set this plan up, according to the subject, a dossier should be compiled on each reflecting his work and leisure habits, where he was likely to be on the night in question, etc., and how to isolate each individual from friends and family.

The subject furthermore requested that similar plans be set up for the Federal Bureau of Investigation and the Washington, D.C., police.

The subject asked if The Directory had sufficient manpower for this operation, and if not, would The Directory consider additional manpower from Chicago and New York with the understanding that The Directory would clear each individual thus assigned.

Subject advised that the Boston Committee had raised $143,000 to date through bank holdups, New York, $187,-

000 and Chicago, $359,000. Los Angeles, he advised, would report an appreciable sum shortly.

On a separate sheet, subject requested layout and photos of street in front of the Russian Embassy, and a plot map of adjacent buildings and those across the street. Subject asked for the approximate arrival and departure time each day of the Russian ambassador.

Taped telephone conversation at 2:20 A.M. between Assistant FBI Director Markinson and the Los Angeles SAC:

MARKINSON: . . . C-77 was trapped temporarily—we don't know the circumstances—by a man we have identified as the owner of the newsstand. He pulled a knife on her and one of the agents running the surveillance was about to enter the store—he would have used some pretext or other—when the pick-up woman interceded. We don't have an ident on her as yet but she passed the envelope to a dark-featured man, about fifty, in a limousine at the northeast corner of Lafayette Square, near the White House, and surveillance of him led to a modest home in Silver Spring, Maryland. Subsequent investigation has identified him as LUIS PARK DIJON, a member of the French military junta that seized power in Algeria in 1958 in an effort to block France's peace negotiations with the Algerian FLN. After de Gaulle came to power, the subject was one of the generals who organized the OAS, the secret army sworn to keep Algeria French and that instigated a campaign of terror in both France and Algeria.

SAC: Isn't he wanted then by France? For treason?

MARKINSON: We're checking that lead out now, and also whether he's in this country illegally. He hasn't yet made contact with anyone. He returned home immediately after taking delivery and his bedroom light was turned off at 12:34. Please ask Agent Ripley to express the Bureau's appreciation to C-77.

SAC: He'll be happy to do that.

MARKINSON: I reviewed the case today and failed to find a report about the unknown party who signaled the subject, Vincent Dearborn, when he put the helicopter down on Ventura Boulevard that night . . .

SAC: We've got two agents working leads.

MARKINSON: Nothing?

SAC: Nothing . . . One thing more. We may've got a bad break tonight. About an hour ago the Marine base at Barstow phoned to report a truckload of weapons and ammo was heisted by three or four men who apparently had inside help. We've notified all law enforcement agencies and we've got six agents on the scene now. We don't know, of course, whether the job was pulled by the Committee . . .

MARKINSON: A truckload? We've got to recover it—

SAC:—if we locate it.

MARKINSON: No ifs. You know that. By the way, tell Rip to arrange with C-77 to talk with FBI agents in other cities. We can't wait every time for the informant to return to Los Angeles to report.

SAC: I've discussed this with Ripley and he considers such a course hazardous for the informant.

MARKINSON: He considers! Will you inform Ripley for me—

SAC: I already have and he won't—

MARKINSON: Does he have a romantic interest in the informant?

SAC: I haven't gone into that. I believe it might be the wrong approach since he is producing maximum results.

MARKINSON: Ask him. Impress on him that the Bureau will tolerate no personal relationship between an agent and an informant.

SAC: I'll do whatever you instruct but it will grieve me to repeat his answer to you.

Teletype received at 3:40 A.M. from the Chicago Field division:

SAC, LOS ANGELES. SURVEILLANCE OF SUBJECT RONALD ASTERISKAN LED AGENTS TO 8 O'CLOCK MEETING LAST NIGHT OF TEN MEMBERS, CHICAGO COMMITTEE, BELIEVED TO CONSTITUTE PLANNING SECTION. SURVEILLANCE BEGUN AT ONCE ON ALL TEN IN ATTEMPT TO IDENTIFY THEM. SUBJECT HELD LENGTHY DISCUSSION YESTERDAY AFTERNOON WITH JAMES RANDOLPH LINCOLN. SOURCE CLOSE TO LINCOLN REPORTED ASTERISKAN ADVISED LINCOLN THAT COMMITTEE PLANNED TO STAGE DEMONSTRATION FOR WELFARE REFORM AND WOULD FINANCE LINCOLN IF HE WOULD LEAD DEMONSTRATION. SOURCE SAID LINCOLN

191

AGREED. SOURCE REPORTED NO MENTION WAS
MADE OF REVOLUTIONARY ACTIVITIES AND
LINCOLN WAS LED TO BELIEVE PURPOSE OF
DEMONSTRATION SOLELY TO CALL ATTENTION
TO POVERTY PROGRAM. REPORT FOLLOWS.

SAC, CHICAGO

Taped telephone conversation at 11:44 A.M. between Assistant Director Markinson and Ted Somerset, White House liaison:

MARKINSON: . . . He's wanted by the French government for treason. The Bureau would like, however, to continue a surveillance on him until such time as we're convinced he can lead to no further members in the Directory and can produce no additional pertinent information. At that time the Bureau will notify the proper French authorities so that they may seek extradition. Since this is a policy matter, however, that involves a friendly nation, the Director would like the President's counsel, and if the President believes we should inform the French government immediately . . .

51

RIP LAY STRETCHED out naked, sweating, every window in the apartment open, with not a baby breath of air stirring. He could not remember a hotter September although every September he said that. Twice this night Pandemonium, who believed in togetherness, had tried to join him, only to be removed to the chair assigned to him as his bed. The last time, Pandemonium had grumbled. After all, with great effort, he had dragged a dead sea gull into the apartment the day before and placed it proudly at Rip's feet. He shared his bird catch with Rip who stealthily buried it at night back of the apartment. Rip blamed the condition of the yard, when the apartment manager grew curious, on gophers. "Pretty big gophers," the manager had remarked.

Tonight Rip had left the office a few minutes after Washington Field had reported Chris had returned safely to the hotel. As long

192

as he had been in the Bureau, spies had used Washington's newsstands as mail drops. It had become such standard espionage practice that even the sales people were aware of it. In New York and Chicago, the spies used cracks in old buildings in fair weather, but Washington's cloak-and-dagger operators preferred the magazine routine.

For the last hour, Rip had debated about withdrawing from the case. Full well he knew the Bureau regulation to the effect that an agent should never develop a close personal relationship with an informant. An agent must remain objective, free of emotions that might influence his judgment. The overwhelming, immediate question was: Could he send Christina Roberts to her death if it were essential to the security of the nation, or in gathering evidence vital to the prosecution of those who had plotted to overthrow the government?

Bureau discipline was strict, even severe. From the beginning, at the FBI Academy in Quantico, Virginia, he had rebelled inwardly, and still did, while at the same time recognizing that an investigative agency could operate efficiently and with integrity only if it maintained rigid safeguards for protecting itself, its own men and women, and the innocent citizens it dealt with by the thousands every day. Two or three agents had left the Bureau in the Hoover years to write books about what the authors termed the tyranny and dictatorship. They were mistaken in their phraseology, Rip thought, but the discipline was unquestionably there, and for decades had molded a corps of investigators without parallel in history, with a fantastic record for solving crimes.

Rip had come to accept it as a part of his profession. More than Markinson or the SAC realized, he was distressed by his maverick violations of the rules. Perhaps he had felt too deeply and strongly about the handling of the case. Especially, the compulsion to protect Chris was overpowering. Had he gone too far? Would he have experienced this same feeling if she were a man, an ex-convict, a run-of-the-mill informant? Of course, he would not have felt as he did, but at the same time he had safeguarded informants of every stripe to the fullest in the past.

Eventually he decided that the question of sending Chris to her death was mostly theoretical. He had already placed her in a hazardous situation from which there was no escape. The possibility of discovery was a fifth horseman of the Apocalypse riding ever closer. The pattern had been cast, there was no changing it. Events—not he—would determine the course, factors over which he would have little or no control. The business of planting an informant, and working with the person, was a stark, unhappy one at the best, tragic at the worst.

Ultimately he reached a decision: He would continue to direct the investigation—because he had to, because the compulsion was too great to repress. A strange compulsion, it was, partly the exciting call of the manhunt, being enmeshed in a case to the point where his every thought and emotion were a part of it; partly because he knew the case thoroughly and could work it as no one new could; and partly, he had to admit, because of his love for this forthright girl he had disliked at the beginning. He must somehow bring her safely through the weeks ahead. He must keep himself in a position to look after her.

He was distressed by the quarrel he had had with her over Winnie Tipton, a quarrel in the midst of their first expression of love. He asked himself once more what he would do if he were in Chris's place? Would he go to Hartman and betray the girl? To be honest, if he were Chris—with her background and outlook—he would not. As an FBI agent, however—if he himself were a plant inside the Committee —he would have no choice. He would disclose to Hartman every word Winnie said. Not to save himself, not that at all, but he could not blow the investigation to protect Winnie Tipton, and jeopardize the lives of thousands.

Some day he must explain his rationale to Chris so that she would understand, even if she could not accept his reasoning. He would tell her he admired her for her ethics—ethics which forbade her to betray a friend even at risk to herself. But he would point out that there was a greater *ethos* in one's responsibility to mankind. His old university philosophy professor would have called it by the Latin term, *summum bonum, the highest good, the final value*.

He tried to put all of this out of mind, to sleep. He hunted for a pleasant thought and remembered his mother's letter which had been in the mailbox when he returned home. For a few thankful moments, the letter took him out of the vicious, sordid, and at times mad world in which he walked day after day, and he escaped to the serene, happy moments of commonplace days in which little things were the bright woof of life.

A week ago she had celebrated her birthday, and he had sent a check for $25. Now she had written: "I got the old ranch clock fixed with the check and it does fine now. I don't remember of it ever being

194

fixed in its likely ninety years of existence. It was like some person who never goes to the Dr. I'd been coddling it along but finally its arteries got clogged and its heart beat faint and it just quit ticking and breathing. It now strikes. I hadn't heard its voice for years. It's a low soothing strike, not loud and clangy. It and the cuckoo keep pace. The cuckoo reminds me of a cheerful little boy. It defers to its elders and lets the old clock strike first . . . How's Peg . . . When are you going to marry that girl? . . ."

He thought then about how he would approach Peg. She would wish Chris and him all happiness, and mean it. She was quite a girl.

Hours later, thrashing about, he awoke. *Chris.* He was mumbling her name. He switched on the light. The old, cheap alarm said it was 3:50.

Oh, Chris. If anything should happen to you . . .

He lay there awhile, his eyes taking in his belongings as though he were seeing them for the first time. It was a lonesome, dreary, tired place. Comfortable, yes. But functional rather than cheerful. Neat, because he was made that way—no clothes draped over the furniture, no papers scattered about. Neither was there any evidence of hobbies. He did not have time for them. He was twenty-nine years old and all he had was a cat!

He had not thought much about it before, not until Chris came along. Now he *was* thinking about it, a home, a real home, with Chris in it, and laughter and love. Chris in a blue dress cooking dinner; Chris in jeans digging the flower bed; Chris beside him in the car, hair blowing in the wind, going wherever the road led; Chris, always there when he came home. Chris . . . Chris . . . Chris . . .

52

THE AFTERNOON WAS graying into twilight, and the sun was a slash of red behind the thin gauze of smog. A homer was hit and the delirium peculiar to a crowd at a baseball game brought one runner in, then two. The pandemonium per person was greater than at Dodger Stadium since these were young and well-worked lungs. One more inning and the Little League game would be over.

Slowly Chris approached the scene, uncertain of what lay ahead, of Max's intent and mood. His tone had been curt over the phone. He had asked her to meet him at this unlikely place. She had never heard him express the slightest interest in Little League baseball.

Her tired eyes sorted through the milling parents and youngsters, and landed and stayed with a bright red pants suit that eeled around people, coming her way. With dread, Chris waited. Not since the third grade, when a boy had delighted in stoning her, had Chris feared any individual as much as Tico.

"Thought you'd never get here," Tico said and started away, her words slurred. In the distance, the other side of the diamond, Chris saw Max holding binoculars pointed down into the Los Angeles River. Years ago the city had paved the floor and the sides of the river to curb its tendency to meander, dig new channels and scramble the metropolitan scenery. Except for an occasional heavy winter rain, and in the spring when the snow melted in the distant mountains, the bed was bone dry.

At sound of them, Max turned and handed the binoculars back to the boy he had borrowed them from. He didn't thank him. Why should he? The peasants were there to serve him. With a nod, he walked a short distance away from the crowd, then turned on Chris.

"You had dinner a few nights ago with Winnie."

Her heartbeat throbbed in her hearing. Unsure of her voice, she nodded. She returned the cold stare of his inquisition.

"What'd you talk about?"

She managed to look properly mystified. Her voice rose in slight anger. "What d'you mean, what'd we talk about? What is this anyway?"

Tico swung toward her. "She told you she was tailing out. And you didn't say one damn word about it!"

"What's she screaming about?" Chris shouted at Max.

"You ought to know. Winnie told you."

"Damn right, she did!" Tico shouted.

Chris turned her back on them and started away. "I've had a belly full of you!"

Max grabbed her. "No, you don't!"

His fingers dug into her flesh, but she yanked free, and stood and stared defiantly.

Unexpectedly he broke into a smile. "Come on, Chris, let's play it cool. I didn't mean to get rough. It's just that . . . you know, you

196

understand. Maybe you were too scared to tell us. Be honest and no harm's done. Just tell us what she said. We won't hold it against you."

Not much, mister, she thought.

"Go on, Chris."

"So what do I tell you? I say she told me nothing about running out and you think I'm lying. I can't win."

"Nothing about going to the FBI?"

"The FBI! Those pigs?"

"What about the bank job?" Tico asked.

"What bank job?"

"The Crenshaw bank."

"What's Winnie got to do with that? I read in the paper—this girl—then Max said at the meeting there'd been a casualty . . ."

"You don't know nothing about nothing," Tico jabbed sarcastically. "I'll bet you and her were planning to tail out together."

"She wouldn't talk even if she did run out," Chris said.

Max studied her a moment. "What makes you so sure?"

"She's not the kind."

Tico said: "You're going to get the same if we find out you were in on it with her. Max gave you a chance."

"Thanks," Chris said.

"Forget it, Chris," Max told her, putting an arm about her. "I didn't mean to be rough on you. I thought maybe you could help us. Remember something. But if you can't . . . We haven't talked with Winnie yet. But we're going to." He added: "You did a good job for us in New York."

She thought she was going to stop breathing. *They were going to talk with Winnie.*

Chris managed to say: "One more rousting around like this and you can get a new postman."

Max laughed and squeezed her. "Oh, come on, darling. You understand. We had to know what was going on. You're doing a great job."

She forced herself to drop her head on his shoulder and sniffle a little. Then she looked up, catching him exchanging a message with Tico. She didn't let on. "I understand," she whispered. He squeezed her again.

"I could vomit," Tico said.

Chris raised her head long enough to invite her to do so.

These days Chris was scraping deep down for the courage she

197

needed. Exhaustion had sapped most of it away. If she could have, she would have tossed in the towel. Nights now she slept fitfully, and in New York the day before, there had been the usual nerve wracking telephone calls with their directions and orders.

As per Max's instructions she had checked into Hotel Lexington at 48th and Lexington with its interior Moorish arches and wooden beams. It was Sunday and New York's deserted streets gave one the strange, eerie feeling that a catastrophe had befallen the city, the same as had the great centers of antiquity, and no one would ever return.

She was having midafternoon coffee and peach pie at the Huddle when she was summoned to the phone. She was to report immediately to the Cattleman restaurant. She wrote the address on a slip of paper, 5 East 45th Street. She could walk it if she couldn't find a taxi. She was to enter the restaurant, sit at the bar near the cash register, and wait for further instructions.

She did walk the few blocks, and it was as if she were passing one blast furnace after another. The pavement and buildings exuded the heat sucked out of the interiors by myriad air cooling systems. A long canopy extending to the street marked the Cattleman, and at the entrance was a cigar store Indian. Though her mind was straitlaced with her mission, she recalled Roz's hoary joke explaining why there were so few cigar store Indians extant. They had all died of lung cancer. How did one explain at a time such as this remembering something that far out of left field? Did the mind revolt and insist on a moment of escape?

She had the impression inside of gas lights, red carpeting, red booths, a grandfather clock, a case with Western firearms. A painting of a nude hung behind the cash register. She ordered a Coke and nursed it for the next half hour. In the semi dark she saw mask-like faces and heard scrambled talk. At last the call came. She was to go outside and leave Max's envelope in the red stagecoach parked on the street. The red one, not the yellow. "A stagecoach!" she heard herself exclaiming. A stagecoach in New York?

Emerging from the dark into the brilliant sun she was blinded for a moment, then saw two stagecoaches beyond the canopy . . . each with two real live horses munching oats from feed bags . . . pigeons on the pavement eating what the horses spilled . . . a bearded driver in Levi's . . . a sign on the back of one coach, "Caution: Horses" . . . another sign advertising the Cattleman . . . a little girl, laughing, waiting for a ride.

198

As if in a dream, she went to the red coach, and pretending to look inside, left the envelope on the floor. She turned then toward Madison Avenue, and once, unable to resist the urge to glance back, saw a young couple getting in the coach. Their backs were to her.

She had no way of knowing it then but she had just passed on Max's plans for the kidnaping and possible execution of the Russian Ambassador in Washington.

53

IN THE SAME spot where Max had stood with the binoculars, Rip crouched low, staring into the night. Overhead a rocking chair moon hung like a tinsel decoration at Christmastime, with the stars vivid in a black velvet sky. A hot, dry Santa Ana wind from the desert, that smarted his face and summoned childhood memories, had blown away the smog. On the distant hills, disembodied lights marked the Los Angeles aqueduct, a waterfall spilling down out of the hills to the valley floor.

A few feet away Lee Jetzel stretched prone, head raised, also staring into the night. Despite Jetzel's inexperience, Rip had chosen him for what might be a dangerous mission. He had a quick mind and an easygoing way. No matter how critical the situation, he was never up-tight. Rip could depend upon his reactions to be correct in a moment of crisis when there was no time for analysis, when a man moved in accord with the way he had programed himself all his life.

A few hours ago, while a Little League game was in its fifth inning, Rip had sauntered out on this ledge with a sack of popcorn that he munched as he nonchalantly looked up and down the dry river. Not too far distant, he had spotted a large trailer truck and cab parked in a recess only a few feet from the river bed. At twilight he and Jetzel had reconnoitered as closely as they dared, thinking likely there would be a guard or two on duty. Through binoculars they saw a name they could not make out on the big rig's side but in huge letters were the words: DANGER—EXPLOSIVES. Rip felt certain the rig held the weapons and ammunition taken in the raid on the Marine base at Barstow.

By phoning city offices, the two learned that the contractors who had paved the river's bed and sides years ago had built this off-ramp for their heavy equipment. They had paved a slight incline that led to a small parking area that was a few feet above the concrete trough that was the Los Angeles River. The rig had been driven down the river from a service road and up the incline to this parking spot. Since city equipment was left here occasionally, no one would suspect one more truck. Aside from small boys hiking the river, the only other persons who might come across the cab and rig would be city employees who would assume that construction was under way requiring blasting. Someone was always blasting.

Now it was nearing midnight and the two were growing increasingly restless. For the last three hours they had had the rig under surveillance. Somewhere there had to be a guard, someone sleeping inside, someone high up hidden in the scrub growth. At a strange, indefinable sound nearby, they tensed, then relaxed when a scrawny mongrel happened on them, turned tail and fled.

The evening before, at 8:14 to be exact, Chris had sent an urgent message through Barney to the effect she must make contact at once with Rip. Rip had notified Barney he would be shopping shortly before 9 at a nearby Safeway supermarket.

He was wheeling a basket when he saw her at the far end of the aisle. Their eyes met briefly, then she resumed looking over packaged breakfast foods. Her lips were moving. She remembered to forego contractions. "I am being followed. The man is standing at checkout. He can see both of us in the overhead mirror. But I am too far away for him to see me talking."

The mirror, a convex one, was near the ceiling at the back of the market, placed there so the checkers could spot shoplifters. It was popeyed and consequently distorted.

She put two packages of corn flakes in her cart, and moved on to a refrigerated bin of frozen foods. She related then seeing Max with the binoculars. Midway in her account she stopped the store manager to ask the whereabouts of the Swanson TV dinners. Rip selected a can of Yuban coffee and wheeled several feet closer. He stopped to look over the powdered milk.

She continued to report. Once when a young couple blocked out Rip's view she had to break off and begin over. She recited almost verbatim the conversation with Max and Tico about Winnie, then picked up several packages of peas. Afterwards she went to the far

200

end of the bin where she pretended she couldn't make up her mind about choosing TV dinners.

"I am scared, Rip. I have never been so scared. I have to talk with Winnie. I must warn her. I could never live with myself . . ."

A teen-age girl came between them. "Excuse me," she said, picking up four enchilada dinners. By the time the girl was gone, Rip was almost abreast of Chris.

As he passed her, he whispered: "She flew to Seattle yesterday. Nobody talked to her. She's okay. I love you."

He was gone then, heading for checkout. She sagged with relief, but the relief was too great, too sudden. No power could have stopped her. She broke down and cried unrestrainedly.

At 2 A.M. Rip held a whispered conference with Jetzel and they decided to move on the rig. They slipped furtively back to their car on the street, drove over a bridge across the river, and parked. It was mostly open country with a small, aging house here and there, and a tilting barn or two left over from another time. It was eerie. No lights burned, no voices sounded, no animals even seemed about. On foot they made their way quietly to a point almost directly above the rig, and began a slow descent. No matter how careful they were, they sent a pebble rolling or scuffed against a dry bush that snapped loudly in their hearing. Each time they would stop to listen. They were no more than a minute away when they saw the glow of a cigarette directly behind the vehicle, and came to an abrupt halt. Almost simultaneously, a gruff voice called: "Hey, you guys up there. Get out of here. Don't you know this is city property? You're trespassing."

A form took shape and a gun reflected what faint light there was. The light came and went as the gun moved. The form was tall and bulky.

"Who're you?" Rip called out, slipping into brush.

"A police officer, that's who. Now come on and get out of here before I haul you in."

Rip shouted: "We're from the Marine base. We've come to get our ammo."

The pause was long, then: "You've got the wrong rig. This is a private contractor's."

"We're Marines," Rip yelled. "We're coming down."

The gunfire was little more than a popping firecracker. Rip felt the air split near him. Neither he nor Jetzel could answer the fire. The man stood too close to the rig. One errant shot and the whole truck would go up killing them all.

Rip's hand went scrambling over the ground and found a short piece of wood. He tossed it several feet from him. The man whirled and fired in the direction of the sound. He took two steps away from the rig. Rip and Jetzel slid down the incline and sought coverage in heavy scrub. Now they had the man at the angle they wanted him, away from the truck and in the clear. Both fired several quick rounds. Deliberately they shot over and around him.

The man returned the fire, but frightened, shot wildly; then he panicked and started climbing, clawing at the brush, grabbing anything to get a hand hold and to reach the street above. Rip and Jetzel piled on down the hill and climbed into the cab. From a trousers' pocket Rip took the duplicate set of ignition keys he had got from the Marine base.

"You know how to run one of these jobs?" Jetzel asked. Rip only laughed. He was feeling good. They had checkmated the Committee once more.

The motor started easily but when he put on the brakes for a gentle descent, they failed to hold completely and the rig skidded dangerously, the brakes screaming. At the foot, when they rolled into the smooth surface of the river bed, he sagged with relief. One more bounce and the ammo might have gone up. Now it would be easy going to the service road out.

Then they heard the crack of a rifle and metal struck metal close to them. "Get out!" Rip yelled. "Get out!" They both piled out and ran with a speed neither realized he could muster. The rifle fire continued. They slowed somewhat, and then a little more, their lungs about to burst, their muscles refusing to take one more spurt. Finally they fell and lay prostrate, their hearts pounding. The rifle fire found its mark, and the truck went up with an explosion that shook the ground they were lying on. A second explosion followed, and a third, and the sky was lighted with flash after flash. The roar, channeled by the river's concrete walls, caught them up with tornado effect, beat against them, and deafened them. Fragments cascaded down in a shower. They cringed and shook in shock and pain. And still explosion followed explosion.

When there were no more blasts, they rose to take inventory and look back. An inferno leaped toward the sky, burning their faces. They searched their bloodied bodies but the wounds were only surface ones. They exercised muscles and bones and found all in order. With each step they hurt until they could have screamed but they plodded on down the river bed looking for a way out. In the background was the wail of police and fire sirens, the muted thunder of cars, and the occasional high shrill call of a man or woman.

Their eyes met briefly. Neither had said a word. Rip shook his head in dismay, gave his shoulders a French shrug of resignation, and they staggered on.

54

DURING THE WEEKS that followed, developments broke rapidly, and each day the pattern for revolution as determined by Max Hartman and Dr. George Henry Beaumont became as freshly and rigidly set as markings in new concrete.

Chris continued her flights, and the photo copies stacked ever higher of the messages exchanged between Hartman and the Committees in the eastern cities. Rip lip read the information Chris picked up directly. Desperately he wanted to set up a meeting with her in the Little Cove but since the Winnie Tipton episode he feared to take an unnecessary risk until such time as one might be essential to the investigation. He still limped slightly from the torture his body had taken the night he and Jetzel had tried to recover the big rig. The Bureau had censured him for his failure to deliver the cargo intact back to the Marines. He should have known the fleeing guard would explode it. His judgment, the Bureau said, had been in error.

Without protest, he accepted the reprimand. At one time he would have pointed out that it was easier for a supervisor sitting on his butt in a comfortable Washington office to make a correct decision than a man under fire. But he recognized now that this was the Bureau's method of keeping an agent keyed up, of never permitting him to forget that his decisions, regardless of the circumstances under which they were reached, could be the difference between life and death for someone.

The newspapers had cloaked the story in mystery. Reporters surmised that a Mafia mob had raided the ordnance depot and a rival gang had tried to hijack the loot. All crimes were pinned on the Mafia these days. At one time the Al Capone mob perpetrated all the gangster shoot outs, and then it was the mysterious Syndicate. The names changed with the passing of eras. The newspapers and movies came up with the same old plots and the same villains but they gave the villains different names.

At a conference this sun-washed day in early October, with the first good smell of fall in the air, Rip briefed the twenty-three agents working the case. He summarized the latest developments:

IN GENERAL: C-77 reported that subject Max Hartman had been furious with the guard who had fired the ammo cargo. This act, he said, could have resulted in an investigation that might have led to the Committee. If the guard had been caught and grilled, Hartman believed he would have talked. Hartman ordered raids on ordnance depots postponed until two or three days prior to the takeover. It was too difficult, he said, to conceal weapons and ammunition taken in such raids . . .

Bank holdups in the Los Angeles area continued at the rate of three a week. It was impossible to determine how many of these, if any, have been undertaken by the Committee . . .

Interviews with more than a hundred parties and the working of all possible leads have proven negative in determining the person who signaled the helicopter pilot during the moving of the Golden State bank . . .

Surveillances being run on known members of the Committee in all cities have led to fifty-seven others to date. Most of these fifty-seven, in turn, have been placed under surveillance.

NEW YORK DEVELOPMENTS: Agents were continuing to check lists of major contributors to political campaign funds to determine the identity of the apparent leader of the New York Committee whose nickname was Boogie or a nickname that ended in Oogie . . .

Subject Hartman has mentioned several times the proposed kidnaping of the Russian Ambassador, which will take place in Washington but will be plotted and directed by New York, apparently because of insufficient manpower in the capital. No date has been set and the purpose of such a kidnaping has not been revealed. The State Department has been notified, and will be kept apprised of developments. The State Department will keep the Russian Embassy fully informed . . .

WASHINGTON, D.C., DEVELOPMENTS: The Directory has delivered to Hartman, through C-77, photographs and architects' plans of twenty-one buildings to be blown up. It should be noted that the term, *blown up,* as used by the subject, may be misleading. Plans to date call for minimal destruction in most locations with the avowed purpose being to give the impression that Washington was being destroyed . . .

The President has advised the Bureau through White House liaison that information about the whereabouts of General Luis Park Dijon need not be furnished the French government until such time as he is arrested. At that time, the French authorities must be notified . . .

Washington Field has determined that General Dijon has recruited an unknown number of veterans of the notorious French 10th Parachute Division that admittedly engaged in torture during the Algerian war. Their role in the proposed revolution has not been determined, and no messages between subject Hartman and General Dijon have mentioned their specific use . . .

The Bureau has requested Interpol to attempt to identify the white mercenaries being recruited in Europe by Henri Brouay of Brussels. State has determined that approximately sixty have been signed up to date, that they will be paid $5,000 each, the money to be deposited in a Zurich bank the same day they arrive in the United States. Their arrival date has been set for three days preceding the proposed revolution. Immigration has advised the Bureau that it will be difficult to intercept them unless the Bureau furnishes Immigration with photos since the passports and visas will be forged and aliases used.

CHICAGO DEVELOPMENTS: The Chicago Committee has advised Hartman that a wealthy industrialist has contributed $50,000 on the promise he will be repaid and given a cabinet post . . .

The number of bank robberies has been increasing in the Chicago area. The Finance Section of the Committee has reported a total of $487,500 on hand . . .

The black leader, James Randolph Lincoln, has set a date of November 9 for the poverty group demonstration of 100,000 in Washington. He will address a rally at 11 A.M. on the Mall. If the original plans of the Los Angeles Committee still hold—that he will be assassinated at the rally by an individual posing as an FBI agent—then apparently Hartman has set the night of November 9–10 for the attempted revolution.

The night of November 9.

Assistant Director Markinson arrived that evening from Washington to discuss the timing for the arrest of the principals.

"What about the head of the Zero Section?" Markinson asked, plunging headlong into a review of the case. "Any possible ident?"

Rip shook his head. "The informant saw him only once, at a distance, in the dark of a deserted store building."

Markinson paced about, thinking aloud. "There's Boogie, too. We have no ident on him—or the fellow who's going to kill James Randolph Lincoln. Can't we talk Lincoln out of making that speech at the last minute if we can't get an ident on the prospective assassin?"

"The police tried once in Chicago," Rip said. "No dice."

"He doesn't trust—"

"It's not that. But he's like Martin Luther King. He's going out there no matter what."

"We need a little more time, a little more . . ."

"We've pressed our luck pretty far," the SAC argued. "We must be awfully close to the point where they'll start bombing and killing."

"What about that?" Markinson asked Rip.

"Well, from what the informant tells me, Hartman doesn't want to call attention to the Committee before he's ready for the take over. The informant says he plans to synchronize everything for what he calls D Day. That way it'll look like the whole country's under attack—with bombings and assassinations in all the principal cities about the time he starts the mob of one hundred thousand running down Pennsylvania Avenue. However . . ."

He trailed off in thought. "However what?" Markinson asked irritably. He disliked people who failed to finish sentences.

"He may not be able to control his people. Take Boone. Hartman's got his own security watching Boone because the fellow would blow up his mother. He's itching to blow up something and he doesn't much care what."

"We've got fair evidence," Markinson said, debating with himself. "A few overt acts, definite intent, a stack of photo copies, and a good, solid, reliable witness in the informant. We've nailed down most of the members in Los Angeles—but we haven't gone as far as I would like in the other cities. And then there's Boogie. We've got to know who Boogie is."

206

"Don't you think we can identify him after we apprehend the others," the SAC said. "Someone's going to talk."

"Not necessarily—and if we leave one top man free, he could re-establish the Committee in time, start all over, and the next time we might not have as effective an informant. Then there's Lincoln. We can't let him get gunned down. If we can't locate the assassin . . . And the head of the Zero Section. He'll be a threat to the informant if we pick up the others and he's left to roam about. Once we start making arrests, he's certain to know . . ."

He took a deep breath, straightened his shoulders. "What about it, Ripley? How's the informant doing? Can she hold out another few weeks?"

"She can hold out as long as we want her to. But . . ."

He hesitated. "Get along with it," Markinson said. "But what?"

"They've almost trapped her a couple times, and it's getting riskier every day. Tico Sharman's convinced she's just what she is, an informant."

"We've placed her in jeopardy a long time," the SAC said. "She's going to make a mistake, or someone is."

"Is she willing to continue?" Markinson asked, and when Rip nodded, Markinson continued: "Are *you* willing for her to?"

"If you want the truth, I wish I could get her out of it—but we're riding a tiger."

"You've got something going with her?"

"I don't believe," Rip said slowly, "that the Bureau has any right to delve into my personal life as long as my actions do not reflect unfavorably on the Bureau."

"What if you had to make a decision that would send her to her death?"

Rip shot him a scathing look. "That's one of those loaded questions they toss you in law school!"

"Don't you think you should have removed yourself from the case?"

"Do you have any reason to think—?"

The SAC interrupted. "I assure you Rip's personal feelings haven't influenced his handling of the informant or the case."

"I was only asking," Markinson said cryptically. "Now about the timing, we will continue on a day-to-day basis. If we get evidence they plan to bomb or kill before they move on Washington, we'll have to work fast." He turned to Rip. "I want you to have all procedures and plans on a ready basis so that we can apprehend the subjects within an hour after the decision is made."

"You can have them now," Rip said with quiet effect. Markinson turned to study him. He saw only a very blank face.

When Rip had gone, the SAC said: "I've always believed we had a place in the new Bureau for men like Ripley who would stand up to the Bureau, and"—he smiled, which was difficult for him—"and for men like you, Ed, to ride herd on them.

"But," he added, "I don't think you should have your heart set on getting an invitation to his wedding."

55

DIRECTOR, WASHINGTON. C-77 HAS JUST COME INTO INFORMATION UNKNOWN NUMBER OF PALESTINIAN GUERRILLA FIGHTERS HAVE BEEN RECRUITED BY COMMITTEE FROM BLACK SEPTEMBER EXTREMIST MOVEMENT WHICH STAGED KIDNAPING OF ISRAELI ATHLETES AND COACHES AT 1972 OLYMPICS IN MUNICH THAT RESULTED IN DEATHS OF 11 ISRAELIS. ACCORDING TO C-77 THEY HAVE BEEN UNDERGOING TRAINING IN SOUTHERN LEBANON AND INDOCTRINATION TO EFFECT THEY WILL BE FIGHTING THE "ENEMY" SINCE THE UNITED STATES PROVIDES ARMS FOR ISRAEL. C-77 QUOTES HARTMAN AS STATING HE HAS PROMISED THEM HE WILL DROP ISRAEL TO SUPPORT PALESTINIANS WHEN HE SEIZES CONTROL OF GOVERNMENT. C-77 ADVISES FURTHERMORE HARTMAN "EXCEEDINGLY HIGH" OVER OBTAINING PALESTINIANS SINCE THEY WILL BE FIGHTING FOR A "CAUSE". C-77 WILL TRY TO OBTAIN INFORMATION WHICH MIGHT LEAD TO APPREHENSION OF GUERRILLA FIGHTERS AT IMMIGRATION . . .

SAC, LOS ANGELES

SAC, LOS ANGELES. WINIFRED TIPTON HAS PUR-
CHASED WESTERN AIRLINES TICKET FOR
FLIGHT 639 SCHEDULED TO DEPART SEATTLE
6:30 P.M. ARRIVE LOS ANGELES 8:39. NO REASON
FOR DEPARTURE KNOWN. IN ACCORDANCE
WITH INSTRUCTIONS SET FORTH IN YOUR LEAD
ONLY PHYSICAL SURVEILLANCE CONDUCTED
ON SUBJECT.

SAC, SEATTLE

THE STREET WAS well lighted and several people were about, late
workers hurrying home, couples setting out on dates, a great Dane
walking his human, and a tornado sweeping past on a tricycle. The
cars bumped noisily over a street that had been recently dug up and
badly repaved.

The taxi driver approached the curb hesitantly, searching for a
number, and then Winnie got out clutching a small overnight case
and an armload of miscellany. She managed to extract a bill from
her purse. When the driver noticed her hand trembling, he glanced up
at her face and recorded it. Most fares were only indistinct bodies
and if they had faces at all, they were blurred when recalled.

Scarcely had the taxi pulled away when she heard behind her a
man's soft voice: "Hello, Winnie."

Her body turned in one sudden, involuntary movement, and a
package fell to the ground.

His voice was as cold as his features. "What'd you come back for,
Winnie?"

Her mind disintegrated. A small voice deep within her screamed
for her to run. Run! it called.

"Chris says you went to the FBI." His words cut like a scalpel.

"You're lying," she whispered. "Chris would not do that. She
would not do that ever, ever."

"It's true," he continued.

She summoned all the strength she could muster. "I wouldn't do
that, Max. You gotta believe me. I wouldn't do that."

"You still love me?"

She nodded, staring at him, praying to find the old Max of the long
weekends. "I didn't run out on you, Max. I just went to Seattle to
visit my cousin."

"Chris said you tried to get her to go along with you."

"I didn't tell Chris anything—ever. You're making it up!"

"Am I, Winnie? Am I?"

"You're making it all up."

"Ask Chris. You told her we were going to hold up the Crenshaw bank. Why would you tell her that?"

"Oh, God, I love you, Max. I love you!"

"Chris says . . ."

"I know you, Max. I know you. You're trying to get me to say something against Chris."

He stood motionless, bulking big against the dusk of the sky, royal palms soaring behind him. A Honda roared by and a sports car backfired. Two teen-age girls passed, laughing. A dog barked, a tuffy-haired boy wheeled by, and television sets came on for the evening.

She got hold of her thinking. "We were so much in love once," she said softly. "So much. I don't know what happened. I don't know . . . what happens between people. You'll never know how I worshiped you. You were the first man—"

"Goodbye, Winnie." Swiftly, he walked to his car. Before she could comprehend, two men came up, one on either side. She started to scream, and a towel was stuffed into her mouth, and the next second she was pushed hard and fell into a car.

From the sidewalk an old man watched, puzzled, as the car took off. The old fellow shook his head, and walked on. He had not lived this long by sticking his nose into other people's affairs.

When the phone call came, Rip was having a hamburger dinner at Ship's in Westwood. Between bites he checked on the Dodgers, the Angels, Snuffy Smith, Blondie, IBM, and Eastman Kodak. Newspapers had changed greatly since he was a boy. In that era, they had offered readers a goodly quota of murders and scandals on page one. Now they had moved such stories to the inside pages and devoted themselves to more constructive news, such as wars, revolutions, riots, and assassinations.

Within minutes, he was speeding over the San Diego Freeway in the direction of Long Beach. A steady stream of reports came in from the two agents running the surveillance on Winnie Tipton. They had followed her since her arrival at International Airport. Rip had no idea why she had returned to Los Angeles. In the movies, people

210

behaved with some degree of logic. In real life, their motivations were often obscure.

"We're going by Imperial exit," Unit 14, the surveillance car, reported. "We're running a passing play." Interpreted, that meant the agents would speed by the car in question between off ramps, then slow down to let it pass. By running this pattern, the people in the car being watched were not likely to "make" the tail agents. A primary advantage, also, was that the agents could take stock of Winnie Tipton's situation. While dark had fallen, they could catch a glimpse of her when the car passed under the big overhead lights that shone above the billboard-like freeway signs.

"She's sitting upright in the back seat beside a man in his twenties or thirties. The driver's about the same age—but it's too dark to get descriptions. About all we can say is that the girl appears alive. They're running about sixty miles an hour in the middle lane. Traffic is fairly light, but there are enough cars on the freeway so that there's not much chance we'll be 'made.'"

Then, a few minutes later: "We're leaving the freeway at the Rosecrans exit . . . traffic is heavy . . . we're not passing . . . the car could turn off at any intersection . . .

"Car is turning into a plant but I can't find the name. We don't dare follow. We're going to park on the street. There's a sign. ADC Laboratory. There are several buildings, dark inside, lighted outside. They're parking in front of a strange-looking one, two or three stories high. The men are taking her inside. She's struggling. They have hold of her arms, one on each side. What do we do? Sit here? Go in after them?"

Rip was at least five minutes away. He was sweating. "Go in as plant security officers. Get tough with them, then tell them you're giving them a break—to get off the property—and you'll take the girl home. Act like you think it's a family quarrel. Downplay it. Then hold Tipton until I get there. Don't question her. Don't even talk to her."

Pushing a little harder on the accelerator, he moved the speedometer up to 80, and prayed there was no traffic officer clocking him. He concentrated on how he would handle the situation if she elected to remain with the agents. Under no circumstances would he reveal his identity but what would he do with her? He would have one woman on his hands to ice away for the next three weeks, a naïve, emotional, talkative woman.

She fought like a wildcat, and her small, slender body that looked so delicate exploded with fury and power. It thrashed about with unbelievable thrust. She half slipped out of their grasp. "Grab her feet," said one fellow, "and I'll get her arms. Grab 'em hard. Hold it! I haven't got her arms pinned back yet. We've got to carry her."

"Don't hit her!" shouted the other. "Max said not to hit her."

"Okay, okay. It's dark as hell in here. If we had a light."

"Here we are. Can you handle her? I know where the light is."

Suddenly, the place was harshly illuminated. It was like a corridor, only high, perhaps two stories high, and there was a heavy, bolted, vault-like steel door before them. She continued the motions of struggling but the body was spent. She thought she was going to faint. If she could only talk, she might persuade them. She would offer them money. Her parents could get together $10,000. They would have to borrow to do it but they would. She quit fighting. She was crying, thinking of her mother and father, how much she loved them. She was praying, and then as they unlocked the big massive door and it opened under the power of a hidden mechanism, and she saw the blackness inside, the screams welled up but found no outlet. She was in hysteria when they literally threw her into the dark, and the big door, taking its time, closed behind her. She tore the towel out of her mouth, and stood listening to the quiet. She had the impression she was inside a huge chamber. It had the feel of a great cave. But it was so black she could see nothing. Her fingers explored the wall. It was concrete, straight up, and went as high as she could reach.

Then she heard the mounting thunder, as on a far-off horizon, and it quickly swelled until it swept about her, shaking her, battering her body as well as her mind and hearing, a great awesome roar unlike anything she had ever heard before, and it swelled and swelled until there was no hearing, and any second her head would explode.

Rip parked across the street from the agents' car. He could not find the Committee's and assumed the two men had taken off. He dared not work on that supposition, though, and was reconnoitering when he neared the strange oversized gramophone-like structure and one of the agents burst out. "Rip!" he yelled. "For Heaven's sake, hurry it up, man!"

On the run, Rip followed him into the building. "We had trouble getting in," the agent said breathlessly, hurrying down a narrow hall, "and when we did, they'd put her into this tornado machine and taken off. We can't find the controls."

"Tornado machine?" Rip asked.

"Yeah. They test planes in there. Try to wreck them with every kind of storm known to man. Hurricanes, everything."

When they got to the high-ceilinged corridor, the other agent had located the controls and shut them off. Frantically, they pressed this and that button until the great door began moving on its own. Rushing in, they shouted in the dark, fumbled around with their hands, then Rip managed to get a match struck, and in the second before the light flickered out, they saw what looked like a bundle of clothing.

56

RIP WAS ALONE in the big room of many desks. In disgust, he snapped off the recorder. His mind was too fogged to continue dictating. He rose and stretched and rubbed his stubble. His nails raked his face and he looked at them. They were claws; he hadn't had time to clip them.

He walked briskly up and down the long room, then broke into a smile. He must be a ludicrous figure. But the stratagem had worked. The blood began flowing again.

Chris. He hoped she was sleeping. But it was difficult to sleep not knowing what the morrow might bring. He wondered if she wanted children. He thought she would but then he didn't know why he thought that. Perhaps because he wanted a boy and a girl. One boy, one girl, one dog, one cat, that would be the ideal home.

He fell back into the swivel and his hands sorted through the teletypes and reports. They came faster than he could handle them, than the twenty-two agents working with him could. A report from Washington. A photographer had telephoned the FBI to advise he had been commissioned to photograph eighteen rooftops along Pennsylvania Avenue. No reason had been given, and he had thought it odd. A teletype from New York. An informant working inside the Mafia had reported that five Mafia leaders would meet tomorrow to consider "co-operation" with the Committee. And a teletype from the Bureau relaying a report from the U. S. Embassy in Montevideo, Uruguay. Ten Tupamaros guerrillas—six experts in kidnaping, four in explosives—had disappeared and were rumored headed for the United States on a "mission."

He sat up straight, threw his shoulders back, took a breath deep enough for a 30-yard pass, and resumed dictating:

". . . The aforesaid agents removed the subject from the test chamber and found her unconscious but alive although her pulse rate was extremely low. She did not respond to immediate first aid that was applied. Plant Security Officer Donald O. Siegler appeared, and was advised of the identity of the agents but not of the nature of the case or the Bureau's interest in the subject. He summoned Dr. Rudolph T. Oxnard who advised that he could find no external evidence of serious injuries but that there might be internal ones. He stated that the subject was suffering deep shock, and should be removed to a hospital. At the request of the agents, he obtained an isolated room at the South Bay Hospital and called an ambulance.

"Special Agent Martha Leamington was requested by phone to report to the hospital and stay with the subject. SA Leamington was instructed to withhold her identity from the subject, and if questioned to advise the subject that she had been sent by 'friends' to look after her but that the 'friends' did not want to be known at this particular time. SA Leamington was further instructed to remove the subject as soon as the subject was able to a motel on the desert outside of Phoenix, Arizona, and to persuade the subject that for her own safety she should stay there without communication with anyone until such time as the subject would be safe. SA Leamington was further instructed to remain with the subject at all times. The Phoenix Field division will be advised when the subject and SA Leamington take up residence at the motel.

"Investigation by physical surveillance is being continued to determine the identity of the two men who placed the subject in the test chamber, more accurately known as an aerodynamic laboratory.

"Security Officer Siegler agreed to remove all traces of entry into the plant, including the test laboratory, and to hold in confidence the events of the night."

He stopped the recorder. Max Hartman would expect to read in the newspapers about such a bizarre murder. What would he do when no story appeared? Probably nothing, since inquiries could

214

prove dangerous. He would be baffled but consider the Tipton matter a closed book.

Rip resumed dictating: "Officer Siegler advised that this particular aerodynamic laboratory was devised to test structural metals to determine their breaking point, and was a combination of sound and wind pressure. The sound pressure subjected metals to levels of one hundred and sixty decibels, about the equal of fifty thousand radios turned to full volume. The wind pressure test could be developed to the equivalent of approximately one hundred and fifty average hurricanes."

He leaned back in the swivel and shook his head. He had had a part in saving a girl's life, and he would put her away where she would be safe. And then one day he would arrest her.

A strange business.

57

OSCAR PEDERSON said in a low, conspiratorial tone: "We've got a post office set up in Washington. She's a sandwich girl. You know, got a truck she drives from building to building for coffee breaks and lunch. You can leave messages with her."

"You know her, Chris," put in Max. "You met her at the newsstand that night."

The woman who looked like a chicken chasing a worm!

"What's she in it for?" demanded Tico.

"Thrills, excitement," said Max. "Her picture in the paper with a tommy gun and the caption, 'Freedom Fighter.' She fought with the Spanish Loyalists. Ran guns for the Hungarian uprising. Was in Israel's six-day war. The first time I give a state dinner at the White House, I'm going to have her beside me."

"The hell you are," said Tico.

They were in a plane flying through the night over the Pacific Ocean off the California coast. Given only an hour's notice, the members of the Planning Section had boarded the plane at the Santa Monica Airport for their last meeting prior to the revolution. The pilot had instructions to fly a hundred miles offshore back and forth between San Diego and San Francisco until ordered to return to Santa Monica.

215

Max had not offered to drive her to the airport. Not only was he busy eighteen hours a day, and totally absorbed, but also, less attentive. He had let her know that Tico had spent the last two weekends aboard his boat, and tonight when Chris met him at the ramp, he barely nodded. Halfway up he had called to her: "Tico's having a party on my boat after the meeting." When Chris protested that she was too weary, he flipped his cigarette away in anger. "I want you there, you hear?"

Outside, a thin crescent moon hung like a jewel on velvet. Inside, the plane was brilliantly lighted. Max had brought champagne which added to the excitement induced by the immediacy of the great adventure.

For the first time, Chris feared her memory would fail her. Place names, figures, and plans were tossed out too rapidly for her mind to assimilate. She focused on a grease spot on her dark blue pants suit. When she stared at an inanimate object, she remembered better than when she looked at faces. The spot in itself, though, bothered her. "It'll never show on a galloping horse," her mother would say.

Max had a map of Washington and environs taped over a window, and talking, pointed to places. "We'll mount machine guns at the circles, and on the rooftops along Pennsylvania Avenue, put sharpshooters to pick off police officers trying to control the mob. And here at National and Dulles airports, Boone is all set to blow up the runways—"

"Nothing to it," Boone said. "Nothing at all. We'll smash up a plane or two."

"—and we'll seize these buildings, mostly with veterans from the old French 10th Parachute division from Algeria. We won't try to take buildings like the Department of Justice. You can't, without an army. They're too big. But we'll seal them off, and Boone will sabotage the communications inside so the FBI and other agencies can't send or receive."

"I'm going to use a nipple time bomb to knock out—" Boone began.

"Later, Boone, later," Max said. The last thing he wanted was for Boone or Dr. Beaumont to start one of their endless dissertations. "Now the same night we're taking over Washington, we've got fireworks going off in every major city. We'll destroy the aqueducts that bring water into Los Angeles from the Colorado River and Owens Valley—"

216

"Nothing to it," said Boone. "We'll set it up in advance, use a chemical action, time delay process—"

"—and wreck the New York subway system," Max continued, overlapping, "and run some of those little tram cars that carry luggage up under the big 747s at O'Hare in Chicago and blow the planes up. I won't go on—but as you can see, it's principally psychological. It won't help us militarily, but it'll give the country the impression we've got the strength to move everywhere. Not alone in Washington. We want to—"

"—scare the hell out of them," Tico said.

"Now about the Russian Ambassador," Max continued, sipping champagne. "Dr. Beaumont has drawn up the plans for the kidnaping the afternoon of November 8. It's a diversionary tactic, of course, and should create a real panic situation between the United States and Russia but more importantly, it will focus the nation's attention on something so dramatic that people's minds will be occupied."

"What're you going to do with him?" Pederson asked, miffed that he had not been assigned to draw the plans.

"We have several alternatives depending upon the course of events," Dr. Beaumont answered. He paused to get his breath. His emphysema was worse tonight. "We will free him if all goes well. But if we need to gain a key installation or the enemy is slow in surrendering, we will advise the rascals that we intend to execute him within twenty-four hours if our demands are not met. And we will do exactly that, my friends. The Tupamaros have employed this technique very effectively, and we have engaged them to handle this particular operation."

"How much is that costing us?" Chris asked.

"Ten thousand dollars a man," Max told her, irritated that she would ask. "Now we go to the White House. When we start the operation at one A.M., we'll have between sixty and seventy white African mercenaries, Palestinian guerrillas, Mafia, and our own people ready to move on the White House and kidnap the President. They have a deadline of forty minutes. At one-forty, they'll withdraw if they see they can't take the White House. By that time the White House should be able to pull in some troops, and we don't want any pitched battles if we can help it. We've got a floating type of revolution. Pull back if you see you're in trouble, advance at the weak spots, and don't sacrifice men over a target that's mostly psychological such as the Capitol or the White House.

"Of course, we'd like to have physical possession of the President, so that he could turn the office over to Dr. Beaumont in ceremonies the next day, and give the revolution an aura of respectability. If we do succeed in kidnaping him, and he won't co-operate, we'll zero him. If he plays ball, we'll see that he collects his pension the same as the other presidents."

"Decent of you," Tico said.

Max ignored her. "Now to the Pentagon. There are certain key places we must take and hold—the Washington police, the FBI, the media, and the Pentagon. We have assigned the Pentagon to the Black September Palestinian guerrillas who will be working with a sizable corps of our own people. For the Palestinians, the attack on the Pentagon will be in the nature of a holy war. As you know, the American military is their sworn enemy, the ally of Israel. They'd like nothing better than to capture the Pentagon, and they've got an excellent chance. They'll take it by surprise, racing up and down the corridors firing wildly, killing anyone who gets in their way. I don't think they can hold it very long but a few hours will be all we need.

"Our Washington people tell us we have friends in the Pentagon's communication room, and when we give the word, we'll control it. And while we're talking about communications, Boone's men will knock out Washington's phone system—"

"Nothing to it," said Boone, forgetting himself and taking his pet grenade out of his pocket. He returned it quickly when Max scowled.

"We ourselves will keep in touch through radios equipped to scramble the conversation and then de-scramble it at our command post."

He advised that General Dijon had assigned special jobs to the Rengo Sekigun and the Tupamaros. They would accompany the Committee people in calling on the high military commanders to support the revolution. If the generals and admirals refused, the terrorists would execute them on the spot.

The Friends of the Revolution, Max continued, would be posted according to their special interests. The Mafia, for instance, would support the French Algerian veterans in sealing off the Department of Justice.

The Planning Section members would leave for Washington three days in advance. Max said he would assign them hotels when they departed the plane in Washington. They would operate the same as they had in Los Angeles.

"What about the guillotine?" asked Tico tauntingly of Dr. Beaumont.

With effort, he drew himself up. "Max and I have given the guillotine a considerable amount of thought, and I have yielded to Max in regard to carting the enemies of the state off to a stadium. We have decided that we will mount one guillotine on the steps of the Capitol and behead some important names. This will be for the benefit of the television cameras—to inform the people of the fate awaiting the enemies of the state. In my inaugural message I will cite the employment of the guillotine as a symbol that the French Revolution continues to live in the hearts of all good Americans who stand for what it achieved—"

"We'll eliminate most of the opposition on the spot," Max said. "I don't want to get bogged down with trials and delayed executions. It gives people too much time to think—to react negatively. But if somebody's dead, shot down during the fighting, no one thinks much about it a month later. We've got a list of recalcitrants who must be eliminated and the Zero Section will hunt them down the second day."

Chris tensed at mention of the Zero Section. She had thought that the section head would surely attend this final meeting. She was tempted to ask Max about him. Wouldn't it be perfectly natural for her to say: "Is there a rule against the head of the Zero Section attending our meetings? All the other heads do." She must come up with some remark, too, that would lead Max into disclosing whom they had chosen to shoot down the young black, James Randolph Lincoln.

"I must admit," Max continued, "that I don't like the guillotine but I have to agree with Dr. Beaumont that the visual effect will be staggering. It'll put the fear of God into people who might move against us."

For the next two hours they talked, and when it was near 11, Max moved to adjourn. They stood in a circle the best they could in the aisle, and one put out his hand flat, and another put his hand over the first until they formed a wheel with spokes. "To the revolution!" There was nervousness, and expectancy, and a knowledge that when the sun came up November 10 some among them would be dead.

They were exhausted when they left the plane. Max came down the ramp behind her. "You may want to write Winnie's parents a note of condolence. She had an accident—or had you heard?"

219

Before she could catch herself, she burst into uncontrollable sobbing. If she had been rested, not exhausted . . .

"I know," he said laconically. "I loved her. I loved the kid."

58

BY THE TIME she reached Max's boat, clouds had obscured the crescent moon. All the way along the finger slip, the dark hulks of small craft, barely discernible in the pitch blackness, bobbed gently. No lights burned, and it was like walking through a ghost city in the dead of night. When she neared Max's boat, she grew apprehensive. There was no evidence of guests, no signs of a party.

She called out uneasily, and Max, materializing on the deck, stood silent and waited, then led the way down to the cabin below. A twisted, grotesque lamp, fashioned out of driftwood, lighted one corner.

"Where's the party?" she asked.

"Make yourself comfortable. That chair over there's the best." The flame of a match put to a cigarette lighted up the prominent, handsome bone structure. She had known that face so well that she had not focused on it in a long time. There was no evil there, only a good face that would attract most any woman if she did not know the man.

He continued: "Tico's got an old college friend you haven't seen since you were in school together." He called out: "Tico!"

An old college friend! Her legs threatened to buckle and she sat quickly.

He handed her a large manila envelope. She was leaving for Chicago the next day. "Last trip," he commented. "I want you to stay close to me in Washington. Have you asked the airline about getting time off?"

She nodded, and at that moment, Tico entered, feigning gaiety. She was followed by a girl about Chris's age, who had a nondescript, pallid face that would be difficult to remember. "Surprise!" Tico said. "Look who's here."

Chris stared hard at the face, and desperately racked her brain. Max stood watching, as one would actors in a play.

"You know each other, of course," Tico said lightly.

"It's been some time," Chris remarked.

"Yes, hasn't it?" the other girl answered in a cool, contemporary tone.

Tico moved to draw the curtains back from a window. "Isn't that funny? You two have never met, have you? I can't imagine."

Chris said to the girl: "I'm sorry. Should I know you?"

"Rose Abatto," Tico said. "She was Howie's girl."

Chris forced a smile. "Howie Spelvin. I don't think our paths crossed."

"I guess not," Rose said.

Tico laughed. "Strange. I thought you two surely would've met the night Howie burned down the Bank of America. Rose was with him that night."

"Oh?" Chris felt the tremble in her legs.

Rose sat and tugged at her hot pants. She talked in the hesitant manner of one who has walked into a taut situation she knows nothing about. "I didn't know what I was getting into that night. Howie said, come on—"

"You were his spotter that night, weren't you, Chris?" Tico bit the words off. "Isn't that what you told us?"

Chris let her anger flare. "I didn't tell you anything, Tico—but yes, I was with Howie that night. *I was the only person with Howie before and after the bank burned.*"

Rose looked from one to the other. "I don't understand . . ."

"I do." Chris swung on Tico. "You've been trying to catch me up on something ever since I came into this organization." She turned to Max. "I've flown twenty-three missions for you—I counted them up today—and I'm finished. I won't take it any more. I'm going to sit it out the rest of the way. All these booby traps . . . if I haven't proven myself by now . . ."

Tico cut in. "Talk, talk, talk. That's it, bluff your way out. You weren't with Howie that night. You lied—but why did you lie? I'll tell you why—to convince us you were one of us. You used Howie Spelvin to work your way in—and you never even knew him!"

Chris handed the envelope for the Chicago delivery to Max and started to go. "Get someone else to do your dirty work," she snapped.

Max called out: "Wait a minute, Chris. We've got to finish this. Rose hasn't any reason to lie."

"And I have?" Chris shouted.

221

"Damn right!" Tico said.

Chris stopped dead still, and fingering the cross at her throat, said quietly: "Ask Rose if she's got a police record. Ask the Santa Barbara pigs who was with Howie that night. They'll tell you who was with Howie. They've got it all down in black and white. Go ahead, pick up the phone, tell them you're a newspaper calling, tell them anything, ask the pigs. I dare you."

Max stubbed out the cigarette. "She's right, Tico. She's right. I'd forgotten. I checked the records."

Rose raised her voice. "Now you're calling me a liar! Ask her what kind of a birthmark Howie had on his hip."

"I never examined his hip!" Chris shouted.

Max roared to Tico: "Get her out of here!"

He followed Chris up on deck. "Tico brought the charge. It was something I couldn't brush off."

He proffered the envelope. She bit her lip, glanced up into those blue, innocent, appealing eyes—confound those eyes!—and slowly accepted the envelope.

"You never hold it against me," he said. "Sometimes I wonder about that."

Never glancing back, she took the finger slip to her parked car. She was spent but exhilarated.

59

November 5

LOS ANGELES—

DIRECTOR. C-77 HAS ADVISED THAT 18 MEMBERS OF RENGO SEKIGUN, JAPANESE TERRORIST ORGANIZATION WHICH RECENTLY EXECUTED 14 OF OWN MEMBERS, WILL ARRIVE NOV. 7 AT UNKNOWN PORTS OF ENTRY. IMMIGRATION HAS BEEN NOTIFIED. C-77 HAS FURTHER ADVISED THAT HARTMAN HAS ENLISTED UNKNOWN NUMBER FROM FOLLOWING SOUTH AMERICAN TER-

RORIST GROUPS: PUNTO ZERO, VENEZUELA; MONTORISTAS, ARGENTINA; AND MR-8, BRAZIL. AS FAR AS C-77 KNOWS, NOV. 8 REMAINS DATE FOR KIDNAPING OF RUSSIAN AMBASSADOR. HOUR AND PLACE UNKNOWN.

SAC, LOS ANGELES

NEW YORK—

From report dated this day:

"In accord with Bureau instructions, this field division assigned 30 agents to develop backgrounds of 44 members, New York Committee of Public Safety, but check failed to disclose any subject with nickname of Boogie or variations or any subject with similar proper name. Investigation continuing in effort to establish identity of Boogie . . ."

WASHINGTON—

From report dated this day:

"An electronic surveillance placed by permission granted by Federal Court, Washington, D.C., under Omnibus Crime Control Act of 1968 on GENERAL LUIS PARK DIJON has reflected that General Dijon will coordinate and command all foreign units, including former African white mercenaries, Palestinian guerrillas, the Tupamaros of Uruguay, and groups from other South American countries and Japan. All units, according to this informant (the electronic surveillance) will be housed in motels on outskirts of city . . ."

LOS ANGELES—

DIRECTOR. RE YOUR INQUIRY. THIS FIELD DIVISION HAS IDENTIFIED TWO SUBJECTS WHO ATTEMPTED TO MURDER WINIFRED TIPTON,

DEFECTED MEMBER OF COMMITTEE, BUT 24-HOUR SURVEILLANCE HAS FAILED TO LEAD TO ZERO SECTION HEAD. TIPTON CONTINUES TO SHOW PROGRESS AND WILL BE MOVED TOMORROW TO MOTEL NEAR PHOENIX, ARIZONA. TIPTON HAS AGREED TO THIS MOVE AND HAS ACCEPTED SA LEAMINGTON'S EXPLANATION THAT "FRIENDS" ARE ASSISTING HER. BACKGROUNDS OF SUBJECTS WHO ATTEMPTED TO MURDER HER FOLLOW . . .

SAC, LOS ANGELES

BUREAU, WASHINGTON—

Memo dictated this day to the Director:

C-77 has advised that the following time schedule has been set by subject Max Hartman for the proposed revolution, and the informant believes these are firm dates:

Nov. 7—All personnel scheduled to participate will arrive in Washington, including members of the Committee from Los Angeles, Chicago and New York, and the terrorist groups from other countries.

Nov. 8—The Russian ambassador will be kidnaped. Approximately 100,000 who will march in the Poverty demonstration will arrive Nov. 7 and 8 and be bivouacked on the Mall by agreement with the Washington, D.C., police.

Nov. 9—James Randolph Lincoln will address the Poverty demonstrators from the Capitol steps at 11 A.M. He will be assassinated at approximately 11:10 A.M. By 11:30 agents provocateur will start the mob moving down Pennsylvania Avenue. For the remainder of the day the city will be looted and burned.

Nov. 10—At 1 A.M. the Committee will begin the take-over of the government.

Agents, acting on information furnished by C-77, are believed to have identified virtually all members of the Committee in Los Angeles, Chicago, New York and Washington, D.C. with the exception of the following: Boogie, the head of the Los Angeles Zero Section, and the "hit" man assigned to attempt to kill Lincoln.

When these have been identified, or when it is necessary to avoid loss of life, Bureau agents working simultaneously in the above cities will apprehend all subjects.

It should be noted that C-77, by acting as a courier, has provided the Bureau with services tantamount to the Bureau having an informant in each separate Committee. It is believed that not in the history of the Bureau has an informant produced so much high level information in such an important case.

AD Markinson

BUREAU, WASHINGTON

Taped conversation between Assistant Director Markinson, the Los Angeles SAC, and SA Ripley:

SAC: Ripley thinks it's highly dangerous for the informant and—

MARKINSON: I know there's danger but I believe it's minimal. Is he standing by? Put him on, will you? . . . Ripley, I want to explain my reasoning in proposing this step. We're powerless to protect James Randolph Lincoln when he speaks. In a mob of 100,000, well, I needn't tell you . . . Now what I propose is that you set forth a lead for Chicago Field to advise Lincoln that the Bureau has come into information about a plot against his life and try to persuade him to call off the demonstration, and if he won't do that, which he won't, of course, get him to cancel his speech.

RIPLEY: What if it got back to the Committee we'd been to Lincoln? Wouldn't they be suspicious—think there was a leak somewhere?

MARKINSON: The agents could get a promise from Lincoln to hold the talk in confidence and from what we know about him, I believe he would.

225

RIP: It could slip out. He's talking with the Committee people every day about the demonstration since they're putting up the money for it and insist on being consulted.

MARKINSON: The Chicago agents doing the interviewing can be vague with Lincoln. They don't have to pinpoint the time the assassin plans to strike. They can say Lincoln will be in danger from the time he arrives in Washington until he leaves. If something does slip out, the Committee will think it's just one more threat. After all, the Chicago police have had three or four threats against his life. I don't see how the Committee could figure that this referred to their plot.

RIP: I don't know . . .

MARKINSON: I'm not going to override you, Ripley. It's your decision. But if we go up until the last minute, and don't have an ident on the party assigned to kill Lincoln, we're in trouble.

CHICAGO—

SAC, LOS ANGELES. JAMES RANDOLPH LINCOLN, AFTER PROMISING TO HOLD INTERVIEW IN STRICT CONFIDENCE, WAS ADVISED BUREAU HAD LEARNED OF PLOT AGAINST HIS LIFE. HE REFUSED TO CANCEL DEMONSTRATION. HE SAID THAT "IF HIS TIME HAS COME" HE WAS READY TO GO. HE STATED FURTHERMORE HE WAS UNAFRAID AND IF GOD "HAS OTHER PLANS FOR ME I WILL DIE IN PEACE AND GO TO MY GOD AND MY CHRIST." HE SAID MOREOVER HE BELIEVED A MAN'S LIFE WAS FOREORDAINED AND IT WAS A SIN TO ATTEMPT TO ESCAPE "THE WRITING IN HEAVEN." HE REFUSED ALL PROTECTION. HE SAID PROTECTION WOULD INDICATE TO HIS PEOPLE HE WAS AFRAID AND HE WAS NOT. HE SAID HIS PEOPLE WOULD LOOK AFTER HIM AND PROTECT HIM FROM ANY KILLER. AGENTS EXPLAINED THAT A KILLER COULD FIRE A SHOT WITHIN SECONDS AND BEFORE HIS PEOPLE COULD INTERFERE. HE REFUSED TO BE DETERRED BUT THANKED THE BUREAU.

SAC, CHICAGO

60

It was the kind of still, pleasantly warm fall day that invited day-dreams and naps. Rip, though, was scarcely conscious of the day. He dug rapidly in the soft sands of Pequeño Cove with a flat rock, and when he glanced back and saw Chris in her boat about to ride in on a wave, he worked more frantically.

"Hi," she called. "What're you doing?"

He covered the hole, and rising turned about. Their eyes touched with a smile, and then they were in each other's arms, holding each as if they could stop time, stop the world.

"Burying a sea gull," he said, letting her go. "Somebody shot it and it washed up here. Somebody getting in a little target practice."

Her face clouded. "Why, why? I keep asking myself why."

He shrugged. "It's a violent age." She stood framed by the blue, blue sky, her figure leaner than ever and her face haggard. He saw hairline wrinkles where there had been none.

Her voice fell. "Winnie's dead. I suppose you know."

He walked toward the rocks they used as seats. Following, she put a hand on his arm. "How did she die, Rip? I've got to know."

He stared out over the ocean to the far horizon where a tanker on its way to San Pedro was a toy boat. "She isn't dead, Chris. She's all right—"

"But Max said—"

"Don't ask questions. I'll tell you later—all about it."

She started to cry. She was constantly near the breaking point. He took her into his arms but this time held her gently. She mumbled to herself her happiness, then pulling back, wiping away the tears, smiling, she said: "You didn't tell me Howie Spelvin had a birthmark on his hip."

"A what on where?"

She told him about the trap set by Tico. "I don't know what would have happened if I hadn't had a criminal record."

At a distant drone overhead, they moved back under the archway, and stood facing each other. He, too, had lost weight. He hitched his belt a notch tighter. His eyes looked sunken and burned, and he talked and moved with effort. But nothing took away, she thought, the strength of the man. Through the years he would wear well.

She reported with the clarity and detail of one who possesses a near photographic mind on the salient points discussed at the meeting: mounting guns on the rooftops and at the circles, the buildings that would be seized and sealed off, what would be taking place simultaneously in other cities, the planned kidnaping of the Russian Ambassador, and the attempt to capture the White House and the President.

"The guillotine," she said. "I forgot the guillotine. They bought one in France—did you know that France still uses the guillotine?— and it's in New York. They're going to erect it on the Capitol steps. And they've got several tanks lined up somewhere or other. Max didn't say where."

"Tanks!" Rip exclaimed in disbelief.

"They're at some army installation, and somebody's going to turn them over at the last moment."

"How many?"

"I don't know. Max had taken Dr. Beaumont off to one side, and I didn't hear much, but enough to know that it was definite, they were getting tanks."

Rip thought that over a moment, then asked: "Nothing yet on the Zero Section?"

She shook her head. "I know what you're thinking. They'll come for me when this is over if you don't get them all."

"No, no!"

"Don't lie to me, Rip. We said we'd be honest with each other."

"Okay, so I'm worried. But we've still got three days. When do you leave?"

"Tomorrow. Twelve forty-five P.M." A message would be waiting for her at Dulles Airport about where to report.

"I called my parents last night. It was two A.M. here. Five A.M. back there. It frightened them but I had to talk with them. And after breakfast I phoned my nephews before they took off for school. You'd think *I* was going to the guillotine."

"Don't, Chris," he whispered. "Don't."

She laughed. "I'm scared green. Funny, growing up, I read about Joan of Arc and all the other brave women of history, and some girls

228

wanted to be like them but I never did. I guess something was missing in me. I wanted to be like my mother, be kind and thoughtful and strong willed. I wanted to get married and have a home and babies. I had a dreadful fear of never getting married, never finding a man I loved. Really loved. Some girls are born for careers. I have a friend, she'd die if she had to stay home. But I'm not that way. I go out and get on the plane and there are all those strangers, and I smile and they smile back at me, and then they troop off, and sometimes I ask myself what kind of a life is this, one batch of strangers after another . . ."

"No more strangers," Rip said. "No more after—what say?—end of the week? I'll need two days to write a final report."

"Saturday. Four o'clock? Where?"

"Make it North Carolina—and then we'll see my mother on our way back to L.A. You're much like her . . ."

She was near tears. "I know," he said, taking her in his arms. "I know."

"I want to say something," she whispered. "I've got to say it. Maybe I shouldn't. But if anything happens to me . . . I know it won't but if it does, don't ever feel you had any part in it. I went into this because I wanted to. It could've been another FBI man. Not you. But you were the one—and I'm glad. But all this, it's none of your doing. It just happened . . . I'm not making much sense—and darn it, I had it all worked out so well last night when I couldn't sleep."

He raised her head and kissed her.

61

NOVEMBER 7

WASHINGTON–

The night the Poverty demonstrators began drifting in was cold, drizzling, and miserable. They came in cars that should have been put to rest long ago, and astride coughing, rumbling cycles, and hobbling on sore feet, and a few, with a sense of the dramatic, on mule and horseback.

Within 24 hours, 100,000 or more would be bedded down on the

Mall, and spilling over into the West and East Potomac parks. The fortunate ones would be sleeping in cars parked on the adjacent streets, and in sleeping bags. Others would be crowded together on the soggy grass, rolled up in blankets, and some only in newspapers. They would awaken sore and aching, clothes smelling, their mouths foul, and hungry. But few would regret coming. They were here for The Cause. And rising from where he had slept on the soaked earth with them would be James Randolph Lincoln. Like Gandhi, what his people did not have, he would not.

In an overheated, stuffy Washington Field conference room, Rip listened as Markinson talked. A score of others, including the Washington SAC, the assistant SAC, and Markinson's own aides from the Bureau, sat at attention. Markinson tolerated no slouching. Washington Field, which was housed in the old Post Office Building, was the local FBI office. The Bureau itself, down Pennsylvania Avenue in the Department of Justice Building, was what a corporation would term the national headquarters.

Rip's gaze wandered about. The building was decrepit, the walls gray with the years, the floors creaking at the joints. A few modern touches had been added, fluorescent lights in long, rectangular sections and venetian window shades. It all brought back memories. He had started his career in Washington Field. Then he had had a wry sense of humor that he never had quite outgrown, nor did he want to. He recalled the time he approached in the best spy tradition the Russian guards on duty outside the Russian Embassy on 16th Street, handed one a blank sheet of paper, and hastily slipped away. He knew the guard would have to turn in the sheet since an inside guard kept constant surveillance on the two posted outside, and the fellow was certain to be grilled about why anyone would hand him a blank sheet of paper. That would be sufficient to start a big Russian espionage investigation.

"We've brought Special Agent John Ripley in from Los Angeles," Markinson said, "to maintain liaison with the informant. Ripley."

Rip glanced about. Every eye was upon him, sizing him up. He had a reputation but in the FBI a reputation called for day-to-day proof. "The informant and Miss Sharman arrived on the same flight at Dulles Airport at eight-forty P.M.," he said slowly, concisely. "The principal subject, Max Hartman, had Hertz cars waiting for them, one for each, and when they reached the cars, a newspaper vendor handed them orders from Hartman instructing them to check into the Sheraton-Carlton."

The Sheraton-Carlton, steeped in tradition, was one of Washington's better hostelries.

From a distance, lost in a crowd, Rip had watched Chris come down the ramp. She was in a see-through raincoat and a rain hood. She walked straight, head held high as usual, but unsmiling. He had followed her through the airport and to the hotel.

He found it difficult to refer to her as an informant. It was as if she were an inanimate object, an automobile, a house. He felt her in his arms, hers about him, holding him tightly, as if never to let him go.

He continued: "They were assigned adjacent rooms on the second floor. At 10:40 Hartman placed a call to each from his room in the Statler-Hilton, asking them to meet him in Lafayette Square at 11 P.M." The Statler-Hilton was only a short distance removed, on the same side of the street. Lafayette Park was across Pennsylvania Avenue from the White House and two blocks from the Sheraton-Carlton. "We know that the informant and Miss Sharman will act separately as couriers in carrying messages from Hartman and General Dijon to their sublieutenants and what you might call their troops."

Rip would run a quasi-surveillance on Chris. She would post him, by means they had worked out, about her destinations, and on such trips he would not follow her. If, however, she was unable for any reason to alert him, he would. Hence, he would not be trailing her consistently, and accordingly, would not be conspicuous—in case the Committee was running its own tail job on her and watching for an FBI one. He would insist, too, on operating alone. Surveillances invariably were team ones, and a lone man would hardly be suspect.

As Markinson was quick to point out, Rip had opposed a surveillance once in the past. But now, with conditions changed, with Chris herself operating alone, Rip had every confidence he could bring it off. He had had to talk like a Dutch uncle, though, to convince Markinson he needed to work alone. He didn't tell Markinson that he wanted to make his own decisions if a crisis should develop. He alone would shoulder the awesome responsibility for her life.

The Washington SAC took over. He was a lean, tall man who had been a minister before studying law and entering the Bureau. "We've covered all the motels in the metropolitan Washington area," he informed Rip, "and found several with large blocs of reservations

231

for the next two nights. Supposedly tourist parties. We have these motels under surveillance. A few suspected mercenaries have checked in—but not many. We don't have any leads on the tanks the informant reported on but we're in the process of checking all military installations—and, of course, we have informed the Department of Defense."

"Tanks?" asked one agent. "How can they get tanks?"

"It'd have to be an inside job," Rip answered. "Someone leaves a gate open—and commits treason—or a commanding officer defects."

The SAC reported that intercepted cables, sent by General Dijon in a code that had been quickly broken, had disclosed he had requested fourteen tank drivers from the Palestinian guerrillas.

Few revolutions had succeeded without the use of tanks, the SAC pointed out. Their employment was almost standard procedure. A few tanks with their guns pointed on a presidential palace usually persuaded the occupant that the time had come to resign. In South America, even palaces prepared for such attacks fell.

The military had informed him, the SAC said, that their greatest concern centered around the possible destruction of the White House by a terrorist commanding a tank assault. "In the kind of set-up we have here," the SAC said, "it's questionable whether General Dijon or Hartman can control their men. Terrorists simply don't obey orders."

Other reports followed from agents heading up various phases of the investigation. The high points included:

Immigration had advised that the following had been refused admission: seventeen white African mercenaries at New York and Boston; twelve Palestinian guerrillas (five in New York, three in Detroit, two in Laredo, and two in El Paso); and six French citizens, believed to have fought with the French 10th Parachute Division in Algeria, all at New York. No Tupamaros had been intercepted. Once again, Immigration pointed out the difficulty in identifying suspected mercenaries without photographs.

An electronic surveillance "informant" (wiretap) had disclosed that General Dijon would command the military operations from a mobile unit, a small van parked presently in a Takoma Park residential garage, which would be moved the night of November 9 to Lafayette Square across from the White House. Hartman would work out of the same command unit. General Dijon had informed him that in strictly military matters he would brook no interference.

No information had been developed concerning Hartman's head-quarters for the next two days. It seemed unlikely that he and Dr. Beaumont would use their hotel rooms since they would have to operate through a switchboard and a public lobby.

The Bureau had called in 2,000 agents out of a total of 8,000 from field offices as far away as Anchorage, and police departments, sheriff's offices and other law-enforcement agencies from New York City to Atlanta were making 16,000 officers available. The Department of Defense was moving 60,000 men into marshaling areas surrounding Washington, 50 to 100 miles distant, and if needed, would ferry them to the capital by helicopter. (Rip feared that with so many moving on Washington, some would grow suspicious and talk, perhaps to the media. Yet 700,000 had worked during World War II on the atom bomb and kept it a secret.)

The deployment of agents, peace officers, and troops had been ordered, the SAC pointed out, as a back-up measure in case the round-up of the revolutionaries failed, or the Committee had forces standing by that the Bureau knew nothing about. It would take only a few Boones at large to blow up buildings, and a few guerrillas running wild with machine guns to fell hundreds, perhaps thousands.

When the reports had been given, Markinson took charge. "We have worked out a plan for handling Lincoln and the crowd if we still haven't located the would-be killer before Lincoln starts talking. So far we have no leads on the prospective assassin. No leads whatsoever."

He looked disapprovingly at Rip. "The informant knows," Rip said, "that we need this information—and also the identity of the Zero Section head—but I've warned her at the same time not to ask questions . . ."

"I didn't say I wanted her to," Markinson replied with asperity. "The fact remains, though, we do not know. So here is the plan we've worked out with the Director. We're going to post agents with Lincoln even though he protests, and put up a bulletproof podium. We'll instruct the agents with him—we'll have one on each side of him—to push him down at the first shot—if the assassin opens fire when he's on his way to or from the podium—and try to protect him if the gunman missed. We're hoping we don't have a repeat of the assassination attempt on Governor Wallace during the '72 campaign.

"The Director has come up with a ploy we have never used. We will ask the Reverend Billy Graham to get up on the platform just

233

before Lincoln speaks and tell the crowd of the assassination plan and the *agents provocateur* who will spread the rumor the FBI killed Lincoln. Dr. Graham commands their respect and I don't think we'll have much trouble with the crowd if they know the truth.

"However, we are setting up barricades on Pennsylvania Avenue and at four or five streets bisecting it. No, no one will man the barricades. The President doesn't want any shooting—and neither does the Director. The mob, of course, can go down other streets if it takes off despite Dr. Graham's plea, but at least we will divide them and spread them out a little, and maybe the FBI and police can control them. But I don't believe we're going to have a rampaging mob on our hands. If you talk to people, explain to them what's going on, well, many are going to listen. Maybe not all but a lot of them. Of course, we'll be criticized. This isn't how an investigative agency is supposed to function in the minds of many people—but we'll give it a try."

Excerpts from electronics surveillance log dated this day recording conversation by parabolic microphone beginning at 11:06 P.M. between Max Hartman, Tico Sharman, and Christina Roberts in Lafayette Park:

HARTMAN: We're going to be working out of this parking garage north of G Street. It's okay. It's owned by one of the Directory. We'll be on the second floor, the only office up there. Come straight up, don't stop down below.

SHARMAN: What do we take? Elevator, steps? I like to know before I go in.

HARTMAN: You walk up the same ramp the cars use, only there's a place to walk. I'd like you there around eight to run instructions to the personnel and personally check the equipment. I mean, just look it over to make certain it's where it's supposed to be. I'll go into detail tomorrow. Now if something happens, and you think we should clear out of the garage, phone me and give me a number to call, any old number, but end the digits with 111. Remember 111. That'll be the signal for us to clear out.

HARTMAN: Libya has a hundred men standing by, mostly demolition experts. They've offered us, also, up to a thousand soldiers. But Dr. Beaumont thinks—and I agree with him—we've already got too many. We can handle only a limited number of men. We can't fight battles, not even street battles. I know I keep saying it but it's got to

234

be quick or we've lost. We've got to take them by surprise before any-one knows what's happening.

HARTMAN: One last thing. We've got a risky situation here in bringing these soldiers-of-fortune in. They're a rough, hard lot, most of them heavy drinkers. I've told their commanders no drinking or carousing with women until we've taken over. But if something does go wrong, and you're caught running messages, I want your solemn pledge you'll take these pills. I've got a couple, and Beaumont has. Boone says he'll use his hand grenade. He's going to take some people with him, he says. What about it, Tico?

SHARMAN: Don't worry. I'm not going to rot in any stinking prison.

HARTMAN: Chris?

ROBERTS: Sure, Max.

HARTMAN: You know what you're saying?

ROBERTS: I'm not going to get hung-up about it before the time comes. You know me, I don't anticipate.

HARTMAN: It's all a part of planning. Good planning. Not that we'll have to take the pills because we've got a perfect escape hatch if we see about three or four in the morning that it's going against us.

ROBERTS: Escape hatch?

HARTMAN: I'll brief you later. Don't worry now. We've got this organized too well for anything to happen.

62

NOVEMBER 8

Awakening at 6, Chris showered and dressed hurriedly. Outside in the never-ending drizzle, she rolled her pants legs up and ran to the Statler-Hilton. She stopped under the marquee to catch her breath, shake out her hair, and empty her shoes.

Inside the hotel, she walked down two short flights of stairs to the coffee shop. She thought Tico would breakfast at the Sheraton-Carlton and wanted to avoid her. She had developed an obsessive fear of Tico whom she considered psychic. How else could one explain Tico's unshakable conviction that Chris was a stool pigeon?

Chris sipped the coffee, then pushed it and the roll aside. Suddenly nauseated, she feared she would throw up. Too long had she repressed her nervous system. Somehow she made her way to the cashier, paid the bill, and once more was back in the drizzle.

Getting her car, she fought a desire to look about her. Rip would be somewhere not too far away, and mere sight of him would help. One more day to go, and then tomorrow morning. Forever, it seemed.

Saturday. Four o'clock? Where?

Make it North Carolina—and then we'll see my mother on our way back to L.A. You're much like her . . .

She was crying. He was taking her in his arms.

At the garage the attendant in the ticket booth followed her trim body up the ramp. Cars roared by, discharging fumes that gagged her. Once a car came down with an animal-like squeal of brakes.

At the second-floor level, she turned right to wrestle with a too-tight door that led into a hole-in-the-wall office. The walls were grimy and plastered with girlie calendars years old, and there was a foul combination of human and car odors. Strands of a broken cobweb hung from a cheap light fixture that held three dirty bulbs. A battered, ancient desk had been cleared occasionally by pushing everything aside from a little square place fronting a creaking swivel chair where Max sat.

"Morning, Max," she said indifferently. The place frightened her. Lenin and Trotsky would have loved it. Why was it that all revolutions were plotted in dark, shabby rooms?

"What's the matter with you?"

"A little sick at my stomach."

"Nerves. I haven't eaten in two days. Don't want anything. I'd ask you to sit down but you can see . . ." He had the only chair. "Where's Tico?"

She shrugged.

"Look, sweetheart, play it cool with her for me, will you?"

"Sure, Max. Cool."

He got down to business. He had six letters of instructions for her to deliver, the first to a motel far out on Wisconsin Avenue. To a Mr. Yamada. "The Rengo whatever it is?" she asked.

He nodded. "Should be eighteen of them. Phone me when you leave there and say only, all okay, if there are eighteen, or two short if only sixteen. Right?"

236

"What's he like? Mr. Yamada?"

"Don't ask me. I've never met any of these characters. You should know, though—and don't go ape on me—he's one of the most feared terrorists in the world. Hunted by the Japanese government—for having masterminded the massacre of twenty-six at the Lod Airport in Tel Aviv."

"Oh, no!"

"Don't worry. He'll be okay with you since you're one of us."

She picked up the envelopes. "What if he wants to talk about it?"

"You know nothing. You're Western Union. Tell them to write out their questions and give them to you, and we'll get back to them."

He rose and went to a map taped to the wall, a map filled with red, blue, and yellow circles. He pointed out six blue ones, indicating the places she would go.

Unexpectedly then he pushed her against the wall and pinned her with his body. She didn't resist. She had learned it was useless and accomplished nothing. He kissed her brutally, savagely. "You're hurting me," she whispered when he surfaced for breath. "You're hurting me."

He eased the pressure slightly. He was breathing hard. "The first big state dinner we have," he said, his voice rising in the exhilaration of the moment, "I want you with me. Do you hear? With *me*."

"You said you wanted the sandwich woman."

He laughed, and with the laugh, his passion ebbed.

"Tico?" she asked.

"I want class."

"Let me go. Please."

He looked down at her. "How about seeing the moon come up from the White House?"

"Don't you ever give up?"

"You've got to keep working the territory. What about it? The White House."

She hesitated, thinking, then whispered: "Okay."

He took an abrupt step backward in disbelief. Then the old cunning surfaced in eyes suddenly gone dark and somber. "I don't believe it."

"It takes time, Max. I told you, it takes time."

His eyes held hers in a firm grip. She dared not look away for fear he would interpret that as a confession. A nagging, fearsome thought

237

skipped through her thinking, and quickly she routed it. If he read her mind . . .

"You never thought I'd make it." The cunning had been displaced by suspicion. The wheels were whirring.

"For Heaven's sake, Max . . ."

"Never thought . . ." He was analyzing, discarding, scanning the alternatives.

"Don't, Max, don't torture me this way. I can't help it if I didn't fall head over heels in love with you the first day. I can't turn it on and off."

"Never thought—but maybe it isn't that." The cunning was back.

"Yeah, maybe it isn't."

Tico burst in and came to an abrupt halt. "Couldn't you wait breakfast for me?" she snapped at Chris. Her eyes swung on pivots from one to the other. "Well, excuse me, I never dreamed . . . it is a little early in the day, you know, for this."

"I've got to go," Chris said, straightening the pants suit and shaking out her hair. "I'll phone."

"Your lips are falling off," Tico said.

She drove erratically. Given time Max would come up with two alternatives. She had given in because (1) she was a scheming, hard woman who would not sell herself cheap on a boat to a man who had little chance of turning his dreams into reality, or (2) she had given a worthless promise knowing he would never sit in the White House. If the second, he would ask himself: Was her move based on a belief the odds still were too great against him, or did she have definite knowledge his plan could not succeed?

No matter which premise he decided was the more likely, she had committed an error. She had committed it thoughtlessly, to escape his savage assault. But no rationalizing could mitigate the seriousness of the error.

She took a firm grip on herself. She had to cool it, and play the rest of the day out with detachment. Her father, in her teen years when she was prone to outbursts, had taught her control, and she had been thankful ever since. A mind ridden with emotion was no mind at all.

If only the blasted rain would stop!

She parked before a Hot Shoppe and went in. She felt contaminated in all the places where his body had pressed hers. She had just

238

ordered when Rip entered and sat at the counter around the corner from her. She pulled her eyes away, and all her love went into the smile she gave the menu. She sobered then, and pretending to read it, moved her lips. "Mr. Yamada. Rengo Sekigun." She repeated the address and name of the motel. Then she synopsized the episode in the garage office. She had debated whether she should. She didn't want to worry him, yet he should know, to weigh the seriousness of it. "I love you, Rip," she ended. "I am living for Saturday."

She still couldn't eat. On the way out her eyes alighted briefly on him. He looked haggard, and she feared he was dangerously tired.

Beyond Dupont Circle she came to Embassy Row and saw the flags of all the far countries she and Rip would one day visit, countries whose names conjured up childhood visions long forgotten.

At the motel she asked the manager for Mr. Yamada's room.

"You a business friend?" he asked, prying. These beautiful dames sure went for those slant-eyed Orientals.

"I'm a tour leader."

"Sure aren't friendly. Sure aren't. Most Japanese are. Had a party in the other day—"

"They're tired. They've had a long trip."

"Not friendly. I was remarking to the missus—"

"Mr. Yamada's room number, please."

Grudgingly he gave it to her, letting her know she had just been classified unfriendly along with the Japanese.

Wearily, she trudged around the court through the steady downfall. Before Mr. Yamada's door she took a deep breath to still her nerves. She noted the tightly drawn drapes, and heard a murmur of voices. When she tapped, the voices went still.

The door opened as if on its own initiative, and there stood a thick-bodied, fierce-looking Samurai warrior from an old woodcut, except he was suited up in modern garb. In introducing herself she could not hold her voice steady. Apparently he understood English because he turned slightly, though keeping her in his sights, and spoke a few words in Japanese into the dark room.

"Mr. Yamada," he said dramatically, and stood aside. She was unprepared for the painfully thin Japanese who took his place, a gaunt individual with a pleasant, sober face, gentle dark brown eyes, and a soft voice. He wore a neat brown suit a little large for him, brown shirt to match, and a skinny brown tie. The Samurai warrior

239

stood behind him, watching her. She had the weird feeling if she made any sharp, sudden movement she might be blasted out of this world.

Arms folded, Mr. Yamada bowed slightly, and she caught a glimpse of a revolver. He spoke little English but compensated with gestures.

"Your friend asked me to give you this," she said, speaking slowly.

He took the envelope. "Friend." He repeated the word for the sound effect. The Samurai warrior translated, then said to her: "He asks, would you honor this temporary home with your presence?"

"I would be the one honored," she said, "but I must beg your forgiveness and most abjectly apologize. I must visit others."

When Mr. Yamada read the note, she saw that it was written in Japanese. He kept repeating: "Ah, good." Finished, he held up all of his fingers to indicate ten, and then three fingers.

"Thirteen," said the Samurai warrior. Nevertheless, she held up her own fingers to confirm the number.

"Ah, good." Mr. Yamada held up five fingers. "Not come. Not come."

"We think the winds of fate have swept them away," the warrior said. "We are sad, and we most humbly apologize."

"I understand," she said, anxious to get away.

"We understand the directions," the warrior continued. "We will be present and our lives are yours."

"Thank you." As she started to leave, Mr. Yamada bowed slightly and she smiled in return.

Across the street, at a service station, she telephoned Max. "Five short," was all she said. He thanked her and hung up. She stood a few minutes in the phone booth, pretending to repair her face, turning slowly to look in all directions. But there was no Rip in sight, and she was disappointed.

So the day went. She crossed the Key Bridge into Arlington County, Virginia (eight Palestinian guerrillas), and drove south on the Fort Myer Drive to the headquarters for the Chicago Committee. Returning to Washington by Roosevelt Bridge, she headed for the Pan-American Building where the contact waited in the foyer (identified later as a runner for the Mafia.) She went north on 16th Street to a small motel (four Tupamaros). She traveled far beyond Silver Spring in Maryland to a deserted warehouse not far from the Baltimore & Ohio railroad tracks (twenty-two white African mercenaries, and artillery pieces beyond count).

240

In no instance did Rip follow her. After each trip she briefed him by lip movement, and informed him of her next destination. Face the direction the car is headed, she constantly reminded herself. That was the arrangement Rip had worked out with her at the Cove. In a phone booth, she was to face the street. She "talked" with him while reading a street guide on a curb, buying a candy bar, getting gas at a service station (standing behind the attendant, presumably talking with him), at lunch (faking conversation with the people in the next booth), and scanning a newspaper. Each time she repeated the conversation. Only twice did she catch a glimpse of him.

Her pants legs were soggy wet, and she was cold and miserable when she completed her last mission. The day had continued dark, the stores burned their lights, and the automobiles had theirs on.

Getting into her car, she spotted a clock in a shop. Five o'clock. She had thought it must be much later. She headed back toward the garage and Max. All day she had dreaded meeting him again.

63

DETECTIVE SERGEANT Jack Eilers, described by a fellow officer as a cadaver with a beating heart, roamed the National Geographic Society's foyer. The big, imposing building, a mecca for thousands of faithful readers who had traveled its beautiful pages, sat diagonally across from the Russian Embassy on 16th Street.

Eilers had never read *The Geographic* although he harbored no prejudice against those who did. The Himalayas and the Hebrides were not his bag. At the present moment, his bag included the embassy and all of 16th Street his eyes could encompass. He saw but did not see the two weary guards hunched in the rain before the embassy gate. Eilers was as good a detective for what he discarded from view when he was on a surveillance as for what he concentrated upon.

Right now two situations held his rapt attention, although anyone entering the Geographic building would never have suspected as much. He had developed disinterestedness in life to a fine art.

A very small driveway curved up before the embassy and the most costly limousine available had slowly nosed up to the ornate door.

The limousine was on time, 5:05 P.M. Eilers had clocked it for three and a half weeks.

Next door was the University Club with a far more spacious driveway. Twenty minutes ago a modestly priced sedan holding three men had come off 16th and parked shortly beyond the entrance. None had gone into the club. All sat slouched and staring in the direction of the embassy.

At 5:10 the Russian Ambassador, who seldom varied his schedule more than a few minutes, emerged, took the few steps necessary to reach the limousine, and slid into the back seat. A Russian security officer trailed him but sat beside the driver. Quickly, the car sped out of the driveway and into the heavy dinner-hour flow of traffic.

By the time the limousine passed the University Club, and the sedan had shot in behind it, Eilers himself had signaled a parked police cruiser. The driver gave the alert over the microphone, and as Eilers scrambled in, swung the car into traffic. They spotted the limousine turning right on M Street with the sedan following.

Traffic on M was not nearly so heavy, permitting the sedan to shoot forward, presumably to pass. Once alongside, however, the sedan careened wildly and struck the embassy car a hard blow, forcing it toward the curb. Simultaneously, there was the wail of sirens, and police and FBI cars rushed the sedan, roaring up from the front and the rear, with officers and agents piling out, shouting commands. Crouching low, they took up posts behind their own cars, ready for a shoot out if that was what the Tupamaros elected. In the background, other officers and agents began clearing the street of people, pushing them back, shouting at them, and when they had them sufficiently far back, erecting barricades.

Simultaneously, too, the Russian Ambassador and the security officer held tommy guns sighted on the sedan, and the driver, braking the car to a lurching stop, swung out of his door with a revolver ready to explode, followed by the other two. The three used their car, too, as a shield, taking up positions carefully chalked out on a blackboard weeks ago when C-77 had first supplied the information the Tupamaros planned to kidnap the ambassador.

The Tupamaros dropped their weapons, raised their hands, and slowly stepped into the street. They were rushed by officers and agents, handcuffed, frisked, and leg chains snapped on. It was over in a matter of minutes.

As they were being taken off, Eilers said to the "ambassador":

242

"Man, what an actor. Always knew you had ham in you but never suspected you were so good. You look more like an ambassador than some of the jerks in the embassies."

The operation had been a combined FBI-Washington police one, and its success based partly on the FBI's study of the modus operandi used by the Tupamaros in their kidnapings in Uruguay.

64

MAX SPOKE IN a slow, normal tone but his words were edged with rage. Most men, Chris thought, took a sadistic pleasure out of letting themselves explode. Max found satisfaction in methodical, thinking control.

"Someone tipped them off," he said. "Had to. You can't explain it any other way. Someone sitting here."

Bodies tightened, rigid bodies, bodies set in concrete. Not a foot moved, not a chair scraped, not a cough was heard, or a breath. They were frozen as if by a time process.

They—the Planning Section—sat on fold-up chairs on the third floor of the garage. It was after 11 P.M. and the cars had gone but their eye-stinging, throat-smarting pollution remained. They—Max, Dr. Beaumont, Chris, Tico, Boone, Vince, and Oscar—sat in a circle in stalls 28 and 29. The parking was convenient. They had lodged their rented cars in adjoining spaces.

"Someone sitting here," Max repeated slowly, looking from one to the next.

Dr. Beaumont cleared his throat, and in so doing, broke the frightening spell. "Hold it, Max, please, before you start making accusations." He spoke with the authority of a president; he looked more like a president than some the nation had had. Yes, Chris thought, if the Committee could succeed, the country would accept him.

He continued: "We're not the only ones who knew. The Tupamaros did."

Max scoffed. "They wouldn't talk."

"They're people," Dr. Beaumont said, "and people talk. Besides, what about the New York Committee members who set up the mechanics?"

243

Max shook his head. "Something's happened all along the way. We steal five million dollars—and it disappears. We send a girl to rob a bank—and it just happens the FBI has it staked out. Just happens. We pick up a mountain of ammo—and a couple of guys who fake it as Marines grab it from us. And now we lose the Russian Ambassador."

He took a labored breath. He had had a long, harried day. Time, growing ever shorter, was in itself a mounting pressure.

"Something always happens." He seemed to talk to himself. "I smell a stool pigeon . . . a stinking stool pigeon."

"You don't have to smell very far," Tico said.

"Go to hell," Chris half-shouted.

Boone interrupted. "I don't like what you said, Miss Sharman."

Dr. Beaumont took over. "Now, now, we're all tired, exhausted. I strongly recommend that we indulge in no accusations. The French Revolution was always tottering because of internal differences, the clash of personalities, insinuations, rumors. We must not have any of that."

Max sat up straighter, as if drawing an even tighter rein. "You're right, absolutely right. Forget what I said. I have every confidence in all of you. It was just that—that there were many strange coincidences but now that we've aired the situation . . . Let's get on with the reports."

Chris had to force herself to concentrate. She had the strongest feeling that each was convinced in his own mind there was a traitor among them. Each was frightened over what the morrow might bring. Each harbored the suspicion the FBI had a blueprint of the operation.

Max was pleased with the statistics compiled by Oscar Pederson that showed 67 Palestinian guerrillas had arrived, 49 white African mercenaries, 13 from the Rengo Sekigun, 12 Tupamaros, 16 other South Americans, and 37 from General Dijon's old French division in Algeria. Besides, Dr. Beaumont had recruited, for his Friends of the Revolution, 26 from the Mafia, U. S. Nazis, the Maoist Revolutionary Union and other dissident organizations. From Los Angeles had come 32 members of the Committee; Chicago, 28; New York, 43; and Washington, D.C., 21.

"One question," Oscar Pederson said. "What about the three Tupamaros the FBI caught? They'll be sweating 'em."

"Forget it," Max advised. "They won't get anything out of them. Besides, they don't know much. They were hired for a kidnaping.

They don't even know what the other Tupamaros are doing or where they are."

No mention was made of James Randolph Lincoln, and Chris felt desperation and despair when the meeting adjourned and she had no clue to the identity of the assigned assassin.

Max urged them to return to their hotel rooms and get some sleep. They would need it. The next night would be a long one. Hopefully, they might end it with breakfast in the White House, the guests of President George Henry Beaumont.

When she started down the ramp, Max stopped her. "I've got a change in plans for you tomorrow. I want you to be at Dulles Airport at noon. A matter of the greatest importance. I'll brief you in the morning. About nine?"

More terrorists were arriving, she thought, and I'm the welcoming committee. Wait until she told her grandchildren about this, how their sweet, old grandmother once consorted with hired gunmen.

She left greatly reassured. Max would not be giving her a key assignment at Dulles Airport if he had the slightest doubt about her.

65

MARKINSON WAS TERSE, concise. He disliked briefing sessions. Invariably they were more discussion than briefing.

"We feel confident we know where the subjects are, with the exception of three, and every weapon and bomb. The informant has supplied us out of her photographic memory with specifics we seldom get in an investigation, and the physical and electronic surveillances have been remarkably productive.

"As a result, we will move to apprehend all subjects at eleven A.M. tomorrow, here and across the nation. The Director, in conference with the President, set the time."

The logistics, he said, would equal or surpass those employed by the Bureau in World War II in capturing German saboteurs and spies. In Washington alone, some two thousand agents and six thousand other peace officers would arrest 344 subjects, seize tremendous quantities of war matériel, and acquire other physical evidence.

Across the country, another 1,200 agents, working in co-operation with local authorities, would be doing the same.

Markinson continued: "The President and the Director believe we dare not wait a minute longer even though we have failed to identify Lincoln's projected assassin, the subject we know as Boogie, and the head of the Los Angeles Zero Section. We are fully cognizant of the fact that this leaves the informant in a highly vulnerable position but the Committee has set the bombings and other terror tactics over the nation for one P.M. our time, and we've got to move. All right, Ripley, tell us about the informant, what you've decided."

Rip corrected him. "Not what I decided, Mr. Markinson. I got the approval of the Director."

"All right, all right."

Rip restrained the irritation he felt. "The problem, obviously, was to get the informant away from the subjects prior to eleven A.M. If she is still running messages, she'll simply return to her hotel at ten forty-five, and go to her room where two women agents will be waiting. They'll leave by the fire escape, get into a waiting Bureau car, and be driven to Dulles where at eleven fifty-five all three will board a plane for North Carolina. The informant will remain in her home town, Clinton, until Saturday."

After she had left Max, and given the doorman at the Sheraton-Carlton the car to park, Rip had seen her stop on a street corner to buy a bouquet of roses from a hippie type. The rain had let up a little, and the weatherman was predicting clearing skies for the next day.

Rip came up alongside her. "Wild night," he said to the fellow who grunted, and opened a soggy cardboard box for Rip to make his choice. She had her flowers and was scrambling in her purse.

"You pick them," Rip told the man, then whispered to Chris: "Eleven o'clock tomorrow morning." Except for the timing, they had set up the arrangement in Los Angeles.

She nodded, found a dollar bill, and handed it to the man who thanked her politely, and then gave Rip his bouquet, wrapped in old newspapers.

She whispered: "I can hardly wait for Saturday."

Paying the fellow, Rip answered: "Me, too."

"Right," said the hippie. "Make love not war."

The Washington SAC broke in. "What if she's with Hartman at the garage when eleven o'clock rolls around?"

246

"She'll go to the powder room and wait."

"You mentioned Saturday," Markinson said. "Where're you keeping her after Saturday?"

"I'm marrying her Saturday, Mr. Markinson, and in doing so I'm relieving the taxpayers of all the money the government would have spent protecting her."

"Very considerate of you," Markinson said.

66

NOVEMBER 9

The sun came up hot but the air was cold and the earth soggy. The clamminess lay on a man's body and permeated his spirits.

The Poverty people began stirring over the vastness of the Mall and the parks that had been blanketed this past night with thousands of them. They drifted early toward the speaker's platform to stake out positions from which they could see this black man who had made senators and congressmen, and even the President, listen.

Lincoln himself arose with them, and breakfasted on a couple of slices of bread, dried meat, and cold coffee. People came by to see him, and he talked with them. "How are you, Brother?" he would ask. It was always brother. Every man was his brother. His leaders kept them moving.

James Randolph Lincoln felt good.

This was the day the Lord had made. He doubted very much if the time had come for the Lord to take him. The Lord on high would look after him. This was the day when the meek of the earth would speak out and the high and mighty sitting over there in the Capitol and down at the White House would listen. They would because there were so many of the poor—and each had a vote. Lincoln was a deeply religious man. He placed his faith wholeheartedly in the Lord. But the capital needed to be reminded occasionally that the Lord was undergirded with votes.

Boone, too, rose early, and set off in a truck which carried sufficient explosives to blow half of Washington off the map. At the Lincoln Memorial he met the four Tupamaros. None spoke English, and

Boone was pleased. He thought of himself as the silent type, and preferred similarly gifted associates.

Shortly after 7 o'clock, they began the rounds. They worked mostly outside, drilling holes and breaches in walls and foundations. Inside the buildings, security guards carefully checked everyone's identification but outside no one took the slightest precaution. No one even asked questions. Obviously, they were construction workers doing something or other. If anyone had asked, Boone would have told them he and his men were shoring up the building. They all had cards identifying them and showing that they were in good standing with their unions.

When they went inside, they became government maintenance men with a Civil Service set of cards, and carried the usual paraphernalia.

On this first round, Boone planted no explosives but merely got the cavities ready for the charges that he would tamp in later. He posted signs around each job: KEEP OUT—DANGER—EXPLOSIVES.

Honesty was the best policy.

At Washington Field, in a big command-center type of room, Markinson directed Operation Revolution. His job was to coordinate the movements of the FBI agents, police officers and other law-enforcement men, a problem in logistics even greater than on a battlefield since most units numbered only a few men and were scattered over a wide area.

The command post was as crowded as the Houston Space Center. Agents worked at desks, one to a desk. Each was responsible for from 10 to 50 men in the field. Maps had been taped to the walls. The key map, a layout of Washington and its satellite cities, was studded with pins, red for the "enemy," blue for FBI agents, white for the police, and a large black one for C-77. As Boone moved about, his pin was constantly changed. When Hartman left for the garage, his pin was moved. And so it went. The other maps were small sectional blowups of the city and environs.

Markinson had set 10 A.M. as Trial Alert. At that minute, every unit in the field would be checked to determine if the men were in place.

It was a chess game with Markinson moving approximately 8,000 pawns within a period of a few minutes following 11 A.M. At the same time he had a mob of 100,000 to control. If one explosion alone was not checkmated, the devastation could be enormous. The chance for error was great.

With Markinson, of course, there was no possibility. With himself as well as his men, he tolerated no error. If one should somehow inexplicably happen, God forbid, the rumor in the field office was that only Bureau regulations would preclude him from employing Dr. George Henry Beaumont's guillotine to rectify the matter.

Dr. Beaumont arose late and breakfasted leisurely in his beautifully appointed suite at the Mayflower Hotel. He thought what a shame it was he had wasted all those years teaching. He had been predestined for this kind of luxurious and gentlemanly living.

The Committee had thought it best that he remain out of sight. He must not be associated with the necessary plotting, violence, and murder. He must not provide a shred of evidence to any probing newspaperman that he was not what he seemed, one of the nation's most respected and eminent historians, the author of numerous scholarly works, a great and good man.

He had only one regret. He would be unable to watch the erection of the guillotine on the Capitol steps. Along with the rest of the nation, of course, he would see the guillotining over the television networks. But spoiled, no doubt, by those horrible commercials they insisted on running.

67

IN THE DARK, this was a mounting nightmare. In the sunlight, it was a bad play. She was climbing the same ramp as yesterday. The checker was following her with his lecherous, tight, little eyes. She was struggling with the door to the garage office, and there sat Max shaving with the electric razor. He looked a little more beaten, his eyes faintly blood shot. He said the same hello and asked with the same indifference how she was.

"Scared," Chris said. "Tell me, aren't you just a little scared?"

"I hadn't thought about it. I suppose I would be if I thought about it." He added pointedly: "There's a full moon Saturday."

"I won't forget."

"Why fake it? You know—and I know—you won't be there."

"I told you—" She steeled herself to take the trembling from her lips.

"You're a pretty fair actress—but you need more experience."

She sat a moment in shock. "Don't hurt me, Max."

"I'd suggest you practice up on your damns. They don't sound right coming from you."

"Look, Max, I don't like it—this business of tearing everyone apart to see what makes them tick. Let's forget me, what do you say? I'm here to run your dirty errands . . ."

He stared a second, his lips grim, then handed her an envelope. At the National Gallery of Art, at 10:15, a man would be studying Raphael's painting, *St. George and the Dragon*. When he saw her, he would turn, pass by her, and she was to slip him the letter. Afterwards, she was to proceed to Dulles Airport.

Next Max gave her a thick, manila envelope. "Call me from a pay phone when you get to the airport and tell me the phone number, then stay close by the phone. I'll ring it around noon, and if I say okay, give this"—he indicated the envelope—"to this man."

He placed a half-page clipping before her from a Montevideo newspaper. The clipping contained a photograph of a man handsome in the sleek, Latin pattern of the 1950s. She knew no Spanish but saw the word, Tupamaros.

"It's got five thousand dollars in it. A lot of money. We could've done better asking the Mafia for a killer, but I don't like the Mafia, and this guy, it's not just a killing to him. It's a cause. It means something. I like people this means something to."

The last remark seemed directed at her.

"Walk by him and slip it to him. Don't say anything and then come back here."

She rose. "If there's nothing else—"

"Aren't you curious?" His tone was deadly, probing. She shook inwardly. He suspected she knew something that he did not. "Don't you want to know why we're paying him five thousand dollars—and getting him out of town?"

"Not particularly," she replied in a monotone.

"He's just killed a man—and you don't give a damn?"

250

"It's nothing to me."

At the door she turned to surprise him staring at her and through her.

He took a phone call, then glanced down on the street below. She had parked a short distance from the garage entrance. She stood by the car, reading the clipping. It was odd that her lips always moved when she read. A hangover from childhood, like biting one's fingernails, a habit difficult to correct.

She was a beautiful woman, and never more so than this morning. The sun shot dancing rays across her dark hair, and the dark blue pants suit accented her curves. She could be provocative in the most innocent, unassuming way, and all the more desirable because she had not set out to create or call attention to her sexuality. He knew she had no intention of spending a night with him at the White House, and he knew why. She thought the revolution would fail.

If she believed that, though, why was she staying—working so hard? In the debacle, she might be killed or have to flee the country with the rest of them. She was remaining in the movement because . . .

He refused to believe it.

A light flashed, something like the reflection from a mirror. He explored farther down the street, and when the light flashed again, his search went to a second-floor office. A man stood in the window with binoculars focused on Christina Roberts.

She started around the car to the driver's seat. On the way she shifted her purse, and the clipping dropped out of her hand to the gutter. She failed to notice.

And then it hit him, a memory. A memory weeks old. He had had a stack of clippings about the Tupamaros—their methods, and organization, and how they had shaken the Uruguayan government to its very foundation. He had asked if she knew Spanish and could translate them.

She had stood down there on the sidewalk reading the clipping— and she did not know Spanish. She had not been reading Spanish.

She drove away, and then he saw a man—not the one with the binoculars—a man of about thirty, neatly dressed, coming down the street. Max might have missed him if it had not been for his odd gait. Without pausing, the man picked up the clipping and continued in the same direction.

251

Max swung about. He was livid. At that moment, Tico burst through the door, and at sight of him, stopped short. On the run, he grabbed her roughly by the arm and shoved her ahead of him out of the door. She shouted at him.

"She's blown us," he yelled above the roar of a car shooting up the ramp. "The damn, stinking broad's blown us to hell!"

68

CHRIS TURNED RIGHT, going south. Traffic moved slowly, delayed by mobs of the Poverty people trekking toward the Mall, but she was only vaguely conscious of cars and pedestrians.

Only one more hour to go and she would be out of this madness. One more hour. Hold on, girl, hold on.

She wondered if her legs would hold up that long. Inside them was this trembling and pounding, and back with Max they had seemed about to buckle. The cause was only partly fear. It was exhaustion, too, and now with an hour to go, exhilaration. By midafternoon she would be home hugging her mother and father, and plunging into arrangements for the wedding. Three days she had. If she had her choice, she would say the vows quietly before a minister with only her parents and a few close friends present. Her mother, though, would be heartbroken. A wedding was a time for the train and veil, and boutonniered ushers, and the altar banked with flowers, and a crowded church. She could not deny her mother that pleasure. But the selection of a wedding dress would be the fastest on record. Forget the train. Maybe, the veil, too. No, her mother would insist on a veil.

Now that she thought about it, she and Rip had never discussed what kind of a wedding they would have. There hadn't been time. When he called tonight, she would explain. She couldn't let him arrive Saturday morning and walk into all of this. What if he balked, though? Most men, she believed, disliked formal weddings. But Rip, even if he didn't care for the idea, would go along with her.

One minute she was happy, then the next, when her thoughts whirled back to the immediate present, the old fear lay heavy. Her heart beat hard with the knowledge she knew the identity of Lincoln's killer. She had had no idea where Rip had been when she mouthed the message and then repeated it. She had thought he might not be about, but then in the rear-view mirror, when she stopped at the next corner, she had seen the agent pick up the clipping.

Straight ahead, six city blocks wide, lay the National Gallery of Art, a gleaming rose-white marble palace. She was early, and took her time finding a parking space. She still had eight minutes. She might as well lean back and enjoy the sunshine. The first thing she was going to do at home was wash and set her hair. It was a mess.

Rip's calm, methodical voice over the Bureau car's radio phone belied the excitement he felt. "Hartman gave her a package containing five thousand dollars to hand the man at noon at Dulles Airport when and if Hartman ordered her to do so. Obviously Hartman would give the order only if the party succeeded in assassinating Lincoln . . ."

Sitting behind the wheel of the parked car, he took his time with the report. There was no urgency. She had given him her destination as the National Art Gallery and the rendezvous time as 10:15. He wanted only to be there when she left, and follow her to her hotel, to assure himself that she had completed her last assignment in safety. When she stepped through the hotel doors and took the elevator to her room, it would be the end of the twentieth week, plus two days. Saturday was not far away.

"The informant asked what disposal she should make of the five thousand dollars, and requested that the agents meeting her in her hotel room instruct her . . . The informant has not yet identified the head of the Los Angeles Zero Section or the party identified only as Boogie."

In the command room, Markinson studied the newspaper clipping. The photograph was sharp and clear. Immediately he ordered five hundred agents and police officers to assemble at the Mall, the most he could spare. Each would have a photo copy of the picture. Since even five hundred men in a mob of 100,000 might have difficulty in locating the would-be assassin, Markinson ordered another 10,000 photo copies to be distributed to all law-enforcement agencies, transportation centers, and media on the Atlantic seacoast.

253

He must be prepared for the eventuality that the Uruguayan terrorist would succeed in murdering Lincoln—and escaping.

Tico wanted to hunt Chris down then and there and kill her. Tico wanted to murder Chris herself. She had her .22 RG-10 Saturday Night Special out checking it over.

Max infuriated her. There he was, sitting behind the wheel, driving slowly, acting as if all their plans had not been dashed against the rocks. "Death's too good for her," she muttered, returning the weapon to her purse. "Got to torture her! Torture her!"

"Will you shut up! I'm thinking."

He pulled the car up in the driveway before a hotel, and handing the doorman a five-dollar bill, asked if he might leave the car long enough to place a phone call. "Take your time," the doorman told him.

Inside the phone booth, he dialed and when a girl's voice came over, asked: "Is this 444-1111?" She seemed startled. "What was the number?" He repeated it, and she informed him he had made a mistake. "Oh," he said, "I'm sorry. I was calling 444-1111."

He hung up in the knowledge he had set in motion the windup of the entire operation. The girl was a secretary, a member of the Directory. She had the name and location of everyone. She would call them as rapidly as possible and ask the same question: "Is this 444-1111?" They were the code words.

He returned slowly to the car. His entire insides had fallen apart. This could not be happening. They had been so close, so near. He had checked and double-checked everyone . . . He had trouble moving, and his mind was clogged. He rubbed his eyes to clear it but nothing did any good. If he had a good, stiff drink . . .

"Now do we go after her?" Tico asked, glancing at her watch. "We've just got time to catch her at the Gallery."

Max nodded.

69

RIP GREW UNEASIER by the minute. By now Chris should have come down the bank of steps and turned right toward her car. He was parked a half block from the National Gallery of Art. He would give her five minutes more, then saunter through the hall where *St. George and the Dragon* hung.

He tensed when an urgent voice said over the radio phone: "Washington 14. Come in, Washington 14."

"Fourteen in," he answered.

Unit 11, running the surveillance on the garage, advised that subjects Hartman and Sharman had checked out. "They left on the run a few minutes after the informant departed, and stopped at a hotel where Hartman placed a call from a phone booth to an unidentified party. An agent in an adjoining booth learned that he asked if this was number 444-1111. The other party apparently said it was not because Hartman said he was sorry, and hung up. He left without dialing again. The number is the police department's emergency one. Hold on, 14."

There was a moment's break, and then Unit 11 continued: "We followed the subjects to the Department of Justice Building where Hartman contacted Boone a few minutes ago in the courtyard. Boone followed him out, leaving his crew behind. Boone is now driving Hartman's rental car, a 1972 black Mercury, southwest on Pennsylvania Avenue. Hartman and Sharman are in the back seat. We are now passing Archives. They are turning at 6th, pulling up . . ."

Rip watched as Boone swung the car expertly alongside the curb before the National Gallery and braked it to an abrupt halt. Barely had he stopped before Tico burst out the far door, and running up the steps, reached the portico with its massive marble columns, and disappeared.

Rip gripped the steering wheel, forced aside every thought in a struggle to put the pieces together: their sudden departure from the garage office, the police emergency number which had to be code, stopping to take Boone off his job at a critical time when every minute counted, and now their arrival at the Gallery where obviously they had come to talk with Chris.

Something of major moment had happened, and a trembling began deep inside him, and spread. No matter how he arranged the pieces, they didn't fit.

Chris was leaving the ground floor rest room when Tico spotted her and screamed her name. Everywhere people turned to stare.

255

Chris froze, with fear welling up in her for no reason except that sight of Tico automatically instilled it.

Tico descended on her, face livid and movements uneven. "Come on, come on. Max wants to see you. He's out in the car."

Chris heard the repressed anger and hatred as if Tico had expressed them. "What about?" Chris asked coolly, feigning a plastic calm she did not feel.

"How the hell would I know?" She seized Chris by an arm and started propelling her by sheer force toward the door. "Come on, get the lead out of your butt. Max wants you . . . on the double." They emerged into the warm sunshine.

A red flag went up. "I shouldn't see Max. I think I'm being followed."

"You damn little liar! You can make up lies faster than a tote board can figure the horses."

"Get your filthy hands off me!" Chris yelled, going on the attack.

Tico was stopped by momentary shock. Max called Chris's name from where he stood outside the car. On impulse Chris shook Tico off and went running down the bank of steps. She slowed at sight of Boone behind the wheel. He was staring straight ahead. Another flag went up. He was fond of her, and should have nodded.

"Get in," Max said firmly, and when she hesitated, continued: "I'm glad we found you. The airport deal's off."

He stated it matter-of-factly, and the red flags went down.

Rip was sweating, though the day continued brisk. He had a good view of their car, and saw Chris get into the back seat with Max. Tico sat beside Boone. Rip had noted Chris's hesitation by the marble columns and lip read her when she had told Tico to take her hands off her. Then Max had called, and Chris had reacted normally. When she got into the car, she had given no indication she might be in trouble. Nonetheless, this was not according to the script. She should have gone quietly to her hotel room.

Oh, God, he thought, don't let anything happen.

He said into the phone: "Unit 11, Unit 11. I'm taking over primary surveillance but please continue behind me and run a pattern play on parallel streets if possible."

Boone shot the car into the steady flow of traffic. Constitution was clogged with the Poverty people and the curious. Rip waited but a few seconds and then followed. He had decided to run the risk of being made.

He said: "Washington 14 reporting in, following subjects Hartman, Sharman and Boone, and informant. Animated conversation seems to be taking place in car. Hartman has moved over, and is sitting very close to informant. Sharman is leaning over the back seat gesturing wildly, as if in anger. Subject car is turning northeast on Pennsylvania, and proceeding at twenty-five miles an hour."

Control took over. "All units, all units. Stand by on alert. All surveillances are now reporting increased activity among subjects at every location. Order to apprehend may be advanced if activity continues. This is not such an order but only for your information."

"I told you!" Tico screamed. "I told you she was a no good, double-crossing stoolie! But no, you wanted her on your boat so badly you couldn't see straight!"

"Shut up!" Max shouted back, then unexpectedly quieted. They passed the Archives and the Department of Justice on Pennsylvania Avenue.

"What're you talking about?" Chris shouted. "What's going on?" Instinctively she knew she had been blown. This was no test run. This was neither the time nor the place to check anyone out.

"Crazy!" Tico said. "You catch her robbing a blind man and—"

"Shut up!" Max repeated. Before Chris could react, his hands went up her legs, then up over her body, searching for a strapped-on microphone. She flailed at him with her fists until he grabbed and held them. "I wanted you, dammit, I wanted you bad. I thought one day you'd want me . . ."

Tico had her Saturday Night Special out. "I could kill you right here and now." She pointed it at Chris's head. "Man, how I'd love to kill you!"

Her hand shook, and her index finger was taut about the trigger. "But it's too good for you," she continued, lowering the gun and turning to Max. "Torture her, Max. She's got it coming. Tell Boone to make her die slow."

"Five million bucks," Max said. "The Russian Ambassador, the girl dead at the bank . . ."

Chris rallied herself. She had to attack if she were to save herself. "What about them? What do I know about them that you don't?"

257

"Where you going, Boone?" Max asked. "You don't turn here. Get back on Pennsylvania and hurry it up."

"You want we should get a ticket?" Boone retorted.

"Where're we going?" Tico asked.

Max ignored her. "Boone—"

Boone knew what was coming. "I got a new way. Worked it out all by myself. Take her maybe twenty-four, maybe thirty-six hours to conk off."

She stared at Boone in shock. He could not be referring to her. He was her friend. And then out on the periphery of her thoughts, the realization grew that Boone was head of Zero as well as Ordnance. All along it should have been evident—his nature, his love for violence and death.

"It's a beaut," he added.

"Spare me the details," Max said. "Just do it."

"Max!" Chris screamed. "What've I done? You got to tell me, Max. You believe this harpy . . ."

He stared at Chris. "Just do it, Boone. The longer it takes the better."

Dr. Beaumont stood quietly at the cashier's office in the Mayflower Hotel waiting his turn to pay. His heart was as heavy as his cases. He had not many active years left. Max, of course, could one day try again.

President Beaumont. It had such a pleasant ring. President Beaumont. Ah, well, so it goes.

What had happened? No doubt, a traitor. There was that fellow in the French Revolution, year of 1793 . . . he couldn't remember his name, but he had betrayed the Girondists and sold out boot and kettle to the Jacobins.

Two young men, neatly attired and brisk with the importance of their duties, came through the door, and at sight of him, hesitated in the background.

Dr. Beaumont raised his voice. "I'm the one you're looking for, gentlemen. Dr. George Henry Beaumont. If you will give me a minute to settle this account . . . and then we can get on with your business."

He mumbled to himself. "Always did want to know what Robespierre was thinking when he rode to the guillotine."

258

Rip never took his eyes from the car ahead, and once caught a glimpse of Chris. Hartman had moved away from her.

Rip said into the mike: "We're still heading northeast on Pennsylvania . . . passing the White House . . . the Executive Office building . . ."

The second he cleared, the radio came alive. "All units, all units. Begin apprehensions at once in case titled Committee of Public Safety, et cetera. Repeat. Begin arrests at once. For your information —Juan Corderas, Tupamaro guerrilla, who informant reported had been assigned to assassinate James Randolph Lincoln, was shot and killed when agents demanded his surrender on the Mall at ten forty-six A.M. today. He resisted arrest, pulled weapon and got off one round before being killed . . ."

When the radio quieted, Rip said: "Washington 11, Washington 11. Subject car is now entering Washington Circle. Please keep close to me . . . Control, come in. Come in, Control. Advise Washington 20 that I request arrest of subjects now being tailed held in abeyance. Advise Washington 20 that I consider apprehension of subjects at this time highly dangerous to informant."

Washington 20 was Markinson. Although the FBI band had never been broken, the Bureau took care in using names.

Shortly after rounding the circle, where traffic was running heavy, Boone drove the subject car alongside a curb painted red, and braked it to an abrupt stop. While Rip drove past, frantically seeking a space where he could park without appearing suspicious, everyone scrambled out of the car. When he got a second view, while parking around the corner on New Hampshire, he saw only Tico standing at the back of the car waving traffic on.

Control came over. "Washington 20 assigns the responsibility for the timing and the apprehension of the subjects in question to Washington 14."

Unit 11 took over. "Unit 14, Unit 14. We just passed subject car, and all occupants except Sharman are gathered on far side. They seem to be just standing there except for Boone who is kneeling. Hartman appears to have informant's arms pinned behind her and is holding her . . ."

Rip died a little.

He could see only Tico, who now ran to the far side of the car, the blind side to him, and disappeared. On that side was a sidewalk, and anyone walking it would easily be discernible.

259

Chris, Chris . . .

"Unit 14, Unit 14. Passed car again but saw no one. Everyone's vanished. Shall we go in for a closer look?"

"Wait a couple of minutes," Rip advised. It was possible this was a trap to determine if they were being tailed.

Rip checked his watch's second hand. Never had 120 seconds gone so slowly. Everything in him cried out that he should rush the car, he should find her, he should take desperate measures . . . if Max indeed had her arms pinned, then he knew, and there was no longer any point in being discreet . . . but to shoot it out with Max and the others might mean instant death for Chris . . . take it easy, take it easy.

He said into the mike: "Let's go—but watch it! The subjects are all armed, and Boone will blow the whole place up if he figures they're trapped."

Rip raced for a point some distance behind the car, to throw off anyone watching. Once in the rear, he walked slowly down the sidewalk. There was no one around the car. Absolutely no one.

The other surveillance unit double parked with red lights flashing, and the agents tumbled out, and came around the subject car, meeting Rip. It was then Rip noticed the car had been parked a good three feet from the red curb.

His heart pounded. At his feet was a large, covered manhole.

70

IN PITCH BLACKNESS, Chris struggled through a torrent of water that rose above her knees and threatened to buckle her. She clawed the rough concrete for support but found none. She could barely stand upright. Her jaw cried out in pain where it had cracked against the manhole when Max had upended her and slipped her through it head first into Boone's arms. Boone had almost dropped her as he felt his way down the cast iron steps, more than a foot apart, into the storm drain. As he took the last few, she saw the water coming closer, and was screaming with sheer panic when he uprighted her. She had had the sensation she was about to faint, knowing that if she did, she would fall into the rushing water and drown.

If she could only see . . . but that would help little. Since a child she had suffered from claustrophobia. There had been the time she had run shrieking to her mother after being locked in a clothes closet by playmates. Now she experienced the same horror. Her chest seemed about to cave in, and her breath was coming spasmodically, but worse was the pandemonium of her thoughts . . . certain the water would rise and the conduit grow smaller and she would drown.

Ahead of her by a few steps was Boone, sloshing and tapping the wall with something metallic. Behind her was Max who shoved her every time she paused. Once she stopped to catch her breath and take stock, and he pushed her so hard she fell, and floundered in the water trying to get a footing on the slick bottom.

Not since a child had she permitted herself to give way to her emotions, and she had scorned women who did. Now she was doing exactly that. She had to get a grip on herself. But the darkness, the water plowing through her legs from the steady rain of yesterday, her soggy clothes, and the searing pain in her jaw and back of her head—they could not be dismissed. Yet she was going to die very shortly unless she tamed the chaos—and that realization sobered her.

Rip. Surely he had followed. He must have been waiting when she left the gallery. He could not have known then, however, that the play they had constructed so carefully scene by scene had reached an unexpected climax.

Saturday, four o'clock, the wedding . . . a misty dream without body . . . a dream barely remembered . . .

That spot below the knee of her new pants suit . . . she had tried washing it out . . . it had seemed important . . . why did it even cross her mind? . . . nothing was important . . . except Rip . . . Rip . . .

And Roz . . . would Roz come back? . . . lasagne and spaghetti and pizza . . . her nephews . . . she'd take them to the very next circus . . . and Clinton with the old courthouse on the town square . . . Hardee's drive-in . . . her mother and father . . . with so much love to give . . . asking nothing . . . Rip . . . Rip . . .

Ahead was a pinpoint light shining down out of another manhole, quite theatrical, like a baby spotlight, and her spirits soared. Nearing it, she heard the roar of traffic overhead, muted at first, then swelling, like the strange rumble of a far-off monster out of another era. The concrete tube trembled under its stomping feet.

261

"Okay," Max said. "We'll make a stop here. I've got something to say."

They gathered in the faint light which oddly turned their faces a pale green. They looked unreal to each other. Boone held his grenade to keep it from getting wet, and Tico breathed heavily, unaccustomed to the exercise.

The light was a magnet that drew Chris's eyes upward. Up there was freedom. She could almost reach up and touch it. She wanted to cry out, to scream, but no one would hear, and if someone possibly did, he wasn't likely to place the sound.

"This is a drainage conduit running to the Potomac River," he said. "There's no sewage in it, so you don't have to worry about methane gas. The pipe'll get bigger soon—to about ten by six feet. But these storm drains sometimes break with the shifting of the ground. That's why Boone's tapping the wall, so we won't kill ourselves by stepping into a big drop. We'd figured we might have to make this run tonight if things didn't work out and we would have had flashlights then, but nobody thought we'd be here today."

He continued talking calmly, quietly. He could have been Napoleon sitting a horse at Waterloo. He considered himself a good military tactician, and as any general would who launched an offensive, had planned for defeat and retreat. After a careful survey, he had chosen Washington's drainage system, extensive along the Potomac River, as the best escape route. Years ago, in a look forward unique in big city planning, Washington had inaugurated a drainage system separate from its sewage one. While an inch of rainfall would drop one billion point two gallons of water on the city, and fill the storm conduits, Hartman had gambled that this would not happen. He had almost lost. He could not have fled the day before with the steady downpour taxing the drainage system nearly to capacity. Even today, the run off from yesterday continued fairly heavy. He had picked up the idea of using the system from a group of Los Angeles militants who had planned to enter the city's sewers, equipped with gas masks to protect them from the deadly methane gas, to blow up a police station. They never succeeded, however, in locating their objective from underground. While Hartman had never considered "attacking" Washington through any such plan, which Boone said was crazy and infeasible, the thought had stayed with him that if his dream burst he might escape through a storm drain. The airports and railroad stations would be under heavy surveillance, and if he fled by car, there would be too many officers on the lookout. But who would ever suspect a motorboat chugging away at normal speed down the Potomac River toward the ocean?

"I rented a motorboat and tied it up about where we'll come out," he said.

"Did you tell her?" Tico asked sarcastically. "So the whole Navy will be waiting for us out there? Battleships, aircraft carriers . . ."

He shot her a devastating glance.

"We've got a trump card to play if we do run into trouble. No one's going to shoot us if it means shooting her." He indicated Chris. "So I want her breathing when we go down the river. You understand, Boone? And you, Tico?"

He turned to Chris. "You're going to get it no matter what happens. It's just a matter of time, but I'd play it cool if I were you and make it easy on yourself. I don't mind knocking you around if I have to."

Boone interrupted. "I could start now. Takes twenty-four hours . . ."

"You'll start when I tell you. You got that?"

His right hand shot out toward her then, and before she knew what he was doing, seized the chain about her neck holding the little cross, and with a hard yank, snapped it. He tossed the cross and chain into the water.

"Lot of good that'll do you," he said. She bit her lips and turned away as tears came into her eyes.

"Let's get moving," he said, and they headed again into the darkness.

71

RIP KNEW HE had very little time. He looked about frantically and spotted an outdoor telephone a short distance down New Hampshire. He shouted at one of the other surveillance agents to bring his car, tossed him the keys, and ran the distance.

Impatiently he dialed and waited. Seconds seemed like hours. He was about to explode. He explained what he wanted to one operator at the Department of Sanitary Engineering, then to another. He told them it could be a matter of life and death. He wanted to add, for someone I love.

Shouldn't he have gone down the manhole after her? But that would have been crazy. They would have killed him while he was descending, before he got a shot off.

Then he got through to a quick-minded engineer. The storm drain emptied into the Potomac River shortly below the mouth of Rock Creek. How long would it take the party to reach the Potomac?

"I need about forty or fifty minutes," Rip said.

"That's stretching it," answered the engineer. "We ourselves could make it in a lot less but of course with two women—and considerable water—and if they don't have flashlights—or do they?"

"We don't know." Rip repeated: "I've got to have forty minutes."

"Well, I wish you luck—you'll need it."

Next Rip called Markinson, and had to wait. He stared at the second hand going around on his watch. In the background were the first reports filtering in. The Rengo Sekigun terrorists were shooting it out at the motel. Four believed dead, two wounded. One police officer killed, one agent wounded. One section of the Palestinian guerrillas was fighting a street battle. Two officers and one agent reported wounded. The white African mercenaries were surrendering. They were paid to fight, not commit suicide. Several times before they had surrendered. It was all in a day's work. General Dijon's veterans of the 10th Parachute Division felt the same. Four Tupamaros were believed to have escaped. The FBI agents rounding up the Committee members had met with little resistance.

Markinson came on the line with three of his key men. They talked into a squawkbox. "They're armed," Rip said, "and Boone's got a hand grenade on him. It's not just a matter of a shoot out. He'll blow them all up if he figures they're trapped."

"I can't believe he'd blow himself up," said one agent.

"He doesn't give a damn," Rip retorted. "The problem is how do we separate the informant from them? How do we get her off to one side?"

"You're assuming she's still alive," an agent said.

"She's valuable to them alive," Rip countered.

Another agent said: "What about letting them go down the Potomac and waiting for a break?"

Markinson hastily nixed the suggestion. "We should apprehend

264

them as soon as possible after they leave the conduit. We'd have a stable situation then, not a moving one. One that we can control."

They conferred a few minutes more, setting plans, and then Markinson said slowly, feeling his way, which was unlike him: "We've had differences, Ripley. We still do. But I'm sorry it had to turn out this way."

He hung up abruptly.

Rip continued standing with his hand on the phone. He was watching a newspaper boy on the corner. A boy. He remembered Chris had told him about sitting at a sidewalk café in Venice, and a boy had run past her, and dropped a rose on her table.

72

ON AND ON they struggled, quiet for the most part. It was too difficult to shout back and forth, and they needed their strength to cope with the ever-rising waters. Although the conduit had increased in size, the water level had risen until it was well above Chris's knees, and it was becoming ever more difficult to move her feet and legs. She would take one premeditated step at a time, then brace herself against the torrent with her legs before making the next move. Soon the muscles reached a stage of painful exhaustion. She couldn't continue much longer. Her legs would certainly give way.

Or her nerves. Boone's incessant tapping on the concrete wall frayed them, and the constant sloshing. If she only had a cup of hot coffee. It was difficult to act defiant when the act was powered by will alone. Suddenly the little things in life meant so much . . . coffee, warmth, dry clothes, sunshine, a bath, resting after a hard day.

They rounded a curve or corner, apparently, because a round circle of light took shape in the far distance. A very small circle that increased in diameter with each step. She could have screamed with joy. Daylight was up ahead, sunshine, a return to a normal world. Whatever fears might lay ahead could not be as desperate as those she had suffered in the dark.

Max called to Boone to stop, and they gathered near Max. She felt Boone's arm slip about her and a hand working over her. It was as if a snake had risen up out of the water. She let out a low scream, and struggled loose after thrashing about for a moment. "What's going on?" Max demanded.

"Nothing," she said quickly. Boone had liked her. If later she could talk with him alone . . . it was a faint hope but she had reached the stage when she clutched at every possibility.

Max said: "I want a straight answer, Roberts." He had never called her Roberts before. "Is there a tail job on us?"

"To quote your girl friend," she answered readily, "how the hell would I know?"

Tico said: "You going to let her get by with that?"

"Go to hell," Chris said. It was strange talking to disembodied voices in the dark. So strange. Strange as in a bad dream—people she knew and communicated with but non-people, voices without reality. Even her own voice saying words some strange force had put in her mouth, not her words. Never had she quite realized how much it meant in the way of communication to see the other person, the expression of the eyes and lips which said as much as the spoken word. Suddenly, as in the last moments of a nightmare, she wanted to scream, to struggle, to break through into reality.

"I think there is," Max continued, "and if you try anything, Roberts . . ."

"Give me a gun and I'll kill the pigs," Chris replied.

"Don't let her snow you," Tico said.

"You would," Max said. "You'd kill a cop to save your skin."

"Anything wrong with that?" Chris retorted.

"I've known a lot of broads but you . . ." His tone said he did not believe her, not that she had anticipated that he would, but what else was there to do but continue the act? There was always the faint possibility that by defiance alone she might persuade him he was wrong about her. If it were something Tico had told him . . . she had no idea what had given her away.

"Okay, Boone," Max said, "let's move it."

The conduit reached the seawall which confined the river. The torrent gushed out of the pipe, and dropped into the Potomac, where it was quietly absorbed.

Near the opening, Max stopped to reconnoiter. Across the Potomac the woods of Theodore Roosevelt Island had been reduced by the time of the year to skeletal forms that looked macabre silhouetted against the pale blue sky. The island was quite near, only a short canoe trip away. Strangely, nothing moved on the quiet, well mannered river which here was called the Georgetown Channel. Upstream, Rock Creek poured into it.

For a long time Max stared at the very limited view before him. He crossed off the island as a danger point. An observer with binoculars might be watching from there but hardly marksmen. The police and FBI would post them much closer, perhaps on the Rock Creek and Potomac Parkway, a busy thoroughfare that paralleled the river, and was separated from the seawall by a grassy strip of varying width.

He took a labored breath. "The boat's to the left. You go first, Roberts—and remember I've got a gun." He indicated a shoulder holster. "You remember the sea lions, how I brought them down? I like a moving target."

"She'll make a break," Tico prophesied.

Max shook his head. "I know what you're thinking, Roberts. As long as you can stay alive, you've got a chance. Right? Okay, so you go ahead and do what I tell you. You stay with me, Tico—and Boone, you bring up the rear. All right, Roberts."

She waded past Boone as quickly as she could, but discovered she would be washed away if she didn't brace herself against the torrent. Boone grabbed her to steady her, and she thanked him and he was pleased. At the opening, she looked down at small ledges jutting forth from the wall that served as footholds. Directly beneath was a narrow strip of mud that lay between the wall and the water. On the last foothold she slipped and dropped to the earth. A pain shot from her ankle up through her leg and into her thigh. She limped a few steps and the pain grew excruciating. She would walk, though, she told herself; she would walk if it killed her. Because somewhere out there was Rip. Her clothing clung to her body and water streamed out of her shoes. The weight of the water alone impeded her walk. And the sunshine, though weak, was blinding.

"Come on," Max said behind her. "Get moving. You can wring yourself out in the boat."

From above came the roar of the parkway, and overhead a jet boomed through the clouds. There were faint voices all around but coming from a considerable distance. Still, voices however far away were reassuring. It would have been horrible if she had died back

267

there in that dark worm hole . . . as if it mattered where one died
. . . but it did.

She saw the boy then, a very small boy, not more than seven or
eight. He had his back to them and was kneeling in the mud sorting
stones. Her gaze skimmed by him a short distance to a motorboat
that had been tied to an iron bar jutting from the seawall.

Max and Tico followed so closely they stepped a time or two on
her heels. No one said a word. The scream had gone out of the pain
in her ankle. Perhaps she was less aware of it because of her concentration on the immediate scene. If she could only spot it, there had
to be some way to escape them.

Taking her by surprise, the boy materialized by her side. He had
large blue eyes, a dirty face, and tousled hair. "Hello, lady," he said.
"You're pretty. You look like my mother. Here, lady." He offered
her a smooth, flat stone which she took.

"Thank you," she told him.

"Get away, kid," Max said sternly. "We're busy. Go on, beat it."

The boy took her hand in his and tagged along. Her heart leaped.
She felt a tiny scrap of paper in her hand as the boy withdrew his.

Max shoved him. "Beat it, kid, beat it."

The boy cowered as they passed him. "Goodbye, lady," he called.

"Goodbye," she answered.

"Give me that rock," Max said. She handed it to him. "Keep going," he ordered, examining it, then tossing it into the water.

73

RIP FOCUSED THE binoculars to bring Chris and the others up sharply.
She looked little like the Chris of an hour ago. Her face and eyes
were drawn, and she bit her lips as if in pain. She limped a little as
she picked her way around puddles, and it was evident she favored
her right foot. He experienced an overwhelming desire to go rushing
from his hideout in a clump of bushes, and grab her. Why not? he
asked himself. A daring act like that would probably take the others
by such surprise they would not have time to harm her.

Probably. That was the trouble, it was only a probable.

The others followed her so closely they looked like a pack of people lifted off a subway train at rush hour. Max was wary, searching the scene constantly, from his immediate area to the parkway above. Tico said something about food, her strident voice rising clearly, but Rip couldn't hear Max's answer. Boone carried the grenade in his right hand, the way a boy would a baseball.

Even while he watched them, Rip rechecked the plans he had so hurriedly drawn. He was disturbed by the haste with which he had worked. He needed a few hours—time to think his way through all contingencies. Instead he had had minutes. He had reasoned that Max would travel south on the Potomac toward the ocean. Northward, beyond the Francis Scott Key Bridge, the river was difficult to navigate because of rocks and boulders. He had considered moving the boat, and hence trapping Hartman and the others, but they would simply have walked to a nearby dock, and taking Chris along, rented another. An expert marksman might have picked them off when they emerged from the conduit, before Hartman, Boone, or Tico could react, but an agent had no right under law to hunt down subjects and kill them. Before opening fire he must identify himself as a federal officer, and give the subjects an opportunity to surrender. Only if they went for a weapon or attempted to escape, would he be justified in firing. Although the criminal had the advantage when an agent thus identified himself, Rip felt strongly that the law was good and just. A peace officer was not judge and jury, not a hunter bent on killing human game.

And yet if he thought Hartman this minute was about to murder Chris, he would shoot to kill, and the ethics and legality of his split-second decision would eventually have been debated in criminology classes. Even with all the laws, each man still had his own.

He continued to search through his plan step by step for a flaw, an error in thinking, a move Hartman might make that had not been foreseen, the impossible happening, such as an innocent person getting in the way, a sudden change in the weather, the faint telltale noise of a kicked pebble, all the scores of big and small eventualities.

He moistened his dry lips and took a deep breath. Now that he had seen her, he pushed his emotions aside. He must be detached and objective. If he were not, he would maximize the risk to her life.

Nearing the boat, Chris lost a shoe in the mud. In exasperation she kicked the other off. She kept her right hand, which still held the

269

note, in her jacket pocket, and prayed no one would think it an awkward place at this particular time to keep a hand. Plowing through the mud, one needed hands and arms available as stabilizers.

Her chance to read the note came unexpectedly. Struggling to bring the boat about, Max and Boone had their backs to her. Tico herself had lost a shoe and was not about to desert it. While Tico wavered on one foot, trying to recover the shoe, Chris sneaked a glance at the note, printed in block letters: *HIT THE WATER WHEN YOU PASS KENNEDY CENTER AND KEEP UNDER AS LONG AS YOU CAN.*

Rip watched as Max took over the wheel, set Chris beside him, Boone behind her, and Tico alongside Boone. Rip waited until the engine roar came over, then said softly to the microphone hidden in his upper coat pocket: "All units, party is now heading out into river. Informant has received and read message. She is sitting alongside Hartman who is at the wheel. Repeat, party is now . . ."

"I can't stand these slimy things," Chris said, struggling out of her wet pants.

She let them drop to the bottom of the boat. She was left bare below the waist except for bikini briefs. She was behaving completely out of character which any other time would have tipped Max off. His thoughts were centered now on the river's shoreline. His eyes skimmed one side, then the other. He kept the motorboat operating at moderate speed.

In the near distance, on an unpretentious bluff, rose an imposing, marble edifice that was the Kennedy Center. Its terrace, with its colored, dancing fountains and miniature trees, overhung the parkway. She had gone there with Sarah, and they had toured the interior, walked the long concourse with its marble walls and gold columns, seen the theaters, and eventually drifted out on the terrace.

A lone man stood there now.

Surreptitiously she unbuttoned her jacket.

There was no sound except the rhythmic *chug chug* of the engine and the soft breaking of water. Max kept the boat in dead center and his hands set firmly on the wheel.

"I don't like it," he said over his shoulder to Tico.

"Don't like what?"

"Nobody's on the river."

When they neared Kennedy Center, Chris began breathing heavily, then gasping, doubled up.

"What's with you?" Max asked.

"She's up to something," Tico said.

Chris breathed as if each breath would be her last.

Below the Kennedy Center's terrace was the steady rush of traffic on the parkway, and halfway below the parkway and the river, Rip sat on the grassy ground, a tourist enjoying the view.

Into the mike, he said: "Washington one, come in Washington one."

"All set," answered Washington one, two agents sprawled on the bottom of a motorboat tied up directly below him.

He proceeded to check on four boats and three units of agents on foot, two on this side and the third on Roosevelt Island. He watched Max and party come into view. Chris was doubled up in seeming pain, and he felt the grab in his stomach. If she were ill . . .

"I got to get air," she gasped, slipping off her jacket.

She gasped again, and doubled up, and rolled over the side of the boat, and fell with a splash into the water. Tico yelled and Max left the wheel to look overboard. Boone stared into the rain-muddied waters, saw her swimming, and shouting, fired a shot. By then she was a good fifteen feet away. The boat was rocking too much for an accurate shot, especially one discharged into water which by its very movement distorted the target. When she surfaced, he fired again, and she went under. Max returned to the wheel, and wrestling with it, spun the boat about. He'd run her down, he'd split her head wide open.

Then a bullet struck the bow broadside, and the boat lurched and for a moment he lost control. He shouted at Boone. Where had the shot come from? Boone yelled back that he didn't know. He couldn't spot anyone. Up ahead, Chris surfaced again. They had gained on her. Once more Boone fired wildly, and again she went under. A second slug ripped into the bow, and several others struck the side below the waterline, pinging every foot or so. By now Max had lost control

271

and water was spurting in. Boone screamed words Max never heard. Tico was shrieking in panic.

The lone man with the high powered rifle up on the terrace of Kennedy Center lay the weapon down. The boat was capsizing. Its three occupants were swimming in circles.

The man, an FBI marksman, smiled. He had a dollar bet with a fellow agent to the effect he couldn't sink a boat with six shots.

Rip could see their lips moving. They were shouting to each other. He said into the radio: "All units, Plan A in effect. Repeat, all units, Plan A in effect."

The motorboats shot forth from their hiding places. Agents appeared on the seawall, guns drawn.

Frantically, Rip scanned the water for Chris, and when he failed to find her, it was as if someone had clubbed him. Back and forth he skimmed the surface.

The other three were swimming toward shore. Boone held the grenade high out of the water but couldn't swim with it and dropped it. A boat raced down on him, and two agents hauled him up, pinned his hands behind him, handcuffed him, and snapped on leg chains.

Another boat picked up Max, and another Tico. Neither resisted. The whole operation had taken less than five minutes.

And then Rip located Chris. She was swimming downstream to get out of the range of the operation. Before Rip could direct a unit to her rescue, the agents in the fourth motorboat were racing in that direction.

The tension that he had lived with for so long broke, and for the first time in days, he breathed easy. He should feel good, and exhilarated, and happy. But it was going to take a little time to get the old body and brain accustomed to the old stand-by emotions. He had taken too many punches.

The moment she stepped wringing wet from the boat, their arms went about each other, then he was wrapping his coat about her.

"Four o'clock Saturday," he said.

She tried smiling. "Don't you dare be late."

Then she was trudging toward the parked Bureau car up on the parkway. "Get her to a hospital for a check-up," Rip told the agent driving the car, "and if she's okay, get her on the next plane out."

The fear still haunted him that someone might come gunning for her, even though all the known members of the Zero Section had been apprehended. "Ask one of the women agents to get her some clothes, and I'll reimburse her."

He hurried down the shoreline to the marshaling point where Hartman, Boone, and Miss Sharman were being held. "You understand," he said abruptly, studying them one by one, "that we are Federal officers, FBI agents, and we have placed you under arrest. Anything you say may be used against you . . . you have a right to counsel . . ."

74

By 3 o'clock that afternoon, the Committee of Public Safety had passed into history. Eight of the Rengo Sekigun had fought to the death, and four of the Palestinian guerrillas. One agent and two police officers had been killed, and three wounded. The Committee members, the white African mercenaries, and the veterans of General Dijon's 10th Parachute Division had surrendered peacefully. General Dijon himself had accepted arrest with the same military bearing and dignity that had marked his misguided and ill-fated career.

In searching Max Hartman, William Boone, and Tico Sharman, agents had found two suicide pills on each. The three had had no chance to swallow them, since the action in the closing minutes aboard boat had been too frantic, but Rip had his doubts about whether they would have under any circumstances. They were scarcely of the mettle of individuals who risk all for a cause and die heroically. The U. S. Commissioner set bond of $500,000 each for the three and Dr. Beaumont.

Still unidentified was the subject known in the files only as Boogie. The Bureau would work for years, if necessary, to locate him.

Late in the afternoon, Markinson sent word he wished to see Rip, and knowing the reason why, Rip dragged his tired, battered, sleepless body through the Department of Justice and up an old, creaky elevator. Markinson sat behind a large, highly polished, scarless desk, clean except for a file folder and a letter. He did not invite Rip to sit.

He picked up the letter. "I have a letter here for you from the Director," he said brusquely, biting his words off clean. "The Bureau has no recourse but to take strong disciplinary action in your case."

He reached over to hand Rip the letter. "You have openly flouted the rules and regulations, and refused to consult with the Bureau in matters of the greatest importance. Vital matters. The Bureau cannot tolerate such violations regardless of whether the investigation of the case worked out satisfactorily. The Bureau cannot permit its agents to take matters in their own hands, even if the action was conceived in all good conscience. I don't need to go into the details of your case because you know . . ."

He hesitated, a stern judge about to deliver sentence. "You are being demoted and suspended for forty days."

"And transferred?" Rip asked.

Markinson shook his head. "The Bureau under Mr. Hoover would have transferred you but the new Bureau does not consider a transfer as proper action to take in disciplinary matters." He cleared his throat. "However," he continued, "as a purely routine measure, you will be assigned to the El Paso office."

Without comment, Rip slipped the letter into his coat pocket. It would be a good souvenir to read in his old age. He was relieved he would remain in the Southwest. He had told Chris he would probably be assigned as resident agent in Nome, Alaska. For a short time in Hoover's era, agents in the doghouse with the Bureau had been dispatched to Butte, Montana. Eventually, however, Montanans had objected to having their state treated as America's Siberia.

Rip was at the door when Markinson stopped him. "Ripley," he said, still brusque, "speaking as a private citizen, and not as an assistant to the director of this Bureau—you did one hell of a job!"

75

CHRIS HAD NEVER been in Arizona before, and the desert south of Tucson was alien to her, so unlike her North Carolina. This was the land, though, that Rip loved, and his happiness at being back again was hers.

They drove in a rented car through a country strange to her, a country of giant sahuaro cacti with their gnarled arms reaching skyward, prickly pears, Spanish daggers and cottonwoods along dry, parched arroyos. When he turned the car off the highway, and they crept over a washboard trail that grew ever narrower, he pointed out places of his boyhood. Here in Skull Canyon he had helped the sheriff's deputies round up three rustlers using a two-ton truck . . . here was where he had run out of gas in the caterpillar . . . Old Man Frazier had lived up in Rattlesnake Canyon . . . he had been caretaker for an old mine . . . and way up in the Volcano Mountain foothills, the Ochoas fired pottery they sold in town . . . he had gone to the senior prom with one of the Ochoa girls.

Once he said: "I hope you like El Paso."

"I'd like any place where you were." She hesitated. "But I thought I read somewhere, the Bureau quit packing its bad boys off to another city."

Rip smiled. "In my case they made an exception."

Miles later he drew the car up before a low, flat-roofed, adobe house. A sad house, it seemed to her, but to him a home of happy memories. It sat well back from the trail, the yard barren except for a few cacti and some scraggly desert growth. Strung about the place was a wire fence badly in need of repairs.

His mother came hurrying to meet them, taking long strides, a tall, thin woman with a face sand blasted by the desert. He picked her up and swung her about. "Now put me down," she said, pretending annoyance.

"This is my girl," he said, introducing Chris.

His mother smoothed out her dress, patted her hair, and sized up Chris. "You'll do," she said. "You'll do."

Rip laughed. "She means you're beautiful."

Chris hugged her, and his mother warmed to her. Chris's eyes went to an old car to one side of the house, far back. "Why, there's your old car. Just like you told me."

"Never touched it," said his mother. "Always figured he would be coming back. Come on in and have a bite. It's about supper time."

"Let me help," Chris said.

A collie dog came racing from nowhere and sprung on Rip. The dog's happiness knew no bounds. "That's Tom's grandson," explained his mother. "Keeps me company. Tom was Johnny's dog for fourteen years."

Chris looked at Rip, puzzled. "She means me," he whispered.

"Tom helped me bring him up," she continued, leading the way toward the house. "I read they don't have many dogs in the cities. No wonder all those crimes. A boy needs a dog."

"I want to ask a favor, Mrs. Ripley," Chris said. "Can we have one of Tom's great grandsons—when the time comes?"

She had her arm about Rip. She reached up to kiss him.